Guitarded

CHURCHILL FORRESTER

ISBN 978-1-956010-61-9 (paperback)
ISBN 978-1-956010-62-6 (digital)

Rushmore Press LLC
1 800 460 9188
www.rushmorepress.com

Printed in the United States of America

guitarded / gui-ˈtär-dᵊd / adj. **1.** any emotional or mental state characterized by an unreasonable and persistent desire and effort to play or learn to play any form of the guitar: a stringed musical instrument played by picking, plucking, or strumming; despite the absolute and utter lack of any ability, dexterity, proficiency, skill, or talent otherwise necessary to do so. **2.** An irrational obsession to acquire or accumulate a collection of guitars. **3.** Tami Cooper's antagonistic characterization of her husband, Paul Edward Cooper.

Chapter 1

How is it that some women always manage to get their way?

Tami's first text reads, "Call me as soon as you find out if you got a second interview." Her second text follows immediately. It reads, "We need this! Please don't screw it up. I'm counting on you. Don't forget the prep sheet I sent you. It's very important that you follow the guidelines. Watch your language. Double-check your appearance. Just believe in yourself and do a two-minute power stance before you go in. You can do this!"

Right. Love you too, darling dear. Speaking of love, why can't you love me more? Even just a little bit?

Maybe it's the age difference. Or maybe it's something else. I don't know. I try not to think about it. Besides, our getting together and then getting married had been her idea, and damn right I jumped on it. Who, in my shoes, wouldn't?

I tap the screen till the text disappears, and I find my way through the smartphone to my secret little file. There she is in that sexy little camisole. A perfect candid of my Tami. The Tami I adore and dream of whenever I dream that she loves me half as much as I love her. And she's never even seen it. Thank God. And in it, she's everything to me: Long hair, silky strands of glowing gold being brushed before bed. Pink lips that glisten. Those glacier-blue eyes. I love this face. So inviting, so forbidden.

Tami is my absolute drug of choice. And this image? About the strongest dosage I'm likely to ever get. I'm absolutely grateful to have it.

Thank God for going digital. No doubt he's got a copy. He would. Not that he needs it. Probably has his own stash of dozens and a lifetime more, for that matter. I want to see them all someday. Preferably, not anytime soon. Not while there's still a chance.

Crap.

Another text. That's just great.

One more glance. Close out the file. Shut it down. Stash the phone. Grab the usual folder of day job crap and move on.

For the third time this week, I'm walking to the butt-ugly excuse for a courthouse for what will undoubtedly be yet another frustrating exercise in futility. Once again, I'm waiting for a sign from God—*anything*—to tell me my prayers have been answered.

Instead, my wife sends me this shit about a prep sheet and a power stance.

I do not need this. Then again, I don't want to end up back in the guest room if all my efforts go south as they so often do.

Great.

Now I'm calculating the probability of chilling out in the guest room if all goes south and trying to figure out just what in the hell might constitute a power stance.

A shrill shriek and I see a strange woman's arms all akimbo, a flailing red scarf, and yet none of it registers in my brain because it's busy searching for whatever a power stance is right up until the moment I'm run over by this wild woman in a wheelchair.

I am on my butt, rolling onto my back, and sliding downhill on a wet tile surface, with its inlay of the mosaic design of the county's lame goat-head logo, as opposed to having some kind of sensible, nonslip surface treatment in anticipation of days such as today.

Normally, this concrete ramp leads up to the entry doors of a former state building, a gull-gray block of bureaucracy now serving as the temporary downtown courthouse. The way up and back down, for that matter, was concrete steps until some jack-ss activists started protesting.

California society today cannot let anybody ever be upset or offended. It's in our amended state constitution. Oh, no. We cannot have any of that anymore. Some county engineer, the one with the short straw in his hand, got tasked with getting some concrete and filling in the steps. Then the county picked another genius to put some mosaic-pattern, tile-like finish on it that made it very smooth; and now, thanks to that same idiot who must think it never rains in California, it's just one big ass-whippin' Slip 'n Slide whenever it rains.

I feel the cold tread of a hard rubber tire roll across my face. The shrieking gives way to what I presume are Spanish curse words, followed by maniacal laughter. Momentum rolls me over her body, and we roll again together, and now she's on top of me as we slide to a stop on the wet sidewalk, all muddy with leaves.

This cannot possibly bode well for me on this day of all days, the one day when, until just a moment ago, everything in my life was supposed to make one final turn for the better. Trouble is, I'm all wet. I'm sore. I'm pissed off. I'm not so sure about anything being right with the universe. That crazy lady who's run me over with her wheelchair aerobatics thinks it's funny.

I don't think it's funny.

Still, she smells nice—if what I smell is her.

She's looking blurry. Bad sign. I feel my face and understand I no longer have my eyeglasses. This can't be good either. I shuffle around, trying to move. But she still has me pinned, and she's trying to get up. She leans on one hand for leverage, and I discover in pain that she's pushing directly on my crotch.

"Hey!" I want to shove her away, but I can't.

"Ooh, I'm sorry," she says in a faint accent, slightly Hispanic, slightly—I don't know—Nashville country singer twang, maybe?

She continues pushing until she manages to roll away.

"I'm so sorry. Really." She's doing a very poor job of trying not to laugh. "I didn't mean to do that. That's just adding insult to injury, I know."

I'm wincing, and she's laughing again.

With two women busting my balls—apparently that's trending now—I'm regretting not being more up to speed on this whole power stance thing. I could have used one a few moments ago.

I manage to get to all fours and crawl around looking for my glasses, sweeping my hand over the slick pavement in front of me, feeling around for them. I crawl toward a reflection in the planter.

"Sorry. That must have really hurt," she giggles.

"Yeah. It does."

I put on my glasses. They're not broken, thank God. The fit's not too bad. I should be okay.

"No worries. Could be worse."

My throbbing tailbone is telling me it's worse. So is the rain that's really coming down.

I get up and retrieve her chair. She's cocooned inside sopping, muddy, baggy sweats; a hooded sweatshirt; darkened deep gray by the rain; with a knit beanie on her head and under the hoodie, and that limp scarf, strangling her like a boa. She still manages a smile.

It's pretty.

C'mon. Focus.

Her right knee looks much larger than her left one. Must be some kind of brace in there. I get up with some struggling.

"Are you okay? Can you get up?"

She raises her arms. "Only if you help me."

I set myself in a weightlifter's squat, take hold of her hands, and stand up. She gets her weight on her good leg and uses the other for balance. I go and pick up the wheelchair dangling over the curb and bring it back to her. She grabs hold and sits.

"Now what?" she asks.

I look around. "We try and get you up this ramp before we melt."

"Not that I mind, but aren't you a little old to be playing Prince Charming?"

"What?"

"Nothing. I'm game if you are."

There's that smile again. Only bit of brightness in all this gloom.

"Let's go."

I begin pushing her up the ramp.

"Andale! Andale!"

I feel the soles of my shoes slip. I keep going. I don't get far. Men in dark suits pass us. They're trying not to slip. They keep their heads down, taking pains not to look.

"Guys? A little help here?" she pleads.

No one looks. No one stops.

"El cabron! Abogados pendejos!" she mutters. "They're all the same."

She turns to look back at me.

"Except you. If you're a lawyer. If not, then you're probably a cop."

"Naw."

"Then ex-cop, right?"

"Would have liked to have been, but naw. Worked in probation once."

"Oh. Well, that's just as good. Maybe better. They got heart. Okay, so what are you?"

"Abogado pendejo."

I slip, again, and we start sliding. I grab the rail, she grabs the rail, and that slows us down; and we sort of skate back to the sidewalk. I look at my watch. We've got maybe five minutes max to get up that ramp and inside and for her to get wherever she's going and for me to get in Department 6 before Chrome Dome takes the bench and starts sanctioning people—me, in particular.

"Now what?"

I walk around the railing and step into the planter. It's mushy, but I get traction. I look around.

Yeah. This could work.

"You're not thinking of pushing me up through all those rose bushes, I hope."

"Nope." I'm looking around, planning our route up the rose bush trail. "I'm thinking we piggyback it."

I see the whites of her big brown eyes.

"Es tu loco?"

"Crazy?"

Good question. I shrug.

"There is that rumor. Never mind all that. I'm going to be late, and I can't be late."

The rain's falling harder.

"And I'm not leaving you here either."

"Wow. Whataya know, a real gentleman," she smiles. "Don't that beat all. That's really nice of you, but I think I can manage. Just get me up and give me a push."

"You sure?"

"Oh, c'mon now. I can't look that helpless. I've been a high school gym teacher for ten years."

"Fair enough."

I get her up, aim her at the door.

"Ready?"

"Andale!"

I give her a push. She hobbles forward, gets two steps away, slips, and promptly face-plants.

"Holy shit!" I go to her. "Are you okay?"

"Ay, Papi! Just help me up. Watch the knee!"

Ah. Not so funny now, is it?

I get her up and guide her over to the railing.

"On second thought, maybe we should try it my way."

"Whatever you say, Prince Charming."

She leans on the rail, struggling to keep her balance.

"Then let's do this."

I look around for my expendable plastic file folder containing all my day-job crap. It's pretty handy, actually. It comes complete with a cover flap—so perfect for these rainy days—particularly so with a parrot decal on the lower right corner of the flap, which some of my peers have taken to calling my folder "Polly Wanna Pocket" because they carry expensive, burnished, hand-tooled leather briefcases from some bullshit plain in Spain where, naturally, it never rains. Fuck them. They're all little sheepy, lazy *baah*-stards who won't think for themselves, who don't like God's best weather, and who are always jealous that I'm always prepared. Until they want something.

Anyway, I find it, pick it up, and walk over to her. The rain is steady.

I squat down with my back to her. She pulls on my shoulders and jumps. I reach back and get a hand under her good knee, and off we go trudging across the tundra. I feel her cheek next to mine. Mile after mile, step after step. About three-fourths of the way up, I lose a shoe in the softer mush and grunt.

"Ay! Are you saying I'm heavy?"

I grunt again. I can't help it. I'm losing my balance.

"Ay! Papi!" she laughs and spurs my thigh with the heel of the running shoe on her good leg. "C'mon, Lil' Pepe! You can do it!"

I really don't need this. I grunt again. Maybe I should just dump her heavy ass right here. No, I can't do that.

What'd she call me?

We're at the top now.

"Hang on," I tell her as I reach out for the little metal box on the wall and slap the metal plate for the ADA automatic door actuator that causes the handicap door to swing open, which takes forever.

I plow through the metal detector, ignoring the security guards who stand there looking even more dopey than usual, and lumber around the corner, pass the exit door, and make my way over to a table against the wall. I use the table for balance and squat again.

"Thank you," she whispers and kisses my wet cheek with cold, wet lips. She slides off. I stand up.

Hot damn!

Mission accomplished.

As I stand here, hands on my hips like Patton watching an advancing column of armor, I think I may just have found something that could pass for my power stance. Or not. I'm not so sure.

"Wait here. I'll be right back."

I shuffle through the exit and out into the rain. It's really coming down. I get my shoe and bang it on the railing to knock most of the mud free. I put it on and carefully go to the sidewalk. I pick up the wheelchair; it's surprisingly light. It takes a moment, but I finally figure out how to fold it. I reach for my Polly Pocket. I put my right arm through the space below the armrests and sling the chair over my shoulder and trudge my way up again, this time without losing a shoe. Now the rain stops.

Nice.

"Good as new," I tell her, tossing my Polly Pocket onto the table and setting the chair down and getting it ready for her.

"Thank you for being so kind. We should do it again some time," she says.

There's that smile.

"Oh, no. I'm good." I smile politely. "Once is fine."

I get my Polly Pocket from the table. She tugs at it, moving my left arm, and then lets it go.

"What?"

"Oh, nothing," she says, smile gone. "I see. That explains it."

"Explains what?"

"Nothing," she mumbles something like "the good ones are always taken."

She sighs and then asks me, "Any idea where Department 9 is?"

"Yep. Third Floor. Same place I'm headed. C'mon, I'll get you up there."

"Sir! Sir! Just a moment, please!"

I turn to face a short, chubby security guard. He looks up.

"I need to wand you, sir. Arms out to the side, please."

Seriously?

He does his sweeping thing with a flattened club that looks like a sawed-off fraternity paddle. He waves it around like he's frosting a giant cake.

"Flip your belt buckle over for me please."

"Right."

I lower my arms and move my drenched tie and twist my dripping belt buckle so he can see behind it.

"Lift your pant legs above your ankles please."

For the love of Christ!

I don't have time for this. I don't have time to argue either.

"Of course."

I have to pull up on my suit pants because they are muddy wet and cling to my legs.

"Clear! Thank you for your cooperation, sir. Have a nice day."

"Thank you, Officer."

I step out of my puddle as he walks away. No need to rush now. We're both late. She'll be okay. She's in a wheelchair. I'm sunk. I'm soaking wet and standing up in a suit soaked in spots with fresh mud. Dripping.

"C'mon, I'll push you to the elevator."

"Thanks."

"No worries."

As I push, I turn my head and glance back. Security people ignore the wet floor. Well, torts are everywhere. That's the law. Every man for himself.

Being this late means the elevator is ours. It's a quiet ride. Neither of us says anything. Eventually the door opens in its own sweet-ass time; and I wheel her out, turn right, and take her to the end of the hall and open the door to Department 9.

"Okay. Good luck."

"Thanks," she says. "You know, you could be a real looker, despite your age and all, if you'd like, you know, smile more."

"Yeah? Why is that?"

"Because, you know, happy people are just good looking in all-around general."

"Oh, really? Then what, pray tell, makes you so happy?"

She smiles. Pretty smile.

"I don't know. Mostly, being myself, I guess."

"Then I'd say your plan works well for you."

"You should try it some time."

So cute. So naive.

The woman's eyes are big, dark brown, and beautiful. That smile of hers wipes me out, and I can't help it. I feel the corner of my mouth crease into a grin—probably a stupid-looking one.

"Yeah, there you go! Like that"

Stupid grin.

"You're much too kind."

"Well, thanks again for the ride, Prince Charming."

She gives me another one of those pretty smiles as I hold the door open for her, and she rolls herself in to the courtroom.

"Always a pleasure, Miss," I say, letting the door close behind her.

Nice meeting you.

Thinking of meetings, I remember my court appearance.

Say adios to the grin.

I'm beating squishy feet over to Department 6 at the opposite end of the hall. I pull open the door, expecting the worst. I see there's still a line. Thank God. Chrome Dome's not on the bench and nowhere in sight. Maybe it won't be so bad.

I get in line as the burly courtroom attendant surveys the just-plain, butt-ugly courtroom. His biceps press tight against the sleeves of his navy blazer. I catch his eye as I pass his desk, waiting with other attorneys as the line inches its way toward the near side of the judge's bench where the clerk who will check us in is seated, awash in manila case files.

"Well, good morning there, Mr. Cooper!" says the court attendant, giving me the once over. "You look like hell, tall guy. Yet you're smiling, almost chipper, and on such a dreary morning."

He's looking out the window behind me at the back of the courtroom.

"And one that must be raining mud, from the looks of you."

"Yeah, well, there's that. Bit of a slip and fall, you might say."

"Say no more. Torts are everywhere. I learned that one from you. Good thing it's Friday then, isn't it?" he says, turning down the volume of his desk radio he's tuned to a jazz station. "Yes, sir, I see you are none the worse for wear and almost chipper. Did you suffer a concussion?"

"I don't think so."

"Win the lottery? Did the county give you a raise?" he laughs.

Several attorneys snicker.

"Wait, the county don't give raises. They give furlough days, I know. Oh, I got it now. Your divorce is final. You're a free man, out dancing in the rain, and your ex done run off with some judge and—*bam*! No mo' alimony! That's it, isn't it?"

That last one has all of us cracking up.

"Not even close, big guy," I say, after regaining my composure.

"Well, something's up. Something big. I can tell. You're not usually this breezy, especially lookin' like you do. You sure you ain't hurt? You look like you're gonna float off any moment." He squints. "You been drinkin' that funny water, again? Sippin' at the joy juice?"

That brings a howl from the line.

"Naw, man, nothing like that."

"You sure now? I need to know these things. I run an honorable courtroom for an honorable judge now."

"Yeah, Dennis, I'm sure."

"All right then. Just checkin'. Gonna keep an eye on you."

"Fair enough."

"I'm just saying this ain't like you. It's my job to notice these things."

"Let's just say, life is good," I say.

"Since when?" chimes someone from the back of the line.

"Oh, I see now. I see. You're in line for a promotion. That's it, ain't it, Mr. Cooper?"

Busted.

I feel my neck grow hot.

"Oh, yeah. I gotcha good this time! Prospect of a promotion can be a powerful drug. I can see it. Well, we won't talk about it. Nice guy makes good and all that. I don't want to jinx it for you. You can tell me all about it on Monday. How'd that be?"

I give him a thumb's up.

"Oh?" asks the impeccably dressed man I've never seen before who is standing behind me.

I think he must be a litigator from one of the big law firms out of LA.

"Promotion to what?" he asks.

"Supervising Deputy County Counsel."

"How interesting," he says in a dead, matter-of-fact tone, smiling.

And then as he looks down at his smartphone, scrolling through an endless stream of texts, he adds politely, "Good luck with that."

"Thank you."

I take a pen from my trusty Polly Pocket and dutifully write the case information on my business card and hand it to the harried, substitute clerk. She takes it, while handling a phone call, flips the page of the morning's calendar, and makes a notation on the page. I wait until she looks up.

"I also need to check in with Departments 5, 7, and 9. I'll be right back. I promise."

She sighs and rolls her eyes.

"Heard it all before, and I don't care. Okay, fine. I'll try and let the judge know. No promises."

"Thank you."

I turn and make my way past the dull, dark line, past the attendant, who gives me a nod; and somebody's cell phone goes off.

I instinctively reach for mine. Of course, it's not there. This is bad. This is really, really bad. I know I had it when I left the office, I know it. I'm sure. No, I'm not.

Crap.

It's gotta be on the sidewalk somewhere. Which means somebody has picked it up and is calling some toll-plus phone-sex hotline in Thailand. That's just great. I walk out and check in with the other departments and return.

Oh, damn.

Chrome Dome is already on the bench. He stops midsentence, glances at the reporter who immediately stops typing, and then he looks at me.

"Just a moment. Nice to have you finally join us, Mr. Cooper. Everyone else, you may have noticed"—he pauses—"is on time. Oh, good lord! What have you been doing? Moonlighting on a garbage truck?"

"I was run—I fell, Your Honor."

"You should be more careful, man. For God's sake, at least invest in an umbrella. You're an attorney, for God's sake! Start looking like one, even if you don't always act like one."

I move to take a seat.

"Don't bother, Mr. Cooper. I'm taking your matter next."

I'm fucked.

He glances at the two lawyers standing before him.

"Counsel waive notice?"

The two attorneys promptly agree to waive notice, stuffing their papers into their briefcases and making brisk getaways.

"Very well. Going back to number four on the calendar. *County of San Gorgonio v. Crenshaw.*"

I approach the counsel table and make way for an elderly woman in a worn shawl knitted from skeins of calico colors now long faded, allowing her to go ahead of me.

"Good morning, Your Honor. Paul Cooper, Deputy County Counsel for Plaintiff, County of San Gorgonio."

"Oh, good lord, I know who you are." He squints. "My lord! You are dripping on the counsel table. Dripping! Have you lost all sense of decorum, sir?"

"Your Honor, if I may—"

"You may not! Your appearance is disgraceful, sir! I take umbrage! Sanctions in the amount of $150 are appropriate. Payable by the end of the day to the state bar's victims' compensation fund." He turns to the woman. "Moving on. Are you Anita Crenshaw, ma'am?"

She nods.

"Is that a yes?"

She nods.

"Well then, speak up. This is a courtroom, not a marijuana dispensary. You'll have to speak up when you make an appearance in my courtroom and that means talk out loud," he says, raising his voice, "loudly enough so that my reporter can make a proper record of these proceedings. Do you understand me?"

"Yes."

"Very well. This matter is on calendar for a preliminary injunction motion. Ms. Crenshaw do you have an attorney?"

The woman shakes her head.

Chrome Dome shakes his head too, mumbling to himself.

Regaining his composure, he resumes, "For the record, I'll take that as a no."

He looks at the clock on the wall.

"Very well. I'm cutting to the chase on this one, Ms. Crenshaw. It would appear that the county has taken extreme umbrage at your insistence on running an unpermitted animal shelter in your home. As much as I love animals, I can see why the county and, undoubtedly, some of your neighbors would be concerned with you keeping a hundred-plus cats in your home."

"I don't keep them. I do not own them." The voice is feeble.

"Oh, good lord, she squeaks. Frankly, Ms. Crenshaw, I could care less. The county's motion is unopposed, and on that basis alone, I should grant it pursuant to the code. From the photos included as exhibits to the county's motion—unopposed motion—you certainly have no trouble feeding them. However, I am going to continue this matter thirty days."

He looks to his clerk.

"Give me a date."

She does.

"Let's make it October 31. I think your cats will see the humor in that, particularly the black ones. That will be at 8:30 a.m., this department. Mr. Cooper will give notice. Ms. Crenshaw, I cannot give you legal advice. I do, however, strongly encourage you to consult a lawyer as soon as possible on this matter."

She turns and walks away.

"Thank you, Your Honor," I say from habit.

"Make the effort to be on time, Mr. Cooper."

"I will."

"And properly attired, if you please, Mr. Cooper."

"Yes, Your Honor."

"Sanctions to be paid by the end of the day."

"Yes, Your Honor."

Fortunately, everything else I have on calendar this morning is routine and goes quickly. All I've got to do now is find my phone. I get off the elevator and head for the exit.

"Sir! Sir! Counselor!"

Oh hell, not again.

I turn and here comes the wand-waving, out-of-breath security guy. I stop. Authority, as they say, always wins.

"Yes, Officer?"

"Sir!" He pulls up on his belt. "During my perimeter sweep of the courthouse exterior for suspicious packages at 0845 hours this date, a suspicious object was observed by this officer lying unattended that appeared to be a cellular phone near a rose bush. Further investigation revealed same. The phone was retrieved and secured by this officer. Subsequently, it was determined it belonged to you."

He pulls a phone out of his pocket and hands it to me.

I look it over.

How about that? It really is mine.

"Excellent work, Officer. Truly, excellent work. I can't thank you enough."

He smiles.

"Oh, no, sir. We cannot accept gratuities."

And I wouldn't think of it.

"I see. Well, how about a handshake then, from a grateful citizen?"

"Oh, that'd be fine, sir."

"Well, then. A handshake it is. Thank you again, Officer."

"It's a privilege to serve, sir."

I smile and head across the foyer and take a seat on a wooden bench around the corner from the elevators. I promise to never think the security dudes are just dopey cop wannabes ever again. The phone seems none the worse for wear and tear, either. Maybe this is a good day.

Oh, look. More messages. Tami. Lucky me. This latest batch asks if I've heard anything yet, tells me that I should have heard something by now. Next, she says she's counting on me and that we need this.

This last text must be the obligatory reminder, "So don't screw this up."

It is.

And to think, she's on my side.

In a way, I almost prefer being abused by some crazy-ass, wild woman in a wheelchair. At least she said "thank you" and even gave me a kiss after running me over.

It's been a while since Tami has kissed me. Even longer since she's let me kiss her.

I can still see the wheelchair jockey's smile. I try, but I can't picture the rest of her face.

Oh, no. Not going there.

Besides, what did she call me? Little Pepe? I need my drug of choice. *Bad.*

I retrieve that sweet digital image and longingly stare at it. She captivates me so. Her eyes show the blue translucence of a glacier—her long, straight hair still shines a golden yellow. She looks so Norwegian or Swedish. I'm still amazed she's not. She's from San Francisco.

Now's a bad time to admit it, but there's this creeping doubt I can never completely shake. What if I've been wrong all this time and it's true that the only way to my wife's heart is through my wallet? If that's true, then I'm in trouble.

Even if it isn't true, as long as she thinks it is—and I'm pretty sure she does—then I'm still in trouble. Maybe after today, I won't have to worry about it. Hope springs eternal and all that.

It's only sprinkling as I leave the courthouse, but the wind picks up. I'm a popsicle by the time I make the short walk back to the office.

Shivering, I check my email on the computer. Usually I do so first thing in the morning, and that's always a bad idea because nothing good has ever come from doing that. Every morning I try not to, and almost every morning I do it anyway.

I keep hoping for deliverance. I like to think it's the romantic in me.

On the other hand, I keep thinking it's never going to get any better here and the clock's run out, so I might as well get used to it. Adapt and succumb. Just tie a knot at the end of the rope I'm hanging from and swing with it. I hate to think it's the cynic in me.

Nothing in the inbox.

Fair enough.

I open the top desk drawer, grab my car keys, and go out to the parking lot where I have spare clothes in the trunk of my car. I'm so cold, I start the car. I fire up the heater and change my clothes from the driver's seat. Why not? I pop the trunk again, rummage through my earthquake kit, and grab some stale energy bars and a sports drink. I enjoy them in the car as I warm up.

She called me "Prince Charming."

Back in my office, I take the files and appearance sheets out of the Polly Pocket, drop it on a chair by the door, and put all that paperwork on my desk so I can update my hard calendar, bill my time, type up and shoot admin a quick email re: sanctions and request reimbursement, and start preparing the notice pleadings. I take off my field jacket and shake it free of the last drops of rain, hang it up on my coat rack, and sit at my desk. It's just another day. I turn and see Ryan standing in my doorway.

"Dude, you look awful! What happened to you?"

"Got caught in the rain. Long story. Got back from court and had to change clothes," I tell him.

"Oh, okay. Not going so well, I take it," he says, fishing.

"Just another romp in the center ring of this circus."

I don't know why, but I feel so sad sometimes.

"Ah." He puts his leather briefcase on the carpet and threads his arms one at a time into the sleeves of his raincoat. "Okay. I was hoping to walk over with you. Next time, then."

I check my email again while he's talking.

"From what I've been hearing, I thought you'd have some news to share by now."

He cinches the belt of his raincoat around his waist and picks up the briefcase.

I see it's a little heavier than usual. He must have a hearing.

Yes!

I point to the screen. "I'm supposed to see Sid as soon as I get back."

"Ah! 'Bout time." He seems relieved. "Don't let me keep you. Cheer up, dude. I've got a good feeling about this."

"Well then, hold that thought," I say, trying to stay positive.

"Absolutely! I really think you're good. I've heard that only five people from the office have applied, and four have already met with

Sid, and they all got the bad news. You're the only one left, dude. Do the math."

"Fair enough." I allow myself a brief smile. "Let's hope you're right. It will go a long way at home and finally make this ring of the circus bearable. I can say thanks then."

"And buy me lunch."

"And buy you lunch."

Ryan steps out and whispers, "Good luck," as he closes the door.

I call Sidney Woo—as in, Chief Deputy County Counsel Sidney Woo—and his secretary Marcie picks up. She says he's in a meeting and to call back in twenty minutes. I tell her I will, and twenty minutes later, I do. Marcie answers again. She says Sid's gone to lunch and has meetings until 4:30 p.m. and to check back then.

Fair enough.

I call back at 4:30 p.m. and get the okay to go upstairs. I check in with Marcie who calls Sid, who gives the okay, and Marcie tells me I can go in. I go into Woo's comparatively plush office and take a seat in front of his desk.

"Give me a minute, Paul," Woo says, staring at his computer screen and tapping on the keyboard.

"Sure. No worries." I look around.

Through the window behind Woo, I see the rain coming down—hard. Woo's attention remains fixed on the computer screen. He's wearing a white long-sleeved dress shirt and a grayish tie. Goes with his salt-and-pepper hair cut short, much shorter than mine. I think I'm getting grayer by the minute. I notice the grayish tie has images of small fish all over it.

He's not wearing eyeglasses, so I assume he's got contact lenses. We can't be too far apart in age, though I think he looks younger, certainly more fit, and more of the outdoors type. Maybe I should get outdoors more. Work less. Or not.

There's no success in working less.

I have never been in Woo's office before. There's a sepia-toned poster on the wall to my right. A big man with a broad, bushy, mustachioed grin wearing a hat with an even broader brim and a creased crown stands tall and proud, holding a rainbow trout in each hand. There's a fly rod and reel tucked between his right thumb and forefinger.

Copies of the *Idaho Fly Fishing Journal* and a thin paperback, *The Finer Points of Roll Casting* by Ross Richards, are stacked on the small, circular conference table below the poster.

"There. It's sent."

He turns and faces me. He blinks.

"Where's your suit?"

"Got caught in the rain on the way to court. Totally soaked. Had to change when I got back. This is all I had."

"You didn't have a spare suit?"

"Not with me. No."

Woo shakes his head.

"That will not do, Mister. That will not do at all. Unsat." He sighs. "Totally unsat. Going forward, you will maintain a spare suit and appropriate spare footwear at all times. We are professional here, and here, we always maintain a professional appearance. At all times. Especially while in the public eye."

So says the guy in the full-color fish tie. A bulging-eye trout tie, perhaps?

"What about an umbrella? You did have an umbrella, didn't you?"

"No, I did not. And it would not have made any difference in any event. I slipped and fell on the ramp. Well, I slipped and got run over by a woman in a wheelchair and fell."

He blinks. He blinks again.

"Some woman called here earlier. Something about . . . oh, yes. I remember now, something utterly ridiculous. Something about a Prince Charming."

He leans forward and squints. He stares at me with his dark eyes. He gets all bug-eyed.

"That was you? Oh, no. Tell me you did not give that woman a piggyback ride."

"I gave that woman a piggyback ride."

"You did no such thing."

Apparently, this guy is stone deaf.

He shakes his head.

"Oh, Paul. Paul! What were you thinking?"

"Before or after I did all that rolling and tumbling?"

Chapter 2

"Oh, good lord! Imagine the liability, Paul! What if you had dropped her? What if she had fallen?"

Probably not a good time to mention the face-plant.

"What then? Would Prince Charming magically appear with checkbook in hand? Such an unbelievable lapse in judgment, Paul." He rubs his dark, beady eyes. "Well, in any event, let's put that behind us now, shall we?"

He waves a hand.

"So, wading back into the stream, thanks for coming up. What else is new with you?"

"Nothing, just yet."

I'm trying to be nonchalant, but it's not working, I'm much too type A, and I'm feeling uneasy. My heart is pounding like the rain, and like the rain, I can't stop it. Not a good sign.

Oh, what the hell.

I don't know what else to do so I point to the poster.

"Hemingway?"

Woo grins.

"Indeed! Full marks! Yes. That is most certainly a picture of Ernest Hemingway. One of many and, as you may have guessed, certainly my favorite."

"I vaguely remember him being a blue water marlin kind of guy."

"Indeed he was. Among many other things. So, Paul." He stares at me with a silly looking grin, like he's about to give a speech. "So here we are. I just sent out the email to staff announcing the supervising deputy for our new program, the nuisance abatement team."

He leans back in his chair.

"I don't mind telling you that it will be modeled in very large part—well, almost entirely, I should say—on your proposal which, by the way, I also don't mind telling you, was excellent, even if it was a bit unconventional. I caution you on that, however. I do. Frankly, it's a bit too much of the maverick, if you ask me."

"How so?"

He clears his throat.

"Well, in a word, that's not the sort of approach we prefer here at County Counsel. We're far more conventional. We prefer consensus—one office, one mind. You seem to be more of the maverick, if you will."

"An outlier."

He looks puzzled, as if he doesn't recognize the word *outlier*.

"Anyway, as I was saying, my hat's off to you, Paul." He nods. "You really took the laboring oar and, fortunately, caught the CAO's eye and delivered on this project. As you must undoubtedly know, the CAO's excited as all get out. The Board wants it up and running yesterday. You can take pride in knowing that. Truly you can."

"Okay."

"You've been with us—what now, seven, eight years roughly?"

"About that, yes."

More like nine years, nine months, and twenty-one days. Not that this idiot would know.

"Impressive. Most impressive," he says, nodding.

He pauses to look at me and shrugs.

"Then again, no reason it shouldn't be. It's not like you're new to this stuff. After all, that is why we brought you in."

Woo takes a breath and smiles.

"So, Paul. The news you have no doubt been waiting for. The long and the short of it is this—the decision's been made, and I do not mind telling you directly that it's not you."

Did I hear him right?

I'm not sure I heard him right. I think he's waiting for me to react more.

I don't.

He blinks, breaks silence, and rambles on.

"The county's bringing in someone from the outside as a new Chief Deputy for Litigation, and so the promotion position and the program are being blended into that unit. The Board's new mood du jour is that we need to start recovering judgments for a change rather than paying them."

My jaws clench and lock. I mentally flip that switch, the switch I believe that we all have—that we all must have—to go into pure, stone-cold survival mode. Only this time, it takes an excruciating amount of effort for me to do it. I think I can hear one of my molars cracking.

Yeah. I heard him right. Why am I still here? It's over. Go home.

No more pounding heart. No more anxiety.

I wish.

My heart pounds harder still. Anxiety's through the roof. No good days with Tami anymore.

Tami's gonna be shittin' bricks now—bloody big-ass bricks!

I allow myself a slight nod and no more, fearing the release of the floodgates of questions and criticisms and God only knows what I might say.

I muster the will to say, "Fair enough," while managing to keep looking Woo in the eye.

He keeps looking me in the eye. Neither of us blinks. Neither of us flinches. Neither of us moves.

Maybe now's a good time to punch him out.

"Any questions?" Woo asks after far too long a pause. "Not that I have any answers for you necessarily, you understand."

I think his fake smile borders on being evil.

"I do understand, and yes, I do have questions."

"Good. Fire away."

"Who is it?"

"More like 'who are they?' Darrell Huntington, for one."

"I don't think I know him."

"Correct. You don't." Woo gives a faint smile.

Cocksucker.

"He's an outsider. Coming on board as a new chief deputy." He gives a stupid little flash of a grin. "More of a favor to the CAO, but you did not hear that from me."

"When's he start?"

"Monday. Which reminds me," he says, snapping his fingers. "I need to have Marcie calendar a meeting for the two of you to get acquainted. The CAO is anxious to get him up to speed. Supervisor Terry is anxious to see results in his district. And you. You're still our man, Paul. I mean that, truly I do. You're our guy. Like I said, you delivered, so we're expecting great things from you. Great things."

"Right. And you say that with a straight face."

"I know. Anything else?"

"Yes."

Are you insane?

"All right then. Make your cast and drop the fly," he chuckles to himself.

He would.

Asshole.

"How about you get around to telling me who you promoted."

"I was about to. However, I didn't promote anyone. Our county counsel did that."

"Okay, fair enough. So who got it? You know, instead of me."

"That would be Jessica Carrigan."

Never heard of her either. I hate having to remind myself to breathe. But I do, and I do. Getting all cottony in the mouth now.

"Is she an outsider, too?"

"Oh, no. Of course not." He gives me a strange look. "Frankly, Paul. I am very surprised at you. No reason you shouldn't know her. She's been here, oh, I'd say at least five years. Maybe more. She's very dynamic. Very capable."

"At what? If I may ask."

"You think you're being funny, no doubt."

"No. I think I'm being quite serious. What exactly does she do so, dynamically?"

"Well, for starters, she's officially our office's legislative liaison. She analyzes legislation pending before the Assembly and Senate houses for the County Counsel and the Board. She also coordinates on behalf of our office with the other offices of county counsel and the league—the league of cities—that is—she's our office's eyes and ears in Sacramento."

"Okay, so the translation is she's all privilege and politics. Pure and simple."

"Excuse me?"

"Privilege and politics. She's a hack and a fair hair. Bet she's never been in a courtroom. Never tried a single case."

He waves me off.

"Well, has she?"

"Oh, don't be so ridiculous. Not all lawyers need be in courtrooms. You know that."

"Then the answer is no."

"Paul, it doesn't make a damn bit of difference what the answer is."

"It does to me. It's taken me years to get through all the bullshit and the meddling and the committees to get the county code rewritten to have any teeth at all for any meaningful land use enforcement. More importantly, those who've never been in a courtroom have no business supervising those of us who earn our livings there. Even those of us who'll never rank among the jury trial gods. Maybe, especially so. The job's hard enough."

"Nobody cares, Paul! You're missing the bigger picture here. The bigger picture. We're fly-fishing here, Paul, not noodling around in the mud like some cap-busting rednecks who have no clue how they made it to the evening news. I understand that you are in the trenches. I get it. You're neck-deep in the mud. I said I get it. Whoop-de-do. So what? None of that matters. It's not the big picture here."

"But it's the trenches where we make it or break it. That's where the appellate opinions come from and the legislation that follows. That's 'so what.'"

"I'm telling you, Paul. For your own good. You have got to get out of the mud once in a while. Get some fresh air. Mingle in the office. You don't . . . participate enough."

"I'm in court nearly every day as it is. You people in admin took away our admin leave, there's no overtime. We can bill till doomsday, but it's all smoke and mirrors. No money ever really changes hands. Who has time for this crap? I don't have time for this crap."

"Well, Paul, you need to make time. Follow Jessica's example. She is the chairperson of our Millennial Relations Committee."

"Millennial what?"

"Millennial Relations Committee. It's a truly splendid mentoring program for assisting new attorneys to adapt to the requirements of the office and for our administration to better understand their needs in terms of flexible schedules, time off, and so forth."

I shake my head.

"More handholding, participation trophies, and butt-wiping, you mean. What the hell's wrong with you people? I never got anything like that in my whole life! And I'll bet neither did you! Admit it! Every attorney job I ever got always started the same damn way. Some jaded old bat threw a stack of files on my desk and said, 'Oh! By the way, young man, you're late! You were due in Department Such and Such thirty-five minutes ago. I had lil' Miss Sweet Cheeks call the department and ask ever so sweetly for second call and tell them that you were on your way, speeding ticket in hand. The file is in their somewhere. Good luck, Tiger. Give 'em hell.'"

"Now that is funny."

"I get it now. You've never been a litigation associate, have you? You've never been in a courtroom yourself, outside of jury duty, have you?"

"Anyway, as I was about to say, she also serves on our Diversity Committee. As a member of the Holiday Party Planning Committee, she supervises all our fundraising projects for the year-end holiday party."

"Yeah? What holiday is that, exactly?"

He rolls his eyes.

"Now. Now. We can't go there. You know very well what holidays I mean. We just call them collectively 'the holidays.'" He grins. "You know that."

"No I don't. I celebrate Christmas, and I celebrate it at home, thank you. I don't live here, despite all the hours I put in."

"Very well then. Whatever floats your boat, Paul. The point, which you would do well to remember, is this—Jessica reaches out. She gets involved. She demonstrates real leadership."

"Which you would do well to remember doesn't have a damn thing to do with the practice of law. Or is the practice of law not really part of the big picture here? Go ahead. I'll wait."

Crickets and a poker face.

Finally, Woo speaks.

"They key word in the term 'county counsel' is *counsel*, not litigate."

"And you say that with a straight face."

"Yes, I know. Goes with the territory," he says, keeping a straight face.

"Fair enough. Then what about a reassignment?"

"For who?"

"For whom? For me."

"Why would you want to be reassigned?"

"Because none of this shit's gonna work."

He waves a hand. "Oh, that's crazy talk. You're not crazy, are you?"

I shake my head. "That's the rumor. But no. I don't think so."

"Well, that's a relief."

"For you. You wanna know what's crazy? Promoting a political hack over me to run my own program that you acknowledged that I created for legally addressing all the nuisance cases and real quality-of-life issues we have running rampant all over the unincorporated areas of this county. That's crazy! But no, everybody is rumormongering that I'm the crazy one. They're the ones who are effin' crazy around here!"

"Now that's just crazy talk, and you know it."

"Really? This Jessica doesn't know squat about litigation, and yet she's apparently my new boss. Like the rest of you, her ideas and decisions and rubber-stamping of the bureaucracy of county departments will get the county screwed in court every time. But nobody gives a shit because it's not their money or your money. No, it's the county's money, and all of you, ivory-tower, political-wannabe dimwits must think it grows on trees. Maybe it comes from breathing all that rarefied air at the top or up the supervisors' backsides. Now how is that not stupid and crazy as fuck?"

He lets that one sit a minute, then sighs.

"Well, first of all, we dimwits are much smarter than you. Second, her background does not concern you. She got the promotion. That's it. That's all you ever need to know. Third, yes. She is your new boss, administratively speaking. Deal with it. The day-to-day stuff is still yours to manage certainly. You can deal with that too."

Woo smiles. He's obviously pleased with himself.

"That said, I suggest you suck it up, big man that you are, and find a way to make it work. Besides, she remains the legislative liaison for our office. That's primary. Obviously, she'll be juggling the two assignments. The new title certainly can't hurt her in Sacramento. There's that."

He's turning toward the window behind him.

"Yes, I see that could well work to our advantage. Anyway," he says, back still turned toward me, "like I said, Paul—although perhaps not quite so enthusiastically now—you are still our guy. For the time being, at least. Don't go getting all bent out of shape over this. It's not a big deal. No big deal. None at all."

He stares at the ceiling.

"Let me put it this way, Paul. Follow along with me here. None of the big kahunas, none of the really big fish you need to worry about here, none of them are ever going to strike at the whiny teensie, oh-so-weensie, little fly you're floating, so you might as well reel it in." He grins. "Just reel it all the way back in, Paul!"

He stares at me with that must-be-patented poker face of his.

"Honestly, Paul, let's just say it's in your best interest to make this thing work."

Something gnawing at my gut tells me this is not the hill I want to die on and that I'm better off pursuing a reassignment another way at another time. Survival matters. I think it's coming from something I read in Sun Tzu's book. I know. Tami made me read it. Twice.

"I see."

"Good. I truly hope you do. You know what might help you gain some perspective on the bigger picture here?"

"Apparently not. No."

"The Diversity Committee."

So help me God, I want to strangle you, Woo.

"Yes, Paul. I want you to reach out to Jessica. The committee does excellent work promoting diversity within the office. Though, I can't say its offerings have improved my waistline any."

He chuckles at his little joke.

"Fat chance."

"Very well. Is there anything else?"

"No."

"Very well," he says, almost sounding like Chrome Dome.

Then I remember. *Duh.*

I heard they're both former navy men.

"Thanks again, Paul, for coming up. I think you needed this opportunity to vent. I do. Truly. And that is precisely why I will overlook your unprofessional conduct and extremely offensive language. This time. Just this one time. Do you understand me, Paul?"

"I do."

"Good. Very good. Next time? There will be serious discipline, up to and including termination. Do you understand me, Paul?"

"Yes. I do. I understand you, loud and clear."

"Good. I think this has been a good discussion overall. And all things considered, I want to thank you for your patience today. It has been hectic, I admit. I do apologize for that. I do."

"No problem."

I stand up to leave.

"Paul."

"What?"

He's keeping that straight-face thing going.

"For what it's worth, this promotion isn't right for you."

Not again.

"It's not?"

"No. Not at all."

My head's spinning. I have no idea how to slow it down other than just leave and call it a day.

"Well, I'm not sure why, but okay. If you say so."

"Paul, if it helps you, imagine this—sometimes I get tired of wading out into fast-moving water, so I treat myself to a river guide and do some drift boat fishing on a dory. With a properly built and beautifully balanced boat and an experienced guide on the oars, I don't need to know anything about the boat, the water, or, for that matter, the fish in order to tell my guide to 'go here' or to 'go over there' and try fishing from a new spot. That's just giving direction. Any fly-fisherman can do that.

"But what I'm telling you, Paul, is that the real skill—the technical craft—is in building the boat and handling the oars.

Moving that load about in a current. Keeping it under control. Staying afloat in the right spot.

"And in a way, that's exactly what you've done here, Paul. You've done both of those things. You've done them amazingly well. You are a true technical craftsman. Not only that, but you went out of the box on this. Completely out of the box. That just isn't done. Not here. That takes real creativity. That takes guts and ingenuity. It's pure innovation. And that never happens here and for good reason. Not to mention you undoubtedly enjoyed a fair degree of luck, timing, and a pretty damn heavy mood swing among the Board."

He chuckles to himself. Again.

"However, in all seriousness, Paul. This program, once it's in place and with you working it, like my guide works his boat and oars, well, then, just about anybody—and I do mean anybody—can give simple direction. Simple steering orders, 'go here,' 'now, go there.'" He leans back in his chair. "Pardon the pun, Paul, but do you get my drift? In other words, anybody can do that job of supervision. Just like anybody can supervise, Paul. But not just anybody can build a river-worthy boat and pull on those oars."

"So I'm a boatbuilder and an oar puller."

"Of the highest order. One of the best I've seen in a long time."

Woo leans further back in chair, and it creaks under his weight. His eyes are closed like he's napping in a little boat, rocking ever so gently with little creaking noises.

He blinks.

"I must also mention to you, Paul, that the boatman and I are a team, just as we in this county law office are a team. The boatman never wanders off to chase his fancy. He never does. He awaits— indeed, he anticipates—my instructions. You, of course, must learn to do the same. You went off chasing this nuisance thing, and in the end you got lucky. Very, very lucky. Far luckier than you know. You will do well to remember that whether on the river or in this office, we must constantly be in touch with the ebb and flow of the consensus that drives us, no less than that of the river's current, so that we may keep our course."

"I see."

"I'm very pleased that you do."

"So on top of everything else, you're telling me I'm not a team player?"

Woo sits up.

"Oh, on the contrary! The issue here is, just whose team are you on? The answer is, of course, that we have only one team here. Make sure you're on it, Mister. Make sure you're on it at all times."

Breathe. Just breathe.

"We do not suffer fools here, Mister. We pride ourselves on maintaining a united front. Consensus is king. All individual effort is guided—directed, if you will—for the common good of our client departments and the uniformity and unity of this office. All things inure to the benefit of the county as a whole. You must decide who you are. Who are you going to be? Your continued success here depends upon your willingness to consent, to conform, choosing to adapt and to fit into the roles and responsibilities assigned to you while you're here. For however long you are here. In a word, loyalty. We will—and we *do*—demand your loyalty here, Mister. Remember that. No mavericks, no renegades, no trailblazers, no knights errant. Not here. Not ever."

Oh boy.

Something tells me now is a good time to pause a bit, so I do, before saying what's next on my mind.

"Well, okay, then." I take another breath. "Next question. Just for my own edification, if anybody can supervise, why does it sound like it wouldn't be me in any event?"

"Well now, Paul, this may not be the best time."

"As good a time as any, and I'll just keep asking."

"Very well then, Mister. For starters, let's just say that you lack, hmm, how do I best say it?"

Well, for starters, asshole, try plain, fucking English.

"You lack finesse, Paul."

"Finesse?"

"Exactly, Paul. Finesse."

"Finesse for what?"

"Well, for starters, handling what we here like to refer to as 'massaging negative information.' Obviously. You see, presenting negative information demands a certain finesse, a certain, delicacy. You, sir, do not have it. Diplomacy might even be a better word."

"Are you saying I can't be diplomatic?"

"In a word, yes."

"That's a load of crap! If the news is bad, then it's bad, for Christ's sake. Wrapping it around a turd and then dipping it into a bowl of marine varnish and sprinkling it with glitter and pixie dust doesn't change a damn thing! It's still a turd wrapped in bad news. Let me break it down for you. Shit that gets sent off somewhere at the speed of light is still just shit when it gets there. So you're better off skipping all that stuff and just lay it out in the open, up front!"

Woo squints.

"That and, as you may not have noticed, you're certainly much too direct. Too confrontational. Perhaps that's appropriate in a courtroom. I wouldn't know. I do know, however, that you are downright and unpleasantly blunt. Curt. Abrupt. Short. Abrasive. Much too much so. We on this floor call that rudeness. By the way, Paul, has anyone ever told you to your face that you, Mister, are a 'bull in a china shop'?"

No way. I am not copping out to that with this guy.

"Now, I'm a bull?"

"In a china shop! A very delicately balanced china shop, I might add. Besides, you can't just waltz in here thinking you're a hero, the new marshal in town, and just change things just because you want to or think you can—or for whatever reason!"

"Okay. So if I understand your having told me, I think you said, 'the decision's been made and it's not you,' that was your way of being delicate? Your style of diplomacy?"

He blinks.

"No. Of course not. None of that applies to you in this context."

"And why the hell not?"

"Well, first of all, you are not in a position of authority here! You—and you will do well to remember this, Mister—are simply a worker bee. As such, you fulfill a subservient role here and, yes, you have done so with remarkable rigor. Judicial notice taken! Second, as anyone who's ever spoken with you for more than thirty seconds understands, you are a much rougher breed of man, less cultured, less refined, more rugged."

"And a worker bee?"

"Yes. I mean, Jesus, just look at yourself!"

"We went through this already."

"Never mind that. I'm referring to how you so often appear these days. Usually your collar's unbuttoned, your tie loosened, the sleeves of your shirt are rolled up. Who dresses like that anymore? Nobody here—nobody except you, and you're not RFK running for President back in, in 1968. Why is that, do you suppose?"

"Well, for one thing, I was eight years old in 1968. 1968 is long past. RFK is dead, and I was in the third grade when RFK got shot in LA."

"No, no. That's not what I mean. You know what I mean. Anyway, let me tell you what I mean. Worker bees and drones. The 'roll up your sleeves,' 'get down to business,' 'dig yourself a hole' kind of working man. Blue-collar thinking. Certainly not professional legal advisors to the key decision-makers within the leading body of our local governments."

"And a bull, remember? You also said I was a bull."

He chuckles a bit and, with a grin, shakes his head.

"And you dare question me. A superior officer. There's the bull in you, right there. So thickheaded. Yes, Paul, a bull, you are most definitely a bull. You will also do as well to remember that we do not need any bulls—or bullies, for that matter—here. No way, Mister.

Not in this office. Keep that in mind and tread lightly, Mister. Tread very lightly."

Yeah? Well, I call bullshit!

"Woo, I've never bullied anyone in my entire life. This is total bullshit, and you know it! Hell, Woo! I've spent most of my life—from the third grade on—a skinny kid with glasses, fighting off bullies!"

I'm pissed.

"So tell me, Woo, what were you as a kid? What was your life like from the third grade on? Who was fightin' your battles?"

His grin is long gone by now.

"Thank you for that, Mr. Cooper. So much for treading lightly, I see. However, your personal problems make no difference to me. None. None at all. Now. That said, I strongly encourage you to reach out to Jessica. Damn!" He snaps his fingers again. "As soon as she gets back from maternity leave. Damn! I forgot all about that. She's out of the office starting this afternoon. She left just not too long ago, shortly after I had met with her. She's having twins, I'll have you know. She's very excited. We are all very excited for her."

"Okay."

So what? Reach out, right? Fat chance.

"Oh! There's just one more thing, Paul."

"Okay," I tell him, stopping at the door. "Name it."

"No more of this Don Quixote nonsense. You want to save damsels in distress? Do it on your own time and on your own dime. Are we clear on that?"

"Absolutely."

"Good. Very good. Oh, one more thing!"

"Certainly."

"Keep a spare suit on hand at all times. We don't run safaris here."

"Naturally."

"And one more thing."

"Seriously?"

What the fuck are you, a clown?

"Yes. You need a hobby, Paul."

"What?"

"A hobby. You need to get yourself a hobby, Paul."

"A hobby?" Now I blink. I'm beginning to think he really is insane.

"I need a hobby? Oh!" I snap my fingers. "I get it. You mean like developing policies and procedures for coordinating efforts of various county departments responsible for enforcing different titles of our code? Developing case assessment plans and evaluation criteria? Making that"—I hold my tongue to check my language—"code workable to begin with? You mean stuff like that?"

Woo, still squinting, shakes his head.

"Mmm, no."

He slowly looks about his office.

"I'm thinking more along the lines of, you know, something outside of work, something totally unrelated to work. Something to refresh the soul."

"I see. Any suggestions? You know, other than fishing. I don't like the smell of fish. And I sure as hell don't have the money or tools or wood or whatever to build any boats."

"Mmm. Well," he says, still staring at me, "in that case, use your best judgment. Focus on something that interests you. It will do wonders for your health, not to mention your sanity, which, now that I think about it, is your health and, honestly, your attitude. Trust me on this. You'll see."

"My attitude?"

Woo nods. "Oh yes. Especially your attitude."

"Okay then. A hobby."

Oh, bite me, boat boy.

"Yeah. I'll get right on that."

Probably right around doomsday, you know, if that works for you, fly guy.

"Good! See that you do, Paul."

"All right, sir. Thank you for your time."

Yeah. In your ass.

"Don't mention it. Have a good weekend, Paul, and you can leave the door open."

I step out. Marcie's gone. It's dead quiet. I realize most everyone on the floor has gone.

Duh. County workers.

"You've got two weeks, Paul."

Two weeks? Two weeks for what?

I turn around. "I'm sorry, what?"

"I said you've got two weeks. Two weeks from today and then report back to me by email on your choice of hobby."

"You're serious."

He nods.

I shrug. "Fair enough."

I go back to my office. Fortunately for me, it's five minutes to 5:00 p.m. on a Friday. The whole floor is deserted.

Déjà vu.

All over again.

So that's it? Wham, bam, thank you, ma'am? I'm a boatbuilder?

But I had come through. So how the hell can this be? I delivered! He even said so! It was textbook all the way. Not even Coach could fault me. Put in the effort and get the rewards. That's how it works. That's how I work it. Everybody knows that. Do what you're told. Check. Go along with the program. Check. Fit in. Check. Be a team player. Check. Check and, again, check. Promotion's *mine*. That's how this shit works! Do the chore—get the cookie. Check.

What the hell am I missing? My promotion . . .

I sit at my desk in a stone-mode stupor and automatically reach for another case folder as if on autopilot and then catch myself.

Fuck it.

It can wait till Monday. I turn to the computer and wiggle the mouse to find the cursor on the screen, click the time sheet icon, and finish billing my time for the day. Then I click on the media player.

I adjust the volume and lean back in my chair to listen to a random CD of old '80s rock and roll.

I feel the vibration of my phone against my belt.

Crap.

Chapter 3

I assume Tami's calling or texting, and I ignore it. I can't deal with her now. I just can't. The vibration changes to a ringtone. It's not Tami.

Saved by a ringtone.

"Hey, Princess," I answer.

"Hey, Papa, wazzup?"

"I don't know. You called me."

"Papa! It's a greeting, not a question to be taken literally."

"Okay."

I put the phone on speaker and set it down by the keyboard and lower the computer's volume.

"What's that noise?"

"Computer music."

"Oh? Who are you listening to?"

"I don't know. Somebody, rock and roll, something."

"What's the song?"

"Not sure. Had a guitar in it, I think."

"Are you having a bad day, Papa?"

I shrug.

"Not at all. Day's same as any other."

"Okay, Papa. You don't have to tell me. Are you working late again, tonight? It's Friday."

"I don't think so."

"You don't think it's Friday or you don't think you'll be working late?"

"I don't think I'll be working late. Apparently, it's Friday somewhere."

"Yes it is! It's Friday for both of us. Be sure to do something fun."

"Okay."

And just how am I supposed to get ahead and pay for someone's college "doing something fun"?

"Good. Oh! Give me your email again. I want to send you a video. I've learned a new song on my guitar."

"When did you get a guitar?"

"Papa! A couple of months ago. Did you forget already?"

"Apparently, yes. I've been busy."

"It's okay. Your email, please?"

"Right."

I give her my office email address.

"I think I got it. I'm sending it now. Watch it. Then email me back and go home and do something fun and call me right back if you don't get it in a minute or so, okay?"

"I will."

"Be sure to watch it, okay?"

"I promise."

"Good. And, Papa?"

"Yes?"

"Please don't take this the wrong way, but I think maybe you need a hobby. You sound really stressed. Did you and Mother have another fight about your job?"

"No, Princess."

Not yet. But I'm sure one's coming.

"Papa, are you okay?"

"I'm fine."

Oh, crap. I used Shelley Lynne's "F" word.

"Papa, when people say they're fine, they're really saying they're hurt or angry. Which is it? 'Cause you are *so* not fine."

I turn away from the phone, sigh, and run my hands through my thinning hair and take a deep breath, then another, rub my face, and slowly exhale. I need to get the tone of my voice just right.

"Neither. It's all good," I say.

That's much better. Maybe I can skate through this.

"Papa, I know you are working much too hard. You are not taking care of yourself. You're not eating veggies, drinking coconut water, and taking vitamins like I told you to. Mother's probably still pushing you about work, which isn't fair, you're probably not standing up to her, and you don't have to talk about it. I just want you to find something fun you can do for yourself."

"Fair enough, Princess. I'll think about it."

"No, seriously, Papa. I mean it. You are really stressed. I hear it in your voice. Maybe you can try guitar. It relaxes me before exams or when I get stuck writing a paper, and playing it is really cheap fun. I don't have to go anywhere special, and I don't need anyone else to do it with. And, Papa, I'm never bored anymore. It's perfect. I think you should give it a try, okay? Seriously."

"Okay, I'll think about it."

"Okay, Papa. I'll talk to you later. Love you, Papa."

I hear the click that means we're disconnected before the words "I love you, too, Princess," make it out of my mouth.

I open her email and click on the attached video. I see Shelley Lynne sitting cross-legged on her bed with a small acoustic guitar in her lap.

"Hi, Papa! I just learned this. I hope you like it."

She looks at the fretboard and forms a chord with her left hand. She starts finger-picking a melody with her right hand and messes up.

"Wait," she says and starts over and plays the melody straight through, smiling. "I did it!"

I hear another girl's voice from off-screen, "That was totally cool. You nailed it."

That must be her roommate.

"Thanks. This is so fun," her voice rises. "Papa! Did you get it? Reply back and tell me if you know the name of the song, okay? Love you, Papa, bye."

The video stops.

I'm all smiles, and I reply that I got it. At least I think I do. I'm not completely sure. I type what I think is the song's name. I tell her how much I appreciate her calls and the video and hope she'll send others when she can, if it's not too much bother and if it doesn't interfere with her studies. I tell her that I've had a pretty good day and that I love her so much. I hit Send, and then I watch it again. I watch it a few more times. Then I email it to my computer at home.

I watch it one more time and shut down the computer. I get my keys and check to see that I have everything—phone, wallet, ID badge, house keys, and suit jacket because I sure as hell don't want to have to come back up here till Monday and maybe not even then—and I leave.

The parking lot is nearly empty as I walk to my car in the light rain. I can hear Tami's nagging voice in the vibration of my phone. Her text message says, "Call me now!"

Nope! Not going there! I'm a bull in a china shop, and Tami's not at all fond of animals.

I open the driver's door and get in. Sitting behind the steering wheel, I watch the raindrops sliding down the windshield. The patter of the drops sounds like a clock ticking, and I think time's a wasting. But I have no action plan, no task list—nothing for handling this situation.

I had assumed the promotion was mine all along—do the chore, get the cookie. I had allowed myself too much stock in Ryan's reading of the tea leaves, as he likes to describe it, and I feel guilty and stupid and used. Now I remember the county's unwritten personnel rule for promotions, HR 100.1: "Never ever, ever, apply for anything until your boss tells you it's okay to do so."

Duh. A little late.

My forearms feel like lead weighing down against my thighs. It takes too much effort to move, so I let the feeling of paralysis spread over me. I can no longer focus on the raindrops. There is only the vague blur of dark and light shapes that seem to slide about the glass and the muddled sound of distant voices in my head, all clamoring for attention and obedience.

The noise is not coming from a runaway clock but from my teeth chattering. The voices are fading. Another fifty-plus-hour workweek has come and gone, and once again I don't have anything to show for it. Once again, someone else will reap the work's harvest—*my* work's harvest. This time, it will be someone I've never even met.

Why am I always doing this?

Then I remember why, and how she's been texting me all day.

I do not want to admit—*can't* admit—what cannot possibly ever, ever be true; all these years and longer, I've been chasing the wrong carrot. It can't be true. It just can't.

No. That I've gotten this far must mean something. It tells me that I'm right and that there's got to be a way out because if I am wrong, then it's all been for naught and I have no idea what the real carrot is. There must be a way. I just to need to keep on gutting it out.

After all, what can the F-4 Phantom II jet teach us about reaching goals? Why, given enough power, you can get damn near anything off the ground and make it fly. See? There you go. Success principle number whatever. Outlook determines outcome. It's all a matter of power. That's all it is—willpower. Need to get me some more of that willpower.

But a hobby? What a joke! Hobbies cost money. They're worthless.

I wonder whose voice that is and whether I should even be listening to it. It's not like I don't know about hobbies. I've had plenty—more than plenty. Tami's gonna shit when I tell her that I must get another one.

Tami.

I still have to figure out how to face her. I can't go on like this. Every time I deliver, she demands more. But she's so worth it.

And so far out of my league.

She can still have any man she wants. Even now. Yet she gave me a shot. I know she hasn't given up on me yet.

Damn it! I came so close this time.

I gotta turn this around somehow. Manna from heaven doesn't fall very often, but when it does—take it. Take it and show the world you earned it!

Earned it.

Damn right I earned it! That promotion is mine! I created the damn position from scratch.

Fuck you, Woo! You power-grubbin', damn little, brook-babblin', bastardly little fuck! That was my cookie! My fuckin' cookie!

I'm quivering. My left shirt sleeve is soaked. So is my left pant leg.

Duh.

Driver door's is still open. I look back. My suit jacket is on a hanger over the rear seat. I don't remember taking it off or hanging it up. My raincoat's back in my office.

Just go home. Figure all this out later.

I close my door and start the car. The radio blasts and jolts me, and I jump. I turn it down, push different channel buttons, not liking what I hear, and then I hear a melody. And just as it grabs me, it ends.

Shit!

A man's high-pitched voice, with a British accent, charges from the radio speakers.

"Did you hear that, man? Are you getting it, man? That sound? That guitar sound? I'm telling you, man, that was the sound. That sound had a voice, yeah? It was talkin' to me, and it was sayin', 'Listen to me, I'm your path to freedom.' That was it. Everything changed after that."

"What were the sounds, the voices, then of the shipyard?" his interviewer asks.

"Well, if you ask me it wasn't freedom. All manner of sadness and 'Lad, here you'll stay,' yeah? Sounds of ''Ard work and pure labor and nothin' much else to ever show for it.' And a little bit of 'A pint for ya troubles.' Remember, this was a time when, you know, musicians on both sides of the pond were discovering the electric guitar, you know. Some were junk. Some rang out like church bells. 'Course, I was just a lad at the time. No way me family could ever afford one, you know, not even a cheap one. I could hear the records at night, you know, with me window open. Somebody had a record player and they was playin' their records. I'd stay up and listen."

The sound comes back on the radio; it's distant but alluring.

"I took a job on the docks, so I could save up for one, and I did."

In the background, I hear what sounds like a foghorn and seagulls calling, a blast from maybe a tugboat's whistle, and then a blend of guitar sounds in the mix.

"I wanted that pure tone, you know, to play that, and me life became a quest to play like that—to capture that tone, you know? I mean that's the whole thing. And I did, man. Made it me life."

And you succeeded—at least until your troubles with your drug addiction," the interviewer's voice cuts in.

"I was working the docks, yeah, you know playing clubs, and someone turned me onto the 'Mighty O.'"

"You mean opium."

"Yeah, I mean opium. 'Course I mean opium. It was, you know, any—*bleep*—that—*bleep*—ing good should have a—*bleep*—ing warning on it, you know?"

"But music saved you."

"No, man, sod off, music. Man, the—*bleep*—ing guitar saved me. Without mine, I'd still be on the Mersey docks, you know?"

The guitar's fade-in is followed with applause and the announcer's voice, "Rock 'n' Roll Hall of Famer, guitarist Gordon Stewart remembering the time he first heard an electric guitar. For *Pioneers of Sound,* this is Jason Weinberg. You're listening to California Public Radio."

I turn it off.

Fuck you, Woo! Hobby my ass.

Where did I go wrong? What did I miss? That promotion was mine. It *is* mine. I earned it. Pure and simple. How's a hobby gonna make any difference now? It's not. It can't. There's just no sense to this—to any of it. None at all. Maybe he's just messing with me.

Prick.

Maybe that's it. Put me in a round room and tell me to piss in a corner. Got to be some kind of test.

Prick weenie.

But why?

Oh, who the fuck knows? Will you just go home, man? Figure this shit it out on Monday.

Monday. Right. When I meet what's-his-name. Already forgot his name. Maybe that's it. Forget what I know. Forget all of it. Let what's-his-name figure it out.

My future changed today.

And none of this shit matters anymore.

In my head, though, I can still hear that guitar bit—such beautiful, clear sounds. Like the voice of God. And I can't shake it.

Seriously. Like the voice of God.

As pissed off as I am, I want to hear it again. I wish I knew the song. I wonder if Shelley Lynne would ever want to learn it. Probably not.

Then again . . .

No, probably not. Maybe I can learn something like it.

Oh, get serious, you dumb ass.

Now that voice I know. Yay! Coach is back. Just what I need.

Not!

His voice is always lurking in the back of my head somewhere. He's been dead, what, maybe three years already? I stop to think about it. Yeah. Something like that. But here he is, like always, like he's never left—always popping out from time to time, sniping me, reminding me how stupid I am, how I'm always effing up this, that, and the other thing.

Good 'ol Coach.

All that "Your worthless, I wash my hands of you" shit—that's all I had ever heard from him as far back as I can remember.

There's a sound of laughter—only I'm not laughing, so it must be an echo of him—and then a "woompf" sound.

Shit.

I've just backhanded the empty passenger seat. So lame. As if I could actually smack a dead guy. In his case, yeah, I sure as hell would like to. If ever there was a dead guy deserving a good whacking, then Coach would be that guy.

I want to whack him like he whacked those beer cans he made me chase after.

"You gotta produce!" he'd say.

"Produce" my ass.

"Fuck you, Coach! I did produce! I did! You know damn well I did! Even you'd have to be proud of me this time! You know it's true! I did everything I was supposed do—every shit thing those pricks demanded! The whole time they're judging me, just like you said. Remember, Coach? Huh? Yeah. I learned. I produced when all the time they were just watchin' me, grading me. Judging me. You know it too!"

Shit!

"Shit, Coach! You should be pulling for me for once! Why couldn't you pull for me just this once? Would it have fuckin' killed you, taken you away from your precious golf game?"

I catch myself looking at the empty passenger seat, as if he's been sitting here with me the whole time.

Okay, this pounding on and talking to a dead guy in my head can't be good, even if it is Coach. Even if he does really deserve it . . . and more. Fuck! I wonder if anybody heard me.

I feel the spike in my pulse and the rapid shallowness of my breathing.

C'mon, man. Get a grip and breathe.

Maybe I should try yoga. Maybe that's the fairy in me—if there is a fairy in me. I don't think there is. Coach always complained he was never too sure. Maybe that's Coach just butting in again. *Fairy* was always his word. Back in the day. He was always warning me not to become a fairy.

Feeling somewhat calmer now—although I can't say that I'm ever really calm—I drive out of the parking lot.

Before long, I pull into a fast food place. Then it's a burger, fries, and a chocolate shake—okay, two chocolate shakes.

Fuck it.

Back through the drive-through for another chocolate shake and then back onto the street. Driving comatose, I think of what Shelley Lynne said. I think of her video.

Then I think about how today was supposed to be my day, all the promises made and not kept.

So help me God, I am not a loser. I'm not worthless! I'm not!

Well, I'm not dead either. But if I were, I could finally beat the shit out of Coach. But I'm not. This can still be my day. But I have no idea how. I think of Woo's shit-stupid command.

You want a fucking hobby, Woo? I catch sight of the big red sign. *Fine, I got your hobby right here.*

I'm driving into a Strummin' City Music Emporium parking lot.

Huh.

I didn't even know this place existed.

Chapter 4

I wander in. I find the guitar section and enter through the blast of noise and move among the mass of bodies—mostly scrawny young men in their late teens—and I trust I'll find whatever it is I'm looking for.

I have no idea what I'm looking for.

Crowded rows of amplifiers leave only narrow aisles to wander through and an occasional bench where one can sit, plug in, and zone out.

The walls are plastered floor to ceiling with guitars of every shape and size and color. They're matched by the variety of players scattered about the dingy, carpeted floor. Everywhere I look, I see them strumming, picking, and shredding every style known and a few, I guess, that never will be.

I'm the oldest guy in here, and I feel like a misplaced mannequin—a soaking wet one.

Okay, so maybe this is a mistake.

I'm not sure what to do. Then I realize I'm the oldest guy here and that means I don't have to do anything. My age alone says I probably have a job and credit cards, and they'll come to me.

Sure enough, a stout man with a graying ponytail and who's sleeved with tats on each arm from wrist to bicep and hand-trucking a stack of brown boxes wheels up to me and stops close enough to avoid having to yell.

"Hey, how's it going?"

"Okay."

"Awesome. Thanks for coming in. Feel free to grab one and play it."

I look around. "I-I, wouldn't even know where to begin."

"I can help with that. I'm Kerry, by the way."

"Paul. Nice to meet you."

"Ditto. Is the guitar for you or someone else?"

My goofy grin—the one I can't control—betrays me.

"Right on. I take it this is all new, right?"

I start to say something, but the words aren't there.

Kerry grins.

"Got it. Starting from scratch. Okay, what was the last song you listened to with a guitar in it?"

"I . . . I couldn't even tell ya," I say, holding up both hands.

"Okay," he smiles. "Let's make this easy. Something basic but fun."

He parks the hand truck, and I follow him. Kerry holds up the plastic key card hanging around his neck to a wall pad, waits for the click, and then leads me into a secure, windowed, wood-paneled room.

"We're going to need some quiet."

"That works."

"First off, Paul, let's see if I can put you at ease. Obviously, you look like a man who can easily afford anything we've got here. I'm not nearly as interested in selling you your last guitar as I am in helping you discover what it is that you want and then letting you take it from there."

"I appreciate that."

"Good. Let's make this easy." He picks up a small guitar. "You want an electric, right?"

I have no idea. I shrug.

"Okay, sure."

"Awesome. Okay then, as you can see, this is a simple, classic design. It's a solid-body electric with a single cutaway."

He studies me for a moment, puts a strap on the guitar, and then plugs one end of a cable into the guitar and the other end into a small amplifier on the floor.

"This is a basic model." He hands it to me. "Here. Slip the strap over your head like this and let the guitar hang in front of you like so. We call this the classic position."

The guitar is heavier than I expected. My pulse quickens.

"This is the easiest placement for learning to play. I highly recommend that you use this position whether standing or sitting and always with a strap on the guitar—first, so you can keep the guitar in this position without constantly shuffling to readjust everything and, second, to keep from dropping it."

He picks up another one just like it, plugs it in, and sits across from me.

"Everything you need is right here."

He takes a pick from his rear pocket.

"Hold it between thumb and forefinger like so," he says and hands it to me.

He takes another pick for himself.

"Now strum the strings like this," he says as he strums.

I strum.

"Cool. See. You're 'Strummin' City' cool now, bro!"

Kerry points one index finger at the guitar I'm wearing and his other index finger at the amp.

"Hear that?"

"Yes."

"What you're hearing is a clean tone. No distortion. No fuzzy, staticky buzz."

"Like a bell?"

"Yeah! Like a bell. Exactly!"

Kerry reaches over to my guitar and flips a toggle switch.

"Now, this guitar has two humbucker pick-ups." He points to them. "That's these black bars with the rows of metal dots that look like the heads of nails."

"I see them."

They look awesome.

"Anytime you run an electric current over a magnet, you create a hum, if it's strong enough, then you get feedback and other nasty sounds. So to overcome that, the guitar gods created pick-ups designed to 'buck' the hum—hence the humbucker moniker."

He adjusts a volume knob on the amp.

"Okay, strum it again."

I strum it again.

"Sounds different than before, right?"

"Right."

"We call that sound 'warm' or 'fat,' and it comes off this pick-up here, the one closest to the neck. What you've got in your left hand is the neck of the guitar." He points. "Now, flip the toggle down and try it."

I do.

"We call that twangy sound 'bright,' and it comes off this other pick-up, the one closest to the bridge, back here, near the lower bout of the body." He gives the bridge on my guitar a light tap. "That's the treble pick-up. Flip the switch to the middle position, and the sound is coming off both pick-ups together."

He points again.

"On this side of the pick-up switch is the volume knob, and on the other is the tone. Go ahead and try them."

I try them.

"That's it. No muss, no fuss. It's a simple, sweet little axe. Add a strap, a cable, a pick, and a practice amp—and you're truckin'. It can't get any easier. From here out, it's all just bigger and badder. More bells and whistles, better components, and big, big bucks—as much as you want to spend. No reason at all to go there, until you get really, really, good or you just got an ego thing for burnin' up the bucks."

"How much for this set up?"

"With tax, I'll have you out the door with everything here and a gig bag for her"—he points to my guitar—"what's her name?"

"Huh?"

Kerry grins.

"I'll let you in on a little secret tradition. Every guitarist names his guitar after a woman. Well, usually a woman, you know."

"Actually, I don't know."

He looks at me.

"Okay," he says and holds up his guitar by the neck, tracing the outline of the body with his other hand. "Not unlike a woman's body, all soft curves. Upper bout, here, the half where the neck joins the body, then the hourglass curve called, appropriately enough, the waist. Then that nice, fat round bottom that luthiers call the lower bout. See where I'm going with this?"

"Not really."

"Oh!" he gasps.

"Wait. I'm not gay."

"Okay. Then whatever name pops into your head, man."

"Bonnie Lee."

"Nice! Bonnie Lee Burgundy."

I try to hold back the grin. The stomach churning starts again. There's nothing I can do about it. I have nothing in my pockets but my keys and wallet.

"You're good with the burgundy, right? Or do you want Bonnie Lee White or Bonnie Lee Black?"

"Burgundy's good. And why did I name her again?"

"The love affair, man. You'll see."

"That's funny."

"Maybe so, but it's true. You'll see."

"Okay," I said. "So like with fights and stuff?"

"All that. You'll see. All right. I can check you out. With everything here and the gig bag, you're looking at less than three bills."

"Okay."

"But if you got a minute, I'm happy to show you some basic chords that sound so good together, to get you going."

"Sure."

"I call these 'lifeline chords' because sooner or later, everyone forgets there's no shortcuts and wants to throw in the towel."

"Yeah?"

"Oh yeah. I'll show you a couple of chord progressions. Each one takes four chords from a major scale. That's why they sound so good together. They fit harmonically, and you can change the order you play them, and they'll still sound good. Add a strumming pattern, and you've got yourself a song. A few hundred at least and many, no doubt, that you've probably grown up to listening to them on the radio."

"Sounds great."

"Oh, it is. You'll see."

Kerry walks me through the major chords in standard tuning, which he says is the key of E (D, C, G, and D) and then through A, E, G, and D. He says we'll skip F for now. Which is good, because I remember F is bad—very bad—and I don't want to go there if I don't have to.

"Anything else I can do for you before you show me the money?"

I think about it, and then I get that choking sensation again when I think about taking lessons. Deep breath.

"Yeah. Any chance of teaching me a really simple song?"

"Sure. Ever hear of 'Amazing Grace'?"

"Yes."

"Cool. 'Amazing Grace' is four chords—E minor, that's just the E chord I showed you without the index finger, G, C, and D. I've already showed you those. So taking it really slow here goes. Follow along."

I try to follow along. It's not so bad; I mean it's not like taking lessons. Not really. He's just helping me, that's all.

It's okay. I'm okay.

It's just some help from someone nice, just to get by, that's all. We go over it a couple of times, I'm stumbling and fumbling my way through the chord changes—Kerry calls them transitions—and I feel my vision begin to blur.

Shit.

I need to breathe.

"Hey! I know, right? Amazing Grace!" Kerry says. "Man, I feel the same way! I'm so like you, you know. Guys like us, we get such zap from a guitar—any guitar. Such power! Such magic!"

I nod, catching my breath, so grateful he hasn't caught on to me. He keeps working with me, reminding me to take it slow. It's not so bad.

It's okay, man. Relax. It's okay. Relax—*what the fuck does that word even mean?*

"Okay, man. The rest is just practice. I promise. Trust me. It'll come. Just keep practicing a little bit every day. That's all it is—practice," he smiles, then nods.

He looks like he's waiting for me to say something. I don't have anything to say.

"Practice all damn day like it's your religion."

"Fair enough. I'll practice."

I let the "all damn day" part pass. For now.

"Good. Trust me. You'll feel like an idiot at first like you're not making any progress, like you can't do it. Totally normal, man. Everybody rides that train. That's just the way it is. That's when 90 percent of the beginners quit."

"Really?"

"For sure. There are absolutely no shortcuts. None."

"Well, I don't intend to quit," I say, as I try forming a chord and strumming it.

"Yeah! That's it. Just like that. Just keep at it, man. Do not stop—ever. Then one day, *bam*! It all starts falling into place. Trust me. Chord changes that seemed impossible will come naturally. They just will. You'll wonder what took you so long. But you gotta put in the time and keep practicing, especially when you don't want to. I can't stress that enough. Okay?

"Fair enough."

"Right on. I'll shut up now. Let me get a gig bag for Bonnie Lee, and then I'll take your money."

I nod without looking up, still fumbling with the chord shapes, trying to make the fingers of my left hand do things they don't want to do. I'm not going to admit that I'm already wondering whether or not I am totally dorky stupid for doing this. I hear Tami and Coach criticizing me in my head. I don't dare tell this guy that I've got no business doing this.

The back of my neck is getting hot like it's on fire. It hurts. I'm sweating, and I want to rip my shirt off.

I look at Bonnie Lee hanging from my shoulder. But I am doing this. I'm feeling sweaty. I'm doing it. And I keep on doing it.

This is so insane!

I stop and rub the hot back of my hot neck. My vision starts blurring so I close my eyes and start taking deep breaths. I go back to the same chord, strumming it over and over with my eyes closed. I focus on the strumming sound. For a minute, I forget everything but this one chord I'm strumming. For an instant, it's all wickedly forbidden fun.

Then I start remembering.

Too bad the good memories aren't nearly as strong as the painful ones. I thought I had finally managed to forget them over the years.

No. Not now. Please, not now!

I don't dare move my fretting fingers. I'm feeling almost happy, and that's the best you can ever allow yourself to feel when you know that in the end, it's just gonna be taken away from you anyway.

Kerry comes back.

"Okay, let's get all this up front and check you out."

"Sounds good."

My pits are drenched with sweat.

He hands me a printed card.

"Here's a chord chart and lyric sheet for 'Amazing Grace' with the lifeline chords on the back. Right now, you've had a magic moment here with Bonnie Lee, and somewhere between here and getting her home, that magic moment's gonna take a magical, mystery detour and be lost for what'll seem like forever."

I smile. I like his humor.

"You mean like the honeymoon's over?"

"No, not exactly," he says. "I'm giving you this card because I want to keep happy, repeat customers and not make frustrated quitters."

"Fair enough."

"Hey, Paul. Can I ask you a personal question?"

Shit. Here it comes.

"Yeah. I suppose."

"Cool. What do you do for a living?"

My shoulders sag.

"Oh, that. I'm a lawyer."

"Thought so. Anyway, here's why I asked. My bet's that you didn't become a lawyer overnight. Am I right about that?"

"You are."

"Same thing here. You won't become a guitarist overnight either, regardless of talent. Talent is practice. I'm talking technical skill here. It takes disciplined practice. It takes time—lots and lots of time. Go slow. Be steady. Don't ever, ever quit," he smiles. "Chicks dig licks. Remember that."

Not that it will ever do me a damn bit of good, but what the hell. For you, I'll play along.

"Okay. Chicks dig licks."

It sounds fun to say it even though it's ludicrous as hell and I don't think it will ever come true for me. Tami's not into guitars.

Tami's not into anything—'cept maybe Tami. Better to just humor this guy and get the hell out of here before I do anything else stupid.

Too late.

"Chicks dig licks!" the words just fly right out of my mouth.

"Yeah, man!" Kerry grins. "All the way to the bank, brother! Remember that. If you can remember that, and all this will stay fun forever. The magic moment will come back, and when it does, it will never, ever leave you."

"Okay."

"Right on! Let's get you out of here before you decide to buy a piano."

I sigh in relief.

"Deal!"

I follow him to the cash register and see a freckled ninety-pound kid with forty pounds of stringy, bleached hair, wrenching screeches from a neon-blue electric guitar as he nags at a frazzled woman who could only be his overworked, underpaid, unloved, single mother and who's clutching at her battered purse as she slumps onto a bench.

"You're good, right?" Kerry asks me as he's already moving toward them. "I need to put her out of her misery."

"I'm good. Better hurry. And give her a discount."

He smiles and writes "Practice!" on a business card and hands it to me.

"All right, Paul You're all set. Keep it fun!"

I pay up and notice the frazzled woman's face. I study that face. Something is familiar about it.

Don't do this, man! Walk away. Mind your own business.

I walk over to her and interrupt.

"Good evening, ma'am."

I wink at Kerry.

"I'm Paul, and I am the SoCal District Manager for Strummin' City. Allow me to assist."

I move over to shithead junior and reach for the price tag and glance at it.

Okay, not bad.

I steal a glance at the woman.

Shit. There's no way.

It's gonna be way too tough on her. But not this time. Not on my watch.

"Thought so. Here's the problem. This model is being discontinued. The sticker price is cut to 75 percent off." I hold the sticker up. "This one's the wrong one."

Kerry coughs.

"So let me ask you, ma'am, twenty-five bucks a month for a total of four months—that's a hundred bucks and not a penny more, including tax. Does that work for you?"

She looks up, eyes wide open, and blinks.

I see she's dressed like a waitress—striped skirt, with two large pockets in front, and a couple of ketchup stains. Pretty sure it ain't blood, but what do I know? She's wearing a white short-sleeved blouse, and her dark hair is up in a bun. White work shoes. Stained. Dirty.

Déjà vu.

She nods.

"Yes. I-I . . . thank you."

Her voice is barely audible.

"Okay then. I'll have my man Kerry here take care of you."

Shithead junior is next.

"And you, pal."

I sit next to him, almost knocking his bony little ass off the bench. I make sure the frazzled woman's behind me and cannot hear me when I start talking to him.

"You need to understand how this is the biggest deal of your fuckin' puny lifetime. Your time is now, son, just like it was when Jimi up there, when he was about your age"—I point up at the poster—"I'm talkin' about that Jimi, and I know you know what I'm talking about here. That means you gotta be a whole lotta like Jimi up there on that wall. Swear to God Almighty, don't even think of fucking this up, kid. I want to see your face on the cover of that same magazine in about five years."

I point at the poster again.

"Understand? No fuckin' excuses. You'll be walkin' outta here tonight with everything you need because I'm you fairy goddaddy. So get on it. You practice an hour a day, after homework, and three hours every Saturday and Sunday after cleaning up your room. Don't even think of giving your mother any shit about chores. You want more than this, you gotta earn it by how well you play. I mean it."

Only now do I get a really good look at his face. One eye is puffy, yellowish below the lower lid. Old bruise. Shiner on the other eye is fresh. He pulls a pair of eyeglasses out of his worn slacks. He's not even in jeans. He puts them on. Whoa! Dark plastic "just beat my ass" frames. Scratched lenses. His wide-eyed stare is frozen. He's scared shitless.

Shit.

I got him all wrong.

Fuck!

I got about a split second to maybe fix this or lose him for good.

I smile and nod. "Near-sighted?"

He nods.

"Yeah, me too, buddy." I point at the ice blue axe in his hands. "I heard something pretty decent there. Show me something."

He takes off his glasses, puts them back in his pants pocket, and then he does. Slowly, a little timid at first; then forgetting I'm there, his fretting fingers move fluidly, pressing strings near frets, no misses. No buzzing. His right hand holds the pick deftly without squeezing the shit out of it, the way I was doing a moment ago. He stops, mumbles something in a wheezy voice, and looks up but avoids my eyes.

"Yeah. You got something good there, buddy! Really gnarly good, no lie. Proud of you. I know the effort that takes. You keep doing that," I tell him. "Sounds good, buddy. Real good."

I give him a gentle pat on the knee—probably the only place left that hasn't been hit.

Fair enough.

I move back to the woman.

"Ma'am, I do apologize for the price mix-up. I am so very glad you came in tonight and that I had a chance to meet you and personally get a handle on this."

"Mister, you have no clue. I can't thank you enough."

"No worries. You just did. You ever need anything in the future, you just get in touch with Kerry here, no one else now, just him, and he'll work with you. Just keep it in the ballpark, okay? Don't go crazy on me. That's all I ask."

She shakes her head. "No. Of course not."

"Fair enough."

Kerry's shoving sticks of gum into his mouth and giving me one righteous stink eye.

"Listen," I tell him softly, as I pull him aside. "You take the cash from her, close out the ticket, give her a receipt for the hundred, and bill me the entire difference separately. All of it. You got my card number. Use it. I'm serious. Take care of her."

Kerry moves the wad of gum aside into a cheek and smiles broadly.

"Yes, sir! You got it, Mr. Cooper."

I step back.

"Thank you, Kerry," I say loud enough to be heard by those nearby.

I look over at the not-quite-so-frazzled woman and not so shithead junior.

"All right, y'all. Be good. I'm outta here!"

I walk my treasures out to the car.

Yeah. Too damn familiar. Hey. What's done is done. How many years has it been? Let it go. That's just it. I can't. I don't know how.

Outside in fresh air and on my own, I find myself fighting the feeling of embarrassment that has suddenly overcome me for making a purchase for myself.

I just bought a guitar. I have never done that—ever. And grown men my age, they just don't do this. Yeah. Well, you've done it now, ace.

Coach is silent. Which is, you know, good news 'cuz the motherfucker's like, you know, dead. Tami, on the other hand, ain't dead. She is an altogether different story, and I haven't yet figured out the story I will soon need to tell her. I'm not even sure there is one or that I even can tell it, if there is.

Mechanically then, like an automaton whose battery is about to die, I load up and leave for home where I lose myself attempting to finger my lifeline chord shapes for the next couple of hours.

Chapter 5

I don't hear Tami come home.

"What the hell is this?" she yells.

"'Amazing Grace,'" I say without looking up.

"What?"

"'Amazing Grace'—you know, the bagpipe song."

"No! This! What is all of this?" she yells at me again, making a circling motion with her car keys. "I can *hear* the bagpipe part, all right. Forget that 'screeching moose' shit. What is all this? Why is any of it even here?"

"Well, I would think it would be obvious. But okay. It's exactly what it looks like. This here is an electric guitar. That cute little box over there is a practice amp. That black floppy bag thing over there is a called a gig bag. I'm not sure why, though. Oh, and this"—I hold up my hand—"is the cable connecting the guitar to the amp. Then that chord over there is the power chord running from the practice amp to the electrical outlet at the bottom of that wall right there. That's what all this is obviously."

"No! You don't need any of this! You are a grown man!"

She squares off in the doorway, hands fisted against her firm hips, her pale blue scrubs hugging every curve; her long flax-hued tresses pulled tightly into a ponytail and held there with a pale blue scrunchy.

"Seriously, Paul, level with me. Is this another one of your goddamn midlife meltdowns? Because if it is, then we need to talk!"

"No, it's not. And could you maybe lower your voice a little? Okay, a lot. Because right now? The only person having a meltdown is you."

"You're damn right! I'm bustin' my ass all night in puke and piss and bloody people screaming and dipshit doctors who want me stroking their dicks and you don't answer my calls, you don't answer my texts, and then I come home to this!"

"What doctor?"

"Don't change the subject! Tell me, Paul. Is fifty the new twelve now? Is that it?"

"No, please calm down."

"I don't need to calm down! I'm the not one acting like a child!"

"You're not?"

"Don't even put this on me! You haven't answered my question, Paul. Why is any of this shit even here?"

"Well," I say, lowering my voice to a whisper, "Woo and Shelley Lynne both told me I needed a hobby."

"Are you high?" She moves closer. "Let me see your eyes right now!"

I lean forward and open my eyes as wide as I can.

"No, ma'am. I am not high. But I will be, God willing, as soon as I learn to play this thing."

"No, Paul! You can't play a guitar! You can't play anything!" she says, screaming and flailing her arms. "You have no musical talent! You don't have any talent at all! I made sure of that. I know you, Paul!"

She freezes.

"Wait," she says, "Did you say *hobby*?"

"Yes, ma'am."

Tami thrashes her arms about.

"Don't call me, ma'am!"

"I don't know why not. Nothing else seems to work. I sure as hell can't call you anything sexy, and God forbid, I even think of touching you without permission."

"Don't you *dare* put this on me, Paul! You knew *exactly* what you were getting into. I put you through law school, and this is what I get? Another one of your stupidly expensive hobbies?"

"It's not like that."

"It's not? Oh, really? I see! Whatever happened to cartooning, Mr. Wannabe Animator? And that drawing thingy, that thing with the hole in the middle?"

"You made me send it back."

"Well, of course I made you send it back! That's not the point!" Tami grunts. "And, and flying, huh? Two grand for flying lessons, and you're not even a goddam pilot!"

"I can explain."

"Really? Then explain this, what the fuck are you doing?"

I look at my new hobby stuff. Big sigh.

"Well, like I said. I'm practicing."

"Practicing what? I told you! You have no talent!"

"I told you, 'Amazing Grace.'"

"No no no! That didn't sound anything like 'Amazing Grace'!"

"Well of course not, I mean, you know, not exactly not now. I'm pretty sure it's much slower, you know, being the student version. I'm still learning it. It's going to take some time."

Even though the strap is there, I cradle the neck in the crook of my left elbow and rub my hands together, trying to massage the soreness from the finger of my left hand and the cramp out of my right. I think I'm squeezing the pick too hard again.

"No! It doesn't matter what version it is, Paul! The only thing you're practicing is a bad habit! What are you, fucking 'guitarded' now? Is this your idea of a joke?"

"Okay. Enough is enough. No. It's not a joke, okay? And yes, I'm trying to explain. It's just a hobby. So lighten up."

"Oh! Here we go again with the hobby shit! And no, Paul, you can't explain. You can't! That's the point, Paul. Oh! Photography! Let's not forget, pho-to-gra-phy!"

"Right. You put the kibosh on me putting a darkroom in the garage, remember?"

She moans loudly.

"Oh! Here we go! Well? Somebody had to! And who must that be? Me! As always, me! Why? Because you don't *need* a darkroom. Photography is all digital now, remember? You tried talking me into buying some fancy digital SLR with some super-duper zoomer thing that I wouldn't give in on. We have a computer, Paul! You take the picture. You *save* the picture. On the com-pu-ter! No hassles, no toxic chemicals, no expensive room additions or garage conversions."

"But if it was my hobby, then none of that was ever your call."

"Oh! It's totally my call. And besides—wait. Woo told you to play guitar?"

"No. I told you while you were having your hissy fit. Woo told me to get a hobby. Shelley Lynne suggested I try the guitar."

"Sidney Woo, your boss."

"Yes."

"Told you to get a hobby?"

"Yes. He said it would do wonders for my attitude."

"That makes no sense whatsoever."

"Thank you. I didn't think so either."

"When did Woo tell you to get a hobby?"

"This afternoon. Right after he told me I didn't get the promotion."

Oh, shit. Here it comes.

Tami freezes again.

"Wait. You didn't get the promotion?"

"No, ma'am."

She bites her lower lip, hard, drawing blood.

"Dammit!"

An' thar' she blows.

She touches, then licks her lip.

"And when did you talk to our Little Miss Barbie?"

"Please don't call her that."

"She's my daughter! I'll call her whatever I goddamn want!"

"Mine too now. Remember? I uh-dop-ted her."

We glare at each other.

She looks spent.

Tami crosses her arms, which lifts her amazing breasts, which I dare not look at and imagine them snuggled tightly in the sports bra she wears to work.

"Fine," she says, pausing a while. "And when did you talk to *our* daughter?"

"She called me about five o'clock, just after I got back to my office from meeting with Woo."

"And she told you to start playing guitar?"

"No. She said I needed a hobby. She suggested I try guitar because it's working for her."

"So? She's a nineteen-year-old college freshman! For Christ's sake, Paul, that's fine for her. Not for you! What's your excuse, this time? You're a grown man, not some flippy-dippy college kid! You're way too old for this shit. You need to focus on your career, and you know it."

"My career?"

"Yes, Paul! That was our deal."

"Our deal?"

"Oh, you are such a card. You know very damn well what deal. You owe me, Paul!"

"I owe you?"

"Fuck you, Paul! Don't you dare play stupid with me! I want my payoff."

"Is that what your tantrum's about?"

"It's not about me, Paul! It's about you. You working harder. It's about all those judges who kept telling you how you were wasting yourself at Probation. You want a hobby? Fine. Go back to those judges and start networking through them to move up. Another firm, maybe, or getting on the fast track for judge yourself."

"Judge? I don't remember that ever being part of your deal."

"Well, it is now, Paul. Listen to me!" She sighs and takes a deep breath. She lowers her voice. "You have this brilliant mind, but you're too damn stubborn to use it on anything worthwhile—anything that genuinely matters like putting food on the table or money in the bank or a new car in the garage."

"Brilliant? At what? You bitch at everything I do!"

"Never mind all that now. You're not listening to me, Paul! Listen to me! You have so much potential, Paul. Please. Stop wasting it. I know you better than anyone—anyone! I know you even better than you know yourself. I know what you're capable of, Paul. You need to keep pushing. We need to get you back on track."

She drops her keys into her purse.

"I don't know why you even bothered going to the county."

"Because . . . you . . . told me to!"

"Fine. Whatever. I don't know why you settled for that."

"Whoa whoa whoa! I 'settled'—as you so conveniently choose to describe it now—because you never ever, ever, stopped bitching me about the hours I was working at the firm!"

"Well, why not? They weren't paying you for all those hours!"

"Oh, not again! How many more times do we have to go through this? Nothing ever changes with you, does it? Nothing is ever enough for you, is it? Nothing is ever—nothing I do is ever good enough for you, is it?"

"You're missing the point, Paul."

"What point am I always missing? That I'm not good enough for you? Hell, I got that one loud and clear! Or is it the other one this time? The one where, the one where you nag, nag, nag? The one where you change your mind, flipping on a dime, to some other nag, nag, nag? You mean one of those? Or is there some other point you haven't thought up yet? What am I missing?"

"You don't have to get all worked up about it. Just apply yourself more."

I'm shaking my head.

"You're hopeless."

"I mean it, Paul. Step up your game. Show Woo and whoever they're wrong about you."

"Whomever."

"What?"

"You said 'whoever,' it's 'whomever.' Objective case."

"Whatever! Pay attention to what I am saying! Get active in bar politics. Network. Get on track to be a judge. You could be such a good judge."

"You're clueless."

"I am most certainly not clueless! You're just being stubborn. I know how smart you are. You Am-Jur'd all those law classes on your own. On your own, Paul. Or have you forgotten? You always underestimate yourself, Paul. You need to stop selling yourself so short all the damn time!"

"Okay, fair enough. But I don't want to be a judge. I really don't."

"Oh, here we go again!" she groans. "What do you want to be, Paul? Huh? What is it this time?"

"I don't know."

"You don't know? Oh! That's just great. I swear you're worse than a kid sometimes. Your mind! Oh my god, Paul! It's like, it's all over the map. All this stream of consciousness! If I didn't know you as well as I do, I'd swear you were on crack. One minute you're rambling on about, hell, I don't even—God knows what, bam! Ten seconds later, you segue to something maybe related, hell, I can't tell. All these crazy tangents. I send you to the market for dish soap, toilet paper, and toothpaste. And what happens? It's a fifteen-minute trip at most. Oh, but not for you, is it? Why, Paul, why? Because you get so distracted over—who the hell knows what—and you're off wandering up and down the aisles reading labels. You drive me nuts!"

She unloads a sigh of anguish.

"And then you're always writing yourself notes on napkins and index cards, on the backs of your business cards, and on any scrap of paper you can find. That would be bad enough. But God forbid that you just stop there. Oh, no! No! What do you do? You leave them scattered all over the goddam house! You leaving heaping piles of bits of paper on the armoire! What the fuck is that all about? You frustrate the living shit out of me, Paul! Why can't you just use a notebook like normal people and maybe even keep it with your car keys so you'll stop losing your keys all the time?"

"Okay. I'll get a notebook."

"Do that, Paul. Please do that! And this time, please just try to get fucking normal, for once. Just once! Try focusing all those smarts on something worthwhile. For both of us! You really, really need to focus here, Paul. Find something important, and this time stick with it. For me. For us. For me, especially! Can't you see? Everything that I hope for, everything I dream of, you can be for me. I see you like an amazing work of art, like a sketch, like, like, one of my figure drawings, you know? Like one of those raw sketches of the master before the finished painting."

"One of your figure drawings?"

"Yes!"

"Am I naked?"

"Of course, but that's not the point!"

"Am I holding a guitar?"

"No!"

"What if I added one? You know, like later. Really nice one. Florentine cutaway."

"What the fuck, Paul? Stop being such an ass! Will you just shut up and please listen to me?" She drops a heavy sigh. "No. It's just . . . I see you as what I can make you. Like, like a mannequin of beautiful clay I can mold and sculpt into being. It's like I knew it when I met you, Paul, all those self-help books you were in to. I knew immediately that you needed me."

Tami's head is pointed up, and her eyes are closed. She's reaching upward with her free hand, making grasping, kneading gestures in the air.

This is kinda fun to watch actually. Wait. What was that mannequin crap about again?

"Okay, wait. This mannequin thing. So you're saying, what? That I'm your . . . puppet? Is that it?"

"Mmm . . . maybe, but in a good way. Can't you see? It's not what you think. Just . . . listen to me! Damn it, Paul!"

Another heavy sigh.

"You're not listening! I'm trying to guide you, Paul, to mold you into the man I know you can be—the man I want, the man I need! For me! Can't you see that? Stop all this hobby horseshit nonsense for once. Focus! Focus on becoming a judge. Just . . . be a judge. Do it for me! Your potential is there, Paul, and you would be so damn good at it. I know you will. Do that for me. For us."

"But I don't think I want to be a judge."

"How do you even know? I want you to. I know you, and you . . . you . . . just stop frustrating the hell out of me, Paul! If you could only see how I'm trying to mold you, to build you up into what I know you could be. I can make you everything I've ever hoped for. Everything I want and everything I need. But you've got to listen to me, Paul! You just got to start following instructions and do what I say!"

"Okay. Wait. Back up. You lost me at the mannequin thing. How is any of this even relevant? You bitch me for my past hobbies—particularly the photography—and yet there's no issue with your current hobbies?"

Heavy sigh again.

"Yes. I have my gym and my art class."

"That's right! The nude drawing class! That's it, exactly. You draw nudes with little sticks of charcoal. That's great. Okay. Fine. Nude figure studies. I get that. Knock yourself out with that. I've got no problem with that, well, as long as you're not up there, modelling nude—unless I'm in the class or if you'll model for me and let me take pictures, but as usual I digress. Anyway, yes, I did the same thing, except for the modelling part, only I just used a camera, and still, all these years later, and apart from the mannequin thing which I'm not sure I get, you still go off on me. Why is that?"

She cocks one hot little hip and firmly plants her palm on it.

God, I love it when she does that. Especially in scrubs.

Car keys jangle from her fingers.

"No. First of all, I didn't try to spend a fortune on equipment. I spent thirty bucks, tops. That's it—thirty bucks for charcoal sticks and pencils, conte crayons, two boxes of razor blades, and a few giant pads of smooth newsprint! Here's the best part, you pervert, the models wore their undies, and our drawings, mine especially, don't show every single hair and detail in living color. I'm going for the total here, the spirit of the pose, Paul, with force, using relative long lines of action, all eight parts of the body. I'm telling a story, Paul, through that pose."

She catches her breath and comes back to reality.

Damn. She was really getting hot for a minute there.

"Besides, Paul, their poses weren't come-ons to a herd of horny old men. Men and women, young and old, are in my class. With clothing! Yours was full of fat, ugly, old men with cameras, always gawking at an underfed, drug-addicted, wispy little nubile waif of a maiden with same thousand-yard stare on her face. Sickening."

"Okay. Okay. Modesty matters. I get it!"

She gives me the stink eye.

"So, no, Paulo. As far as my hobbies go, I'm not going there. *We are not going there.* So there."

She waves her cup hand slowly.

"And this? This is all about you. We're talking about you, Paul. Just you. Again, just try to stay focused for once. That means 'shut up and listen to me'!"

She's waving the cup hand higher in the air now—this time, it's like she's painting or something, eyes wide open and staring at the ceiling.

Wow! What a rack.

"If you would just focus for once, you would see how easily you could put all that brainpower of yours, all your powers of observation, to work for something real. Now, Paul. Now is the time to do that. I really think you've got a chance now. So much opportunity for you! I'm not letting you throw it away. Not this time. I'm just not. I've carried you all these years. I can't keep this up, Paul. I just can't. I need you to step in and man up and be my husband. I deserve better, Paul. I do. I really, really do. Okay, yes, so do we. We deserve better. We, baby, *we* deserve better."

"Right. Well, whatever it is that we deserve, I don't think chasing that carrot can bring it. You can dress it up all you want in a black robe or a black muumuu for all I care, and it's still the same carrot. I'm tired of chasing it. I don't want to chase it anymore."

She moves her hands to her hips, looks down, and sighs.

"Like hell you don't," she says in a soft almost whisper.

"Why does it matter so much what I do for a living?"

"Because it does, Paul, and it always has. You know that. You've always known that."

"No, I don't! I have no idea what you're talking about. Hey! Look at me. You're not being fair, Tami. It's not my fault that your old man cut you off. Okay? We've been through that. But he's still the bad guy here. Right, huh? Not me. And that was a long, long time ago. About nineteen years, if my math serves me. And after all this time—after all this time—why can't you just love me for me?"

She doesn't answer. But then she never does. She just looks away. Like always.

Shit. Shit! Shit! Shit! Fine! Fair enough. But I am not giving up. Not by a long shot. We've had some righteous good times and regardless of how few there were, I just know there's got to be more righteous good times ahead. There must be!

"Tami, c'mon! From day one, I've done everything you've ever asked. I love you. I adore you. I cherish you. I've done everything I could to be a good husband to you and a good father to the princess. I have. I know I have. Tell me I have. Haven't I?"

"Of course you have. It's all part of the deal."

"Well then, what about *me*?"

"Really, Paul? Really?"

"Tell me!"

"I can't."

"What do you mean 'you can't'?"

"I just can't. God knows I've tried, Paul. 'From day one,' I've tried."

"That's it?"

"Yes, Paul, that's it."

"Well, shit, that's just awesome!" I catch my breath. "Look, I know we've never really talked about it. I don't know. Maybe we should. It's just not my fault how your dad's been to you."

She squints, looks away again, holds up her free hand, and clenches it into a fist.

"Oh, don't even!"

She slings her purse over her shoulder, leans toward the end table, and reaches down and grabs the bag from the health food store. She looks down on my hobby gear.

"Put your toys away, honey, and clean up your mess. It's past your bedtime."

She steps into the hallway and turns toward the kitchen.

I follow her like a hungry puppy and sit at the kitchen table.

"What else happened today?"

She wipes her mouth with a napkin and puts the cap back on a plastic bottle of some gnarly organic drink that's got a bazillion berries and vegetables in it. It smells like lawn clippings. The price of beauty.

"I went to restock a crash cart and walked in on Dr. Merkle just as he began squealing while his little bubbleheaded bitch was yanking his crank. I never knew you could jerk it that fast. No wonder everybody says he paid for her boobs."

I'm silent. Speaking of boobs, I remind myself that now's not a good time to get caught looking at hers. I don't look.

"Anyway, other people heard him, and he jumped out the door, tripping on his pants, flashing a couple of patients, and shooting off his wad at another, so they all complained. Some maintenance guys refused to clean up the mess. There wasn't much of a mess. Most of it was on some patient's robe. Anyway, a shitload of complaints. Now there's a scandal, and he's on admin leave and that ruby-lipped bitch turns on him, says he was forcing her. And now to shut her up, she gets promoted over me and everybody else who had a chance. Now she's in another building, supervising all the ER nurses. From a private office."

She takes another hit of the nasty juice.

"This shit's getting so old."

"Welcome to the club."

"Oh, not even."

"On the lighter side, I thought I heard a catchy rhyme in there somewhere."

She gives me a look.

"Maybe not. Sorry. I thought there was a song in there."

"Fuck you."

I so wish.

"Oh, take the guest room, you sick bastard."

I sigh and close my eyes. Yeah. I should have seen that one coming. Another deep breath, and I open my eyes. She's gone.

What did she mean by saying I was practicing a bad habit? I've never played long enough to have any habits.

I take everything into the guest room and close the door behind me. There's no point to going upstairs. I know the bedroom door's locked.

I unplug Bonnie Lee and sit with her on the bed. I go back to work at forming chord shapes. My unruly fingers resist. I struggle to get each fingertip onto the string where it belongs and to the fret where it belongs. When I lift them up and put them down again, they either land between the strings or on the wrong strings and move to the wrong frets. This goes on for some time, but I refuse to give up.

I remember I am a grown man and that means Coach is not going to burst in on me. I feel my shoulders relax and my face flush with a wave of embarrassment sweeping over me. God, how I wish I could get over this stuff and just get on with my life.

I must be an even bigger idiot than Coach ever thought. I've been cheated. Kerry was right. Whatever magic I had felt at the store, that little handful of heaven, is long gone. I put the guitar on the stand and stare at it.

"Please don't tell me you're taking her side. You could at least be neutral, you know."

I'm a grown man, and I'm talking to a guitar. This can't be good. Oh, lord, help me. Help me, one time.

It's 2:30 a.m. I close my eyes and rub my sore fingers again for a while. Okay. Break's over. I reach for Bonnie Lee. I try again. By 4:30 a.m., I'm even worse than when I started. All the strings buzz now.

Bonnie Lee can be a cold little bitch.

Chapter 6

Monday morning. I'm up before the 7:00 a.m. alarm. I'm not in the habit of eating breakfast, so I usually manage to get to work by eight. Okay, 8:05 a.m., maybe 8:15 a.m. The weekend is a blurred memory. Somehow, Tami and I had reached some semblance of a truce.

My hobby gear found its way to the garage/unfinished darkroom/cartoon studio/brewery/hangar—whatever Tami's in the mood to call our detached garage. For her part, Tami occasionally cooked our meals and did not yell at me or insult me the few times that we ate together. Sex, of course, was out of the question. That goes without saying. I've been cut off so many times, I'm pretty much resigned to it.

Not that all has been forgiven, not by a long shot. And although she has not said anything definitive and has not issued any ultimatums, that she does not approve of my latest hobby, my steady acclimatization to the guest room has become self-evident.

Make no mistake. I am not at all certain of my future. I want to enjoy the new hobby—at least, I think I do, sort of. Yet the difficulty I continue to experience in changing chords is also self-evident, and that troubles me.

On one hand, the thought of playing a song—just one, particularly one I like—is very appealing. Mesmerizing. On the other hand, the admonition that the necessary skill would not be achieved overnight, especially for someone as uncoordinated as me is utterly discouraging. The questions tormenting my mind are just how long will it take and can I last long enough to get there?

Although Tami does not come right out and say it, I can feel it in my gut that a decision is called for—a choice required—and that the deadline for both is imminent. There's no escape. Until then, I can keep practicing. So I do. Relentlessly. Blindly. I'm driven by an unspoken hope that such furious fretting—no pun intended—might yet pan out for me, giving me a reason, the strength, and sufficient skill to go on. I'll show them. I'll show them all. I'll keep at it till it kills me.

I guess that means I'm in love with two bitches now.

On the other hand, when I pick up her bra that had fallen from the shower door when I opened it and I feel the lace between my fingers and smell something of her in the fabric, I understand it's not too late. I can quit while I'm ahead. Bygones being bygones and all that. No doubt that will be Tami's preference.

I take another whiff.

Oh my god.

Or I can come clean with her and admit that I had simply gotten caught up in a siren's call to something I've got no business pursuing. I'm not at all certain I'd say it that way.

I have plenty of time to think about how I would say it while waiting in Department 3. I should be out of here in ten minutes, but Judge Sawyer decides to handle the telephone appearances first. So I find myself heading for Department 6 by 9:27 a.m. I follow a tall, rather buff-looking sheriff's deputy into the courtroom and know why immediately upon hearing the old coot's raspy voice.

"I am the Reverend Justice! You called me 'Mister,' that's a mistake! You need to know."

"Do I?" Chrome Dome gives the old coot a hard look. "Well now, let's see. *You,* you, mangy mutt, need to know that *you* never interrupt *me* in my courtroom! I am sanctioning *you,* personally, another $250 for your outburst. Unless you are made of cash, which I highly doubt, I suggest that you sit down and shut up. Your attorney, Ms. Wilson, will do your talking for you. Take the hint, Ms. Wilson. Muzzle your mutt or you will also face sanctions."

The coot turns and notices the deputy moving around Dennis, the court attendant. The deputy points to the chair the coot is rising from. The coot sits down.

"Very well. I see Mr. Cooper has finally chosen to grace us with his appearance. Lucky me. So very nice of you to squeeze me into your busy day, Mr. Cooper. This is getting to be a habit with you, I see. Very well. At least you're presentable. You may take your seat at the counsel table."

"Thank you, Your Honor."

I walk up to the plaintiff's side of the table, each step slower and harder to take than the last, looking over the courtroom as I do and taking it all in—the artless walls; the dull colors; the lifeless reporter who never smiles and could use a little lipstick; the insufferable Napoleonic magistrate whose shiny forehead glare is as blinding as any aircraft landing light; the code violator who is just the next miscreant coot in the never-ending line of foul-smelling, foul-looking, and foul-mannered assholes who refuse to obey any laws but those of their own whim; the code violator's attorney who is just the next individual in the never-ending line of arrogant, self-righteous, self-serving, greedy, or, worse yet, crusaders-for-anarchy holders of state bar cards; and I just as soon walk off a cliff as stay here another minute.

I sit down and put the file on the table. I reach for my stomach as if that will stop the gnawing and burning. I know instantly that discomfort will be with me for some time because I won't be saying anything of the sort to Tami after all.

As much as I love her, as much as I have given up for her, I don't want any part of this lawyering crap anymore. I'll do whatever it takes to get by, but beyond that, I'm checking out. I'm done with this madness. I need to make it all go away and without losing her. The thought of it sets my guts on fire.

I'm staring blankly at the table, but I see Bonnie Lee instead. I want to see Tami, but my mind must be playing tricks on me because I see Bonnie Lee instead. And I can feel her neck and her strings, and I imagine how good it will feel to finger the chord shapes correctly, how good that will sound. Someday.

Yeah. Right. Someday.

No! I'm going to see this guitar thing through, come hell or high water. It's the Taurus in me.

God help me. Tami's gonna shit when she finds out. It's the Scorpio in her.

"Oh, good lord! If you don't mind, Mr. Cooper, perhaps you'd care to join us? I would like to proceed with this matter. Unless, of course, there's some other place you need to be."

"No, Your Honor. My apologies."

Chrome Dome looks at the reporter.

"Very well. We're back on the record. Now, as I was saying, we have two matters on calendar this morning for *Mr.* Justice." He stares at the coot who starts to get up, only to have his shoulder meet the grip of the deputy's hand, which shoves him firmly back into the seat.

Chrome Dome smiles and looks at the file.

"Very well. The first matter is case number SGCV-139584, *In Re Appeal of Reverend Justice*—that being *Mr.* Justice's appeal of an administrative hearing officer's ruling upholding an administrative citation, citation number CE 138000091, pursuant to Government Code section 58069.4. And the second is the county's motion for a preliminary injunction, case number SGCV-483186, *County of San Gorgonio v Reverend Justice, et al.*"

Chrome Dome looks up.

"Let me have counsels' appearances, again for the record, please. Obviously, Mr. Justice is present."

I look at opposing counsel as we both stand up.

"Denise Wilson, Legal Aid Services for Reverend Justice, Your Honor."

"On the motion, Deputy County Counsel Paul Cooper appearing for the plaintiff and moving party, the County of San Gorgonio, and for the county as the respondent on the administrative appeal."

"Thank you, Counsel. I'll take the appeal first. Notwithstanding the statute, I prefer not to handle this de novo. It is what it is. I'm very well aware of the facts and the law in this matter. The administrative record speaks for itself, the conclusion is self-evident, and I am prepared to rule on this matter. However, before so doing, I still want to hear from the code enforcement officer. Is he here, Mr. Cooper?"

I look back to the gallery. I see him stand.

"Yes, Your Honor."

"Very well. Officer Hollings, take the witness stand if you would, please. My clerk will swear you in."

The clerk does so, and as directed, the officer spells his first and last name for the record.

"Just so I'm clear, you've issued thirteen citations in all, and the last one is the subject of the instant appeal, correct?"

"Correct."

"You cited him for an illegal business without permits and for operating a pig farm without permits. What's the difference?"

"Two separate violations."

"What separates them?"

"He's got a pig farm, and he's got an illegal business."

"Okay. Who's on first."

"Excuse me?"

"I don't think you have one. Tell me what the illegal business is exactly."

"Exactly?"

Chrome Dome gnaws his lower lip.

"Yes. Exactly."

"Something to do with the pig farm, I guess."

"So now you're guessing. You don't know?"

"I don't know."

"And I don't know is on third," Chrome Dome mumbles to himself. "Tell me, please, what permit does Mr. Justice need?"

"He'd have to get that information from planning. It says so on the citation."

"But do *you* know what permit he needs?"

"No."

"Why not?"

"That's not my job. I don't do planning. I do enforcement."

I watch Chrome Dome slowly inhale and glare at my officer. This will not end well.

"Interesting. Can Mr. Justice get a permit to operate a pig farm on his property?"

"No."

"Why not?"

"Because you cannot have a pig farm in a residential zone," the officer says. "The subject property is in a residential zone. Pig farms are limited to agricultural zones."

"So, to be clear, you cited him for operating a pig farm without permits?

"Correct."

"But there is no permit allowing a pig farm in a residential zone."

"Correct, again. You're batting a thousand there, Your Honor."

"In my courtroom, I always do. So let me hit this one out of the park for you. Officer Hollings, you cited a man thirteen times for not having a permit—a permit that he can't get in the first place. You, sir, are a complete moron." Chrome Dome shakes his head. "Makes you wonder why people hate the government. Step down, carefully, Officer. I don't want you hurting yourself. The bailiff will help you find your way out. Don't ever come back."

He rubs his eyes and mumbles to himself, "Oh my lord. I swear to God, Cooper," but it is just loud enough for his microphone to pick up, so we all hear him. He pauses for a moment.

"Very well. The administrative hearing officer's ruling is reversed in all respects. Ms. Wilson, I will give you the honor of preparing the judgment."

"Yes, Your Honor."

"What's that mean?" the coot asks her, leaning toward her as she leans away from his stench.

"You won," she replies in loud whisper.

The code officer has a wounded look as he leaves the stand and passes the counsel table. There's no point looking at him.

"Ha! You hear that, you tinhorn G-man! I win!"

The coot jumps up, and the deputy slams him down into the chair. He lets out a feeble cry of victory tinged with pain.

"I guess you don't need me for backup, huh?" says the code officer, grinning.

He is a much older man with toothpick arms and a pot belly.

The deputy stares. "No, I got this. You need to leave. Now."

"As to the motion," Chrome Dome continues.

"Your Honor, if I may—"

"No, Ms. Wilson, you may not. Relax. I'm not shutting down any pig farms today."

"But, Your Honor, I think—"

"No, Ms. Wilson, you did not. Even if you had, even if you could, you would have been wrong. As much as it pains me to say it, Mr. Cooper's moving papers are 'right on the money,' as they say."

The coot whispers into her ear, nearly overwhelming her, "Didn't he just say he wasn't shutting me down?"

"Get away from me!"

"But what's he mean?"

The judge smirks and then continues, "What I mean is that you lose, *Mr.* Justice. Although I am not shutting you down today, and notwithstanding the code officer's apparent inability to issue a proper citation for the correct violation, the county code, byzantine as it may be for any reasonable man to follow, nevertheless clearly prohibits you from operating a pig farm on your five-acre, residential parcel. You get five pigs, that's one per acre, and that's all."

He glances at the calendar on the wall behind his clerk.

"I'm giving you ninety days from today to remove the pigs and relocate them to a properly zoned parcel. Or you may want to consider moving lock, stock, and barrel next door to San Bernardino County. They speak your language there, and there is lots of room for your kind there in what undoubtedly must be the last hellhole of the ol' Wild West. No wonder the Earp brothers settled there—a target-rich environment by anyone's standards."

Chrome Dome glances at the reporter.

The reporter nods, and Chrome Dome continues.

"However, if you don't, then I will declare each remaining pig a public nuisance and order this county's animal control people to seize the pigs and auction them off and remit the proceeds to you, less the county's costs of care and feed and costs of any veterinary care required pending completion of the auction. The motion is granted. That will be the order. Mr. Cooper, you may have the honor of preparing that order."

"Yes, Your Honor. Thank you."

"Don't thank me, Mr. Cooper. Ninety days should be a sufficient amount of time for you to file your summary judgment motion and get your animal control people to gear up. I suggest you put them on alert as soon as possible and maybe get some training to your client department. I am not at all fond of repetition."

"Very well, Your Honor." I say, smiling.

Anchors aweigh, asshole!

Chrome Dome gives me a stern look.

"Very well indeed, Mister. I'll set this matter for a status conference re: compliance with injunctive order and a trial setting conference for this matter for December 15, at 8:30 a.m., this department. Mr. Cooper you will give notice."

"Yes, Your Honor."

"For what it's worth, Mr. Cooper, you've been around this block more than a few times. You have skills, sir, and yet here you are, a man of your age, still doing the same entry-level garbage—pun intended—first with the City Attorney's Office and now with County Counsel. You may want to consider growing a pair and manning up to litigating some real cases."

As accustomed as I am to Chrome Dome's insults, this one nails me.

"Or not, judging from your expression. Nevertheless, Mr. Cooper, the view from the gutter never changes. Something to consider."

"Yes, Your Honor," I reply, controlling my tone.

Bite me.

"As to you, Ms. Wilson, see that your client gets a bath. Court is adjourned. Deputy Curtis, thank you for your assistance this morning. Dennis, clear the courtroom and have it fumigated forthwith."

Chrome Dome stands up, unzips his robe, and rushes off the bench and into the hall behind it. The clerk rushes to follow him, difficult as that is for her in spiked heels. Dennis helps the reporter, who's coughing and gasping, gather her computer and stenography machine. I pack up my file and turn to leave. Deputy Curtis is guiding the old coot out. I hear Ms. Wilson fling the door open.

"What an asshole!" she announces to the world as she clears the doorway.

Probably the only time we'll ever agree.

"Okay, Mr. Cooper, you're welcome to stay for the fumigation, but if you have to leave, I understand, knowing how important you are with that new promotion and all."

"Thank you, Dennis. If it wasn't for a meeting, I would stay."

"Life at the top. I get you. Say no more."

"That's kind of you, Dennis. But I didn't get promoted."

He looks down as he takes a breath.

"Say no more. Till next time then."

"Till next time."

"And don't be paying the judge no mind. You know how he gets. His Monday started off bad too."

"No worries, Dennis. It's all good."

Chapter 7

My floor seems more quiet than usual when I get back. Nobody seems overly eager to speak with me, particularly my secretary who is walking into my office and not at all happy about it.

"Here's the copy of that form from the Assessor's Office that you were so hot to trot for."

She drops it on my desk.

"Thanks." I look at it. "Wait, it looks blank. None of the data spaces are legible."

She grunts.

"Well, no beans, bright boy. You should have seen the Assessor's copy. You can barely read it. I don't know why you'd ever want a copy of that."

I close my eyes and count to ten. I remind myself to look for the face of Christ in everyone. Okay. I tried. He's not there.

"I need it as a trial exhibit as I had explained to you when I asked for it. Did you think of trying to make it darker?"

"Don't you be caterwaulin' me, bright boy! You didn't ask me that. You asked for a copy. There's your copy. If you wanted it darker, you should have said so the first time. Really, Paul, you need to think these things through. No wonder you can't get promoted. How long do I have to be stuck with you?"

"I don't know. Maybe until you actually do any work."

She holds up her hand.

"I don't have time for this. I feel sorry for your next secretary. Really, I do. She can't get here soon enough as far as I'm concerned."

She spins a portly pirouette and leaves, leaving the door open.

"Bohica," I mumble to myself. "Bend over. Here it comes again."

I scribble myself a note to stop by the Assessor's Office later and try to get what I need.

Monday, Monday—how much hell can there be? Fresh dread is appearing for me everywhere like a reminder on my computer of a conference call that I don't know anything about slated to begin in less than ten minutes. Of course, there's the meeting later in the morning with Darrell Huntington. I can hardly wait. And there's always my secretary from hell, and she's mine and mine alone.

I print out the email reminder with the call-in number, retrieve the print-out from the printer near a storage cabinet down the hall from my office, grab a legal pad, tear off a sheet, write "conference call" on it with a marker, and tape it to my door.

I dial the number, enter the access code, and listen to the cheerful voice of an invisible woman telling me that I'm the first party on the line and that others would be joining me shortly. Soothing elevator music follows, setting me adrift into a few precious moments where all seems well with the world. I close my eyes and lean against the telephone handset pressed against my ear. I shift around a bit for comfort. I open my eyes at the silence. I check the clock face on my telephone console.

Oh, crap. It's been twenty-eight minutes. This can't be good.

I bring up the conference call email on my screen to forward it to my secretary from hell, not knowing if she's even at her desk, with a request to call the conferencing coordinator and find out what happened and ask what I should do. I worry as I'm about to press Send that she might not be at her desk or even if she were there, she might decide that she does not have time for this either and ignore me altogether. I add some names of other participants to the copy list for my email query and press Send.

In an abundance of caution, I consider forwarding that email in a direct message to those whom I had copied—this time, asking them for their direct assistance. I languish over whether to copy the secretary from hell, ultimately deciding in favor of full disclosure, and finally press Send. By now, over fifty-eight minutes have elapsed.

Within seconds, there's a reply from some private firm participant's secretary with a new call-in number and a polite apology for my inconvenience, which amazes me because it couldn't possibly have been her fault. I reply immediately and convey my gratitude. I hang up and call the new number.

I listen to the cheerful voice of an invisible woman welcoming me to the call and telling me that I am the first party on the line and that others will be joining me shortly. Soothing elevator music follows.

I hang up, and my phone rings. I see Marcie's name on the LED.

I answer with the requisite, perky tone, "Paul Cooper."

"Are you coming to the meeting?"

"Sure. Just finished a conference call." I check my screen, bring up my calendar—nothing. "Where do you need me?"

She had already hung up.

Okay then.

I dial the main reception line and ask our overworked receptionist where Darrell Huntington was having his meeting. She puts me on hold. She comes back and tells me.

I thank her, grab a pad, and go upstairs. I follow the commotion to Huntington's new office. IT techs crawl around the floor with cable. Their pushcart—laden with a computer, monitor, and keyboard—is parked outside. I look at the bright yellow wires dangling from the false ceiling. I have no idea what they're for. The wires' color is cheerful and reminds me of lemon pudding. I'm longing for lunch.

"Yeah. I was kind of wondering about them myself. The wires are up there and," the man in the natty pinstripe suit says as he points at the techs on floor. "They're down there. I'm sure it all makes sense somewhere. It's certainly an insight into how this county works. Maybe, maybe not."

He looks at me and sticks out a hand.

"I'm Darrell Huntington."

"Paul Cooper."

"I know."

We cordially shake hands. I can't help but notice his jet-black hair, so shiny and slick, and his jowly face. His blood-red tie must be silk, and the collar stay is a delicate bar, gold-plated.

Huntington breaks the silence.

"Listen, it's obviously a little crowded here. Why don't we go to your office?"

"Sure. No problem. It's downstairs."

"Lead the way."

Huntington follows me.

"Here, let me make some room," I say, clearing several redwells from a chair. "I don't usually get visitors."

"I understand completely."

"There, a little cramped, but at least it's quiet here."

Huntington closes the door and takes a seat.

"Now, tell me about this amazing program of yours I've been hearing so much about. Go ahead. I'm all ears."

"Sure. What would you like to know?"

"Well, for starters, give me the big picture."

As much as I don't want to, I run it down for him. It's roughly a five-minute presentation.

"I see. There's some potential certainly. Now tell me, what's the biggest obstacle to making all this happen, as you see it, of course."

He smiles like a shark would, if a shark could smile.

"Getting all the county departments with enforcement authority on the same page, coordinating their efforts and resources instead of letting them pursue independent enforcement actions simultaneously."

"And how's that been working out for you?"

"Haven't started yet."

"I see. Sounds like you've got a challenge on your hands."

"Looks that way."

"Good. Make that your focus."

Huntington looks at the bare walls as if making mental notes. Then he looks at me.

"For any chance of real success, this program needs to make money. That's why I am here. I have never practiced nuisance law, and I don't intend to start. I'm strictly plaintiff's personal injury, and I'm damn good at it. I'm also damn good at politics, which should pretty much answer any questions you may have about me or why I'm here. I've made a lot of money, and I'm doing some favors for some people. You might say I'm giving something back to the community."

"Money?"

Huntington laughs.

"That's a good one. I like that. No. Not money. Some time, maybe an assessment or two, and some guidance. A favor for a friend. I'm going to take your program, and I'm going to orchestrate it. I'm going to cherry-pick the cases and go after the real money. I intend to make a great deal of money off you. I thought you should know."

"Fair enough," I say.

Make money off me? This guy's nuts.

"Good. Lean, mean, moneymaking machine. That's your new mission statement. Any questions?"

I'm curious about Jessica but decide now's not the time.

"None."

"Good man. I'll be in touch." He stands. "In the meantime, keep doing whatever you're doing. You don't need my permission. You don't need my input. You don't need to check in with me at all. Just get it done. Get these departments in line. Get operational. Then come see me."

"Will do."

"Good man. While you're at it, put something on these walls—anything. You've got nothing but files everywhere. Too dismal. Get some plants too when you do." He smiles that shark smile again. "You can't make money when you're all cramped and dreary and deprived of oxygen."

"You're right. I've had to change offices three times in the last year, and I just never got around to it."

"TMI."

"I'm sorry?"

"Too much information."

"Oh, got it. Anyway, it's just an office. I don't live here."

Another one of those smiles.

"We may need to change that."

He opens the door.

"This place is a dump, Slugger. Dedumpify. Plants and pictures. Make it happen."

He walks out.

Make it happen? Right.

I clear the computer screen and make an entry on the time sheet. I tear the sheet off the pad, wad it up, and toss it into the wastebasket. I wander over to Ryan's office and peek in.

"Any lunch plans?"

"Nope. You?"

"I need to get the hell away from here. Any interest in Italian?"

"Lil' Italy's?"

"Sure, if that's okay."

"When?"

"Like now."

"Oh, dude! I am all over that. I'll even drive."

"You don't have to drive."

"Yeah I do. You got that 'lost in space' look again."

I shrug.

"Just another day with F Troop."

"It shows." He gets up, grabbing his keys from a drawer. "Let's roll, dude."

Lil' Italy's is a cozy spot, quiet, almost dark, and known for its killer meatball subs—the "Torpedoes"—on the menu. I usually go for the massive pepperoni pizza, also excellent, out of my recurring need for both comfort food and lots of leftovers.

Heaven on earth is an ice-cold cola, chilled to the point of being a near-frozen slush and a hot slice of Mama Luchesi's deep-dish pepperoni, sausage, mushroom, black olive, and pineapple pizza. Together, they work wonders on the soul—mine, especially.

Ryan watches me eat.

"Damn, dude. I guess you needed that."

I nod, sauce oozing at the edge of my dopey grin. I wipe my face.

"You're not exactly suffering."

"Me? Oh, hell no. These meatballs? This sauce? You kiddin' me? They're to die for."

He stops to watch our waitress, Anna—who is twenty years younger at least and for whom he lusts without hope because she also is to die for—as she strolls by carrying a tray of fresh bread and an antipasto salad to the next table over. I watch him lean ever so discreetly for a better angle of view of the adorable Anna leaning over to place the food on the table, her low-cut peasant top working almost as much magic on the two of us as the food.

"And the atmosphere is most excellent as well."

"Don't you know it," he says, eyes locked on her bountiful bosom. "Atmosphere is everything, and everything about the atmosphere here makes me feel young and virile."

For an unguarded moment, I imagine that the atmosphere includes a guitarist, tucked over in that corner to our left, picking pretty on an acoustic twelve-string guitar. Then in a moment of low blood sugar weakness or whatever follows a bellyful of pizza, I see myself playing one in a coffeehouse somewhere. That's a jarring visual, and I'm back to reality. I can't even play a baby electric. Hell, I can't even play. The realization is a shock, and it sends a cold wave of anxiety through me.

"Dude! Don't go all glum on me now."

"What? Oh, no, I'm good. Really, I'm fine."

"Sure, you are." Ryan reaches for his iced tea. "Wherever you were a moment ago, you need go back to that place and stay there. Forever."

"It's not like that. Forget it. Never happen. It's not like that at all."

"Something about it has to happen. For your sake." Ryan nibbles on a slice of dill pickle and drinks some tea. "Look, except for that one shining moment I want to hear more about, you've been looking mighty down lately. What gives?"

"I don't know. Maybe nothing. Everything's shitty at the office. Everything's shitty at home. Just . . . nothing and everything, I guess."

"At home too? Ouch. Probably can't help you there. She's younger than you, right? I've never met her, obviously, but that's what I've heard. That and she's totally gorgeous."

"Yep."

"Yep? Yep to which?"

"Both."

"How much younger?"

"About nine, maybe ten years."

Ryan exhales, whistling soft and low.

"Oh, you sweet stud! Good for you, dude!" He sips his tea. "Someday, you will have to tell me how the two of you got together."

"Yeah. Someday."

"Now about the office scene. What's up with that? Maybe I can help you there."

"Oh, I don't know. They bring me over to do some stuff, and then it seems like everybody—the office, the client people, *everybody*—all take turns getting in the way. It's like they talk change but don't really want change. They'd all rather sit around and BS the issues to death. Like God forbid ever actually getting anything done. And then there's this Huntington guy. I have no idea what that's all about. Other than he's doing somebody a favor. Whatever that means."

"Ah! See? There you go. Except for the Huntington part, you nailed it, dude. Welcome to County Counsel. Look, word is, you came from a long line of doers. If you look around, you'll notice we don't have a lot of them here. There's a reason for that. It's like our staff meetings. You miss most of them because you're in court all the time. A while ago, somebody brought up the process for disqualifying bidders on county contracts. Apparently, there isn't one. Apparently, they've been supposedly working on it for eight or nine years now. Get this. Nobody can explain the holdup.

"All the Admin folk can say is, 'Yeah, we're taking another look at that.' What does that even mean? Somebody mentioned some dude who's always bidding, always coming in lower than anybody else, always getting the jobs, and then always running up change orders and suing the county with every breath he takes. So bizarre. And their answer is always to lament and acknowledge the dude's latest threat and say, 'We'll just see about that,' like they're ready to clobber him.

"But that's just it, dude. They never do. They're permanent sideliners, dude. All talk. All the time. All watching and waiting for everything to go away on its own. Which, unfortunately, given enough time—and I'm talking years here—is what usually ends up happening. That just reinforces the whole process."

"Yep. That whole process pisses me off."

Ryan sips more tea. He gives me a long, blank look.

"What?"

"Listen, if you can hang on till Friday, come on over to Robby's place."

"Robby?"

"*Our* Robby—upstairs, you know, office next to mine."

"Got it. Sorry."

"Nothing to be sorry for, dude. You're obviously having another bad day in what is obviously and inexplicably a never-ending string of bad days. Anyway, Friday night at Robby's, we're getting together for a poker night. Get yourself a party mask and come on over and sit it for a few hands. You can tell us all about your meeting with Woo, the new boss guy Huntington, and whatever else is putting your life in the toilet. Maybe bring me a picture of your wife."

"I'm not so sure that would be a good idea."

"Dude, it'll be good for you! You keep clamming up like today, and you're gonna explode. Besides, I sure as hell don't want to be representing the county in any employment matter involving you."

"Well, crap, Ryan! Why didn't you just say so? On top of everything else, I'm in trouble too?"

"Not at all, dude. Not at all. Forgive me. Bad choice of words. Bad. Very bad. Don't rush off and get all paranoid on me. All my bad. Okay, dude? Listen, I'm just taking the proactive approach here, okay? Bottom line? You took one in the shorts for a team that doesn't deserve to have you on their roster, and I'm saying I don't want to see you unravelling as a result."

"Are you sure I'm not in trouble?"

"Dude, look at me. I'm sure." He waves to Anna.

"What are you doing?"

"Paying the bill. I owe you one for scaring the living shit out of you. That and as much as it's against my better judgment, we've got to get back to where we once belonged."

Anna comes over with a box for my pizza.

"Can I get you anything else, guys?"

"No, Anna darling, we're good. We're very good here. Everything was perfect," Ryan says, handing her two twenties. "You're adorable as ever. Keep the change, and if by chance you have an older sister who's as beautiful and bubbly as you and single, I do hope you will let me know."

"Okay," Anna giggles and adorably so, I think.

"On second thought, may I have a refill of my tea? In a to-go cup?"

"Of course," she says. "I'll be right back."

"Thank you."

We watch her walk away.

"Like I was saying, dude. Poker, Friday night at Robby's."

"I can't."

"Yes, you can. Besides, you owe me."

"For what, lunch?" I reach for my wallet.

"No! Not for lunch, dude. For the bet I lost."

"What bet?"

"My standing bet with Robby. Whenever you walk to court in the morning, we scramble over to the windows and try to watch and when we can, we always bet on which homeless dude you're gonna give money to."

"Are you kidding me?"

"No."

"Why?'

"Dude, I grew up in Vegas. I love gambling. I love the thrill of taking a chance."

"You've got to stop doing that."

"Yeah? You've got to stop being Fr. Flanagan."

"Don't say that. Their lives are all so fucked."

"Okay, I won't say it. But it's still true. Just tell me you'll be at Robby's, Friday night, 7:00 p.m. Eat light. He usually puts out a good spread. Oh, and be sure to get yourself a Halloween mask or something because the one thing you don't have is a poker face."

"Oh, thanks."

"Don't mention it, dude. You know I've got your back."

"A mask?"

"Absolutely. Grab your box. We gotta jet." He trades smiles with Anna as she hands him his to-go cup.

I grab my box, and we jet.

Chapter 8

"Robby's, Friday night at seven. Think about it," Ryan says as we walk to his car.

I think about it throughout the week. I think about it when I buy the stupid mask. I'm still thinking about it when Ryan opens Robby's door. I'm standing at the doorway wanting to turn around and leave.

"Yes, I knew it! C'mon in!"

"If that's Paul, don't let that pussy in!" Robby yells from inside.

Ryan waves his hand.

"Don't listen to him. He's just jealous. C'mon in, get a beer, make yourself a sandwich, get some chips. C'mon in, dude, good to see ya."

"Sure, why not?"

"That's the spirit!"

"Jealous of what?"

Ryan grabs my arm.

"I'll tell ya later. Just trust me. Drop it," he says, giving my arm a squeeze.

"Okay! It's dropped," I mumble.

What the fuck is that all about?

Ryan leads the way from the entry into Robby's den. Robby slaps some cards onto the table.

"What are you, deaf? I told you not to let that pussy in," Robby deadpans.

"I told ya, I told ya! Didn't I tell ya? Pay up. Pay up, dude."

"When I skin your flabby ass, I'll take it out of my winnings." Robby shuffles the deck. "Then and only then will I pay you and not a moment before."

"What? You didn't think I would show up?"

"Of course I did, dude. Come on, you know I believe in you. He doesn't, so I got odds up front and won me a little side bet."

"You got me here . . . just for a bet?"

"No! Nothing like that at all. I got you here because you need to be here. I just made a little money on the side is all. Relax, dude, it's just on the side."

"Can you play?" a stranger with a graying mustache and thinning hair asks me.

"No," I reply.

"No," Robby echoes.

"Got money?"

"Some."

"Okay then. You can play. Sit here." He taps on the table.

"That's AJ. He's an accountant. One of the regulars, so watch yourself," Ryan says, lowering his voice to a whisper. "Please tell me there's a mask in the bag."

I ignore him and move around to AJ's side of the table and take a seat. I lean over and take a garish Halloween mask, a distorted bright yellow face, out of the bag and put it on.

"Oh, dude! That is so killer! You'll take two hands easy without even knowing what you're doing."

The mask turns and stares at AJ.

AJ nods. "Works for me, crazy man. Long as you got cash."

"Whoa, Nellie, dude! Okay, you met AJ. You know me and Robby, and I think you know Danny, right?"

Danny smiles and gives a nod.

"Not really, sorry. I've seen you around though. Fourth floor?"

Danny nods again.

"That's right. Danny's got Clerk of the Board. He does all the county's ordinances."

"Oh, right."

"That mask ain't gonna help you none, son." Robby snaps the cards and slaps the deck on to the green felt of the table. "Cut 'em."

With the deck cut, Robby begins to deal.

"All right, gentlemen, limit of three on the draw. Danny's bet."

"Quarter," said Danny. "What did Woo have to say, Paul?"

"Easy, dude! Give the man a chance now. He just sat down," Ryan says. "Okay, you've been sitting long enough. Spill it!"

"Not much to tell," I say.

It's uncomfortable talking through this mask, but I'm pretty certain getting me to talk is their ruse for getting me to take it off so I'll talk too openly and make for easier pickings. I decide I'm better off with it on and keep going.

"You all got the email I'm sure, except maybe AJ. At least the one I heard about," Ryan says.

"What email?' I ask.

"You didn't get one?" Danny asks.

"No," I reply.

Danny snorts.

"Never mind me," says AJ. "Go on with your story."

"There's not much of a story, really. Woo said they were bringing in someone from the outside as a new Chief Deputy, and sure enough, Monday morning, he was there."

"That Huntington guy in Woo's email?" Danny asks.

"I'm not sure about the email, but yeah, Darrell Huntington."

Robby tilts his head to peer over his sunglasses.

"*The* Darrell Huntington?"

"I don't know. How many of them are there?"

"Only one who'd matter, and you would know if it was him."

I shrug. "I don't know. Flashy dresser. Slicked-back hair. Expensive suit, silk tie?"

"That would be him," Robby says and then chuckles. "Damn."

"What?"

"You'll find out soon enough, son."

"What? I met with him. He told me he's done plaintiff's PI—"

"No shit he's done plaintiff's PI. He's raped automakers for millions," Robby says.

"Yeah, he mentioned he's won some big cases for big money. He didn't get into specifics. He's going to see that the nuisance unit's run like it's a plaintiff's PI firm. He says we're going after big money."

"Ha! That's rich!" Robby laughs. "Yeah, he's going after the big money all right. No wonder they put that sleazy bastard in charge of litigation."

"You lost me on that one," says AJ. "Doesn't he realize we're in San Gorgonio County and not LA? There's no money here. Believe me, I know."

"That's the county for you," Robby says. "Somebody's getting scammed. All right, gents, we've got Danny boy working a straight or better. What's your pleasure, AJ?"

"Interesting. My bet, huh? Okay, I raise a quarter."

Ryan looks at Danny.

"Dude, didn't some big PI dude try that once with LA or Ventura?"

"Maybe. Whatever it is, it's just politics. I wouldn't worry about it. Keep your mouth shut and go along with the program—whatever be the program—and everything will be fine, and before you know it, it'll be quittin' time. You need to trust me on this, sports fans. Just run out the clock. Nothing else matters."

Robby turns to me. "Okay, masked man. What's your play?"

"Oh, my turn? Sorry. Okay then. I guess I'm raising a quarter."

"That's the spirit, crazy masked man. A right natural player, you are," says AJ.

Ryan raises a quarter.

"And I'll raise a quarter," Robby says.

"Quarter. I'm good." Danny says.

"I'll take two," AJ says.

"Two for the Culver City Kid. I'm thinkin' the bean counter is workin' another full-house fantasy here, boys." Robby passes two cards over to him.

"Forget Huntington. What else did Woo say, dude?"

"He said I needed a hobby." I adjust the mask. "I'll take three cards, please."

"Three?" Robby stares at me over his sunglasses.

I nod.

Robby shakes his head.

"Take that stupid mask off, you pussy."

I slowly shake my masked head to signal a *no*. I get rid of three cards, one at a time.

"Yeah, dude, keep it on. Finally, a game that's interesting."

"Yeah, for those who can't play," Robby says.

"Says the man in black and wearing shades," I say.

"Whoa! Listen to the crazy man! Get some, bro!"

Robby raises an eyebrow. "Well, all right, then. Three cards for the masked man."

Robby flicks me three cards.

I nod the mask vigorously, making AJ and Danny laugh. The mask tilts toward my left shoulder as I try to look at the cards without turning them over.

"Get back to Woo, dude. I didn't hear you. What did Woo tell you?" Ryan asks.

"A hobby. Woo told me to get a hobby when he passed me over for the promotion."

"He didn't pass you over, dude. He just delivered the bad news."

"Going with Ryan on that one. Bringing in some higher power like Huntington—that's from on high, man. Woo had no say in it," Danny adds.

"You're probably right. I met with Huntington the following Monday. He said something about giving back to the community, doing some favors. But he was shrewd and kept away from the details," I inform the group, not wanting to argue about it.

I just want the evening over with as soon as possible. "When Woo was giving me the news, he told me Huntington's name. I told Woo I had never heard of him, and then Woo said he hadn't heard of him either."

"There you go. *Favors* is right. All scam," Robby says.

"Dude, did Woo have his fly-tying kit out when you were talking?" Ryan asks.

"Maybe. Crap. I don't remember. He was staring at his computer screen a lot. He was making me sit there and wait while he dicked around before he finally sent out the announcement email."

"I don't know, dude. Maybe you're reading too much into this. I think he was just trying to do you a favor. I think he was dropping hints on how to survive in this office."

"Bingo!" chimes Robby.

"So I'm supposed to just sit around and tie trout flies, is that it?"

"Don't get pissy with me, little man," said Robby.

"Lighten up, Paul," Danny says. "They're probably right on this."

"Dude, just get a hobby like the man said. It's no big deal."

"Yep. Give credit where credit is due. I'm telling you, that man is going to outlast us all," Danny says. "He's like Teflon."

"What does that mean?"

"It means you're taking this the wrong way, Paul."

"I don't think so. He got pretty testy."

Robby snorts. "Oh, hell. Did you ask the man any questions?"

"Sure I did. He asked me if I had any questions."

"Well, shit, man! There's your problem right there. He really didn't mean for you to ask any."

"Really? That's not what he said."

"No shit, Sherlock. Haven't you ever heard of reading between the lines? Hell, the man had one job, and that was giving everyone who applied for the bullshit position the bad news. That's it. You don't fuck with him, and he don't fuck with you. Decision was made before the announcement for applications was ever posted. Don't you have any fucking life experience? Shit."

What the fuck is your problem?

Danny takes another peak at his cards.

"What Robby means to say is that Woo sits back, ties his trout flies, rakes in the deferred comp, and then goes fly-fishing two months out of the year. The man's a political genius, Paul. He's been a Deputy Chief like, I dunno, like forever. He's been through at least four county counsels in his career."

Robby slaps the table.

"Bingo! He shows up, does only what he's told, and not a diddle more. He doesn't take any of the shit personally. He doesn't give a damn. He puts all his energy and passion into what he loves. Take the fuckin' hint, Paul. Be a man and quit your fuckin' whining."

"Fly-fishing?" I can't keep the disdain from my voice.

"Ouch! Still bleeding, are you?" asks AJ.

Robby slaps the table again. "Bingo! You're right, Ryan."

I think Robby's drunk. What the hell. I think he's always drunk. I knew a priest like that once. He hit on my Mom a couple of times before the booze took her beauty. Coach hit him out of the diocese.

"Yep, ol' Ryan my man, this game is finally getting interesting. Dealer takes two," Robby says and then glares at me. "Well, you just gonna sit there and bleed, little man, or are you gonna tell us about the new hobby? Wait! What was the old one you had? Cartooning? Your bet, Danny."

"Something like that," I say.

Be grateful you're drunk, motherfucker.

"Raise a buck," Danny says.

"Big man makes a big move. AJ?"

"Adding a quarter to that."

"Okay, masked man, what's it gonna be?"

"I'll raise a quarter too. Cartooning wasn't a hobby."

"Wait," Ryan said, "all this time I thought you were getting a pilot's license. Whatever happened to that? And I'll raise you fifty cents."

"Well, that's on hold. Guitar is cheaper. I don't have to get a medical exam, and I never have to leave the house."

"Oh, that ought to get the wife dewy all over," says Danny.

"What are you talking about? I call. Guitar? What guitar?" Robby asks.

"Guitar. That's the new hobby. I'm learning to play the guitar."

"What? You?" Robby bursts out with a laugh. "That's too funny."

"Why is that too funny?"

"First, it's cartooning, only that wasn't a hobby, apparently, because you were home brewing beer in your darkroom. Jump in any time here, Ryan—"

"Yeah," I aim the mask at Ryan, "jump in any time."

"Only you weren't brewing, you were learning to fly and, oh, that's right, distilling bourbon in a sour mash copper kettle still you had set up in your garage."

"Hold on a minute. You have a still?" AJ asks. "Can he do that? You know, be a moonshiner and be an attorney with county counsel at the same time?"

"Whoa, everybody! Back the fuck up! I'm not a moonshiner. No, I'm not distilling bourbon or brewing beer. No, I'm not a pilot and probably never will be."

"Wow! Man, I am so sorry I asked. For a guy in your shoes, making your own booze may be the absolute best way to go. Next to that mask thing you got going."

"Listen to AJ, Paul. The man's giving you a pearl of wisdom!" Robby laughs again. "That's why it's too funny and that's why you are never going to learn to play a guitar. You obviously have the attention span of a twelve-year-old and even less discipline, so you can't stick with anything long enough to get it done. Unless it's work related, of course. That and you are just too damn old to be taking on something as complicated as a musical instrument."

"So? What do you know about playing guitar?"

"You kidding me, son?" He laughs again. "I've been playing for"—his voice trails off abruptly—"years. Whole lotta years."

He isn't laughing anymore.

"Fuck it. I need another drink."

He stands up.

"Anyway, if you haven't learned to play by the end of high school, then it just can't happen. Honest truth. Hell, everybody knows that. Music, language—all that shit's gotta be learned in childhood while the brain is ready for it. That's a scientific fact, jack!"

"Yeah? The earth being flat was once a scientific fact."

"Forget it, Paul. You'll never make it. Anybody else need a drink?"

"I'll take another beer, man."

"Are you sure you don't want anything stronger, Danny? I'm gonna get something stronger."

"No, man. A beer'll do me."

"Suit yourself. AJ? How 'bout it, my friend? You up for a beer?"

"Water," he says, not bothering to look up. "Water will be fine."

Robby snaps his fingers.

"Shit! My fuckin' bad. Sorry, man. Senior moment. Totally fuckin' blanked. I am so sorry."

AJ looks up, smiles.

"No worries, brother. I know you didn't mean anything. Hey, tell you what! I'll take one of those bottled sparkling waters if you got any left from last time."

Robby nods.

"Absolutely, my brother!"

Robby then pulls a Jekyll or a Hyde and shoots me a look.

"Oh, how rude of me. How about you, Paul? You wanna orange soda or something? Water, maybe?"

"Actually," I say, with a smile behind my mask, "gee, Robby, an orange soda or root beer or a cherry cola would be, you know, like totally swell."

Ryan grins. Danny and AJ keep their poker faces.

"Cherry cola?" Robby nods. "Okay. Fuck you. Let me see what I got."

"Okay, getting back to the game for a minute. I've lost track. Where are we? Anybody know?" Danny asks.

AJ glances around. He points to Robby's chair.

"Robby called. It's showtime. Soon as Robby's back."

"That sounds about right," Danny says.

Robby comes back with a bottle of beer and a can of soda in one hand and a glass with ice and a bottle of bourbon in the other. His arm cradles a bottle of sparkling water against his side.

"Here you go, gents. A beer and a root beer. Sparkling water."

"Thank you," I say, reaching for the can.

Danny gently clinks his bottle against the bourbon bottle.

Robby nods.

"All right," he says, poring bourbon onto the ice cubes in the glass. "Showdown. Let's see 'em."

Everyone reveals their cards.

"Damn!" says AJ. "Looks like our crazy masked man takes the pot with a full house, kings over nines."

"Didn't see that coming. Here I thought I had it going on with a jack's high straight," Danny says.

"Dude, do you even know what you had?"

I let the mask give Ryan the silent treatment.

"Yeah, I didn't think so. Good for you, dude."

"That is just wrong," says Robby. "So fuckin' wrong."

Finally. It's over.

I take the mask off and wipe my face with a napkin and take a sip of the root beer.

"That's a good soda right there. But, hey, I digress. It's all in the cards, right, boys?" I say. "That and a good poker face or, in my case, a good poker mask. And with that, gentlemen, I will call it a night."

"You pussy. Sit back down! You just got here," Robby says. "Finish your root beer and give us a chance to get our money back."

"Next time, boys."

"What the hell's the rush?"

"Got to get home and practice before—" I catch myself and stop.

Seems I'm doing a lot of that now.

"Before what? Before Mama gets home?" Robby asks.

"Yeah, pretty much."

"Well, okay then. Next time, pussy."

"Your wife's not too fond of the new hobby, I take it," says AJ.

"Not at all."

"That's too bad. Another reason to appreciate being single."

"You play guitar, AJ?"

"Me? Oh, hell no."

"AJ's a drummer. Damn good one too," says Robby, knocking back another bourbon.

"We don't need to go there, brother. I didn't bring up your past, did I?"

"No, you did not. I apologize. I was out of line."

"That'll do. We're good here. It's all good."

I have no idea what's going on, and that's just fine because I'm getting out of here. I pack.

"Good night, all. Have a good weekend."

I get up and put the napkin in my pocket.

"And I play bass, dude. And Danny sings. He sang in his high school choir. Give me a call, dude. We can get together and jam."

"Sure. Sounds good."

I want to be polite but . . .

No. That is so not happening.

"What are you doing? You got him in the band now?"

"It could happen, dude."

"Yeah, that'll be the day."

"Yeah, AJ's right, that'll be the day, all right," I hear Robby say as I pull the front door closed behind me.

That went well. Right. Look at the bright side. I won a few bucks, and I learned my instincts were right. Coming here tonight was a huge mistake.

Chapter 9

My telephone rings. I pick up the receiver and see "Receptionist" on the LED display.

"Hi, there."

"Paul?"

"That's me."

"Aren't you're supposed to say 'this is Paul' when you answer your internal line?"

"Sorry. I figured you'd know it was me like I knew it was you. Okay. You win. Take two. This is Paul. Hi, there."

"There's a code officer here to see you, Paul. Where should the officer go?"

I am so tempted, but I decide to play it straight. "Send him on back to my office."

"He's a she."

"Fair enough. Send *her* on back here."

Next time I'm better off to let it ring. I get up and move the stack of redwells off the chair.

"Hey, look who's here! Come on down. Have a seat."

"Thanks." The officer notices all the files everywhere and seems to have second thoughts. "I can come back later. You look busy."

"Up to you. It's just another Monday as far as I'm concerned. I'm here all day."

"Well, if you got a minute. I just want to run something by you real quick."

"Sure. What do you have for me?"

"Well, I finished my investigation of the complaint."

I smile politely.

Sure you did.

"It's a land use violation, and the owner is not in compliance. He's running an illegal business out of the house that's on the property. It's a single-story wood-frame stucco dwelling in a residential zone, and we need to really hammer him. The neighborhood's not zoned commercial, and several neighbors have complained to the board for, well, it's been going on about, I'd say, six or eight months now."

"Owner information?"

"Right here," she says, shuffling through a folder of loose papers.

She pulls a sheet from the pile and hands it to me. I start copying the name and other information onto a legal pad.

"Name of the business?"

"I don't know."

No surprise there.

I put my pen down and look up.

"What kind of business are we talking about?"

There's a blank look on her face.

"Take your time," I tell her.

"I think it's a computer business," she finally says as she shrugs. "I'm not really sure. There's lots and lots of cables and stuff on these huge wooden things, you know—spools. Yeah, I think they're called spools."

She fishes out a color photo from her pile of stuff and shows it to me. I look at it and see stacks of large wooden spools coiled with an unknown length of bright orange cables that, by my guess, must be at least three inches in diameter. The spools dwarf the white utility pickup truck parked next to them. I notice that the truck's rear license plate is obscured from view by a blurry stripe that must be part of the chain-link fence dominating the foreground of the photograph.

"Your cable guy does something with all this cable, and you're thinking he's into computers. What about this truck? Any name on the door?"

"I don't know."

"Okay. Any more pictures of the truck?"

"No, just this one."

"Take down the license number?"

"No."

"No?"

"No. I couldn't get any closer."

"I see."

"I just assumed the truck belonged to the property owner—well, *trucks*, actually. There are three trucks altogether on the property."

"Three trucks?"

"Yes. Three white trucks."

"Three white trucks. Like a business."

"Exactly."

"Did you knock on the door, talk to anybody, ask for consent to enter and inspect—anything like that?"

"No."

"Interview any of the neighbors?"

"No."

"Who lives in the house?"

"I don't think anybody lives there."

"What makes you think so?"

"There never seems to be anybody around."

"Just the trucks and all that yellow cable stuff?"

"Exactly."

"Got it. How about the Fictitious Business Name database? Run the owner's name through that?"

"No."

God help me. I so hate it here.

"Fair enough." I turn to my computer. "Let's try that. Maybe we'll get lucky."

"Maybe."

I bring up the database, type in the name, and wait.

"Well, what do you know? We have a winner! Aurelio Contreras dba Tres Rios Communications, Inc. How about that, huh? Different address though."

"Oh, that's where he used to be."

"Used to be? Whataya mean 'used to be'? You know this guy?"

"Yes."

"You've talked to him before?"

"Yeah. Once or twice. I cited him a couple of times at the old place. Same thing."

I stand up and stretch.

"Tell you what. Here's what I need from you if you expect me to, as you say, *hammer* this guy. Go talk to him. Ask him for consent to inspect the house, the interior of the house, the yard—the works. If he says yes, then inspect and document the inspection with good photos. And by that, I mean don't shoot photos through a chain-link fence. If he says no, then write up a declaration for an administrative inspection warrant. With me so far?"

Blank stare.

"Good. Then talk to the neighbors to get whatever else you need for the warrant declaration, and I will help you get an administrative inspection warrant. By either of those two methods, go onto the property. Write down the license numbers of all of the trucks and take pictures of all of the trucks and all their license plates. Run the plates and get the registration information for each vehicle. I can't make it any plainer than that. Go to the Assessor's Office and find out who pays the property taxes on this parcel. Get copies of the checks."

I jot down some notes.

"Ask your owner guy why the trucks are there. See if the company name is on the door of the trucks. Take pictures of that.

Ask him what the yellow cable is for. Ask him what his business is. Do that. Can you do that?"

"Well, yeah. Maybe I could do all of that." She looked at her watch. "That's an awful lot to do."

"Yes it is." I smile politely again. "Lunchtime?"

"Yeah, pretty close. Maybe I can just talk him into leaving. I'd like to resolve this with a lot less paperwork."

"Hey, no worries. I understand. Too many complaints, too little time. I get it. Let me know how that works out for ya."

"Yeah, okay."

"Enjoy your lunch."

"Thanks."

"Anytime at all."

I smile as she gets up to leave and tear the page from my legal pad and wad it up. She hears the noise and turns back. I hold my smile and flick the crumpled wad into a wastebasket. I tell her to have a nice day as she walks out.

I glance at my calendar. Wow. Time files when you're having fun. I swivel to the computer and bring Woo up on email. Subject: Hobby Report. I type the word *guitar* in the memo space and press Send.

I'm beginning to look forward to Fridays almost as much as I hate them for reminding me another Monday always looms just around the corner.

Woo's email reply: "Splendid choice!"

He follows with another email. He thinks it's a great idea and insists I play something at his Hoedown Harvest BBQ party on Halloween weekend.

Fat chance.

I email back and tell him no thanks. There's no way I can be ready by then. He replies that is nonsense, says he insists and that he won't take no for an answer. I tell him to pound sand. Then I think better of it, and I hit the Delete button.

Everything is peachy again until my screen lights up seconds later and there's a flurry of incoming email beeps. Woo has announced officewide that I'm taking up guitar and have volunteered to give a brief concert at his party and will be joining his party's very own house band, which, apparently—as this is news to me because I never go to these things—is led by Robby Sherwood.

Everybody else is responding and dumping in their two cents' worth, starting with the "gossip girls"—my name for all the office busy bodies.

Woo sends another message, also officewide. Apparently, I have a new hit single entitled "Pound Sand," which I have most graciously agreed to perform live at the hoedown.

Oh shit!

What the hell key did I really press?

I pull up my sent messages, and there it is, in pristine, unmistakable black and white—me telling Woo to pound sand.

My phone is ringing. I'm frozen to my chair. My phone is still ringing, screaming rings. Robby's name is on the LED. I feel a sharp kick in my chest and my hands tingle. My body is paralyzed with what I'm thinking is a massive adrenaline dump. I fumble with the handset, drop it, and I hear the ping of the hands-free tone.

"Cooper! Who the hell do you think you are?"

"Cooper," I finally manage to mumble. "Who the hell else would I think I am?"

"Fuck you, funny boy!"

I'm not trying to be funny. I'm trying to function. But my body has a mind of its own, and it won't let me. I'm all cotton-mouthed and couldn't talk if I tried. And I'm trying to talk, and I can't, and I think I've been harpooned. I feel like I'm bleeding invisibly—or maybe, internally—and I can't do anything except sit here and take it.

"I know you're there! Is this your idea of a joke? You jackass!"

"Of course I'm here. Where the hell else would I be on a Monday? This place is its own special purgatory, and no, this is not my idea of a joke. For your amusement and information, I am not a jackass."

I want to say more, but my tongue is stuck to the roof of my mouth.

"You balls-less bastard! I'm gonna kick your ass!"

Is it the rage in his voice that slurs his words or has he been drinking? I'm pretty sure that you can't drink in the office. Not this office, anyway. I must remember that this is government and not the private sector. Everybody knows that.

I'm wrestling my tongue and blurt out sounds and syllables and manage to say the first thing that comes to my mind.

"Are you drunk?"

There's a split second of silence then this piercing, shrieking yell, like a Scot's battle cry minus the bagpipes. It sounds vaguely reminiscent of an elephant giving birth. Another burst of . . . silence. I'm certain by now Robby's on his way down here to kick my ass. No worries. First, it's not like I can feel all that much right now, should he succeed. Two, he won't succeed because I will be waiting to bushwhack the little bastard.

Ryan's in my doorway. He's out of breath.

"What did you do?" he asks.

I shrug. "I dunno. Gimme a hint?"

"What did you say to Robby? He's up there screaming like he's got rabies."

"Okay."

"Okay? Talk to me, dude. What the hell happened?"

I nod at the computer.

He looks at the monitor.

"Were you thinking out loud again?"

I shrug again. My tongue is swollen, and I'm smacking it against my lips. Ryan looks around and spots a bottle of water. He opens it and hands it to me. I mug it with both hands and drink like I'm dying in a desert.

Relief! Oh thank God!

Robby's still on the phone, screaming incoherently. I knock back several slugs of water.

"It's Robbie," I say, holding up the receiver, which I put it to my ear. "And if you are, boozer, then you sure as shit better bring somebody sober cuz I've had it with you and your shit and I ain't takin' none of it no more. Bingo! There it is, boozer. Ain't wastin' time with you no more. Your move."

I hang up.

"What the fuck, dude?"

I look up at him and grin.

"Woo emailed me and said he wanted me to play at his party. I said no. And he insisted cuz he's pushy that way. And I was thinking out loud, and I thought I hit the Delete key, only I'm guessing I didn't hit the Delete key."

I take another slug of water.

"Damn. I was so sure I had hit that Delete key. Swear to God I did. But that's just my guess and then that bottle-boozin', lil' willy of a bastard Robby calls me. Well, by then I couldn't talk, and when I could talk, he sounds drunk, so I ask him, 'Are you drunk?' Obviously, a perfectly logical thing to do on my part. Don't ya think?"

Ryan sits down.

"Oh, dude."

"Yeah. Well, there's that."

"I don't see how you can fix this, dude."

"Nothing to fix. Fuck him. Hell. Fuck both them bastards!"

I sit still, close my eyes, and let the waves of whatever is this buzzing sensation wash over me.

"No, no. You don't understand. Damn it, dude! We've talked about this!" He takes a moment. "Okay. Don't send anymore emails. Nothing to nobody. Understand? Stay off the phone. Keep your mouth shut. Be at my place at 9:00 a.m. on Saturday with your guitar. I will email you directions and my cell number. Try not to fuck up anything else till then."

"Fair enough."

I stop answering my phone. I hibernate in my office. Now my secretary smiles at me. I stay off the fourth floor. I manage to get through the week despite a lot of razzing in the elevator from people I don't know and normally never see. Admin's keeping quiet, and I take that as a good sign.

◆ ◆ ◆ ◆ ◆

Saturday's come, and I'm none the worse for wear. On the road, I am constantly rechecking the directions and keeping my eyes on the curving road. The scenery has turned from dull brown to deep green, though the leaves of many oaks and other trees have turned to colors of rust, russet brown, and gold.

Intriguing how these colors match up here in apple country, at the base of the mountain. I have not been up here in a long time, and I've never been to Ryan's, and I fall in love with the place the minute I turn onto his winding gravel drive and pull up to a barn.

Ryan lives in a barn. How cool is that?

I park next to a sporty four-wheel drive. I assume it's a four-wheel drive, and I assume it's his. I get out of my car and take the gig bag from the back seat. I walk to the center of the barn where a massive door has been slid open along a metal rail embedded in the cement floor.

"Hello?" I say.

"Hey! You made it!" Ryan calls out from a loft above. "Be right down."

He comes down with a couple of microphone stands and a coil of cable.

"This place is amazing," I say, looking around. "This used to be a barn, right? I mean, it's a barn. I don't know what I mean."

"It's been a lot of things, dude. Apple-packing shed, horse barn, tractor barn, country store—you name it."

"You fixed it up? I mean, all the conversion work, construction stuff."

I look around. Then I think of permits and approvals and code violations and notice that discomfort in my stomach.

"Dude, will you lighten up? I know what you're thinking. I see it in your face. Everything here"—he waves—"as far as your darting eyes can see in any direction you choose to look is fully permitted and approved by County Planning, Building, and Safety, the Inland Counties Temperance Committee, and every musician's four-wheeling club in the country. So there."

"I'm sorry."

"I know," he grunts, giving my shoulder a congenial shake. "You're a piece of work, dude. Anyway, you are safe here. At least until Robby arrives. You'll be on your own then. You might want to stay near that shovel over there."

"Like I told him, his move."

"Oh, relax, dude! I'm just teasing you. You'll be fine. He's just really pissed. You called him out, and he blew up. He'll get over it. Besides, he's Woo's fair-haired boy, so nothing's gonna happen to him. Next time, though, try keeping your mouth shut and look the other way. Yes, he drinks. Yes, he's a functioning alcoholic. Yes, everybody knows it."

I shrug.

"Everybody but you apparently. You need to spend less time in the stacks and more time with actual people. Just so you know, Robby's an office legend. He's been a kick-ass litigator for nearly thirty-some years, and he's won far more cases than maybe is fair—and I never said that—and he's saved the county tons and tons of money in the process. That and he's damn near a closet rock-god guitarist who can make his axe wail and moan and scream as well as any hot porn star."

I blink.

"What?"

"Nothing."

"Yes, dude. I'm occasionally fond of porn. I also have a pulse. You happy now?"

"I didn't say anything!"

"Oh, c'mon, dude! Your face! Your body language. Look at yourself! Christ, your eyebrows alone work harder than any sailor flagging semaphore signals. Go look in a mirror once in a while."

"Sorry."

"And stop apologizing all the time. That's even more annoying."

"Sorry."

The word's out before I can do anything.

Ryan shakes his head.

"Just shut up. Relax. In fact, stay away from the coffee. And the Cokes. You know what? Come here. I got something for you."

I follow him into a kitchen. I look back, and there are no doors that I can see.

"Have a seat."

I sit on a wooden shaker-style chair at a rustic-looking table. He pulls a plastic gallon jug marked "Cider" from a refrigerator. He pours it into a saucepan and puts the pan on the stove on low heat. He gets a box of something from a cupboard, then he's back to the fridge for some apple slices and what looks like a new, unopened jar of caramel sauce from a walk-in pantry.

"Something smells really good," I say, trying to be cheerful and sound appreciative.

"Yeah? Right on."

"Forgive me, I know this will sound stupid, but I really love what you've done with the place."

Ryan busts up laughing.

"Okay, over in that drawer are place mats. Go pick one you like and bring it over to the table."

I do as he says and find a nice red one. Bright red. Cheerful. I come back, put it on the table, and sit down. Ryan brings over a large mug and a small plate of sliced apples with caramel sauce.

"I don't know if you've had breakfast or not," he says, seeing me shake my head, and he looks at me for a second. "Okay then, here's your breakfast and hot-spiced cider with a cinnamon stick. You're gonna want to let that cool, dude. Start with the apples."

"Thank you."

I start with the apples, dipping the slices into the warm caramel and work my way up to the cider. It's delicious. It has a different smell though. I'm not sure what it is. Anyway, it's delicious and ridiculously sweet, and I love it like a kid with a mouthful of candy. I finish the mug, and Ryan immediately refills it. I finish that one, and he immediately refills it again. I finish it and begin feeling light-headed in a rather cozy kind of way.

"So what's the plan?" I ask, feeling warm and really good.

"This," he says with a grin.

"This what?"

"Mellow your ass out."

I think about this. I didn't know my ass needed mellowing. Interesting concept. Anyway, the cider is most excellent, but I don't get why it's thick, why it's creamy.

"Why is the cider creamy?"

"Because it's got a dollop of heavy cream in it."

"Oh, okay. What else does it have in it? It's most excellent."

"Cider, honey, cinnamon, brown sugar, maple sugar, maple syrup, and four shots of maple-flavored bourbon."

"Oh okay."

"How do you like them apples?"

"Delisshusss."

"Good. Feeling' mellow yet?"

"Yep."

I sip the syrupy sweetness. I close my eyes and enjoy the sweet warmth of this elixir.

Mellow. Mmm. Melodious. Mellomius. Mellow are us. Mapleous. Mapleous Themonius mellonious. Mapleonious. Mmmmm.

I hear Ryan's voice too.

"Good to hear it. You know, you've been wrapped a little too tight lately."

Wrapped! Tightly. Wrapped so, so tightly. Wrapped. Trapped. Trapped so tightly.

Ryan's whistle noise and his nudge make me open my eyes.

"Hey, welcome back. Stay with me here. Okay?"

Ryan smiles.

"Hey, over here. Look at me, dude. Here's the deal. You're going to take it easy today. The boys from the poker game ought to be here in an hour. I got a little stage set up out back on the main floor. There's an outdoor kitchen there with chili cooking in a Crock-Pot. There's a bathtub full of ice with all kinds of soda, beer, and bottled water. There's a table with chips and dips and munchies. This is a partyin' up and chillin' down kinda day. With me so far?"

"Yep. I'm with you all the way."

"Good deal. Another thing. The poker boys are all closet pro musicians. I already told you about Robby. You need to know they've all been at it most of their lives. You are just getting started. Point is—and why I had you come early—is to get you geared up and comfortable. This is not a competition. I don't want you getting discouraged and all depressed and worked up over this thing. It's all about having fun."

"Okay."

"Good. C'mon out. Let's get you amped up," he chuckles a bit. "Okay, bad choice of words. I'll set you up and you can show me what you've been doing on your guitar."

"Okay."

We go back out. All that sugar has got me goosed a bit, and I'm a little unsteady.

"When you play, do you sit or stand?"

I think about this for a minute. I'm usually sitting on the corner of the bed.

"Sit."

"Thought you might. Here's a folding chair, make yourself comfortable."

I take the chair, unfold it, and sit down. Ryan opens my gig bag and hands me Bonnie Lee. I slip through the strap and get my position right. She feels good in my arms. I'm hoping that after our last fight, she'll be nice to me this morning and let me play.

"So how is this thing, you know, with the poker boys supposed to work?"

"We all sort of warm up at first, everybody doing his own thing. Then depending on feel and everybody's mood, we'll pick a song we like, something pretty easy at first just to get everybody blended together. AJ will give us a beat to start us off. I'll come in with the bass line. You and Robby will come in with the guitars. You'll play rhythm. That means you play the harmony line. All that really means is you just cycle through a series of chords keeping to my bass line—you know, *one*, two, three, four, *one*, two, three, four, like that. Emphasis will be on the one count. The cheat is to play a chord for three beats, change chords on the four beat, and then strum the new chord on the next *one* beat. It's simple and I'll walk you through it."

I have no idea what any of what he just said means. So I nod, pretending I do. "Fake it till you make it"—Tami's always telling me that.

"Robby will play the melody and do the solos. Danny'll sing, of course, and hopefully, we'll all start the song together, end the song together, get along, get a good vibe going, and have a lot of fun."

"Okay. Let's hope so."

'C'mon, dude. Have some more cider. Stay mellow."

"I am. I'm just a little nervous about this."

"No shit. It shows. Relax. Shake it off. It's not an audition. Just do what you can. It's all about having fun," he says, kneeling to plug the amp into my guitar. He turns on the amp. I carefully make a D chord shape and strum. He adjusts the volume, just enough so we can still talk easily.

"You're all set, dude. Go ahead and show me what you're working on."

Chapter 10

So I do. I start with the D, strum it, stop; change to an A, strum it, stop; switch to a C, strum it, stop; and switch to a G, strum it, stop; and switch back to a D to start over. Each time I do, it takes a minute or so to get the fingers of my left hand in the right position on the fretboard for each chord.

"Good. Keep going."

I keep going and lose myself in concentration.

I feel the electricity running through the amp and the guitar, and it speaks of power. I realize I don't use the amp at home. That way, Tami can't hear me. That also means that I can hardly hear myself. But now? I can hear myself. I hear the sound of the strings and not so much the sound of my fingers on the strings.

Brave New World.

I hear the buzz when I screw up too, and I hate that godawful sound, so I really take my time to get every chord perfect. I need it perfect. I mean *absolutely per-fect.* Like Coach always said, "Make it perfect." Everything has got to be perfect. Anything less is failure. *Total failure.* I do not need to be reminded. I heard it all, over and over and over and over and over—"You are a worthless failure to me."

I try to relax and breathe and then hope I can get it right. I do each finger one at a time and then adjust them to get the shape right, and then I strum the chord and listen for a second or two, enjoying what Kerry had called the sustain. And the sound is sweet. I like that sound. It's all I want to hear. So I keep repeating my little drill.

It's a cold morning, but the sun is bright. I notice for the first time the wood grain in Bonnie Lee's mahogany body shines through the brilliant, glassy color. It's stained a burgundy color and coated with what I'm guessing is a clear plastic of some kind. Maybe it's a varnish. I don't know. Pretty damn thick to be a varnish.

Unfortunately, the body with its uber smoothness feels more like glass than wood. I can't help but wonder about the wood itself and what it would be like to touch it instead of the cold and perfectly smooth plastic. Would it be anything like the rosewood fretboard? Between the fret wires, the fretboard feels fairly smooth but not at all glassy and, as far as I can tell, has no coating at all.

I think it's been a month—maybe two—and I still can't play a song yet. I can do a strum pattern. I can finger a chord shape one finger at a time. I know that's the wrong way to do it. But I can't help it. I'm still learning a few chords and how to form them.

I can't do a strum pattern and switch chords at the same time to save my life. It's all I can do to just play the down strums then stop and switch chords before making the next down strum. Maybe that's what Tami meant by bad habits.

I haven't figured out yet how to get both hands working at the same time. I thought it would be automatic somehow, but it's not happening. I'm beginning to think this is a huge mistake. I begin to sweat. My hands go clammy. There's this fuzziness and I flinch, and my vision begins to blur. I realize I'm holding my breath. I breathe.

I breathe a series of long, slow, deep breaths. I put the pick in my mouth and rub my right palm across my right thigh pushing against the fabric of my denim jeans. Then I hold Bonnie Lee with my right hand so I won't drop her. She's small but heavy, and I let go of her neck with my left and rub that palm across my left thigh. I feel her weight pulling at my left shoulder and realize the strap is keeping her from falling. I'm such an idiot!

I take a deep breath then another one and another. I switch to my lifeline chords, D, C, G, and back to D. As long as I go slow, really slow, I'm okay. I can't fret the three strings of each note at the same time. I put the middle finger down first then follow with my first and ring fingers, almost one right after the other—almost. Usually, not even close.

The goal is to get them pressing down on the correct strings in the correct fret spaces as close to simultaneously as possible and then strum the correct number of strings: four for the D chord, five for the C chord, and all six for the G chord. So much to do at once, and it all has to happen at once, and that's not happening at all. It's like that old pat-the-belly and rub-the-head and "do it all at the same time" trick. Never got that one right either.

The instant I try to do it right, it all falls apart.

D-C-G.

D-C-G.

One by one like a faucet drip.

Then there's laughter in the distance, and now it's loud. I stop and look up. Oh boy, Robby's here.

"What's that riff you're playing there, funny boy?"

I don't know what a riff is. I look for the shovel cuz I've decided I want to hit him with it.

"Just practicing my lifeline chords."

"Lifeline?" he howls. "Lifeline. Ha! I gotta remember that one. Not bad, funny boy. Not bad at all."

Then he has a puzzled look.

"Hang on a sec, you were serious, weren't you?"

No matter what I say, I'm hosed.

"You're pathetic, Paul, you know that?"

"That's one of the rumors."

"Yeah? Well"—he gives me another once-over and aims his guitar case at Bonnie Lee—"if you gotta be pathetic, son, at least you've got a decent beginner's axe to do it with. I'll give you that much."

Yeah. Whatever. Lord, please turn the other cheek so you're not looking when I wallop him in the face with the shovel. I promise I'll start going to Mass again.

"Mornin' all."

"AJ!" Robby says as they fist bump.

"Any coffee?" AJ asks, yawning.

"Got it right here," Danny says, as if on cue, coming through the doorway. "Man! Check this place out."

"Never mind coffee, what about doughnuts? Who brought doughnuts?" Robby demands. "I will not play without doughnuts—real doughnuts, no doughnut holes. It's in my rider. Real doughnuts. Fresh. Very fresh. Jelly-filled, even."

I perk up at the mention of doughnuts.

"Ryan, where are my doughnuts?" Robby yells.

"Chill out, dude. They're right here," Ryan says, walking in with a stack of pink cardboard boxes.

"About time. When did you get them?" Robby starts digging into the first box just as Ryan sets them down."

"Just now."

"You've been gone all this time?" I ask.

"Yeah. You were busy practicing your lifeline chords."

Oh crap. Here we go again.

Robby does a double take.

"You know about those?"

"Sure. All beginners are doing that now." Ryan winks at me. "Nothing you old pros would ever need to know about."

"Huh."

I stand up slowly, making sure the strap holds, and take a glazed donut.

"Mmmm. Coffee, coffee, coffee," AJ says, a cup in each hand, walking over to the drums. "Hey, Ryan, nice kit."

"Thanks, dude. Nothing fancy, just the basics."

"Hey, man. Nothing wrong with the basics."

AJ sets his cups down on a small table. He takes out a leather case that's protruding from a back pocket of his jeans, opens it, and takes out a pair of sticks. He sits down on the stool behind the bass drum. I see his right knee bob and hear a muted *thump-thump-thump*. He taps lightly on an upright drum, puts his wallet on it, and then taps it again with the sticks. Then he taps on two smaller ones on a rack above the bass.

"Nice bark to the toms," he says to himself.

Holding a stick in each hand, he begins twirling them—first one hand, then the other, then both at the same time.

"All right, pops," he says in a near whisper. "Let me show you my chops. Some rolls, some paradiddles."

He keeps playing.

"Work in the high hat and the cymbals."

He alternates between tapping drums and cymbals. Then he closes his eyes and *bam*! He goes to town. He is amazing.

"Oh yeah! Oh yeah! Wake me up, baby!"

Robby's plugged in and rips into a solo of cascading notes, the fingers of his left hand flying up and down the fretboard. His guitar has the same body shape as mine, but I think all similarity starts and ends there.

They're in sync with one another, and I think I recognize the rock and roll song they're playing. All that's missing is the high-pitched wailing vocal which, *duh*, Danny immediately supplies. Talk about timing! And he's loud enough, even without a mic. There isn't an ounce of shyness in that man, and I hate him.

Then I hear this booming—only it's different than the drums. It can't be Robby. No, it's Ryan on the bass. I get it. This is Woo's house band. I would have known that if I ever went to his stupid hoedowns, but I never do. It's the hermit in me.

I realize now why Robby is so pissed at me, and I don't think it's his drinking. It's because these guys are tight. Woo's little house band is a thing. No wonder. They sound unbelievably good together. I get it. Woo's set me up to fail. Ryan's hoping for a good vibe.

Yeah right. Good vibe my ass.

Ryan was just being considerate. He's like that. Only it won't matter how nice Ryan is to me or how much he's my friend. It's obvious I don't belong here.

I don't belong here. I don't belong anywhere I've ever been. I'm just a worthless POS like Coach always said I was. My vision blurs again, and it's hard to breathe and that stupid "light show" problem I have with my eyes when I'm really stressed starts happening. I'm glad I'm sitting down and not in my office having to read something on a computer screen.

This time, it's bad, and I can't blink it away, shake it off—nothing. Maybe I should see a doctor. Maybe I should have had some more of Ryan's cider.

They finish. No—don't do that, keep going! I'd rather be a fly on the wall and just listen. Maybe then I'd get my eyesight back. Later on, I could crawl down the wall and maybe work my way up to third assistant drumstick caddy or guitar-cable-dragging dude. But actually play? With these guys? That's insane. No wonder Robby laughed at me at the poker game.

"That was awesome," I say with admiration.

"That was nothing," Robby says in his patented fuck-you tone. "Hell, we ain't even warm yet."

"Right."

I believe every word. Again, I carefully stand up, relying on my peripheral vision and slip the strap over my head. Maybe I should get my eyes checked.

"Hey, what are you doing?" Ryan asks.

"Going home. I get it. I don't belong."

"Dude, you can't go."

"Sure he can, son. Let him go."

"Robby's right. We all know I don't belong here. Not unless I'm carrying your guitar cases or getting you guys coffee. You guys need a roadie, gimme a call."

"C'mon, dude. It's not that way at all."

"Yeah it is. Look, I'll fall on the sword with Woo on Monday, all right?"

"Now you're talking sense, son. You do that!" Robby laughs.

Danny waves Robby off and gives me the icy stare.

"Paul, what planet are you on?"

"Uh, dumb question. Earth."

"Yeah? Well start acting like it."

"Now you sound like my wife."

"Well, there you go, Paul. No shit. Maybe I can get through to you now. You need to understand that here on planet earth, in our never-ending fight for survival—hell, let alone any real success—the first casualties are always our values and principles. Always. And yeah, if you're blessed by God, you may even get a chance to buy some of them back. But's that rare."

"No way. No way am I selling out."

Danny shakes his head.

"No, no. Of course not. The hell you're not. It's a given, Paul. Everybody does. Even you. You'd know that if you ever got of your headspace more often. In any event, you'll have to. There is no other way. Law of club and fang, remember? The only issues remaining are when and at what price. Okay. You're holding out for a better price. Bully for you, Paul. Ryan's right. You are the patron saint of stubborn. I see it. Maybe it's coming from all the time you spend stuck inside your own head. I don't know. But keep in mind, you can't bargain forever. You will run out of time, Paul, and they will crush you at the buzzer. Game over."

"So what am I supposed to do?" I feel myself shaking. "You heard Robby. Seriously. What the hell chance have I got?"

"Actually, Paul, that's not how this thing goes down. Don't listen to Robby. Listen to me. Listen to me very carefully—"

"Ah, fuck him! Let him find out!"

"Danny, I got nothing here."

"Forget Robby, he's still pissed at you."

"Damn straight, you fuckin' crooner king!"

"Hey! Have a beer!"

"Have a beer? Fuck you too, Danny!" Robby blinks. "Fuck. I think I will have a beer. Maybe two beers. Maybe three or four even, motherfucker! Tell me to have a beer."

He heads to the tub piled high with ice and bottlenecks and reaches in with both hands.

"Like I was saying, Paul, it's not a matter of falling on the sword. You screwed up big time. You told Woo to pound sand in an office email that went officewide. Then with that fiasco on the phone with Robby, suddenly a lot more people know, and unfortunately for you, it's gotten outside the office, and now a whole lot more people know. People outside the office who shouldn't know anything about inside the office now know everything. That means you have embarrassed Woo and badly. Now, I don't believe you meant to do that."

"Honestly, I didn't. I was . . . I was thinking out loud, that's all. I thought I hit the Delete key. I-I don't know what happened. Only that it did."

"That's right. It did. That's my point. You got him, and now he gets you. Quid pro quo. You're in the octagon now, my friend. This is the deal. You man up and you rise to the occasion, either as part of this band or you go down in flames trying. The worse the humiliation, the better, and you do it on his turf and on his terms. Humiliation in front of everyone, and only then will the debt be paid. You follow?"

"This is crazy."

"Yes it is. Again, get out of your head. What you also need to understand is that we're all old white guys grossly outnumbered in a diverse world of all-assuming, inexperienced, and unknowing millennials where each of us is far more expendable than any of them ever will be and far more expendable than any of us ever wants to admit. The pendulum of the world clock is swinging the other way now, and you don't want to get hit with it."

"Yeah, but Woo's an old—" I catch myself.

"That's right. Only that's not the point here, Paul. Forget Woo for the moment. There's a bigger picture here, bigger than any of us ever want to admit. Okay? First, like I said, it's open season on old white guys now, especially those of us in the cheap seats. Pendulum is swinging, man. There it is. Just putting it out there. Get used to it.

"Second, not all is lost. There's plenty of good dead-end assignments in County Counsel where you can disappear and cocoon yourself in comfort. The caveat, of course, is that you must learn to stay satisfied with silence and enjoy the invisibility. Knowing you, that may not work, especially given recent events.

"Third, that said, if it won't work for you, then don't be afraid to pull the pin and retire now. Will it be enough? Probably not. Will you need to pick up another job, preferably with some benefits, if possible, until Medicare hits? Most definitely.

"The upside to all this is that you will be free to do something of your own choosing. The key fact here—and you especially need to remember this—is that your health will not improve with age. Hate to break it to you so bluntly, Paul, but it's all downhill from here, and it won't be long before you're sliding the rest of the way to St. Peter in your own shit.

"Now, getting back to Woo. Woo has something none of us have, and that's the power and privilege of rank. You forget that. You don't want Woo for an enemy. None of us do. Trust me. Robby will probably retire in two, maybe three years tops, if his drinking doesn't derail him first. My money's on derailment. Even then, Woo will probably have his back because Woo owes him.

"It's the other way around for you and me and your bohemian buddy here. What I am saying is this—if you want to quit, that's fine. But you might as well quit the office too while you're at it. Believe me, you'll wish you had. Assuming, of course, they haven't already worked out the plan to fire you. They may be slow and timid, but they're not stupid. They will take however long they need to line up the votes, win the hearts and minds, and then you're gone. You do not want that to happen, Paul. You want to go out of here on your own terms."

He looks over at Ryan.

"Am I missing anything here, Ryan?"

Ryan shakes his head.

Seeing that sends another chill up my spine.

"Life's not a spectator sport, Paul. Let's have some fun! Strap her back on. This party's just getting started." Danny looks over his shoulder and yells out to Robby. "Hey, Rummy! You drunk yet?"

"I'm working on it, asshole Crooner King . . . fuckin' asshole!"

"Good! Let me know when you get there. I'll have a chore for you!"

"Fuck you! I ain't teachin' that punk-ass pussy how to play!"

Danny grins and turns to Ryan. He lowers his voice.

"Okay, bohemian maestro, serious business here. We need three easy—and I mean ridiculously and insanely fucking easy— rockabilly tunes from the '50s. Something with three simple major chords. Preferably two, if you can swing it. No B or F notes, no barre chords, and absolutely no minors other than E minor or A minor. Preferably songs sharing all the same chords. You with me?"

"I'm all over it, dude."

"Outstanding. Robby's right about one thing. He's not about to teach Paul how to play. So here's the plan. Ryan's going to give me the songs and the chords. I'm going to have Robby go over those chords, the transitions, and the strum patterns that he prefers with Ryan so Ryan can better anticipate Robby's changes on lead. Robby will buy that for sure."

Danny looks at me.

"Ryan's then going to teach the chords and the strumming patterns to you." He looks at Ryan. "Robby is always shit-faced, but he's never stupid either. If you think any of the strumming patterns are overdone, they are. I need you to simplify the ever-living holy shit out of them for Paul's sake as much as you can. Got it?"

Ryan nods. "Like I said, dude, I'm all over it."

Danny grins again.

"Okay. Good. We're in agreement." He faces me. "I hear you're a nice guy, Paul. Good for you. As you are about to find out, if you can stay that way, you'll always have friends."

"Thanks. Thanks a lot."

I feel awful for thinking I hated this guy.

"You're welcome."

"So, AJ, I'm thinking we switch it up for this year's hoedown. You up for some rockabilly?"

"Yeah, Danny, I'm up for it," AJ laughs. "Nice change of pace. I can use the rest."

"Outstanding. How about it, Robby? Are you up to being the star again this year on some rockabilly with all the solo room you can handle?"

Robby squints when he looks at Danny, then at AJ, who gives him a slight nod. Robby's thinking.

"Maybe. Will junior be able to keep up?"

"What do you fuckin' care if he keeps up or not? Either way, you win. All I want to know and all I'm asking you, my good lightnin' man, is simply this—the game is five-man rockabilly. Now, are you all in or not?"

"Oh, hell, son, I'm *all* in!"

"And how did I know that?" Danny says to me quietly and smiles.

I can't help but smile back and wonder if I haven't just met another devil. Fuckers are everywhere.

✦✦✦✦✦✦

My curiosity still lingers Monday morning through my court appearances. My phone's ringing as I enter my office when I get back from court. I round the desk and reach for it. Too late. Not a second later, I hear the cigarette cough and exasperated raspy voice of the secretary from hell yelling at me.

"Hey, Paul! If you're in there, answer your phone!"

I'm about to yell back, only I remember Danny's lecture and I see the straw I'm assuming he has taped to my computer monitor as a reminder for me to suck it up.

Then I hear grumbling just loud enough for anyone within ear shot to hear, "It's bad enough I got this, and now I gotta answer his telephone too? This is ridiculous! Hello? Yes? Lemme see."

My internal line buzzes. I let it buzz some more and then pick up.

"Whataya know, you are there, finally. Go ahead, please!"

Click.

"Paul?"

"Yes."

"Sid wants to know if you're coming up for the ten o'clock?"

"I didn't know there was a ten o'clock. Where do I find it?"

"CA."

"Thanks. Oh, Marcie, any chance you know what this is about? There's nothing on my calendar."

"The meeting notice says ordinance review."

"Okay. Thank you."

"You're welcome."

Click.

Chapter 11

What ordinance review? I grab a legal pad and head up to the admin conference room. Woo's there, along with two other chief deputies and the Assistant County Counsel, Edgar Huffman, and about a dozen or so deputies in the office, most of whom I don't know and have never even met as they're scattered about other floors and departments in the county. I realize, looking around, that neither Ryan nor Robby are here.

"Oh, good. You can make it," says Huffman, blinking at me through his thick horn-rim eyeglasses, which he then takes off and waves around to make a point.

"C'mon in, Paul. Find a chair, if you can. We seem to have a full house, this morning," he says, looking about again, waiting for everyone to chuckle at his joke.

The people around the table chuckle at his joke. He smiles.

He turns to Woo who's seated next to him and mumbles, "It is Paul, right? Isn't that what you said?"

Woo nods.

"Good. Good."

He puts on his glasses and retrieves a mechanical pencil from his trademark pocket saver. He's wearing a white short-sleeved dress shirt with a very narrow, black tie with skinny, little, silver stripes. The shirt matches his snow-white crew-cut hair. The thick frames of his eyeglasses match the color of his tie. He looks more like an accountant circa 1950 than a lawyer. I remember hearing somewhere that he was a CPA who later went to law school. I've heard that he spends most of his time working with the assessor and the county's treasurer. I also remember hearing somewhere that he's never seen the inside of a courtroom.

There are no chairs. I stand in the doorway.

"Sid has suggested this meeting, and he's asked all of you to attend this morning. I think this meeting is a marvelous idea. I do. I think this is a marvelous idea for not only maintaining consensus within the office but to further our working relationships. Don't you agree?"

There are nods and affirmative mumbles.

"Good. What we—I'm sorry—what Sid has asked was for each of you to review and comment on a parking enforcement ordinance that, I believe . . ."

Huffman flips through a pile of papers.

"Yes, I see it now, here it is. Good. Paul has been working on it, I believe."

He turns to Woo.

"Is that who has been working on this ordinance?"

Woo nods.

Huffman nods but looks constipated.

He turns to Woo.

"Isn't he a litigator?"

He looks at me.

"You're a litigator, aren't you, Paul? What's your assignment in the office?"

"Yes, sir. Litigating code enforcement and nuisance abatement cases."

Huffman looks more constipated.

"Oh, oh well then." He looks at Woo. "If he's a litigator, then why is he drafting an ordinance? Litigators don't draft ordinances."

"Paul, perhaps you would like to brief Edgar, briefly, as to why you are drafting a parking ordinance?"

"Absolutely, sir," I say. "I drafted a parking enforcement ordinance at the request of my client department in response to a direct request from Fifth District, Edgar."

"I see. I see." He looks at the papers then back at Woo. "Oh well, we can't have that."

He looks around and then turns to Woo.

"Did you know about this, Sid?"

Sid shakes his head.

I realize that Danny isn't here either. He's the ordinance guru and represents the clerk of the Board of Supervisors.

Huffman opens a red folder. The red folder is empty.

"I don't see a report from Danny on this. Have you seen a report from Danny on this?"

He stares at the empty red folder, as if waiting for a piece of paper to magically appear and make everything better.

"There's no report here." He turns to Woo. "Did he go through channels? I don't think he went through channels. Shouldn't we wait until the ordinance is properly assigned and the draft goes through channels at the proper time?"

Now Woo is the one who looks constipated.

"Yes, we could do that. We could certainly do that. Although, in all honesty, I'm not sure that we need to do that. After all, we're all here now, and you did ask for several of us to take a look at it."

"Well, that's true. No, I thought you asked for it to be looked at."

Woo, still looking constipated, nods.

"Even so, since we're all here now, perhaps for Paul's benefit, we can go around the room and give everyone an opportunity to comment on the proposed ordinance. I think it would be instructive for Paul to learn something of the process, get a sense of where we are on this. I think that would be very helpful for Paul. I think that would be very helpful indeed. Don't you think that would be very helpful?"

He turns his head from side to side as he speaks, as if appealing to as many as possible for support. Some woman mumbles that it would be very helpful, then another voice chimes in saying that it would be very helpful indeed, and pretty soon, they are all nodding, turning to one another, mumbling and grunting and whispering and pleased to agree among themselves that it would be very helpful.

Huffman no longer looks constipated. He looks content with that pleased look of one who has just been relieved of a great load. He smiles, and he turns his head from side to side as if to savor the comfort of the sudden rise in consensus and prolong that joy for as long as possible.

"Well, as long you think it would be helpful," he says, his head on a swivel, inviting another round of responses to which other voices that heretofore had been timid and held in reserve suddenly speak up to be counted.

Huffman smiles, well pleased.

"I agree," he announces with an imperial tone in his voice. "I think it would be very helpful if each of you share your comments. Who would like to start?"

"I will start," announces a shrewish-looking bookworm in her late sixties with an over-dyed bob of hideous red hair whom I have never met and who is squirming in her chair and who looks like she's been waiting the last two months for a chance to pee.

"I am concerned about due process," she says, looking around but not at me, letting the words hang there as if in a low earth orbit of their own—a cue to the others to change their expressions from deep comfort to dire concern. "This is a street parking ordinance after all, and yet it calls for the towing of vehicles. That's private property. Can we legally tow private vehicles? I'm not sure we've ever done that."

That starts a titter among the flock. Now Woo looks well pleased.

He would. He's a prick.

"That's a good point. That's a very good point. Have we ever towed private vehicles? I don't think we've ever done that. I think there may be some counties that do. I know the City of San Gorgonio certainly does," Huffman says.

"But that's the city," Woo says.

"Exactly my point. I don't think we've ever done that," Huffman says, tapping at his copy of the ordinance. "Paul, do you think you can shed some light on that issue?"

All eyes are on me.

"Absolutely. The statutory authority for the towing of private vehicles by a local agency—defined to include a city, a county, and a city and county—of this state is set forth in the state's Vehicle Code, section 22650, et seq."

I look at the shrew who looks like she still needs to pee.

"And you are?"

"Myrtle Potts," she announces with an indignant look that scolds me for not knowing.

"Oh, Myrtle represents the library and the museum, and she handles backup for the clerk of the Board," Huffman announces, apparently for my benefit.

"Fair enough."

I get it. She must be one of the channels I didn't go through. Like I ever knew there were any such channels to begin with. Like the policies you're supposed to know but don't because none of them are written down. None of them are written down because most of these people have been here for twenty years or more. They already know them.

Chapter 12

It was a time when everybody came out of the juvenile dependency unit; and they all grew up in the same culture, speaking the same language, and drinking the same bottled water from the same water cooler. They made up the same policies together, and now you never learn about them until somebody tells you that whatever you've done isn't done that way. Like everything else around here—it's just assumed that you know.

"Do you know Myrtle? Have you met Myrtle?" Huffman asks.

"No and no. In fact, except for knowing who you are and knowing who Sid is, I don't know any of these people any more than I know that homeless guy staring at you through that window."

All eyes turn to the homeless guy.

Huffman turns to Woo again.

"Can't we do something about that?"

Woo says he doesn't know.

"We could, if we had a decent trespassing ordinance," I say. "My guess is that we don't. We've probably never done that before either. Probably because the ordinance we do have is preempted by state law and has been for more than twenty years and which, apparently, doesn't get enforced either because no one bothers to post or give the proper warnings as required."

If these bastards want a fight, I've got one.

"Is that true?" Huffman asks Woo. "Because, obviously, if that's true, then he would have a good point, wouldn't he? I don't know. I'm just thinking out loud here. I'm wondering. No, that's a good point. Paul has a good point, I think."

Huffman makes a point of telling Woo, "Can we have someone look into that?"

He does a head swing like he's watching a tennis match, looking for volunteers. No one does. I'm betting no one ever does. Probably how they all got up here and then stayed here so long. Probably the single most important criterion for those who survived long enough to get promoted.

"We can certainly look into that, Edgar. I believe Fifth District made some inquiries a few years ago. We can certainly revisit the issue."

"What about him?" I ask, nodding to the homeless guy staring back at us from the tree outside the window. "Is he going to revisit the issue? You want to invite him to the meeting? Get his viewpoint, reach consensus? He certainly looks harmless enough."

"What do you mean harmless?" asks someone from the peanut gallery. "He's four stories off the ground!"

"I certainly don't think he's harmless," Myrtle snaps, clutching her sweater and closing it tightly about her throat. "I don't think he looks harmless at all. Look at him! For the love of God, he's in a tree! We're on the fourth floor!"

"Regardless of how he looks, I think if we all ignore him, he will eventually move on or fall off or what have you or we can continue looking at him as he continues looking at us. We can continue giving him all the attention he wants. I don't think that would be productive. I don't think that would be productive at all," Woo says.

"Well, that's a good point too."

The peanut gallery is all atwitter.

"Maybe if we closed the blinds?"

"Just close the blinds."

Tweet. Tweet.

"Yes, I think we should just close the blinds."

"Can't someone please close the blinds?"

Tweet. Tweet.

The homeless guy unzips his pants. Got to give the guy kudos for keeping his balance. Someone closes the blinds as the homeless guy urinates on the window.

Impressive.

That tree limb must be six or seven feet away. Either he has an extremely full bladder or he's got serious skills.

"Oh my god! That's so disgusting!" Myrtle's on a soapbox.

"Can't we do something about that?" Edgar mumbles.

"Getting back to the matter at hand," Woo says, amid a rise of laughter from some of the hardier menfolk in the flock. "Certainly, no pun intended—"

"No, Sid, that . . . that was a good pun."

"One of your better puns, Sid, I dare say."

"Damn good pun, old man!"

"Yes, a very good pun. Too bad for the window though. Until the next budget adjustment, it's not likely to be cleaned anytime soon."

"All right, thank you all for that. As I said, no, no, I won't say it again."

Cue restrained, muffled laughter.

"Okay, people. We need to concentrate here. We need to refocus. We're here critiquing Paul's draft. We need to stay focused and get a grip on this thing."

Some of the older farts in the room are laughing uncontrollably now. Edgar is blushing. Myrtle's face flushes a deep red and then goes utterly pale. She struggles for a breath and then shrieks across the table.

"Please! I am appalled!"

"Excuse me. Hello? I too am shocked, and I most certainly agree with my colleague, Myrtle. And furthermore, I will respectfully remind our more experienced and, hopefully, much wiser male members—"

Another outbreak of laughter.

The speaking woman's face reddens. She scowls. Hell hath no fury like a woman scorned or, at least, one who insists on acting like one.

"Colleagues! Might I remind my colleagues of the male-identifying genders, particularly those of the so-called baby boomer generation, of the county's sexual harassment policy. Consider, if you will, all of you, just how obviously and grossly that very policy is being violated here. Violated, I remind you, in a continuing and ongoing manner in this meeting, even as I began to speak in defense of my sister colleagues. I expect and demand that such violative behavior cease and desist immediately. Immediately!"

The woman with the harsh crewcut—so proudly, so blatantly butch—and ear piercings that look like a rivet repair job to both of her ears has moved to stand behind the seated Myrtle. She's attempting to make eye contact with every person present as she continues to speak.

"Further, I trust, Mr. Huffman, that you, as the senior leader present, will enforce the county policy with rigor, promptly and vigorously."

I think the owlish eyeglasses are a little too big for her little rat face and seem just about to slide off her narrow, crooked nose at any moment.

Sudden outbreak of sheer silence.

Woo and Huffman are pale.

Uneasy silence.

Huffman clears his throat.

"A very good point. A point very well taken. Yes, there will indeed be action taken."

"Thank you. Now, I believe sister Myrtle had some comments concerning the ordinance. Myrtle, please continue."

"Yes. Yes, I do. Thank you. Now, I also have concerns about respecting constitutional safeguards with respect to the inspection provision relating to inoperable vehicles." She eyeballs Edgar.

"You know, I was thinking about that too an attractive American Indian woman in her early thirties adds, seated at the far end of the table. "I believe we need to add some language here. Something straightforward."

There is a refreshing mix of poise and confidence in her voice. Her ebony hair is long and straight. She wears bracelets that look made of silver and turquoise, and I wonder if they are.

"You can do that, can't you, Paul?"

"Fair enough. I'd be happy to do that for you," I say, and for her alone, I smile politely.

I know the text of my ordinance draft expressly spells out the requirements relating to consent and administrative inspection warrants in those circumstances where consent is denied. I know that as certainly as I know that most of these commodores have not even bothered to read so much as a complete page of it.

Whatever.

I'm more than willing to make as much of this ordinance as repetitive, monotonous, tedious, insistent, and continually dull and constant, on one hand; and as completely redundant, unnecessary, needless, and unessential, on the other hand, as anyone cares to insist on making it. Tautology is a litigator's stock in trade.

"Then we can move on," she says.

"That's a good idea. I agree. Let's do that." Huffman begins to fidget.

I think his attention span is shot.

"Paul, if you can get back to Alicia with some language, that would be great." He looks at Woo. "And then, if you can have Danny take a look at it and do his report so everything's ready and we can get it on the agenda and take it to the Board. Thank you everybody. This has been very helpful indeed. Thank you all for coming. Thank you, Alicia."

"No problem," she says, as she and the others at the table start to get up.

Huffman hesitates, then turns to Woo.

"Shouldn't we at least call the sheriff?"

I smile, hoping I have dodged a bullet, and step out of the herd's way to avoid the stampede heading my way.

Somehow, I manage to skate the rest of the day.

Having done so is a pleasing thought, and I take it home with me. I see Shelley Lynne's car in the driveway. I feel even more pleasant.

"Hi, Papa," she says, greeting with me a soft tone in her voice.

I see her eyes are red. We hug. She holds me tight.

It's enough for me just to hold her.

"You okay, Princess?" I whisper.

I feel her pony-tailed head bobbing.

"Okay," I say.

As much as I want to know what's troubling her, I also want the hug. I want that more. I'm selfish that way. It's not like there's a hug store anywhere nearby. And if I push, she'll tune me out, like her mother, and that'd be the worst of all.

She relaxes, and I let her go.

"So's your mom around?"

"Nope. She said she got a page or text or something. I don't know. She threw her phone in her purse, grabbed her scrubs bag, and tore out. I think she said she had to cover for somebody. I don't know. I never know."

"Okay. So it's just us. Cool. You hungry?"

"Not really."

"Okay. You're probably tired from the drive. I won't ask how long it took ya."

I see a little smile.

"I'm just glad you're home, Princess. I need a friendly face around here."

"Oh, Papa." She lurches and hugs me again, tighter. "You don't know how good that makes me feel."

"That's good to know."

"What I'd really like is to play guitar for a while."

Ahhh. And it was so good while it lasted.

"Sure, no problem. Maybe we can watch a movie or something later."

"Papa, I meant with you! The two of us playing. I've been waiting all week for this!"

"Oh, okay! I'd love that too!"

"Where do you want to set up?"

"All my stuff's in the guest room."

"That works, Papa."

She retrieves her guitar case from her bedroom and brings it into the guest room. She opens it and takes out the small acoustic I had seen on the video. I strapped on Bonnie Lee.

"That's cute, Papa!"

"Thanks. So how do we do this?"

"It's easy, Papa. We just jam. We can start with some chords."

"Okay." I'm feeling a bit apprehensive. "Something easy."

"Of course. Let's start with D."

"Okay," I say and form the shape, making sure I got it, and I start strumming with down strokes.

Shelley Lynne is counting.

"One . . . two . . . three . . . four . . . you know A?"

"Yes," I say, still strumming a D.

"To A. One . . . two . . . three . . . switch!" She makes the change, and I lag behind. "That's okay, Papa. Just keep strumming. Okay . . . two . . . three . . . four . . . back . . . to . . . D and . . . switch!"

I fumble the chord change. My index finger hits the fretboard between the second and third strings and my ring finger lands on the first string at the third fret. And I'm holding my breath again and biting my lower lip.

"Relax, Papa. Deep breath. No need to fight it. Let it flow."

I breathe.

"How do you do it?" I ask.

"I don't know. I just do. It's easy. I just do it."

"Easy for you. Sorry, Princess. I'm just not getting it."

"It's okay, Papa. I'm going too fast."

"I'm not sure that's it. And if it is, then with the way I'm making the changes, we'd have to go so slow and it'd take us five minutes between strums."

"No, Papa," she giggles. "We won't have to go that slow. Here, let me watch you and see what you're doing. Just go ahead and strum a D. At your own pace and when you're ready, switch to A."

I do.

"Okay, do it again, a couple more times, just D to A."

I do it again, a couple more times.

"Hmm," she says, watching. "Okay, this time, just strum once. Now, lift up just your ring finger. Not so high. Okay, lower it, stop just above the string without touching it. Yeah, like that. Now, lift up your middle finger. No, leave your index finger where it is. Press the tip down on the string. That's it. Keep it there on the third string, second fret."

I tense up.

"I'm sorry, Princess. I don't think I have the coordination to do this."

"Trust me, Papa, please. You do. You'll see. Just give yourself a chance. Try it."

I try it and fight the feeling of awkwardness.

"Now what?"

"Okay, now gently and slowly, without moving your index finger, put the middle and ring fingertips on the strings where they belong for a D. Good. Do that again. Again. Again. That's it. Lift up the middle and ring fingers and then put them back down. Good. This time, lift them up . . . put them down, strum. Nice. Lift up, put them down, strum. Nice."

I'm not sure where this is going, but so far so good.

"Okay, now this time, just use index and middle fingers. Index finger stays put. Okay, you don't have to press so hard. Okay, now, leaving your index finger where it is, just switch the middle finger back and forth from the first string to the fourth string, still on the second fret. Yes! Like that, Papa. Keep it slow. Don't rush it."

"Now what?"

"Do it again."

I do.

"Check this out, Papa. Now just use your index finger and your ring finger. Make a D and then gently lift up the middle finger and move it out of the way. Strum the D with just the index and ring fingers fretting their strings. Now slide the index and ring fingers toward the nut—that's where the fretboard joins the head stock—so the ring finger is on the second fret."

I try it. My fingers go everywhere but where they need to. Little pricks. Now I'm getting pissed. It ain't rocket science; it's just music. It's a simple little exercise, and I can't even do it right.

"Papa, you're grinding your teeth. Relax. Try it again."

I try it again. My fingers are stiff little nutcrackers.

"No, Papa, the index finger slides but stays in the second fret. The ring finger slides from the third fret to the second fret and back again. Slide your ring finger to the second fret, and you've got two-thirds of the A major chord. Slide back to the third and you've got two-thirds of the D major chord. Try that."

I try that.

"Notice when these two fingers are in the second fret, how you have to scrunch them closer together to keep the index finger's string from buzzing? See that?"

"I do."

"So keep doing that but slowly. And when you get in position for the D, strum, let it ring out. Slide toward the headstock and make your A chord shape, strum, let it ring. Slide the other way toward the bridge, make your D chord shape, strum, and let it ring."

I slide, strum, and let 'er ring. I'm klutzy, but I'm doing it.

"That's it, Papa. Nice."

I slide, strum, and let 'er ring.

"You're doing it, Papa. One of the secrets of chord transitions is recognizing what the chord shapes share in common, like if one or more fingers stay on the same strings but simply move to an adjacent fret. Take advantage of that."

"Okay."

"Now, all that's left to complete the D and the A and switch between them is your middle finger. So while you slide the index and ring fingers, just let your middle finger hop back and forth between the first and fourth strings, staying on the second fret. When it's on the first string, it's a D. When it hops to the fourth, it's an A. Try it, Papa."

I try it. I'm still a klutz, but I'm getting the idea. It's just that my fingers aren't getting the idea. I can't believe how uncoordinated I am.

"That's it, Papa. Go slow, and just go for smooth. There's no test. This is not your job. Let yourself find the groove in an A and a D."

I unload a sigh that could propel a yacht through a cornfield.

"Relax, Papa. Let the baby steps be fun."

"I'm trying. I really am. I need this to work."

"Okay, I get that. Just don't make it become your work. You already have a job. You don't need another one."

Another deep breath.

Oh, but I do. I do. I do. I just can't tell her that.

So I slide, hop, strum, and let 'er ring. And breathe. I remind myself to breathe. So many yachts to move.

"You're doing great, Papa. Don't be so hard on yourself. Just keep doing that."

"Okay."

"Just do that. Get good at that. Please don't rush it. Speed will come."

"Yeah, so they tell me."

I'm thinking of the guy at Strummin' City. Crap. I can't even remember his name.

"It doesn't matter, Papa. It takes time. A lot of time."

I smile and nod. Yeah, says the twentysomething with talent and grace. And one of the voices in my head reminds me I'm a fiftysomething piece of shit with all the coordination of a guy suffering an epileptic seizure and I should be on my hands and knees grateful that I don't even have epilepsy. I'm so grateful for that, and now I feel grateful. Grateful and guilty. Like an idiot.

"Papa, I started in elementary school. Then middle school. Then high school. I got a ten-year head start. Give yourself a break. All that matters is this moment. Right now. Now and all the nows that will follow."

Another deep breath, another smile.

"Okay, Princess. If you say so."

"Yeah, Papa. I say so. Take it at your own pace. And let it be fun."

"Fair enough. I will. I promise."

"For reals?"

"Yes, for reals. I promise."

"Thank you, Papa." She's looking me in the eye like she's searching. "Make a game out of it, Papa. A simple little game. Middle finger hop-a-thon. Fret finger sliders."

She smiles.

"Trust me."

I nod.

"Oh, I almost forgot. I have something for you. Gimme a minute!"

She dashes out and comes back just as quickly with a paper bag.

"I saw this, and I thought it'd be perfect for you."

She hands me the bag. I take it and know it's a book. I pull it out, and the dust jacket cover's got this sunburned, damn near-nude, surfer-lookin' dude—only he's middle aged, with reddish-blonde dreadlocks playing an acoustic guitar, standing on a stage that seems to float out into an ocean of people. The title is *I Be Diggin' I Be Livin' I Be Irie* by Duggie Meadows.

"He certainly looks like a mellow, happy fellow."

"Yeah, he's all that and a bag of chips. He's totally epic. It's ridiculous," Shelley Lynne laughs.

Her voice is a delight, and it's like she's a little girl again, only a lot smarter, and I love this moment.

"Yeah, and he's all that and a cake of surf wax," she says, laughing again.

I have no idea what she's talking about.

"I don't think I've ever heard of him. He's some kind of rock star, obviously."

"When he's not surfing or saving the environment. And yes you've heard of him. Remember that 'coconut burrito' song you said was so funny and would always make you feel good no matter what?"

I had forgotten that song. Too bad too. It was a really good song.

"You're kidding me. That's him?"

"Yep. That's him. And you know what else?"

"What?"

"The coconut burrito sing is D, A, and G."

"No way!"

"Yes way. So see? Now you've got something to look forward to—you and Duggie strumming the coconut burrito song."

Yeah, like that'll ever happen.

"That could be pretty cool," I tell her.

And it would be too, but for one little problem—that ain't never gonna happen.

I'm staring at the carpet.

"Yes, it totally could. I was worried about you that night I called you and you were still working and having a bad day. I had to get to the bookstore on campus before it closed, and they had this on display. I knew it'd be perfect for you."

"Thank you. This is so very sweet of you. I really appreciate it."

"You're welcome. I hope you like it a lot. I hope you really get into it. He's all about living in the moment and being open to the joy of life because it's really there, even in the hard times."

"Then I probably will," I say and smile.

I open the book, flip through a few pages, and spot the inscription that says,

> Thank you for being my Papa, the best dad ever. Please stay true to your dream, whatever it is. Be happy.
>
> Love,
> Shelley Lynne

"Wow. This really is so very sweet of you. Thanks. Big hug."

"You're welcome so much, Papa." She gives me a terrific hug.

"So Duggie lives?"

"Yes he does, Papa. I want you to live too. That's why I got it. For you."

"I want to live."

Slide, hop, strum, and let 'er ring. And live.

Now that's a chorus I'd love to get all the voices in my head to come together and sing along with me.

Slide, hop, strum, let 'er ring, and live.

Maybe that's the mantra. Make it my new bumper sticker for a new life.

Right. That'll be the day.

I'm starting to sound like Robby when he's carping on me. Which is pretty much whenever I see him. I only wish his playing would rub off on me and stick the same way his criticisms do.

For the life of me, why haven't I punched that bastard into next Tuesday afternoon?

"Okay. Now I'm getting hungry," she says, putting her guitar back into its case.

My fingertips are sore from fretting strings, and I'm relieved the lesson's over. I learned something worth practicing, and if only for a moment, it was even fun.

For a moment, it was fun. Remember that.

"Papa," she says, "you think way too much."

"Yeah. You got me on that one."

"C'mon, let's go get something to eat. My stomach's growling. It's craving real Mexican food. Can we do Consuela's tonight?"

"Oh! Hurt me. Beat me. Twist my arm! Of course!"

I haven't been there in quite a while so it's a good choice, and I can't help but shake my head thinking of Tami's stink eye whenever I suggest to her that we go there. So we never do.

"What is it, Papa?"

"Huh? Oh, nothing, Princess."

"Tell me."

"Your mother hates that place."

"Well, she's not here, is she?"

"Nope."

"Well then, let's go and have some good food."

"Fair enough."

I order the carnitas platter with flour tortillas and an extra bowl of the salsa that they bring with the basket of hot corn chips, and I ask for an extra spoon to go with the extra bowl of salsa.

Shelley Lynne gets shredded beef and chicken tacos and a chile relleno and a cola. I ask her if she minds if I get a margarita. She asks me if I mind if she drives home. I tell her I don't mind at all and she mimics me and says, "Fair enough." I like how it sounds when she says it.

It's a humongous banana-mango margarita—all frozen slushiness, booziness, and deliciousness.

"You're going to be really happy in no time, Papa."

I nod and smile and slurp away.

Princess, from your lips to God's ears!

We eat, and we talk. She chirps on about school, and her bike, and the marching "band-uh," and the football season she doesn't want to ever end and how this weekend is an away game, and her roommate needed to come home, and how she didn't want her roommate driving home from Sac alone, and how the "band-uh" has big plans for Picnic Day this spring.

I listen, and we smile, and I'm grateful there's a lot of that, and I'm grateful for our breezy mood and getting a chance to just hang out together a while in this little mom-and-pop hole in the wall with the most awesome food ever and the big crazy-ass plastic macaws painted in rainbows of color that hang everywhere in this place— and I mean everywhere.

The one over my head must be broken because it's the only one in the place that's hanging upside down. But it looks ever so cool that way. I pretend that I've adopted it because this is my favorite table, and I always ask for this table. I always leave a little of my margarita for this hardiest, hearty-partyin' macaw of macaws and tell the waitresses it's for Dylan, and I point up to the bird. The waitresses always give me a funny look and then look up at the upside-down bird and smile and say, "Ohhh! For Dylan. No problemo, Senor Cooper." Then they laugh. And walk away with the dirty plate and empty salsa cup and down what's left of the margarita before reaching the kitchen.

I'd eat here every day if I could. There's got to be a way to fix Dylan up with a half-burnt stogie tip in his beak and holding a shot glass with tequila in his foot—talon?—and wearing a custom-sized wifebeater that says, "Got Tequila?" on the front.

Tami hates this place.

I cap off the evening with another banana-mango margarita, and life is becoming purely, bodaciously slushy goodness. Shelley Lynne drives us home. I'm so proud of what a good driver she is, and I wish I was a better influence on her than I am when I'm lounging upside down on the passenger side of the car.

She doesn't seem to mind though. She's singing along to Duggie whose music is pulsing the car's sound system to its limits. I'm starting to like this guy. I'm trying not to think about what it's going to be like when she leaves. Then I remember she should be back for Thanksgiving. I am not going to like it when she leaves.

We get home, and I autopilot my way to the guest room.

In the morning, I wake up to muffled remnants of an argument between Shelley Lynne and her mother. I run my fingers through my ever-thinning hair and walk out to the kitchen, still wearing yesterday's clothes.

Tami immediately picks up her keys and tells me she's going to the gym and then to work and that I'm on my own for lunch and dinner. Then she stink-eyes me as usual and tells me to shower and clean up. She storms out.

"Love you too."

She can't hear me. Probably just as well.

Shelley Lynne tells me Nana called and wants to take her shopping. She'll see me later and maybe we can do dinner.

"Sounds good." I give her a hug.

She goes to the door, turns, and says, "Remember to play, not practice. We don't practice anymore. We play. And make it a game. Okay? And read some Duggie if you get a chance."

"Will do, Princess."

I follow her and start to close the door.

"Oh, Papa?" she calls back. "You can skip the shower. You're not working today. Besides, I've smelled worse than you."

She laughs, walks out, and gets into her car. I close the door and watch her drive away. I get a ceramic mug from a cupboard and retrieve the bottle of orange juice from the refrigerator. I sit down at the table and pour myself some juice. I don't remember it ever being this quiet.

The juice tastes good, and now I want some sausage to go with it. We don't have any, so that means a trip to the market and that means a fast food run. I come home with more orange juice—this time, with pulp—and a bag of sausage and egg biscuits. I get full and plop onto the fancy recliner with Duggie's book.

Chapter 14

The book's all right. Interesting guy. Navy brat. Grew up all over the world. He had a Jamaican nanny. Dyslexic before anybody had ever heard the word. He's ancient, which puts him just a few years older than me, but he looks like a twentysomething. Go figure.

He grew up under an iron-willed father. I can relate to that. Except his old man was out skippering boomers in the Atlantic, all silent and submerged for months on end. Duggie's mother was a wealthy socialite with dreams of putting her hubby in the White House when she wasn't on a drinking binge. By his early teens, the little Rastafarian had been a rebellious runaway on three continents.

Out of the blue, he up and steals a page from his father's play book—run silent, run deep—gets a buzz cut, gets quiet, gets serious, and buckles down in school. He goes Ivy League, to his mother's utter delight, and graduates from an established music conservatory, not exactly what mother had in mind, earning a handful of undergraduate and graduate degrees in guitar, music composition, traditional Caribbean and Calypso music, and African music.

On the cover, he looks like a penniless, beachcombin', and bummin' castaway with flaming red dreads. But Sterling magazine ranks him as the fifteenth wealthiest man in the world. Apparently, his easy-go, easy-flow, feel-good music has made him the "Crown Prince of Party" worldwide. I've never heard of the guy. He reminds me of the pirate captain in those rum commercials on late-night TV, only that guy's hair is a lot darker. In all fairness, I do recognize a lot of his music in beer commercials now that Shelley Lynne has played so much of it for me.

It's almost dinnertime, so I clean up and shower anyway and then send her a text. She's thrilled that I liked the book so much that I finished it in one sitting. She's even more thrilled that I like his music. It's light and breezy and mellow and upbeat and damn near hypnotic.

I wonder if they play it in mental institutions. I hope so. I figure my last rational legal act will be getting a court order requiring they play his stuff wherever I'm finally committed.

It's soothing, which is good because Shelley Lynne texts me that her grandparents are taking her out to dinner. They'll be late and that she's probably spending the night with them. The empty, aching feeling is not so bad, and maybe it's just hunger. Thank God for chocolate shakes and cheeseburgers.

Extra pickles. No fries.

Bolstered by Duggie's wisdom and music and a full belly, I latch on to Bonnie Lee and play a D. I slide and hop to an A and strum, let 'er ring, and breathe. I go slow—so slow, big mon—I mean, "ever so methodically mellow" slow, a slo-mo ballet with my ever fretful fretting fingers.

I resist the relentless urge to tell myself how stupid and lame and clumsy and worthless I am. It makes me sweat. I slow down even more so my fingers can move at the same time, and I imagine how much I must look like a man loaded on ludes to someone looking at me through the window. Fortunately, there's no window in the guest room.

I take my watch off so I'll stop looking at it. My fingers hurt, but I ignore that because I read somewhere that pain is good and extreme pain is extremely good because it means weakness is leaving the body and that has to be good because weakness is bad.

I don't remember where I read it because I read everything, but I'm pretty sure that whatever I was reading was talking about the Marines. I think it was a Marine who said it, and I would never argue with the Marines.

I like how D and A sound. They fit, and I remember they're paired up in my lifeline chords that guy at Strummin' City gave me, so I feel good about that.

I don't feel so good about the sound of Tami's car in the driveway. I put Bonnie Lee back into the gig bag. I don't like the sound of her keys clunking on the tile of kitchen counter either. I go out to the kitchen to greet her and get it over with.

"Hey," I say.

She doesn't answer me. She sits down at the table to finish what I'm guessing is some sort of organic juice drink. It's green. I think it's got lawn clippings in it. I notice she's glaring at my fast food trash. I pick it up and toss it into the waste basket.

"Shelley Lynne's having dinner with your folks and will probably stay the night there."

Tami grunts.

"What was this morning's argument all about?"

I get a cold stare.

"You. Her. Everything," she mumbles.

"Oh. Wanna talk about it?"

"Seriously?"

"Yeah."

"Seriously? No. No, Paul. I do not wanna talk about it."

She emphasizes my word *wanna*.

"Okay. Rough night?"

"You think?"

"That would be my guess, yes. Would a back rub help?"

She pauses. I can tell she's tempted. Then she steels up and shakes her head.

I change the subject.

"Shelley Lynne's really quite good playing the guitar. I swear it's like she's a natural at it."

"No argument there," she starts to say something but clams up.

"Were you musical as a kid?"

"No."

"Oh."

"Hello? Of course she's musical, Paul. She's only been at it since the fourth grade. Pay attention," she sighs. "That's why it's too late for you, Paul. Get over it."

She gets up, rinses out the plastic bottle, and drops it into the recycle bin.

"Do yourself a favor and let it go, Paul. I'm tired. Leave me alone. Go hug your damn guitar if you're that needy."

Well. Okay then.

"Good night, Tami."

I can't think of anything else to say and autopilot to the guest room. I want to tell her I love her, but that would be wasted breath. I do as I'm told and hug my guitar. It's cold too. It doesn't help me play any better. I concentrate on doing what Shelley Lynne showed me. I concentrate for a couple of hours.

When I wake up, Shelley Lynne is standing next to me, gently rocking my arm. I look around. I'm in the recliner. The Duggie book is on my chest. I don't remember falling asleep here.

"It's okay, Papa. Don't get up. It's still early."

"What time is it?"

"About six. I have to pick up my roommate and head back to Sac. I just stopped by to say goodbye."

"Oh. Well"—I look around, still dazed—"let me give you some gas money."

"It's okay, Papa, really. I'm fine."

"You sure?"

"Yes, Papa. Granddad gave me plenty. You can chip in next time."

"Okay. How 'bout giving me some gas money?"

She laughs.

"You're funny, Papa." She hugs me. "I'll be home for Thanksgiving."

"Promise?"

"Yes, Papa." She hugs me again. "Love you, Papa. Gotta go."

"I love you too, Princess, so much. Please, please drive safe."

"I will, Papa. I promise."

She's already to the door as I manage to sit up. I'm still foggy as I hear the door close. I get up and get to the door in time to see her back out of the driveway and wave as she drives away. I stand there like I'm half expecting she'll change her mind or something. I get myself some orange juice and sit down.

It doesn't taste as good.

I go back to the guest room and pick up where I left off. As usual, my fingers have forgotten everything, and I can't for the life of me figure out what happened to "slide, hop, strum, let 'er ring, and live." It worked yesterday.

But that was yesterday. And yesterday's gone.

Shit! Why ain't it workin' now?

I squeeze the neck harder and force my fingers into the strings. I'll show the little nutcrackers. I'll make 'em get it right. I grit my teeth and slam each strum. I bark the count like a drill sergeant and I'm really pissed at how slow I have to go. I grip the neck harder. The slide really burns but I don't let up. I should have this by now. I don't.

I try Duggie's song, "Why I Don't Know." Bad move. It's not recognizable as anybody's song when I try to play it. It's not mellow and sweet and joyous and carefree at all. It's not hypnotic at all. It's more like wailing screams. More like tortured chords crying out at semiregular intervals, like I'm choking the guitar with one hand and spanking it with the other and I feel like shit.

Coach always told me I was shit.

That pretty much sends me over the edge. I switch to the "Amazing Grace" chords. That's what I need. I know I can do better with E minor, G, C, and D.

Wrong. So very, very wrong. I ignore the sweat and keep driving. Bad move.

I can't get the transition from D to A right. I can't get any of the transitions right. I can't keep my rhythm straight. Neither hand knows what it's doing. I don't even know what they're doing. Maybe I should just stick to playing a beer keg one mug at a time.

I yank the strap over my head and toss the guitar onto the bed. My left hand is numb. I have no idea where the pick is. I feel short of breath, and I'm drenched in sweat.

And that fucking light show.

I wait for the light show in my eyes to end.

I'm glad Shelley Lynne isn't here to see this. I wish she was here to help me not do this anymore.

Shit.

I wish Tami wasn't watching me from the doorway.

She can laugh like a witch.

I still hear her laughing at me—laughing that sinister cackle laugh, telling me I have no talent whatsoever. I keep hearing it.

I'm still hearing it even as the phone on my desk in my office rings.

It's not even eight o'clock in the morning yet, and my phone's already ringing. God, I hate Mondays. For the love of God, when are they ever gonna run out of Mondays?

On the bright side, the secretary from hell is more late than usual, and I pray she doesn't come in at all. Then, right on cue, I hear the jangling jewelry, the heavy moan, the creak of the chair as she plops down, the crash of her two-ton purse full of make-up and costume jewelry and fashion magazines and six-packs of diet soda, and the sound of her croaking voice demanding coffee.

I answer my phone.

"Paul Cooper."

"Mr. Cooper, this is Deputy Forsythe in Department 21. The judge would like to know why you're not here."

"My apologies. I have nothing on calendar."

"We have a pretrial for Everett Redfern, misdemeanor citation and FTA. How soon can you get here?"

"I am on my way," I say.

"Thank you," she says.

I grab my jacket and tell the secretary from hell where I'm going and why.

"So?" she says. "Good for you. I'm going downstairs to get coffee."

The stench of God's people in the hallway is palpable. A young buck deputy struts out of a courtroom. His uniform is impeccable, his body all buff and bad to the bone, and his head shaved and as shiny as the mirror finish on the toes of his boots.

"Listen up! When I call your name, you will form a single-file line to my left!"

I open the door and enter the chaos of Department 21.

I go directly to the seated bailiff, probably the same young woman who called me. Then I see the other deputy in the courtroom. Maybe she's the one who called me. I don't know any of these people.

Another young woman, probably an attorney given her dark business suit, speaks up.

"Your Honor, I believe that would also be a code enforcement matter handled by the city attorney." She notices me. "Perhaps that's him."

"Are you the city attorney?" the judge asks me, her voice rings with impatience.

"No, Your Honor. Sorry. I'm Paul Cooper. I'm a Deputy County Counsel."

The judge rolls her eyes.

"Same difference."

The deputy seated in front of me speaks up.

"Your Honor, he's here on number 43, *People v. Everett Redfern*."

"Excellent. The court calls number 43, *People v. Redfern*."

"Dolores Alvarado for the defendant, who is present out of custody, Your Honor."

"Paul Cooper for the County. Your Honor, I have no idea what this is about, and I do not have a file for this matter."

"What? Are you kidding me?" She glares down at me. "Unbelievable. Will somebody please give this man the court file? I'll come back to it. Anybody else ready?"

A deputy walks the file over to me. I step aside to review it. Redfern was cited for "street hawking," an infraction violation of the county code. Looks like he later failed to appear for his arraignment. No surprise there. And a bench warrant issued for a misdemeanor FTA. About a year or so later, he gets picked up on the warrant. Great.

I ask the seated deputy for a plea bargain form. She hands me one. I turn to the deputy public defender.

"Miss?"

"Alvarado."

God, I love how criminal lawyers ooze with such self-righteous attitude.

"Any chance we can agree to dismiss the FTA, plead guilty to an infraction, say hundred-dollar fine?" I ask her.

"I will discuss this with my client," she says.

Good poker face.

"Thank you, I really appreciate that."

I don't have a poker face. I just want to get out of here with as little effort as possible.

She swivels and struts her way to the gallery where Redfern is one of a dozen denizens. Nice suit. Modest heels. She bends over to talk to him, and the other denizens leer at her round butt.

What the hell. I leer at her round butt. So beautifully round. I turn away and start filling out the form.

"It's a deal. Here, I'll take that."

"Thank you."

I hand her the form, and she finishes it in a flash. She takes it, has him sign it, she signs it, and hands it back to me.

"Sign here," she says.

I sign.

She rips off the goldenrod copy from the back and hands it to me.

"You can go."

"Thank you kindly."

"Don't mention it." She turns and approaches the counsel table. "That's also my matter, Your Honor. Dolores Alvarado for the defendant, in custody, present and seated in the back row of the jury box, at chair 6."

"Karl Flushing for the People, Your Honor."

"This matter is on for a prepreliminary hearing. And your pleasure, counsel?"

"Your Honor, the defense requests a continuance. There are still lab reports and other discovery outstanding."

"Of course. Time waiver?"

Sweet. I see I'm invisible and free to go. That's a relief. I have my copy, and I leave.

My office desk phone is still ringing when I get back. Apparently, my secretary's none too happy about it.

"Hey, hey, hey," she says, swaying her head side to side like some kind of disenchanted snake charmer, pointing at me, heavy metal bracelets jangling at her chunky wrists. "Look who's decided to mosey on in. Must be nice to have those kind of workin' hours."

"I was in court."

You dumb bitch.

"Uh-huh. Well, now that you're back, maybe you can answer your phone. It's only been ringin' off the hook since you been gone."

"Yeah? So? Who's calling me?"

She gives another head sway.

"I dunno. I don't babysit your phone. I didn't say you could just let it roll over to me. I got my own work to do."

"Yeah? Like what?"

"Oh! Now you're checking up on me? Is that it? Yeah, you start working that angle. See how far you get."

She reaches up, a rattling noise shaking from her wrist, and touches the back of her hand to her forehead.

"I'm feeling a grievance coming on, is what I'm feeling," she says.

"Knock yourself out if you've got strength enough to make the effort."

"Oh, you think I won't?"

"Oh, my bad. I forgot. That's the only work you ever do, isn't it? Don't let the door hit you on the way out."

I put the paperwork on my desk, walk around it, take a seat, and answer my phone.

"Paul Cooper."

"Hey, man! You gotta help me! I'm out here on a warrant, and the sheriff's done up and left me and the owner's yelling at me to leave, and now all his biker buddies are rolling up! Hey! Get away from me! I got a warrant to be here! See for yourself!"

I can hear other voices–loud, mean, angry voices—yelling back, "We're gonna kick your ass if you don't get the hell off this property! This is private property! We don't need to see no papers! Get the hell outta here 'fore I shove that piece a paper right up yer ass!" My heart jumps, and I feel goose bumps on my arms.

"Who is this?" I say, trying to be calm.

"Bill Harding, Code Enforcement. Cooper, you gotta do something. This is getting outta hand!"

"Where are you?"

"Out at the river. Sandy Cove at the Cavanaugh trailer."

There's a trembling in his higher-pitched voice.

"Give me the numbers."

"Two, five, zero, eight, one, Sandpoint Landing!"

"Got it. Help's coming. Now get out of there, Harding."

He doesn't answer. I hear jostling noises, and the voices are distant. I hear something about a tire iron, and I hear him threaten to taser somebody.

Chapter 15

I hang up and call the sheriff's dispatch center and report a code officer's getting his butt beat and I tell the operator where. Between the beeping sounds I'm hearing as my call is recorded, I explain that a deputy had been present during the execution of an administrative inspection warrant and things got ugly as soon as the deputy left. The dispatch center operator takes all the information and says the call has been assigned and that deputies are in en route. There's nothing else I can do at this point. I thank her and the line goes dead before I can hang up.

Nothing else to do but jot down as much as I can remember to update the file and leave myself notes for follow-up. That and worry and wait and find something else to work on.

About twenty minutes go by, and my phone rings again. I don't recognize the number.

"Paul Cooper."

"Mr. Cooper, this is Lieutenant Hood out at Red Rocks Substation. I understand you've got a concern about a warrant."

"No, not about a warrant."

"You reported a code officer getting his butt beat."

"That I did and that he was, and that was my concern not the warrant itself."

"Do you always overreact like that?"

The palms of my hands are moist, and the back of my neck feels like it's on fire, and there's a shortness of breath. I give myself a minute and then a couple more.

He starts up.

"Seems to me—"

"Look, I don't care what it seems like to you. You weren't there, obviously, or the code officer would have mentioned you, which would have meant he probably would not have needed to call me at all. But that's not what I heard. I heard the yelling. I heard the threats. I'd heard some guy yelling at the officer, threatening to shove the warrant up the officer's ass. I heard someone else yelling at the code officer that if he didn't get off the property, the guy yelling was going to kick the officer's ass. I heard enough."

"Well, of course, you know everything, bein's how you're the lawyer and all. Me? I just been a lawman for thirty years, so what the hell do I know? Right? Well, let me tell you what I know. Something you lawyer types often don't know, and that's how boys will be boys. There's such a thing as bluff and bluster."

What?

"Now, you take your boy. All he got was a fat lip. He tried to taser one of Cavanaugh's biker buddies, and they took it away from him. Threw it in the back of his truck. So you see, right there, nobody got his butt beat. My guys took paper on it, and that report will go to the DA who probably won't do anything with it, you understand? It's what we out here in the real world like to call a 'mutual combat, 415, situation.' I'll remind you that disturbing the peace is a simple misdemeanor. No big deal. If you had ever been with the DA's office, you'd know that by now. So, mister big-shot civil lawyer, all in all, you overreacted."

"Sorry. I'm going to disagree with you. First, a fat lip is a battery, and I'll remind you that a battery is also a misdemeanor. Second—and this is the key fact here—that battery against the code enforcement officer means your deputy left that code enforcement officer on his own and unprotected in the middle of an inspection warrant. That's a major problem."

"Well, now hold on a minute, he had another call to handle."

"Well, now, you hold on because that wasn't supposed to happen. My client department paid extra for an overtime slot just to make sure there was no adverse impact on shift coverage to prevent just this type of event from ever happening in the first place."

"Look, I don't think you're hearing me. Number one, those misdemeanors are gonna cancel out. Any lawyer who's ever spent more than ten minutes in a courtroom knows that. Number two, stepping aside the overtime mix-up for a moment, this is not a priority call for us. You and I both know we're not dealing with real crime here. This is just piddly ass nuisance shit. That's all it is. It's not at all important, if you catch my drift. You need to understand that nothing much goes on out here. We're a small station, and we pick our battles."

"You're kidding, right? Tell me you're kidding."

"I kid you not. And you oughta know that ol' man Cavanaugh is a pretty popular local. He's got some pull out here. He's even helped up us out from time to time."

"Now I know you're kidding me."

"No. I am not. I'll even spell it out for ya, son. We let a lot of minor stuff slide, but only the minor stuff, never anything major. We know where to draw the preferable line in the sand and everybody out here knows that."

"Proverbial. I think you mean the proverbial line in the sand."

"Ah, whatever, smart-ass. You know damn well what I mean."

"I know exactly what you mean. You're so far off the reservation, you're no longer accountable. Just doing whatever the hell you want."

"Cooper, I don't think you're hearing me. You need to set aside all them lawyer smarts and law books and learn to read between the lines from the pages of the real world and understand my position."

My fingers are tingling, and I feel light-headed.

"What? Wait! I'm . . . I'm not hearing you? Seriously? Well, hang on a second, Lieutenant, let's try something," I bash the handset of phone against my desk. "How, 'bout now, Lieutenant? Can you hear me now?"

I bash the desk with the phone a few more times.

"How 'bout now? Can you hear me now, tinhorn? Because I can hear you just fine. You said I don't understand your position. I understand your position just fine, Lieutenant. You're a cop! At least you're supposed to be. So start fuckin' actin' like one. Preferably one who isn't one of those 'retired on duty' types."

I take a quick breath.

"For your edification and information, an inspection warrant is a court order, and part of that court order says your guys protect my guy while he conducts the inspection. That's it. End of discussion. Only what do you do? You and your boys ignore that. Now you're telling me, in so many words, that you and your boys don't even have to do that much?"

"I said no such thing, Cooper."

"The hell you didn't! You told me you've got a small station. Your station's so small, you gotta pick your battles. Well, boohoo! You got a station that's so small, you have to let the minor stuff slide. Code violations are piddly ass nuisance shit. So, to you, that means they're minor and don't count, and as long as Cavanaugh breaks only the minor laws and helps you out from time to time, that's okay with you because he's an okay guy, and he helps your boys out."

I take another breath.

"That's a load of tinhorn, Wild West crap in your hat, and you know it! Maybe you should just retire now! Then you can sit in the sand all damn day suckin' down some cold beers and swirlin' little lines in the sand with your fingers when you're not stickin' 'em up your own ass!"

I don't hear anything.

"Hello?"

I look at the screen. It's blank. I start bashing the handset of my phone against my desk. It feels really damn good to do that. Really good.

I liked calling that jackass a tinhorn, too.

I look up midbash at Darryl. and the words leap from my mouth, "What are you looking at?"

I let go of the handset, and it falls to the floor. I hear buzzing from the phone. I regret the words the second they fly, but there was no stopping them, and I know I'm burnt toast.

Fuck me.

Darryl has an amazing poker face. I can read no sign upon it.

Maybe something like a heart attack about now would be nice.

I'm tempted to point at the phone and say something really stupid like bluff and bluster. Boys will be boys. Somehow, I know he'd never buy it. I watch as he slithers into a chair across from my desk. He crosses his legs and adjusts the knot of his impeccable silk tie. In the silence of the room, I can hear my own heartbeat. It sounds like grenades exploding.

Shit.

I sit.

Darryl stares into my eyes, and I blink before he does. He takes a deep breath slowly through his nose and then exhales the same way. He steeples his hands, letting the fingertips tap lightly against each other.

"My, my. I may have misjudged you. Perhaps there is something of a litigator in you after all. Offhand, I'd say you need to give voice to your inner asshole more often. I like it. But that's just me. Oh, don't get me wrong, your sandbagger of a secretary's going to milk this for all its worth. She's already been on the telephone to HR claiming hostile work environment."

Darryl shakes his head.

"Of course, she's much too stupid to understand that only applies in the context of sexual harassment, which, based on her statement so far, obviously is not at issue here. Then again, I'm thinking there's some wiggle room on workplace violence. Nothing substantial from what I've seen so far but enough for HR and Admin to have to do something. So I'm guessing the conniving, lazy-ass bitch just may get some mileage out of this incident after all unfortunately. Of course, if it were me, in my firm, I'd have fired that worthless bitch a long time ago. But again, that's just me."

For the first time, I think, I see him blink. Maybe once.

"Paul, if I heard Woo correctly—and I'm fairly sure that I did—then I want to warn you. I think you're probably looking at some discipline, some kind of anger management, and, most likely some, I don't know, 'go see a shrink' bullshit. Just so you know." He smiles. "But, hey, don't let that worry you. It's all good."

He reaches into his right front suit pants pocket and pulls out a money clip and starts peeling off fifties.

"Tell you what, slugger, I want you to take the rest of the day off. Translation? You're now on, what do they call it here? Oh, that's right, admin leave."

He laughs.

"Admin leave. That's cute. In private practice, I'd just fire your ass. But not for this. Oh, no. Never for something like this. You were making a point with someone you need to rely on to do your job, someone who had obviously dropped the ball. You let him know, in no uncertain terms, and you called him on it, and I like that. You blew off some steam. I get that. Good for you."

I'm thinking maybe this won't be quite so bad.

"Go to the beach," he says, and he has almost an excited look on his face. "Capistrano. Have dinner at The Spinnakers. In fact, there'll be a table waiting. Gorge yourself on the lobster thermidor. Don't even worry about a wine selection. I've got it covered. Hit the road. I've got your cell number. I'll call you with further instructions."

"I'm out of here," I say and stand up.

There's no point in arguing with him or in doing anything other than going along with the program, especially when it's his. Between him and Danny, I'm not sure who the deadlier devil is, and

I'm not in any hurry to find out. I take my keys and cell phone out of a desk drawer.

"Dinner's taken care of. This is just in case. It's always good to have some pin money." He hands me the cash. "I'm betting you don't have twenty bucks on you."

"I don't have any cash on me at all."

"And how'd I know that?" he smiles.

Okay, that's creepy. And familiar.

He takes a slow look around my office. He stops to take in the wall poster I put up. It's a picture of a giant sand dune with footprints and a silhouette of a man at the top of the steep dune in front of more dunes, steeper dunes. Beneath the picture is the word "Problems," and below that a line of text that reads, "I knew I'd have to face a few problems in my life. I just didn't know there would be so many, that they would be so bad or last so long."

Then he looks at me with a squint.

"Funny," he says. "All right. Hit the road. I'll handle things here at the shithole oasis."

I don't waste any time leaving.

I'm not much of a lobster-and-wine guy, but I'm thinking of becoming one. I feel my cell phone vibrate. I check it, but I don't recognize the number. I answer it anyway.

"Hello?"

"Hey, slugger! How ya swingin'?"

"Doing great, Darryl."

"Yeah? How's dinner?"

"Phenomenal."

"That's what I want to hear. Where are you?"

"Oh, I'm still here."

"Excellent."

"Yeah. I'm waiting for the . . . waiting for the wine to wear off before driving home."

"Change of plans, slugger. I've got bad news."

I can feel the lobster starting to crawl its way back up, and it's pissed. My mouth goes totally dry, and I'm reaching for the last of the wine, wishing it was as chilled as when they brought it.

"Slugger, you're better off cabbing on over to the Swallows Inn tonight and driving home in the morning—late morning. Maybe even noonish depending on your hangover."

"I don't really have a hangover."

"Oh, you're gonna want one."

"Oh, crap."

"Yeah, 'fraid so, slugger."

My heart's pounding again, and the lobster's almost to the top of my throat.

"Oh shit!" I look around and lower my voice.

Somebody with a white towel on his arm comes from nowhere and pours me a large glass of ice water. I start drinking it.

"How bad?" I ask in a near whisper.

"Bad enough. Not everyone shares my value of expressing the inner asshole from time to time. Everybody here's a fucking sheep. I also underestimated Woo's influence. Sheriff's people are pissed off at you. Woo's still pissed off at you over the email stunt. Now your client department's pissed off at you."

"Code? What are they pissed about?"

"You making them work. Backstabbin' little shitheads. I should have seen that one coming. Now that you're on admin leave for about two weeks or more, they've suddenly decided they got cases they needed filed yesterday. I'm not buying it though."

"They've been on me for weeks to hold off and not do anything. Not start anything new."

"Then Woo's got 'em drinking out of his water cooler."

Now it sinks in.

"Two weeks? Or more?"

"Easy, slugger. I've got some friends and a couple of my associates looking into it. You should be fine."

"Hell, I don't feel fine."

"That's where the hangover's comin' in, slugger," he laughs. "I see this all working to my advantage."

"Your advantage?"

"That's what I said, slugger, your advantage. I admire your knack for making enemies. I like it."

"I'm not sure I like it. This can't be good."

"Stay with me, slugger."

"I'm here."

"Good. Here's the plan. Have some more wine and then cab over to the Swallow Inn like I said. Room will be waiting. Best night of sleep you'll ever have, bar none. When you crawl into bed, turn off your phone. Don't even think of answering it. You married?"

The munch-mangled lobster is clawing its way up my throat.

"Yeah."

"Oooh! There's a visual I didn't expect. Then in that case, you will by no means ever answer your phone tonight. In fact, when I hang up, you will turn it off. Have you used any credit cards or debit cards tonight?"

"No. Why?"

"That's the first thing your wife will check when you don't answer the phone. Has she called yet?"

"No. She's an RN, works nights."

"You bastard! You are one lucky son of a bitch. You know that? Good. That will buy us some time. Okay, back to the plan. When you get up, get some eats, head on home. Now listen carefully. You've got an appointment tomorrow afternoon at three with a psychologist in Riverside. Name's Dr. Robert B. McGee. Good man. Knows all about the inner asshole and the hypomanic, competitive edge. You'll like him. I will send you the info by text to your phone. Still with me, slugger?"

"Yeah."

"Good man. How you doing on gas for the car?"

"Oh, crap. Maybe a quarter, a little less."

"Okay, don't worry about it. Leave your keys with the manager. I'll have it taken care of. Car will be gassed before you even wake up."

"Okay."

"Relax, slugger. I've got everything under control. This time next year, I'll have you zipping around in a sweet sporty roadster dripping with hot women instead of pushing around in that hybrid wannabe, soccer-mom ride you've got now."

A toweled arm is pouring chilled wine into my glass. The glass is frosting up. I thank him without looking up and reach for the glass as I hear the bottle slide into the silvery bucket with the crunchy ice.

"Sounds like the next bottle of wine's arrived. Excellent. Drink up, slugger."

I can't hear anything, and the swaying screen of my phone is black. I love how the wine swirls around the glass when they pour it, and the next thing I know, I feel myself being poured into the backseat of a banana; and it's dark and, my god, these sheets are marvelous, and I've disappeared into this huge, cushy pillow. And everything goes black, even as it spins.

I'm still spinning when I hear the pounding jack hammer or maybe a baseball bat, and I reach for the pillow and can't find it and sit up in the recliner in my house. I'm fully dressed, and my watch says it's one thirty in the afternoon, and my phone's ringing. I see a text from Ryan that says he's pounding on my front door and for me to stop jerking off and let him in and there's a reminder of an expert witness deposition in Riverside at three. I don't remember scheduling any deposition.

I barely remember the fight with Tami in the doorway as I was coming in and she was going out.

Chapter 16

"Where the hell have you been?"

"What the hell do you care?"

My phone buzzes, and she yanks it out of my hand.

"Give me that. Great. You have a deposition at three? You're drunk."

"No. I'm hungover. There's a difference."

"Don't get smart with me, Paul."

"Then don't get stupid with me, Tami. I'm the lawyer. You're the bitch. Fuck you!"

She freezes. She blinks a few times.

"What is this all about? Why are you doing this?"

Her voice is much softer.

"Rough times at work. Ah, hell! Who am I kidding? Work's in the toilet. Dinner was on the new boss. He bought me wine. He said it's my reward for expressing my inner asshole and pissing people off."

"You're not making any sense, Paul. There's no need to make up stories. A little honesty would be nice."

"Oh! You think? Yeah, I'm diggin' the irony too. Honest-to-God truth, Tami. But you're never satisfied with the truth, are you? All you ever willing to accept is your own jacked-up version of it. So like you're always telling me, there's really no point talking about it. Is there? I want to brush my teeth and take a shower, and unless you intend to join me and suck and fuck me into next weekend, we're done here."

Tami's face goes pale. Then she scowls.

"Fine. I'm leaving. If your new boss takes you to dinner again tonight, I hope you'll have the decency to send me a text and let me know."

"Yes, ma'am."

She slaps me hard across the face.

"Fuck you, Paul!"

◆ ◆ ◆ ◆ ◆ ◆

I remember Ryan's knocking at the door. I sort of crawl my way to the door to let him in. He's talking at me a mile a minute. I have no idea what he's saying. I'm still thinking of Tami and rubbing the left side of my face.

He guides me into the kitchen and rumbles about, poking his head here and there, banging cupboards, slamming drawers, mixing and stirring and pouring, what? Tomato juice? I didn't know we had any.

"Drink this."

I drink this. Tastes like tomato juice. Not sure. Not bad. Not all that good either.

"Finish it."

I finish it.

"Dude, you know you're on admin leave, right?"

"I know."

"Woo's out to get you fired."

"That I didn't know."

Ryan gets a funny look on his face. "Where do you keep your guitar?"

"In the guest room."

"Wait here."

I wait, and he comes back holding a tangle of strings and a busted guitar.

"What happened? Did you do this, dude?"

What the fuck?

"I don't think so."

"What do you mean 'you don't think so'?"

"I mean, I don't fuckin' think so, you deaf? I haven't practiced since Sunday. I totally sucked at it, and I tossed her on the bed."

"You tossed Tami on the bed?"

"Oh, hell no! I never get to touch her. I tossed Bonnie Lee on the bed. I was playing lousy, couldn't get anything right, and . . . and I got mad, and I tossed her on the bed, and Tami laughed her ass off at me when I did."

"Then what happened?"

"I got up Monday morning and put Bonnie Lee in the gig bag. She was fine then. Went to work and started pissing people off by the pound before I even knew I was doing so."

"You're hungover now."

"Well, yeah. You made this for me to drink."

I point to the empty glass.

"Dude, what time did you get home last night?"

"This morning. I got home sometime this morning. Maybe noonish. Shit, I don't remember. I remember I was coming in the door and Tami was going out the door, and we argued and she-bitch slapped me good, and she was pissed off at me. Everybody's pissed off at me, except Darryl. He's proud of me for expressing my inner asshole and pissing people off. He sent me to the beach last night and bought me dinner and wine—*really* good wine, man. I hope I brought some home."

I notice him staring at me like I'm from another planet. I notice his hands, how reverently they hold Bonnie Lee, and I finally notice her—really notice her—how mangled she is.

"I didn't do that."

"I didn't think you would. Tell you what. Let me take her for a while, dude. I know a luthier."

"Okay."

"In the meantime"—he rubs his chin—"I need to figure something out. I've been trying to get a hold of you. I've got the chords for the rockabilly songs for Woo's barbeque. Only you're nowhere to be found. Then I hear about all the stuff you've got going. Too much, dude. There's no time for this. Now you're on admin leave, so in a way, you got time. There's just no guitar to spend it on."

"Yeah, I got all the time in the world and no time at all, and it's all goin' on at the same time. Go figure. What time is it?"

"About two o'clock."

"I need to be in Riverside at three."

"No you don't."

"Oh yeah I do."

I show him my phone. I show him the text message with the address and everything.

"Dude, you're in no shape for a depo."

"It ain't a depo. It's an appointment with a shrink."

"What?"

"Darryl set it up. Well, it's mandatory, something about workplace violence. Maybe the county set it up. I don't know. Whatever. All I know is somehow Darryl pulled strings and picked the guy."

"What?"

"The guy. You know. The guy. The shrink guy. Yeah, Dr. McGee. The guy I have to go see at three."

"What?"

"Oh, c'mon man, cut it out. You're making my head hurt."

I grope my pockets. I stumble around, looking. I know I'm missing something. Car keys. I'm missing car keys.

"Forget it, dude. I'll drive."

He takes my phone.

"What are you doing?"

"Dude, I don't want this disappearing like your car keys."

"Good point. Shit. Now I sound like ol' Huff n' Puffman."

"That's right. I heard about your ordinance review meeting." He shakes his head. "What a clusterfuck."

———— ✦✦✦✦✦ ————

The waiting room for Dr. McGee is tasteful. For a county guy, the place doesn't look county at all. The chair is actually comfy. I need all the comfy I can get. The main wall art is a photo-quality massive framed poster of snow-capped peaks in a pine forest that's bordered in the foreground with white-barked trees with shimmering yellow-gold leaves. I wish I was there. Anywhere but here.

The interior door flies open, and I'm lurching up as Paul Bunyan's lumberjack twin brother fills the doorway. He's huge—Sasquatch huge. Except his reddish-brown beard is neatly trimmed and his matching hair neatly combed. He's got on these huge leather hiking boots with red laces that match his red-and-black checked wool shirt. The shirt sleeves are rolled up at the elbows. He takes a quick glance around the room. No one else is here.

He holds a manila folder against his forehead.

"You must be Paul," he says, looking around the room again.

I'm still the only one here, besides him.

"Yeah, 'fraid so," I say, and I glance around the room like I'm never going to see it again.

"You're probably wondering how I did that. Like some kind of mind magic, eh?"

Oh, what the hell.

"Hey. Works for me, man."

"Let's go, eh." He waves a manila folder. "We're losing daylight."

I don't see how that's possible, but who the hell am I to argue with this guy? I realize I'm relieved to see he's not packing an ax. Bet it's huge.

He reaches for the clipboard with all the forms I've been filling out.

"I'll take that if you're done."

Oh, I'm done. I've been filling out forms for the last half hour. There's a lot of boxes to check on drinking and drugging habits, different kinds of abuse you've inflicted on others or that others have inflicted on you and if you liked it, who else lives in your house and why the hell would you ever let them—stuff like that. There are four pages just on sex. I skipped those. They were too depressing.

Chapter 17

This is all so much bigger than me. I just gave up on the clipboard. Besides, I know everything I've written is an admission, and the county will find a loophole the size of Texas and use every box I've checked against me, which is only as depressing as half of the boxes I've checked.

I follow him into a tiny office where he sits in front of a polished oak rolltop desk. The desk, like him, is way, too big for this office. There are green plants in colorful glazed clay pots everywhere. On top of the desk, plush toys little stuffed huskies—three of them with grey-and-white fur—are harnessed to a little dogsled. The huskies' white-and-blue plastic eyes sparkle, and their little, pink felt tongues stick out of their mouths. I swear the little huskies are smiling at me. I wish I had a dog.

"Sit anywhere you like, eh."

There's a tiny couch and a small rocking chair. I choose the rocker.

"Yeah. Good choice, that chair."

Above the couch is a painting—almost abstract, looks like. I think it is a hockey player, and I think the sweep of line and splashes of color are meant to convey drama and speed. Pretty cool.

There's a small bookcase to my right where plants and wood-carved duck decoys, pretty ones, compete for space with books. The books have titles like *The Path to Happiness Can Get a Little*

Rocky, and *I'm Okay and You're Not and That's Okay Too*, and *Stress Management in 12 Not-So-Easy Steps*, and *All I Really Need to Know I Learned From Getting Hit in the Head with a Hockey Stick*. There are more ducks. On another shelf are two books side by side. They must be companion volumes as they're the same size, the titles are in the same color and type font, and they're by the same author. I find them disturbing, though I am completely clueless as to why. They are *If You Can Believe in Yourself, Then the Sky Is Your Limit* and *Even If You Crash and Burn, It's Never Too Late to Learn to Believe in Yourself*.

There's even a life-sized trout—maybe it's stuffed or maybe it's a model, I can't tell and don't much care. It's leaping upward from the floor, between the chair and the couch, through the splash of a transparent block of acrylic resin that's clear at the top and then tinted in ever-deepening shades of blue and teal toward its pebbly bottom. This place is like some great northern sportsman's lodge stuffed into a college dorm room.

I like it.

That fish thing? Not so much.

I look up and see he's leaning forward, wringing his hands and studying me like I'm a meal or something. I notice he's wearing glasses too—wire frames, aviator-style. There's even a touch of grey in his sideburns. He scratches at his beard.

"You don't look like the violent type to me, eh."

"I'm not. I promise. Really, I'm not."

"Yeah? Okay then. "What's this I hear about you bashing phones? Are you the phone basher? Is that you? What's that all about?"

"No—well, yeah. I mean, no. I mean, yeah, I did it. A couple of times. Okay, it was like several times. You know, I just kinda got in a groove thing, you know, and you know, I just sorta went with it."

I want so much to yell at myself to just shut up, but I keep talking.

"Just, you know, went with it."

"I see." He starts scribbling, fast. "And what do you suppose that's all about?"

I shrug. "I'm not sure."

I talk. He scribbles. He looks at the clipboard. He looks at me. He looks at the clipboard. He scribbles some more.

I can't stand his silence.

"I get a call," I say. "Get the usual song and dance. I'm trying, but I'm not getting through to the guy. Everything's really frustrating. I mean it. Everything I do is just an exercise in frustration and futility. *Everything.* Every damn day. It's like I'm being deliberately set up to fail. and like, everybody's been in on the plan from the day I got there. I got no way out. Everybody I have to deal with at my client department is ignorant, incompetent, and indifferent."

"Give me an example."

I give him an example. I give him several examples. I tell him all about my problems with Reverend Justice and a code officer who keeps issuing unenforceable citations. I tell him about Lieutenant Hood. I tell him about illegible and blank photocopies and my secretary from hell and how she's probably milking some kind of medical leave out of this mess at my expense.

I tell him about Chrome Dome and Woo and about hobbies and other unfinished business, and he scribbles like he's writing a damn bar exam. He never looks up, he just keeps scribbling, so I keep talking. And somewhere, I slip and mention the Coach, and he scribbles a bit more and then stops. He wants me to talk about the Coach.

I tell him about Coach, my father—the high school baseball coach whom I never called Dad again after the sixth grade.

I tell him how Coach, back when he was a teenager, was the golden boy prospect of the Baltimore Orioles. I tell the story about Coach, in his first game in the majors, slides toward second to break up the double play. I tell him how the Yankee shortstop spikes him on the fall. Cracked ankle. Surgery goes sour. His career over before it begins.

I tell him what I can remember of all the long years of my childhood, the Coach slurping back the beers to keep his dream, swatting the empty beer cans from the porch on the house where I grew up. I tell him about Coach swatting the crushed cans with a fungo bat. He drives the cans with long, loping, line drives back—way back, high over my head, "it's outta here!" back, and over the fence a few feet behind me and far back into the neighbor's backyard—the neighbor yelling out "asshole!" the Coach laughing, crumpling the next can, tossing it up, and belting it into the neighbor's yard.

I tell him about growing up a scrawny, asthmatic kid with eyeglasses with black plastic frames that went with my black hair and hid my green eyes and with no major league prospects whatsoever. I tell him about having to gather up all the cans and catch shit from the neighbor as I collected the cans.

Then I remember.

Shit. Fuck. Piss. Cunt. Motherfucker. Tits. I just want to end this.

He waits for me to continue, but I don't.

I can't.

He studies me and scratches at his beard. Same spot as before.

"Okay. We'll come back to that. I think that's enough talking for now, eh. We have one thing left to do today."

He looks at his watch. I don't remember noticing that he was wearing one. He stands up and waves for me to follow.

I follow.

He leads me into another room, and this place looks county. It's just another decrepit conference room with an ugly long table with a fake wood top; way too many chairs; blah-blah walls painted a cheap, dull shade of ick. There's a booklet on the table; inside the booklet and protruding slightly is an answer sheet, the fill-in-the-bubble kind, and a pencil.

"You're kidding, right?"

"Oh, it's no joke, eh. The powers that be who have sent you to me require these tests. This one's a two-hour test. Self-explanatory. Everything is explained on the top page of that booklet, eh. Bathroom is through that door. I suggest you use it first and then take the test. I'll wait till you start, then I'll be back when the time is up."

I keep my mouth shut for a change. I go take a dump and come back. Then I take the test. A bunch of asinine, random, senseless, stupid questions.

"Would I rather tie a shoe or plant a flower?"

"Would I rather drive a car or drive a nail?"

"Sometimes the top of my head hurts. True or False?"

"I think flames are pretty. True or False?"

"Would I rather play with paper airplanes or paper dolls?"

"Would I rather stand with my hands on my hips or with my hands behind my back?"

"I usually feel some kind of pain around my stomach. True or False?"

"Would I rather watch a porn movie or a fireworks display?"

"Would I rather play with a deck of cards or with a book of matches?"

"I like the sound of a dripping faucet. True or False?"

"Would I rather read a map or listen to a speech?"

"Would I rather walk along the beach at sunrise or at sunset?"

"I prefer coffee over orange juice in the morning. True or False?"
Really? This kind of bullshit?
I'd rather take a beating than take this test.
I finish the test anyway. Something about keeping my day job.
Sasquatch strolls in like he said he would.
I don't even look up. I just push the paper and booklet his way.
"Hey, I think that's enough fun for one day, eh?"
I shrug and tell him I'd have rather taken a beating than that stupid test. He thinks that's funny. He hands me a card.
"Next appointment. I'll see you back here day after tomorrow."
I stare at the card. Pretty letters.
"Day after tomorrow," I mumble.
"Yeah, that would be like, Wednesday, eh."
"Day after tomorrow. You mean like this week?"
"Yeah, that's what I mean. Just like I wrote it down for you on the card there, eh."

"Fair enough."

I can hardly see. I can hardly walk. I fall asleep in Ryan's Jeep. When he wakes me up, it's already dark out. He helps me inside.

"Bathroom's in there. Just walk to the night light."

I think I'm on a couch. He smothers me with a cushy blanket. I don't remember there being a nightlight. Somebody moved the couch. I think the recliner is missing.

I wake up in somebody else's house. I sit up, and the blanket, which is a sleeping bag, falls; and it's damn cold. I pull it back up. I let it fall again because I need to use the bathroom. I have no idea whose house this is, but my toothbrush and toothpaste are waiting for me in the bathroom. Ryan's waiting for me when I get out of the bathroom.

"This is your place, right?"

"Yeah, dude."

"What'd you do with the barn?"

"You're at the other end."

"Oh."

"Hungry?"

"A little."

"C'mon."

I follow him and end up in the kitchen I remember. He serves me a small plate of scrambled eggs, a bowl of strawberries and blueberries, and a glass of orange juice.

"Tell me what's going on, dude."

"Man, I am all talked out."

"What happened with you and Tami?"

I shrug. It's getting to be my go-to move.

"What always happens. I practice—I mean play, Shelley Lynne says I'm supposed to play, not practice. Anyway, doesn't matter what I call it. I still suck. Anyway, Tami goes off on me. She's in my face with all this 'you got no talent, no skill, you're too old' crap. And you know what? Damn if she ain't right. I'm just a 'guitard.'"

"Did you just say 'guitard'?"

"Yeah. Bitch called me a guitard. Well, what she actually said was, she asked me if I was 'guitarded.'"

Ryan perks up.

"Bitch?" he asks, and I see his eyebrows rise.

"Wait. That didn't come out right."

"Oh, no! I think it did. I think it came out right on the money. But it doesn't matter what I think, dude, as long as you recognize that's what you're dealing with here."

"Don't bust my chops on that, okay?"

"That's not my doing. Did you hear yourself just now? Word for word. 'Bitch called me a guitard' and 'she asked me if I was guitarded.' Hello! Sounds to me like you finally admitted your dream girl is an Elm Street nightmare!"

We stare into one another's silence.

"I wasn't finished. You interrupted my thought, Ryan. Anyway. As I was trying to tell you, I was mad because she called me guitarded and because, even more so, because I think she's probably right."

"No way. She's wrong, and she's scared, and she's lashing out. Fear does that. What else did she say?"

"That I need to grow up. Act my age. That I embarrass her. How can I embarrass her? I'm in my own house. In a guestroom."

"Go on."

"That's it. Mostly that crap. Same old crap."

"Same as what?

"Doesn't matter. I was stupid to think I could try this again. I'm too old for this crap."

"Dude, there'll be a time that's true. But not yet."

"How do you know?"

"One, you're not dead. Your fingers still work, even if you don't think so. Your eyes still work. Your brain still works—overworks, actually. Whatever. You started once before, you said, right?"

"Yep."

"Okay. When was that?"

"Summer after the sixth grade, 1972.

"And?"

I finished the eggs. Then all the berries right after that. My mouth went wild.

"Dude!"

"What?"

"Talk to me!"

"Nothing to talk about. Truth is, I couldn't do it. Fingers all going every which way, everywhere but where they're supposed to. Strings buzzing like I stuck my head in a beehive. And nothing's changed." I look around. "I want more berries. And then I want to die."

"No. Go back to how it all began. Tell me that part."

I shrug.

"I had a friend, and he had a big brother. And he'd let us hang out with him."

"The big brother?"

"Yes. And he could play guitar. And he was so cool. He really tried to help me. Then they moved away—up and gone like that. One week we're hanging out, next week, I'm staring through the picture window of their empty house and a neighbor lady says she has some stuff for me that they had left behind. Some record albums he let me listen to and an old, beat-up kid's acoustic. But I loved it. Because it was his, and then it was mine. It was special, and it was mine. It was everything."

"Go on."

"He had showed me some chords before, and when he was around, you know, when I was hanging out with him, I could do it. I could actually do it. Not real well, mind you, but so much better than I can now. When he was around, it was like I knew I could do anything. I had no idea how skinny, or dorky, or how four-eyed I was. When he was around, none of that shit ever mattered."

"What happened when he moved away?"

"I took the records to my grandparents' house and hid the guitar under my bed. I'd wait for Saturday mornings when Coach would leave the house to play golf. That was his thing. Then I'd take it out and get up on the bed and practice, trying to hear Tim's voice, close my eyes, and pretend like he was there."

"Tim was the older brother?"

"Yeah."

"Who's the coach?"

"My dad."

"Okay. Then what happened?"

"He threw it in the street. I was trying to get F major . . . there's a reason they call that chord the F chord, and I couldn't get it right. I kept at it and at it and at it. Coach got all pissed. He said, if I were half that stubborn shagging ground balls, that I'd be a star at second base. He said, no kid of his was ever gonna be some sissy-assed, fairy-hair musician."

"The coach dude hated musicians?"

"The coach dude hated everything and everybody. He played in the minors, got to the majors for a couple of games, got hurt, and eventually ended up coaching high school ball and living out of beer cans when he wasn't using them or me or my Mom for batting practice."

"Dude, that's a story that's needed telling for a long time. I hope you told the shrink."

"Not yet."

"Dude, you gotta tell him."

"I couldn't."

"Why not?"

Shrug.

"Oh, dude, you have to tell him. You have to tell him. Every single word. Next appointment? You tell him. If you don't, I sure as hell will. I mean it."

"All right, all right. You chill for a change. I'll tell him. It won't help, but if it will shut you up, I'll tell him."

"Good."

"Yeah. Good. Good for me. Right."

"Tell me something. I saw all those guitar books in your guestroom. What's up with that?"

"Just, you know, trying to learn the only way I can. The only way I know how."

"Amazing," he says, shaking his head. "Seriously, for now? That's all overload. They have their place, sure, don't get me wrong. They're valuable books, all of them. They're helpful, and in time, you'll be using them. But right now? No. Not so much. Set 'em aside for now. Baby steps, dude. You gotta take baby steps."

"Crap. Now you sound like my daughter."

"Whatever, dude. Baby steps—one string, one finger, one note at a time."

I lean back and rub my eyes.

"Why are you pushing yourself so hard, dude?"

"Oh, come on, man. I'm supposed to have a hobby, remember?"

"No, dude. That's not how you mean it. You mean it like, 'Oh? I'm supposed to have a hobby? Fine! I got your hobby, right here, asshole! I'll show you. Happy now, asshole?' You mean it more like that, right?"

I can't hold back the grin, and I nod.

"Got it. Only you're not showing them a damn thing, Paul. That's the problem. You're just punishing yourself. What do you say we rethink this, redirect this energy, and get a vibe you can sail on? What do you say to that, dude?"

I nod and rub my eyes so he can't see them.

"You don't have to hide on me, dude. I'm with you. As I see it, we got two problems to deal with up front. The first is you're in love with a dream."

I'm shaking my head.

"No, I'm in love with my wife."

"That's what I said, dude. It's all just a dream."

"Okay, fine. Have it your way. I'm in love with my dream wife."

"Exactly."

"Exactly. So how's that a problem?"

"The dream ain't real, dude. Like I said, it's a fuckin' nightmare. Yeah, you love her. A blind man can see that. What you can't see is that all the time you're dreaming she loves you back. But here's the catch, it ain't happenin', dude. She's more like a mannequin, and I don't ever see your dream lover making any of your dreams come true."

"It's not like that. It's not."

"Dude! Open your eyes! The cards are on the table, face up. Look at 'em. The cards never lie!"

"No no no, Ryan. You got it all wrong."

"Dude! Hear me out."

"Fine. What's the second problem?"

"Your attitude, dude."

"Ahh! Shit, Ryan! Now you sound like that asshole Woo!"

"Dude. You've dug this hole you're in because you want to stick it to Woo and to Admin over Woo's 'get a hobby' crack when nobody over in Admin knows or even cares. That's the first half of the second problem."

"The second problem has two parts? Kind of overcomplicating this a bit, aren't we?"

"And who's calling the kettle black now? The second half of the second problem comes from you trying to outlast your wife, and that ain't ever gonna happen. She's got you strung up like a puppet."

I'm rubbing the back of my neck. I hear a tea kettle, and Ryan gets up and makes himself a tea. It smells minty, I think, and good. He makes another and brings the mugs with a pair of spoons to the table and gives me one.

"Dude, you got no chance at all unless you can honestly—purely, with no thought of personal gain or outcome whatsoever—develop a sincere, genuine, total infatuation with and love for the guitar."

"That's it?" I say as I stir my tea.

"That's it? Fuckin' A right that's it! That's the bar exam of music for you."

"Great. I'm supposed to fall in love with a guitar, and I can't even play one yet."

"Exactly."

"That makes no sense at all, Ryan."

"Dude, it makes perfect sense. Apart from the fact that, from what you've told me, you did once already. Do you even know that all guitars—*all* guitars—each have their own individual, distinct sound?"

"Well, yeah."

"No, I don't mean how one brand sounds different from another. I mean how two of the same guitars—same maker, same brand, strung alike, tuned alike, with no effects, and with the same amps set the same or no amps at all—do not sound exactly the same. They may be damn close, too close for you to tell the difference, but they do not sound the same."

"Okay, then apparently I don't."

"Now you do."

"Fine," I say and sip tea. "Seeing how I've got no talent, what do I do with this revelation?"

"As far as talent goes, there's what most people think, which is the knack for doing something that comes naturally, and then there's the other kind."

"Bull. What other kind?"

"The kind that says talent is the lazy man's label for practice and the best excuse ever invented not to. Even people with the first kind get better with the second kind. Sometimes, talent comes down to putting in the right kind of hours that it takes to get good. It's how the universe works, dude."

"I'm not so sure."

"It's true. Think about it. Nobody starts off perfect. Perfection's a myth. As for the rest? Just accept it. Understand that it matters to listen, to always get your guitar in tune. Then, be in tune with your guitar. That's really the heart of your 'brave new world,' as you like to call it. That's where you start. It's where every guitarist starts, however famous or obscure they become."

"Okay. Fine. Assuming you're right, then how do I solve this problem?"

"Ask yourself this question, can I love the guitar for no other reason than simply I love the guitar—its look, its feel, and, most importantly, its sound? You gotta ask yourself that one question, dude."

"Okay, and then what?"

"Then we gotta figure a way to get you of your head and into your heart."

"That doesn't make any sense."

"Ahh! You're killing me, dude. You gotta make a decision here. You gotta decide that playing a guitar is what *you*—and nobody but *you*—want to do. You need to want it so bad and so much so that you'll do it anyway, no matter what, never for a moment dreaming you can make a living at it, that you would do it just as a hobby, even if you were an accountant, a truck driver, or just another lawyer."

"That's it?"

Chapter 18

"That's everything, dude."

"Fair enough. Then everything oughta be . . . fair enough, then."

"Keep thinking about it. I'll be back in a minute."

"Okay."

I finish my tea. It's cold. I need to check in with Darryl or at least check my phone. There's a missed call from Darryl, so I call him back. He tells me to lay low, check in with him every morning, and keep my appointments with Dr. McGee. I tell him I will. Then he asks about Woo's barbeque party. My guts knot up. I start to tell him. He cuts me off, telling me to do whatever I have to do. I tell him I will.

Ryan comes back with a small, black guitar case. He puts it on the kitchen table and opens it.

"No pressure or anything, but while you're thinking things over, there's the issue of Woo's barbeque. We still have to deal with that. Danny's plan is to have you join us for three rockabilly songs. Each song has the same three notes, C, D, and G. Same three notes damn near every popular rock 'n' roll song has. Strum pattern is different on all of 'em to be sure. That and some pinky finger tricks are how they can all sound so different even with the same notes. Here's your chance to put your admin leave to good use, dude."

"Don't I need to go home or something?"

"No, you're good right here."

"But Tami," I say and check my phone—nothing.

"No, dude. You're good. You wrote her a note."

"I wrote her a note? When did I write her a note?"

"Last night, while I packed your bags. You told her you were on admin leave, your job's in the toilet, and you were getting away for a few days—maybe a few more—and not to wait up for you."

"No I didn't!"

Ryan stares me down.

"Oh, dude."

"Really, I did?"

"Oh yeah, you did."

"I don't remember doing that."

"That's because I paraphrased and cleaned up the language."

"You cleaned up the language?"

"Not on the note, dude. Now. Just in summarizing for you now, what you wrote in your note. You told it too much like it was. You went totally gonzo, dude. The doctor would be proud."

"Which doctor?"

He just looks at me and shakes his head.

"Never mind."

He picks up the guitar. He looks at it for a moment.

"Take care of him," he mumbles as he hands it to me.

It takes me a minute before I understand he was talking to the guitar about me and not to me about the guitar. Or so I think.

We work on the first strumming pattern, using the first song's first note, a C. We do that for a while, a long while. He keeps it light. He keeps it simple.

He tells me about the folk players' secret of learning a few chords, then learning a few strum patterns, and then learning a few tempos, and then working up to speed. He regales me with stories about music and musicians and rockabilly history. I talk about flying and drawing and trying to brew beer in the garage. We don't talk about work or Tami or Woo.

I get lost in the chords and let go of how bad I am. I'm drawn to the wood and the sound, the tone of this little acoustic, and how the sound of each strum is its own reward.

I keep telling myself that, and I feel I am becoming a wealthy man. Even the buzzes seem okay. I don't care that I still suck. It's okay when I play slow. I know from reading his book that Duggie would say, "It's all irie, mon." I'm making a little progress, but I don't think about it. I just listen and marvel at the tone and the wood and wonder how it all comes together, the sound and the feel of this guitar.

The sound carries me through the day, through the next day, and into my session with the Sasquatch shrink. I settle into the rocker. I like this chair. I'm feelin' irie.

Sasquatch studies me in silence.

"What?"

He leans forward.

"Hmm. Interesting."

"What?"

He taps on a folder. "Says in here, your test results, says in here you have serious women issues."

I shake my head. "No."

"Oh yeah."

"No. Not a chance. Not really."

"Oh yeah. Big time. It says so right here."

"It says what right there?"

"Says here, you are hung up on beautiful, sensuous women even though just looking at them makes you feel totally inadequate and worthless most of the time."

"Oh, no way! That is such bullshit! How can you get any of that out of some bullshit test from questions about tying shoelaces and . . . and . . . whether or not you like playing with fire or drinking orange juice and all that other crazy shit? Fuck that test! How can you get anything like that out of that bullshit test?"

"Oh, you'd be amazed."

I can hardly breathe.

"Seriously?"

"Yeah, that's right. . . . No." He grins. "I'm just pulling your chain, eh. I add that part to all my patients just to get a reaction. Yours was a beaut. So, let's say we talk about your women issues for a while."

Oh, holy shit no!

I'm exhausted and out of breath.

"I don't have any women issues," I mumble through clenched teeth.

Oh, yeah. That oughta convince him real good.

"I see. Is that your legal opinion? Cuz, you know, 'round here, there's no place for that. Just sayin', eh. Anyway, we'll get back to that."

He leans forward again. I hate it when he does that, and he just stares at me some more.

"You don't look like the violent type to me, eh."

"Thank God. By the way, Doc, you said that last time."

He holds up the folder.

"Hey, like I know what I said. You don't have to remind me, eh. The test profiles paint a different picture."

"That I'm the violent type, right?"

"Not exactly. More like the ranting type."

No argument there.

"I'll bet you already knew that, eh. The risk of violence is low, but without some changes in your coping skills, you may become the violent type. You have some significant self-esteem and anger issues stemming from your childhood generally and your father— the Coach, in particular. Like destructive criticism from a parent figure in childhood is some dangerous shit, eh."

He swivels his chair, grunts as he bends down, reaches under his desk, and pulls a bottle of Bull Moose Lager out of a cardboard box that, as it turns out, is a case of beer. He holds the bottle in front of me.

"This is you, eh." He shakes the bottle. "This is you at work, eh. Pressure, pressure, always more pressure. Sooner or later, like this bottle if I keep shaking it, eh, you blow your top."

He bends over again, grunting again, opens the door to the small refrigerator under his desk and puts the bottle inside.

"Here's another one for you. You're a square-peg guy, and everybody's been round-holing you your whole life. So much so, you're doing it to yourself now. Then one day, the fear of dying wakes you up and you begin to question whether you belong in a round hole."

I'm not feelin' so irie anymore. I stare at his minifridge. I want booze. I want some of that frozen concoction that's supposed to help me hang on. I want better living through chemistry. I want an ice-cold bottle of that Bull Moose Lager.

"Why not, eh?"

Sasquatch does another bend and grunt and retrieves two bottles of Bull Moose from his minifridge. He puts one in each hand and then flicks the caps off with his thumbs. He hands one of the bottles to me. It's ice cold.

"Cheers," he says.

It's delicious. God, can the Canucks brew beer.

"What did you want to be, back in the sixth grade, when you grew up?"

"I don't remember wanting to be anything back then. Besides I'm somebody else now."

"Oh, like that phone basher, eh?"

"No."

He stares at me.

"Let's work on remembering back then. We were talking about Coach last session. Let's start there, eh?"

I start there. I tell him about the time Coach took my student acoustic guitar—the one my hero Tim Seville had given me—and threw it into the street just as the punk hot-rodder from two blocks over, that asshole Leonard Jackson, raced down the street and ran over it. All that just because I was trying so hard to learn to play the F major chord instead of throwing a ball against the garage wall and pretending that I was fielding ground balls at second base for the Orioles.

I tell him I never liked the Orioles. I tell him about Tim Seville, all that I can remember. I tell him how cool he was, the older brother of one of my sixth-grade classmates. He was always fixing things around the house for his mother. He was always nice to me. Tim would let me and his little brother hang out with him. Tim was learning to play guitar then. He even taught me a chord or two. I had forgotten those days. Now that I remember them, I miss them. A lot.

I tell Sasquatch how Tim's dad went back to war, somewhere in Southeast Asia, leaving Tim in charge. Tim's dad was a US Air Force pilot. He got shot down and rescued twice, over Laos or Cambodia. He made major and came home a lieutenant colonel. I never met him. I got the news of the transfer to Nellis AFB when the family moved to Nevada to join him.

I tell Sasquatch that I never saw Tim again. I no longer have the note he had written, the one explaining why he was giving me some of his record albums that he knew I liked. He wrote the records would help me through my hard times, as they had helped him. He was also giving me his guitar. It was a cheap kind of student model. He gave it to me because he thought I'd like to have it and because his dad had promised him a new one when they got to Vegas.

It pisses me off remembering how so much important stuff tends to get lost when you move around a lot, especially the good stuff—stuff you want to keep if only you could remember to keep it.

Sasquatch listens and scribbles. We drink another Bull Moose in Tim's honor. I think I like this shrink.

Sasquatch asks, so I tell him about Woo's challenge to get a hobby and Shelley Lynne suggesting I take up guitar and that she doesn't know anything about Tim Seville or my sixth-grade summer of maybe twenty days of heaven and all the hell that followed or that I tried guitar once before. No reason to. It's all new now, and I can share this newness with her and let the past go, except when Sasquatch brings it all back.

Sasquatch listens and scribbles. And then I'm telling him about Woo's hoedown, and the house band, and my shortness of breath, and the light show in my eyes when I'm stressed and anxious, and that makes him stop scribbling.

I answer his questions, he scribbles, and then he looks something up in a thick book and says it might be "migraine aura" and that I need to make an appointment with my doctor and get a referral to an ophthalmologist. He scribbles some more, and our session is over. But I don't want to get out of the chair. I do it anyway. He hands me another appointment card.

Somewhere on the way out, I stop in a hallway and lean against the wall. I close my eyes. I think of Tim strumming something, something he had taught himself. He was pleased, and he was enjoying showing his brother and me. I keep thinking of it until I'm almost reliving it, hearing the sound of his playing.

The sound carries me out of the building. The sound carries me through more days. Somewhere in the mix of days of laying low, between the strumming sessions, I start writing stuff down, lines like lyrics or poetry maybe. Things come to me, and I write them down, images and sketches in words. They keep me going as I struggle to learn to make those sounds for myself.

I think of Tami. I think of what she said about why someone else was promoted and why, in her mind, she wasn't, and I think she said *pig* at one point or maybe it was *men are pigs*. All that mishmash leads me to thinking about bosses and hogs, and I keep writing, I keep writing the images that come to mind. I keep sketching with words.

That remembered or imagined sound I've come to cherish carries me through the medical appointments.

Turns out I suffer migraine auras, and I am totally down with that. If you have to suffer migraines, trust me, this is the bomb. There is no pain. My light show is black and white. The darkest coal blacks and most brilliant whites you can imagine. Usually it's a black-and-yellow halo that people suffering these events experience. But mine consist of expanding crescents of triangular shards of these blacks and whites that flash like gunshots.

No wonder I can't read when the surprise attack comes. I can generally see okay when they go off. Most of the time. These attacks always start in the periphery and slowly expand and move to the center of my visual field. They last anywhere from a few minutes to thirty minutes or more. All I can do is sit back, pretend to relax, make myself breathe, and enjoy the monochromatic kaleidoscope of fireworks in my head. No big deal.

The ophthalmologist is kind and quite patient—considerate, even—answering my questions and explaining that I could never be a pilot now. The news still hurts, sure, but maybe I'm too old for that anyway. There's a lesson to be learned from this, and I should have finished that goal years ago instead of putting it off like so many other things. It won't stop me from learning the guitar, so that's all the more reason to press on. I won't be putting that off anymore.

• ✦✦✦ •

The remembered or imagined sound I've come to cherish carries me through two more rehearsal sessions.

For some reason, Robby's taken to calling me Sky King and sometimes Sky Pilot, laughing that I'll never ever touch the sky. What? Because I look up at the sky now and then?

Fuck him.

Danny calls me the Bard because he thinks there are songs stuffed in my writing and all they need is music to set them free.

Ryan agrees. I'm not so sure. I think they're either conning me for some reason or just being nice. Who knows? They ask to look at my stuff, so I show them all I've written. All this carries me through the rest of the week and the weather's changes that heralds Woo's Halloween barbeque party hoedown.

The autumn air feels so crisp, and the sky turns gray with heavy stratus clouds that anchor against the ridge of the mountain behind the hoedown barn at Granny Smith's Farm. I watch the mist tumble over the ridgeline.

"So whataya think, dude? Good flying weather?" Ryan says, pretending to needle me.

I look up and admire the overcast's low ceiling.

"Maybe for some pattern work or a few touch and goes back in the valley right over the airfield, probably. Up here, probably not. Definitely not."

"Right on. Think you'll ever go back to it?"

"I try not to think about it."

I haven't told him about the migraine auras.

"Well, it's all good. You got another hobby now, dude. Think you're going to like this one more as time goes by. Let it be, and you'll be feeling fine."

"I feel fine now."

"That's the spirit, dude."

"Sky King staring up at the clouds again?" Robby calls out, hauling his guitar case out of his trunk.

I just smile and let it go.

Robby starts walking toward us.

"You boys waiting on me, huh? Sorry I'm late. I had to run an errand."

I suppose that means he ran out of booze. I catch Ryan looking at me.

"Don't go there, dude."

"What?"

"What? You know what. Stop tweeting your thoughts across the universe."

"Am I late?" Robby asks.

There's a boozy-lookin' grin on his face.

"No, dude, you're good. We're all good."

Robby passes me without a word.

"Robby!" Woo yells. "Where you been? Party's not a party without you leading the band!"

Woo ushers Robby into the barn.

"Hey, everyone! Robby's here!" he hollers out to cheers.

Must be something in the cider. I follow.

"You ready?" Ryan asks.

"I was until you asked me if I was ready."

I feel my guts start to knot up. My hands are clammy. My vision blurs a little. I focus on breathing like pretty much everybody's been telling me to do.

A fair-sized crowd has gathered around the stage, and Danny's in his element as unofficial emcee and bandleader. Robby stumbles a bit getting onto the stage. Woo's right there to steady him, and nobody else seems to notice or care.

I see Woo nod to Danny, and he announces me as the newest member of the band and Ryan's favorite shadow. There's some laughter following that comment, and I follow Ryan onto the stage. I'm looking down as I move, making sure not to trip. We gear up. and I head to a stool in the back. But Danny grabs it and moves it up front. He looks back at me with a devilish sort of grin. With a flick of his head, he summons me forward. I move up.

"You're ready, right?"

I just nod and sit on the stool and prop my left leg up and balance the waist of the little acoustic across my thigh. The golden hue of the soundboard in this fading light makes it look so earthy, and the strings glisten. Just noticing these things makes me feel better. I'm vaguely aware that Danny's said something—I have no idea what—there's some laughter and some cheers, and who knows what else. I don't give a rip.

They can all go to hell.

I hear Ryan's bass rumble. It's my cue to start strumming a C. I stare at the fretboard and will my fingers to move. I start strumming. It isn't long before I feel myself falling behind so I focus on strumming the first and last chords only and that seems to help. Robby's solo pleases the crowd, and that helps the most, and then the song's over.

Rockabilly songs are simple, fun, and short. And fast. Deceptively fast. As in "holy shit" fast. Okay, maybe not as fast as bluegrass or that other Irish and Scot stuff that came out of the same hidden hollers in in eastern Tennessee and Kentucky or West Virginia, all that rugged Appalachian Country, that even the US Postal Service still can't find to this day.

Of course, it stands to figure such places were only natural for those same people with their passion for distilled spirits, independent-minded spirit and all, and especially their rabid hatred for any authority in general and government authority most in particular, to roll up them sleeves and get downright serious about moonshinin'. No doubt that's probably the main reason all that area's music is so incredibly fast is they were lit up with moonshine when they made it. The music and the moonshine—anybody's who ever braved a sip a shine can certainly vouch from the taste a th' stuff that it ain't all that far removed from pure gasoline. Ain't no way anyone on crack could ever compete. Not that I would ever know. But I digress.

I've also read somewhere that rockabilly became rock 'n' roll, which makes it real good music for a party. And boy howdy, we have got ourselves a party. I look up and catch my breath. I have to remember to breathe. Everyone's having a good time, and nobody seems particularly interested in me.

Thank God.

I can smell sweet cider and barbeque sauce, and it's all so wonderful, and I'm praying to get through these next two rockabilly songs and then get the hell out of Dodge.

<h1 style="text-align:center">Chapter 19</h1>

I'm sweating up a storm and then the second song is done and then the third, and I'm about to pass out, I'm so exhausted and relieved. I don't see Woo step up to the microphone. But I hear his voice and he's revving up the crowd's applause for the band, that's cool, and then he says he's thrilled that I'm playing a solo, a new song that I wrote myself called "Pound Sand," and that he hopes the lyrics are clean enough for a family show. That gets a laugh.

I'm blinded by a spotlight. Woo moves the microphone stand in front of me.

"Paul Cooper, ladies and gentlemen!" He covers the microphone with his hand and gets into my face. "Pound sand, Paul."

Screw it.

I play a D, then a C, and then a G because, at this moment, that is the easiest order for me to change between those chords.

Hey, if it can work for the rock 'n' roll gods, it's good enough for me.

I play slow—real slow—because I can't play any other way than real slow, mon.

Starting with that D, I strum down so each string sounds individually, and then the sounds blend together at the end. Then I do part of the strumming pattern from the first song, the down-up-down part, because it's the only part I can do right. It comes out in a sort of loping, dum-de-dum kind of sound, and the sound has a nice rolling quality.

Then I switch to C and do it again. When I strum the G, I hit it hard, just two down strums—dum, dum—and yell out, "Pound sand!" Somebody laughs. I do this a couple times and then find the lyrics in my head.

Strumming a D, I sing out, "Has yo' silly o' boss man got you down?"—switch to C—"then you better come around and tell him to"—strum G—"pound sand! Has your ol' lady got you down? Down on the ground? Better come around and tell her tuh pound sand!"

Now it's getting fun, and I drag out the word *sand*. I'm getting brave, and I know that's a dangerous thing. Woo is fuming. Danny's smiling and shaking his head, Ryan's bug-eyed, and Darryl is laughing his ass off.

Good times!

"Get religion, all my lonely people, wherever you come from," I mumble into the mike, pretending I'm like some crazy-ass folk singer—maybe with some curly hair and a harmonica—because I feel like I've lost everything.

And when you lose everything, religion is the only thing left they can't take away. Any folk singer or country singer worth a salty damn knows that.

"Sing the chorus with me, all you lonely people. It's only got two words. Perfect for a protest, maybe even a rally. Maybe even a Halloween hoedown."

There's raucous laughter, and it's okay that there are just as many who are laughing at me as opposed to those who are laughing at my joke, and I'm amazed that a lot of them do sing along.

Oh, well. What the hell.

Who knew, right? Okay, it's probably the spiked cider, I get that, but they're loud little heathens.

Yeah. They're loud and they're having fun, and sometimes that's the best kind of protest you can hope for to wake people up to the stupidity that surrounds them. And the microphone goes dead, and the spotlight goes out, and a good chunk of the crowd goes, "No!" They grumble, and I figure I'm home free. Free at last.

And then some kid, maybe my first fan, asks me to play "Three Blind Mice."

Three Blind Mice?

Woo eggs her on, sweet little girl, can't be more than ten or eleven, maybe eight? I can't tell. But she's adorable.

"Sweetheart, I don't know that one. I just make up protest songs when I need to," I tell her.

Someone in the crowd laughs. I think it's Darryl.

"It's easy. I'll show you," she says.

Woo helps her on stage. The lights come back up, the microphone comes back on, and she shows me. She plays the song, and she's damn good. She's fearless. I don't remember ever being fearless in my whole life.

She gives the guitar back to me and insists I try it. Woo insists I try it. I try it, and I fail miserably. I'm buzzing strings. I can't keep the time. I have no idea what I'm doing wrong. There's something odd about this lil' kiddie diddie of a song, but for the life of me, I have no idea what it is.

"Oh my god, Paul! That's terrible! You're really not any good, are you? Try that again."

I try it again. Damn. I'm getting worse.

"That's not 'Three Blind Mice,' is it? It certainly doesn't sound like it. That sounds terrible. Doesn't that sound terrible? You're choking on a children's song! I should think you'd be totally embarrassed to play like that in public."

"Oh, I am. Totally."

"Well, I should say so."

Love it. Dumbass Woo thinks I'm serious. Not even. The little girl thinks it's funny. It *is* funny. Hell, it's hysterical. But she's so adorable, and her laughter is so sweet. I ask her to show me again. She loves that idea, and she shows me again. She's having a blast and so am I.

I notice Danny, and I give him a wink. He raises his glass and nods. He's smiling. I try it again, and this time, I go with my strengths, which in this case are all the defects in how I play, so I exaggerate them.

The little girl goes nuts.

"No-ohh! Not like that! Like this!" she laughs.

I give her back the guitar, and she nails it, again. I want to be that age again.

"Ohhhh! Like that! I get it, now! Silly me. Let me try it again."

I fumble it up, although I am actually trying this time to do it right, but there's something I'm still not getting, and I'm totally okay with it. It's like part of the song seems to speed up or something. I can't tell what it is.

She tells me I did a little better but not much. I thank her for her help. She says I need lots of help very badly, and it's at that point that she gets promptly carted off by her mother. I think it's her mother.

I stand up and put Ryan's little acoustic back in its case. Danny's made his way to the microphone and rouses the rest of the band into some rock 'n' roll. Everybody's happy. I'm ecstatic.

I come off the stage and see Tami at the back by the door. She's not ecstatic. She's standing there, leaning against the doorjamb, her folded arms tight across her chest. She's standing with all her weight on one shapely leg wrapped tightly in denim, the fabric tucked neatly into calf-high, black leather boots that match her turtleneck sweater. Her other leg angles outward, pivoting on the heel of her boot. Her sculptured eyebrows have the slightest of furrows. Her bountiful lips are pursed thin.

Holy shit she's hot.

She wants to chew me out so bad, I just know it, but I'm not having it. I'm feeling quite good—irie, in fact. So I tell her the one thing that will send her running.

"Hi, babe! You look *so* hot tonight. I'm glad you made it."

That works. Without a word, she spins and strolls out into the darkness. How apropos. It's the place where most ambushes await.

I'm not going into that darkness. I'm going to stick around here a bit longer.

I'm hungry. I get in line for food. It's nearly gone now, and the Granny Smith kid serving up the tri-tip looks bored. He has no idea how lucky he is. I thank him, he gives me a blank look and grunts, and I step aside and start to eat.

There's a meaty blues riff pumping over the sound system, and it's soul stirringly good. Danny's voice is low and growly, and I recognize my lyrics. The band's put my words to music.

> So they called you in, out of the blue
> Decision's been made, and it ain't you
> You had no way a knowin' at your interview
> Little Miss Bubblehead was already chosen.
>
> It just doesn't matter how well you do
> You won't be promoted cuz the job ain't for you
> You're a spot of grease for the grindin' wheel
> Makes no difference what you think or feel
>
> Only a bubblehead can make the boss hog squeal.

Right on cue, Robby rips into a wailing squeal of high notes on the B and high E strings. He's all swagger, piss and venom; and I swear everything that's ever pissed him off in his life is flying out of his fingers, fretting and bending those strings, and the little crowd remaining is on their feet and rocking out.

Woo looks catatonic.

I'm thinking this hobby thing ain't such a bad idea after all. I'm thinking now's a good time to leave. So I do. I walk the mile or so back to Ryan's house alone. The cold breeze is invigorating. I won't even mind if it rains. All the more reason to heat up some cider when I get there.

◆◆◆◆◆

I have a pleasant couple of days for a change. Work eases up, and I swing by my house for replenishment. Tami's waiting. This won't be good.

"Woo must think you're an idiot. That was Woo, right? The one who said you choked on a children's song?"

"Yep."

"This is how you handle a setback in your career, Paul? You choke on a children's song? This is your idea of being a professional?"

She doesn't wait for an answer. That's cool with me because it means I don't have to come up with one.

"The damage is done. Paul, you were so embarrassing up there. Everybody was laughing at you. Why should anyone take you seriously now? You need to do something. Seriously, Paul, what are you going to do about this?"

I rub my chin. I nod. I mull it over.

"Yeah, I know. I'm thinking, you know, maybe practice more and choke less."

Tami's face flushes, her cheeks glowing redder than her lip gloss. It's a very enticing look for her.

Tami shakes her head and wags an index finger in my face. "This is not funny, Paul."

"Nope. It's not. It's serious stuff. I agree."

She glares at me.

"Are you—you're mocking me?" she asks, her voice dropping to a near whisper. "You have no idea, do you? You made a complete ass of yourself in front of everyone you work with."

"I don't care."

"You should care. But you won't. Go ahead. Practice all you want. It won't help. Innate musical ability can't be learned. You have no talent. No sense of rhythm whatsoever. What part of that do you not understand? That little girl? She's got talent. Shelley Lynne? Yeah, she's got talent. Real talent. In spades, Paul. And you? Zilch. You have no talent. None at all. Unless you count making a complete ass of yourself in public a talent. You obviously can't do anything else. You're just so pathetic."

"Says you. Fair enough."

"You're just being stubborn. I swear, you are worse than a child."

"Fair enough."

Tami sighs.

"Look, you've had your fun, Paul. Where did it get you? You're the laughingstock of your office. You let them make you some kind of clown. No more. I'm telling you it's over. It's time you move on. It's time to become a judge."

My turn to sigh.

"We've been through this already. I do not want to become a judge."

"Oh? Then you had better start wanting it. You obviously have no future where you're at."

I turn away.

"Look at me, Paul! You are running out of choices! You are running out of time!" She puts her hand on her chest, just below her throat. "What about me, Paul? I am so running out of patience. Can't you see that?"

I know better than to take that bait.

She takes a deep breath and looks down as she exhales.

"Please understand. I want something better for you, Paul. I want something better," she says, looking up at me again. "For us."

I must be an idiot, like Coach always said. I'm hearing hope. I haven't heard that in a while. I'm hearing a voice in my head tell me she's playing the hope card and I need to cut her off right now and be honest and tell her the judge thing ain't happening—not now, not ever. But I want her so bad, so I can't do that.

"Paul, I need you to become a judge," she says, ever so softly.

"Okay. Fine. I'll start working on that," I force myself to say it.

I'm about to choke.

"And stop all this hobby nonsense."

"No. This"—I struggle to get the words out—"is something I can share with our daughter. So no."

She's thinking, her lips are pursed. She goes to the refrigerator and takes out a bottle of Chardonnay. I take a glass from the cupboard and give it to her.

"All right. But only as long as you make becoming a judge the priority."

"Fair enough," I hear myself say, and I hear a voice in my head tell me I'm pussy whipped.

She sits down and sips wine. I sit down next to her.

"Do you mind?"

"Tami, I want to be with you."

She takes another sip.

"Paul, we're not kids anymore. Okay? Just"—she pauses—"give it a rest."

"So? What's age got to do with it? I love you, Tami. I want to make love to you."

Wow! I actually said that.

I'm more nervous and excited now than I was the first time she said it was really going to happen.

She looks down and closes her eyes. There's a slight shake of her head.

"I said I'd work on becoming a judge. You win. I'm giving you what you want."

"You're not giving me anything yet."

"Don't do that. Please. It's been months."

"No, Paul. You knew what you were getting into when we got married, and I told you over and over how I felt about sex and about what I needed from you and what I could give you in return, and I . . . I never asked you to adopt Shelley Lynne. You did that all on your own. Yes, I am grateful, and she adores you. But that has nothing to do with us. As for us, well . . ." her voice trails off.

"I keep hoping."

"I know you do, and I never should have left that door open. I'm sorry I did."

"Is there someone else?"

She scowls.

"Someone else? No! There will never be anyone else as long as I live."

"Then you do love me."

She lets out a heavy sigh.

"In my own way, yes. But in my own way, Paul!"

I shrug. All these years, and I still have no idea what that means. I don't know what else to do.

"Fair enough," I say.

I don't know what else to say.

"Fair?" She pours herself another glass of wine. "Really, Paul? How would you know what's fair? You leave me a note that says your job's in the toilet, and then I don't hear from you for nearly a week."

She takes a drink and then another.

"Now you diddy bop on back here and dare to ask me to lie down with you and give up my body to you? I can't believe you!"

She refills her glass.

"And taking my pain and putting it into some stupid song. What the hell's wrong with you? That's just mean."

She looks at her glass.

"It's been a long, bad week for both of us, Paul. Let it go, please."

She takes another drink, leans back, and closes her eyes. It's only then I realize how tired she looks. I have no idea what she's thinking and she's in no mood to talk, but on the bright side, at least we're not arguing. I don't want to see one start, and one surely will if I seek to continue the conversation.

"Okay," I say, and I get up. "You're right. I'm sorry. I need to be more thoughtful."

Bullshit.

Off I go to the guestroom. I know the drill. It's only then I realize how tired I am, but I can't sleep.

I lay there and read random pages from the Duggie book. Lingering over the wise words of the maestro of mellow helps me let go of my loneliness and my longings until I'm feeling a sense of gratefulness and find myself swimming in memories of better times.

✦✦✦✦✦

I fall asleep feelin' irie. I wake up still feelin' irie. I show up at Sasquatch the Shrink's office for my next appointment, and I'm still feelin' irie, which makes me feel even more irie. I settle into the rocker.

Fuck it. I like this chair.

Sasquatch the Shrink studies me in silence.

"What?"

"Are you a wimp?"

"Am I a wimp?"

"That's what I said. That's my question. I didn't ask you if you were deaf, eh, I know you can hear me. I asked you if you were a wimp. That's my question. Are you a wimp?"

"Uh, no. Not exactly. No. I mean, well, maybe sometimes. No."

"You hesitated. Now you can't make up your mind. You know what that means, eh? That means you are a wimp. Unless you're bashing phones, eh? Then you're a phone basher. A phone-bashing wimp."

I shrug, and I sigh.

"I am not a wimp," I say.

"Says the phone-bashing wimp slouching in the rocking chair, shoulders sagging, hunched over like an dying old man wimp. Your body language says 'look at me, I'm a wimp,' eh. Even the tone of your voice—it says it too."

"Fine. I'm a wimp."

"No, you're not."

"Then what the hell did you say I was for?"

"Ah, see that anger rising right there? Feel that? No wimp in there, eh? You're like some bull in a pasture and then you get pissed off and then you're the raging bull, eh? Chasing people down the street like they do in Pamplona."

He stares. He looks down and scribbles. He looks up at me again and stares.

"Who are you, eh?"

Don't want to go there because I'm not sure I even know.

"Where are we going with this?" I ask.

"To the ice rink." He stands up.

"Excuse me?"

"Oh, there you go again with the deaf thing, eh, what's up with that? Get up, eh? I told you. We're going to the ice rink. Man you up once and for all."

"Are you nuts?"

Sasquatch the Shrink gives me a look. Instinctively I look at his hands. No ax. Thank God. No ax. I know it's gotta be huge.

"Okay, sorry. Bad choice of words. I'm the one that's nuts, not you."

"You're not nuts because you can't be nuts because you don't have any nuts to be nuts with. We're gonna get you some nuts, eh. Man you up. Give you back what the Coach took away."

"Okay, so setting aside for a moment all of the psychobabble bullshit so colloquially expressed, what exactly are we doing?"

"Put you on the ice and keep you there until you finally grow a pair."

"You know, I'm really getting tired of hearing that. It just so happens, I'll have you know, that I do have a pair actually. It's just that . . . I never get to use them much."

"Oh? Well, then. You're gonna get to use them now, eh."

"On ice? This makes no sense at all. Do you have any idea how lame this sounds?"

"Do you have any idea how lame you sound when you talk like a wimp?"

"I can't ice-skate!"

He laughs.

"Oh! That's a good one right there, eh? No shit you can't skate. Well, we're gonna change all that. Make you skate and man you up. That's two birds with one stone right there and all at the county rate, eh?"

"Dr. McGee, seriously. Stop. Please. This is a really bad idea."

"Oh, listen to you, eh? Whimper, whimper. You know, it's a long walk to Riverside from here, but I could use a little workout. How about it, Wimpy? You want to get in the car or do you want me to sling you over my shoulder and hoof it, prairie style?"

"Can't we talk about this?"

"No, I don't think so."

He reaches for me with one of his man paws.

"Fine. I'll get in the car."

Chapter 20

The ice rink is cold.

Duh.

Should have seen that one coming. Some hockey team is practicing. Some goon body checks another player into the Plexiglas, and it sounds like an explosion. I flinch. Sasquatch the Shrink lets out a roar. I flinch again.

Fuck this!

Then he yells something in hockey-speak. The players on the bench rattle and bang their sticks and cheer and call out his name.

Holy shit! They know this guy?

Then it dawns on me, that painting in the office? It's *him.*

He motions to a trainer, I think, who comes over.

Sasquatch points at me and tells the trainer, "Here's a fresh egg for you, eh. Dress him up and put him in the pan."

He turns to me.

"That means he's gonna put you in skates, and he knows you've never been on the ice. Just do what he says. I'll meet you out on the ice."

I'm in hockey skates, gloves, and all padded up, thank God, and standing next to a gate at the far end of the ice away from the practicing players. Thank God. Sure enough, my worst fears are confirmed when Sasquatch the Hockey Shrink comes flying down the ice from the practice area in a bright red-and-white jersey that looks like the Canadian flag. He slides to an immediate stop just before I think he's about to crash into the gate—of course, he doesn't.

I instinctively flinch. Flinching causes me to lose my balance, and I fall. Sasquatch reaches over the gate and picks me up. I dangle from one of his man paws, and he swings open the gate and pulls me through. The only reason I can't scream is that I managed to knock the wind out of myself.

"Relax, eh?"

He smacks me on the back, and I'm breathing again sorta. He lowers me down so the skate blades touch the ice.

"Okay, I want you to stomp the ice, straight down, with the left blade. Give that a try, eh?"

I do. I feel the blade slip a bit.

"Again."

I do. This time I feel the ice bite.

"Good. Now let go with your left arm and put it on my right forearm and grab the bend in my arm at the elbow."

I do so, and I feel him cradle my elbow with his hand.

"Good."

He lets go of my other arm and positions his arm, and I rest my arm on his and I feel him cradle my other elbow.

"Good. Now I want you to relax. With your right leg, open your stance a bit more, just a little wider than your shoulders, and stomp your right blade straight down into the ice a few times. Give that a try, eh?"

I do.

"Good. Now relax. Breathe. Close your eyes. Flex your knees a bit and feel your butt balance between the blades until you can feel the blades are not moving on their own. Try that."

I have no idea what I am trying to do.

"It may seem awkward at first. That's okay. Trust me, eh. I've got a hold of you and you are fine. Stop holding your breath."

I start breathing.

"That's it. Feel that balance point right there, eh. That's good. Now keep your legs as they are, keep your boots level, and now let your weight shift more to the left blade without leaning the blade. That's good. Now shift back to the center, weight even on both legs, eh. That's good. Now shift more weight to the right blade in the same way. Like that. That's good."

I stiffen up.

"Relax, eh. If you feel the balance shift, then move your weight to get the balance point back underneath you, eh. Always underneath you."

"Okay," I hardly speak.

"I'm proud of you, Paul. You're showing me some real guts right here, eh. It's tough for a tall man at your age getting his first time on the ice."

I keep trying to feel the balance.

"Paul, it's no different than being on a slippery floor. You've done that before, eh?"

"Yeah."

"Then it's no different from that, eh. It feels the same to your brain. Let it feel the same."

"Okay."

"That's it, like that, eh. Now ease up on your grip, let your arms rest on my arms, and let go with your hands. Keep breathing, eh. That's better."

We do the foot stomp drill for a while. I have no idea how long. I feel like we're moving, I feel his arms moving. I hear faint scraping sounds.

"Are we moving? Dr. McGee, are we moving?"

"Relax, eh? You tell me."

I open my eyes, but all I can see is a big ass maple leaf.

"Close your eyes, eh, no cheating. Feel for your balance, eh. If you feel like you're moving, then you're moving. Keep your boots level, keep your weight and balance centered directly under you. At all times. The longer you can keep your eyes closed, the sooner you will get the feel of this, eh."

"Okay." I let out a deep exhale.

"Oh, that's some good courage breathing right there, eh. Good for you, Paul. I'm proud of you."

For an instant, the words sound so good. Yeah, right. I know it's a load of crap. But still . . .

"Hey, no negative thinking allowed, eh? I saw that. That little eyebrow thing you did just then. None of that, eh? I say what I mean, and I mean what I say. You're on the ice now, eh. Start believing in yourself."

"Okay."

"Good. When you feel yourself moving, feel the direction and shift your weight if you need to and keep your balance. Call out the direction, forward, backward, got it?"

"Yeah."

"Okay, then. Talk to me, eh."

I breathe deep. I shift, leaning more toward the balls of my feet.

"Forward."

"Good."

I feel my legs move back.

"We're stopping." I feel the shift and pull my feet back. "Backward."

"Good. You're doing great, Paul. Keep it up."

I have no idea how long I've been doing this. Maybe five minutes? It feels like a month. Make it all stop. Just hang on, do whatever makes him happy until it stops.

"Okay. Open your eyes. Reach out for the wall with your right hand. Good. Now, keep your boots level, just walk off the ice, eh. Sit down there and put the blade guards on."

He joins me on the bench.

"You did just fine out there, Paul. When you're ready, stand up and pay attention to your balance. Keep the palm of one hand sliding along the wall and walk back to the locker room. Take a seat at the first bench, then take off the skates."

"Okay. Where are you going?"

"To the locker room, eh. Same place as you. You don't need me for this Paul. Trust yourself."

He gets up and leaves.

Another deep breath, and I follow. But I can't keep up. I eventually make it back to the locker room. I'm thrilled to get the skates off. I'm drenched in sweat, and I'm freezing.

Dr. McGee turns up the heat for my benefit on the drive back to his office. Neither of us talks. He gives me another appointment card and a note when he parks.

"Here's a list of some videos posted on the internet. They're like home movies, young hockey players learning to skate. Watch a few. Pretend you're watching yourself, eh. Pretend you're watching your hero Tim. Then imagine you're twelve again and trying out for the team, eh. Imagine Tim's helping you."

"I will do that," I say.

No, I won't. It sounds hokey as hell.

"Good. See you next session. Bring a change of clothes too. We'll be on the ice. You'll shower afterward."

I look at the appointment card. Yep. Sure enough, it says the appointment is at the ice rink.

Cue heavy sigh.

"Okay."

"Good. Good session back there, eh. I'm proud of you, Paul."

"Thanks."

Whatever it takes.

"Paul!"

"What?"

"The world's plenty full of people who give up their lives chasing after the approval of others, eh. As long as you're going to insist on being one of them, be careful whose approval you choose."

I nod. He waves and drives off.

I get in my car and crank up the heat. I drive home feeling dazed and confused.

I show up at my shithole office, and I'm still feeling dazed and confused. There's a lunch-sized paper bag on my chair. The bag is neatly folded at the top where a yellow, sticky-note rests.

The handwritten note says, "You're welcome."

I hang up my jacket and peek into the bag. There's a new DVD in there. The price tag's been peeled away, and there's some smiling kids holding guitars on the cover of *Having Fun with Your New Guitar: Easy Basics for Beginners.*

I smile and mutter, "I suck so bad. Please, God, let this work."

"He will, dude," Ryan said, leaning in from the doorway.

"Oh, I sure hope so. By the way, what do I owe you for this?"

"Nothing. It's on me, as long as you promise to use it and stick with it."

"I think I can do that."

"Every day at lunch, dude. Two lessons a week, no more than that. That and practice. Practice slowly. Every day, slowly."

"I can do that."

"Then you'll need this," he says, pulling a small, black case from behind the wall at the doorway. It looks familiar. "It's a loaner. I'm sorry about Bonnie Lee, but she's too thrashed, Paul. My luthier pal said 'no way.' My loaner comes with two nonnegotiable conditions precedent."

"Sure. Name it."

"First, leave it here in your office. Never take it home."

"Fair enough. What's the second?"

"That you practice for half an hour after work, before you leave here for the day."

"I can do that too."

"Deal?"

"Deal."

"Good deal. This way, you've got no problems at home. Buy yourself some peace, dude. Buy yourself some time."

"I can use a lot of both."

"Yes you do. For the next two weeks, thirty minutes at lunch and thirty minutes after work, and that's all. Just do that every workday for the next two weeks. Ten days—that's it, that's all. I'm tellin' ya, dude. Do not overdo this. I'm as serious as the heart attack you're headed for. You overdo this, and you kill the karma and any chance you'll ever have to rewire your hard, stubborn ass."

"Got it."

I'm wondering if he's been talking to Dr. McGee.

"Aces." Ryan moves to the door. He turns and looks at me as he steps through. "It's all up to you now, dude. Later."

"Later. And thanks!"

Ryan nods and closes the door behind him.

Now that I have committed to becoming a judge to make Tami happy, I suggest to her that we go to the upcoming bench-bar dinner and mixer. The thought makes me nauseous, but I do it anyway. Oh, the things we do for love, eh? If doing this makes her happy, then maybe I'll get to be happy too.

I'm still thinking how I will regret this when I hear her say "I'm ready," and then I hear the click of her heels as she strides into the room.

Holy shit.

I'll say she's ready. Oh lord, is she ever. I reach for my chin to find my tongue and put it away and make sure my mouth is closed. "You look beautiful clean to nice."

"What?"

She looks at me like I'm doped to the gills. Might as well be. That's what I get for thinking "you look beautiful tonight" while trying to say "you clean up nice" at about the same time.

From the high-heel, closed-toe pumps—are they satin?—in a lovely shade of lavender, up her shapely long legs to a satiny sleeveless white dress that begins just above her knees and flows into a tapered waist, caressing the curves of her body all the way to a rounded neckline that starts just inside the shoulders. She turns to pick up a clutch that matches her heels as the neckline ends in pleated folds at the small of her back. From the flow of her beribboned golden hair that wraps partway around her neck, to the light touch of makeup on her face, she is all radiance, elegance, and grace. The clutch and her hair ribbon match her shoes. She looks so wonderful, so beyond gorgeous tonight.

She is dressed to kill, and I'm bleeding out on the floor.

She'd make a great Roman goddess. Probably a mean one too—with dead guys everywhere. I'd be on the bottom of that pile. My mouth wide open. My tongue hanging out. Drenched in my own blood.

"Great," that's all I can say.

"Let's go. It won't look good to be late."

"Sure."

"I'll drive," she says, passing me.

"Sure," I say, staring and feasting with my eyes as long as I can, following her out to the car, thrilling at every sensuous swish of her butt and ponytail.

We gotta go to more of these damn dumb bar dinner things.

I enjoy following her with my eyes, and I'm sure every man and some women do too as we walk into the hotel lobby. We're guided toward the ballroom, make our way down the main hall, pass the Presidential Lounge, go around the concierge desk, check her coat, check in at the reception table for our event, and get our table assignment.

Already I can sense it. I'm invisible, and she is a lamp to the moths.

"Do you see anyone you know?" she whispers as we look for our table.

I attempt to be nonchalant as I look around without looking at anyone directly.

"No. Sorry."

"It's okay. It's early yet. Let's see. We're at table 9. There."

She leads. I follow. I will gladly follow her as wonderful as she looks from behind. I wish I could see just as much of her from the front. Not likely. I'll try not to think about it.

She moves around the table to a chair with a good view of the speaker's podium.

"I'll take this one."

I pull the chair out for her, and she accepts it like a throne. She releases the clasp on her clutch, opens it, and removes a small compact. She checks her eyes in the mirror—they're lovely—snaps it shut, and puts it back into the clutch. She takes her hand and puts it lightly atop one of my own, which is on the table because I have no idea where to put my hands except where I can't.

I feel paper. I realize she's pressing money against the back of my hand. I turn it over as she moves and accept the dollar bill. It's probably a twenty.

I don't know why I feel stupid. I never carry cash.

"Sweetheart, please get me a white wine—Chardonnay, if they have it. Leave a dollar for the tip. Put the change in your pocket."

I just smile and get up.

"Paul?"

I look down.

"Be friendly. Say hello to people you meet at the bar. It's important. Mingle a little. And smile, Paul."

I smile. I walk toward the bar.

Cue heavy sigh.

This night's gonna suck.

I take a breath, then another, and another. I look around, smile, and nod to a bunch of strangers who pay no attention to me whatsoever.

Fuck all y'all assholes!

I don't want to mingle. I don't want to be friendly. Everybody here must think I'm an idiot. I want to go home.

I see the bartender put a small black straw into a glass. It reminds me to suck it up; Tami is worth it. She's totally worth it. I'm not about to lose her. I don't give a fuck what deal we made. I'll take any deal as long I have her. I will gladly be pussy-whipped as long as it's her pussy that's whipping me.

I get in line and smile politely. No one is speaking, and that's fine with me. I get the wine. I get my change. I leave the tip. I get the hell out of the line. I make my way back to our table, hoping nobody bumps me, hoping I don't trip, hoping I don't spill the wine. Hoping I don't fuck up anything.

I have to move around tables and people because so many of these stupid people insist on standing in the middle of the only spaces you can walk between the tables instead of exercising simple common sense and stepping aside and leaving some aisle room so foot traffic can flow.

Fuck these people.

I brave the maze.

Keep calm and carry the wine on. I'm on a mission from God. I manage to deliver Tami her wine, and it's still relatively cold. I lean down and carefully set the glass down. The sigh lets itself out. Tami's eyebrows rise and then relax.

I expect her to say something; she's looking at me or is it through me? I hear a man's voice—a confident, assertive voice coming from behind me.

"Good evening, Paul."

Oh, great. Darryl's here. How much fucking worse can this evening get?

I straighten up and turn. He's already moved, so I stop.

Where the fuck did he go?

"Oh, Darryl! Good evening to you." We do the manly handshake thing. "Are you at our table?"

"I am now," he says with that great white grin.

"Oh, well then. Fair enough," I say, not knowing what else to say and making a clumsy gesture in Tami's direction. "Allow me to introduce myself—I mean, my wife, Tami."

Shit. Here we go.

Of course Tami has shifted about in her seat, an upward twist that thrusts her breasts out and up as well. I don't know if that's intended or merely incidental to the economy of her movement or the intensity of my horniness, and she is looking up and smiling at the ever dashing, debonair Darryl as I am sure he is no doubt thinking of himself. I won't let myself think of how he must be thinking of her.

"Tami, this is my new boss, Darryl Huntington."

"Nice to meet you," she says with practiced poise and deliberately wraps both of her hands around her wine glass.

Nice move.

"My pleasure." He points to her glass. "Something decent, I hope."

"I'll know in a moment."

"Of course," Darryl beams.

He studies her, glances at me, and looks at her once more before choosing a chair to my left—not my immediate left but over one—where he can sit directly across from her with the view of her that I want. I feel tense and keep wondering how much worse this evening can get, and Chrome Dome comes to mind. A waiter comes and pours water. I sip water carefully to avoid getting a mouthful of ice or pouring water and ice onto my chin. Another waiter appears, bringing two bottles of wine to the table, one white and one red.

Darryl grabs one and then the other and checks their labels.

"As I expected," he announced. "The house swill."

The waiter attempts to suppress a frown.

Darryl grins and reaches into his pocket.

"Go ahead and leave these," he says. "Don't get me wrong, they're quite drinkable, and I'm sure someone will want them."

He pulls a bill from his gold-plated money clip and hands the money to the waiter.

"Please bring us two bottles of"—he stops and turns to Tami—"Chardonnay, right?"

"Yes. It's fine, really."

"No doubt. But this is a special evening, and you, Mrs. Cooper, deserve so much better."

He turns back to the waiter.

"I want two bottles of Caillet Cellars, Chardonnay, Proprietor's Reserve, from Duane's private stock. Tell him it's for me, and make sure they are well chilled."

"Certainly, sir."

Well, it looks like he now owns the waiter. What else is he going to do?

Tami takes another sip of her merely drinkable Chardonnay.

"As you husband will attest, I am an excellent judge of fine Chardonnay, and I believe you will greatly appreciate the difference."

"I'm sure I will," she says and then turns to me.

I can't read her expression. I hate it when she does this.

I just shrug and say, "I so attest."

She offers a faint smile and sips more wine.

"Good lord! Will wonders never cease?"

The voice is Chrome Dome's, and I cringe.

Chapter 21

"Is that Darryl Huntington sitting at my table? *My* table? By God's grace, it is!"

I look, but I don't see his name card on the table either.

Chrome Dome walks over.

"Oh, please, don't get up on my account. This isn't my courtroom!" Chrome Dome laughs.

No one else does.

"Besides you just sat down and made yourself comfortable. I'm Corley O'Halloran, judge of the superior court in a neighboring county."

He switches his whiskey glass to his left hand, reaches out with his right, and offers it; Darryl offers his in return; and Chrome Dome pumps the hell out of it.

"Mr. Huntington, you are someone I have always wanted to meet."

"It's Darryl, please, and in that case, I have always wanted to meet you, Your Honor."

"Ha! Turning on the charm! I love it! Now tell me, sir, am I to believe you are trying a case here in the humble backwaters of the inland counties? Tell me it's in mine, and I will have it transferred to my department. You just say the word."

"Actually, none. I'm doing a favor for some friends, and so I am helping out over at the County Counsel's Office in San Gorgonio."

Chrome Dome blinks and stumbles back a step.

"Good lord! Everyone knows they need all the help they can get. What a sorry bunch that lot is. But, no. You? You are without a doubt one of the most preeminent trial lawyers of our era in this state, if not the country."

"*The*, actually," he grins.

"What?"

"*The*. You said *one of*. It's *the*—as in, I am *the* most preeminent trial lawyer in the country."

"A-ha! Well, I'll be damned if you're not, by God, sir! Now, that's confidence for you!"

Chrome Dome looks down and notices me.

Just my lucky fucking day.

"What the hell are you doing at my table?"

"Having dinner with my wife, my boss, as assigned, and now, apparently, with you as well. Unless, of course, you'd prefer to have both my wife and me and our meals transferred out of your department and to another table."

I feel a sharp kick to my right leg.

Darryl is chuckling to himself.

Yeah, I've got my inner asshole goin' on.

Chrome Dome is blinking.

"What? Oh, no. No, that won't be necessary. Good lord, Cooper. Where is your sense of humor, man? It's supposed to be a social event. Oh, hell," he says, waving his free hand. "I need another drink. Millicent? Millicent!"

"Stop shouting, dear. I'm right behind you."

A frumpy, elderly woman with a bob of gray-white hair in an old lady's lace dress emerges from behind her husband.

"Oh, there you are indeed, my gal, my love. I need another drink. Please fetch me another bourbon. Make it a double this time and neat, damn it. I want it neat."

"Yes, dear."

"That's a good girl. And when you come back, I want to introduce you to Darryl Huntington." He doesn't notice that she's already walked away. "Wait, my manners."

He blinks. He looks at Darryl.

"What are you drinking, sir?"

"Caillet Cellars."

"What? What's that?"

"Chardonnay, of course."

"Char—wine? Oh no, man. Wine is for women." He turns and notices Tami. "See? Women. *Res ipsa loquitur.*"

He looks at Tami again—this time, a bit closer.

"A very beautiful, very beautiful woman. Miss, are you related to the late Marilyn Monroe, by chance?"

"It's missus, and no, I am not."

"Missus?"

"Yes. I am Mrs. Paul Cooper."

Chrome Dome blinks.

"Oh, good lord."

He looks at me, then Tami, then me, or maybe he's watching a hallucinatory tennis match.

"You finally grew a pair?"

I swallow hard and feel her nails dig into my thigh.

Chrome Dome looks at Darryl.

"Did you know he finally grew a pair? I've been telling him for a month to man up and grow a pair." He looks at me. "Didn't I tell you that?"

"You did."

"Your Honor," Darryl says firmly, "what do you say we take that matter off calendar for the rest of our evening together?"

"Oh, very well."

"Excellent."

Chrome Dome looks at me.

"You do get my point?"

"Yes."

"Very well."

"Excellent."

"Yes, indeed." Chrome Dome looks at me and smirks. "You need to man up and start litigating real cases. None of this ridiculous nuisance nonsense. Understand? Real cases. Learn from him, Cooper! Be a sponge, man! Soak up all the knowledge you can get from this man!"

"Real cases."

"That's right. That's exactly, right."

"Got it."

He's not like *this* in the courtroom—ever. Obviously, booze brings out an entirely different personality in the man. How weird.

"Good! See that you do, sir."

I notice Tami is taking all this in, hiding it all behind a demure smile. I see Darryl taking it all in too.

"No need to worry about my boy Coop, Your Honor. He's got game."

Chrome Dome starts blinking.

"Coop? Coop? You know him already?"

"Indeed. I'm his new boss. We've been getting acquainted this past month or so."

"His boss? Where?"

"At county counsel, as I've mentioned. Let's just say I've signed on for the time being. Coop here is my protégé and next project. I'm going to make a lot of money off him and turn him into a killer in the process."

"Good lord, man."

"Indeed."

Chrome Dome mulls that over—hell, I mull it over. I can see Tami is mulling it over. She's got her own poker face, and it's a damn good one.

"How?" Chrome Dome asks.

"Well, Your Honor, I can't tell you," he says with that great white grin. "As you know, that's all privileged."

"Yes. Yes, of course. Good one. You got me. Judicial notice taken, sir."

Darryl looks around.

"Now, I see my wine is coming, why don't you sit here next to me, the seat of honor for Your Honor, and I can regale you with tales of trials won."

"Thank you, lad. But whiskey, man! You need a whiskey!"

He follows Darryl's gesture and sits down at Darryl's left.

"I prefer Chardonnay, thank you. Particularly in the company of beautiful women."

"Ha, you devil!" Chrome Dome says.

And then, in a mumble loud enough for those present to hear, adds, "I know you've got a pair, by god."

Darryl stands.

"And speaking of beautiful women, I believe your wife has returned with your bourbon."

Chrome Dome starts to stand.

"No, you're fine," Darryl says, gently taking the judge's shoulder.

He takes the bourbon from the judge's wife and sets it down in front of the judge.

"Here's your bourbon, Your Honor. Down the hatch."

He turns to the judge's wife.

"Mrs. O'Halloran, I'm so very pleased to meet you. I am Darryl Huntington. Please, sit next to me. We will enjoy a splendid evening."

"Thank you so kindly, Mr. Huntington."

"Excellent. Please, call me Darryl. By the end of the evening, we will be old friends, I assure you."

"Oh! Darryl, you are such a gentleman," she says wide-eyed and grateful. "Such kindness to an old lady. You just don't see much of that anymore."

She gives a snooty look to her oblivious husband. Probably the only time she'll get away with it.

"And if I may, Mrs. O'Halloran, allow me to present a most lovely couple, I'm sure you'll agree once you have had an opportunity to converse with them, Paul and Tami Cooper."

I stand up and bow slightly and shake hands with the old bat. I can't see Tami and have no idea what she's doing.

"So lovely to meet you both. Oh my, this will be an enchanting evening. I simply love your dress, dear. You look divine."

"Thank you. That's very kind of you."

"And our wine has arrived!" Darryl announces.

"Please open them," he instructs the waiter, who does.

Darryl does the whole cork thing, which I've never really understood—but whatever—and he pronounces the wine excellent.

Duh.

He has it poured for everyone but Chrome Dome who has his bourbon and doesn't drink wine anyway because wine is for women, by god.

"Millicent—may I call you, Millicent?"

"Oh, yes! Please do!" she says, almost squealing with delight at the attention.

"This is a delightful vintage of Chardonnay from Caillet Cellars. You've heard of them, I trust?"

"Oh, yes. Quite the rage, I hear."

"Indeed." Darryl scans the table and raises his glass. "If I may, a toast to our table, a pleasant and cheerful evening, lively conversation, and good health to all."

"Here, here!" Chrome Dome bellows and knocks back another shot.

"Allow me, and it's for the table by the way," he looks at Chrome Dome. "So you're fine, feel free to imbibe to your heart's content."

He then motions to the wine waiter.

"I'll take a bottle of Harper's Creek Bourbon and three more glasses for the table as well."

"Young man, your timing and your taste is impeccable," Chrome Dome says in a soft tone I find surprising.

Darryl's wine selection is delicious. I recognize the flavor from the night in Capistrano. I look at Tami, and I think she's just found nirvana in a glass. Darryl notices too, of course, and makes no effort to suppress his broad grin of pleasure.

An extremely slender young woman in a burgundy pantsuit and modest white blouse approaches us.

"This is? Yes, I see now. Yes, table 9. Good evening. I'm assuming this last seat is mine? I'm supposed to be at table 9," she says.

Her voice has an almost singsong quality like a chant. She sits down before either Darryl or I can get up, which we were doing.

"I'm Janisha Gupta."

"Such a lovely name. You don't hear names like that anymore," Millicent says.

"Indeed. Ms. Gupta, may I have the honor of presenting the Honorable and Mrs. Corley O'Halloran," Darryl says.

"Please call me Millicent, dear."

Chrome Dome blinks.

"I do so love your accent, dear. Where are you from?"

"Good lord, Millicent. Look at her. It's obvious she's from India for God's sake. Look at the dot on her forehead."

For a moment, I think I see a "deer in the headlights" look on Janisha's face. Then her brows narrow, and she has a steely look.

"She's a child. Are your parents attorneys?"

"I am not a child. I am not from India. For your information, I was born in San Francisco. I'm from Sausalito, and I live in LA. My parents are both doctors in the Bay Area. I am an attorney. I am an associate with Grua, Reynolds, and Paschek."

For a second, I think she's gonna finish with a "so there." But she doesn't. Too bad. It would have been smashing good fun.

"Ah, the civil rights firm," Darryl says.

"You know of it?" Janisha asks.

"Good lord! Civil rights? Christ Almighty," interrupts Chrome Dome.

"But I do indeed. I must ask you, Janisha. How is ol' Granola Grua doing these days? We went to law school together quite some time ago—that is, when he wasn't off climbing a rock somewhere."

"Oh, we would never call him that."

"No you can't. I certainly, however, can and I always do." He gives her the great white grin. "I gave him that nickname in our first year. We were starving students to be sure. To date, I think that's all he's ever lived on. If he ran out, he'd just shake some from his beard. He's the one man that money has never changed."

"I did not know that. About the nickname. Or shaking the beard."

"All true. I think we were the hungriest kids there as I recall. Funny, the things we hunger for. Kenny Grua always hungered for justice and righting every wrong, no matter how small or how great the cost."

"You? What do you hunger for?"

Oh, boy. I can see this train wreck coming from a mile away.

"Me?" he says with another great white grin. "What I always hunger for—money."

"I see."

Okay, so I didn't see her dot, but I see her frown. I can see she is disappointed in and disapproves of Darryl. That was disdain I heard in her voice. I also can see past her hunger for justice to her shoulder-length, black hair; her lovely eyes—the whites of which look even bigger, accented as they are by the darkest pupils I have ever seen—and framed by what must be the perfect arch of eyebrows; and skin the color of dark chocolate which sets off the deep red hue of her lipstick. She's yin to Tami's yang. Or is it the other way around?

"Ah, to hell with the fish. I'm in the mood for cherries and chocolate," I say, thinking out loud.

Okay, that gets me a funny look from pretty much everybody.

"And with a charming, if not odd, non sequitur, we have Paul Cooper, and he is here with his lovely wife Tami," says Darryl, continuing the introductions.

Tami and I say hello.

"Very pleased to meet you."

"And I'm Darryl Huntington."

"Good evening."

"It most certainly is, Janisha. It most certainly is."

Amazing. Nothing ever fazes this guy. She's giving him a look branding him untouchable, and he's all charm, all "full speed ahead, damn the torpedoes" charm, scheming to touch her untouchables, no doubt.

"Well, at least she speaks English."

"Another non sequitur."

"Of course I speak English, Your Honor."

It's her tone of voice that suggests she's fluent in loathing as well.

"I also speak French, Spanish, and Italian. Don't say it. I know what you are thinking. I see those very tiny wheels turning in your head. Yes. I also speak Hindi and Punjabi. I learned from my parents. They were born in Jaipur, Rajasthan."

"In India?"

"Of course, India."

"Then I am right. You are an Indian. So many languages. I love French. Please, say something in French."

She does, and she does so, so fast, I have no idea what she said. Of course, the ever-dapper, bon vivant, and debonair Darryl must know and, therefore, must also speak French because he's chuckling to himself. Damn.

"Tres magnifique, mademoiselle," Chrome Dome mumbles with an accent made simply offensive by her own. "Yes, I studied French in college. Back in the day."

"C'est magnifique," she says and then lets rip another line at ten times the speed of his mumble, and now Darryl is laughing out loud.

Chrome Dome, apparently not to be outdone or exposed for his ignorance, looks at Darryl and then starts laughing himself.

"I didn't catch all of that, I'm afraid. What did you say?"

Darryl cuts her off.

"She said that you are unbelievably"—he pauses—"amazing. That she's never met anyone like you before."

He looks at Janisha as if to steer her away from a cliff.

"I'm paraphrasing, of course."

That seems to placate her sense of dignity for now.

"Yes, I am indeed. Thank you. So true and so beautifully spoken. Touché," Chrome Dome mumbles in his sickening blend of arrogant self-approval and faux humility.

I don't know much French, but I know *faux* means "fake." I know that much. And now I know Chrome Dome. He's all bluster and what was the other word? Whatever. Anyway, he's a fake. Total rat bastard fake fraud. I've taken judicial notice, by God. And as he's bowed his head in self-worship, he notices his salad. They are bringing us our salads.

"Good lord. What are those?" He picks at the salad with a fork. "Weeds?"

"Your Honor, I believe it's a mix of baby field greens. Quite the rage in Boston these days. Goes exceptionally well with a side of baked beans. Pity they aren't serving any."

"Oh! Well, in that case . . ."

He shoves a forkful into his mouth and munches. He looks up and gives Janisha a leafy smile.

"Bon appétit."

She glares at him. She glares at Darryl, and then her expression softens.

She looks at Chrome Dome, smiles, and, with a wee flourish of her fork, says "bon appétit" with as beautiful a French accent as I have ever heard in her lilting, singsong voice.

"Such a lovely voice, dear. You should try singing."

"Waiter!" Chrome dome calls out.

At once a waiter is at his side.

"Can I get a side of baked beans, please?"

The waiter's bewildered expression is priceless.

"Excuse me?"

"Baked beans—you know, to go with the salad. Good lord, man! Baked beans. They are supposed to go with the salad."

The waiter gives Darryl the ever-classic "what the fuck?" look.

Darryl moves his hand away from his lips just enough for the waiter to see Darryl rub thumb and forefinger together and give a little nod.

The waiter perks up.

"Yes, of course. Baked beans. Of course. Let me take care of that for you. Forgive me. It may take a few minutes, but I will take care of it."

He steals another look at Darryl who nods approvingly.

"Fine," Chrome dome mumbles. "That will be fine. Thank you."

The waiter disappears.

Janisha gives Darryl a brilliant smile. He returns the favor. He raises his wine glass.

She raises her water tumbler.

"It is a very good evening. A very entertaining evening."

"And to think, we're just getting started," Darryl answers her.

I imagine him imagining himself getting started and giving her the boning of a lifetime later tonight. My fork slips, and I bite my tongue. No time for thinking out loud.

Chapter 22

Darryl pours some wine for himself first and then, ever the gentleman, offers to pour for Millicent, who eagerly accepts.

After the salad—part of which is pasted with dressing on his tie—Chrome Dome wobbles out of his chair and steadies himself.

"My god! Did you feel that earthquake?"

He stumbles off, without waiting for an answer, presumably toward the men's room.

Tami turns to Janisha.

"Please, I love the sound of your name, and forgive me if this is a stupid question, but I'd like to know if your name means something, you know, a special meaning?"

She smiles. Her smile is divine.

"It does. It means 'one who dispels ignorance.'"

"That's lovely. What exactly do you do in your practice?"

"I litigate constitutional civil rights cases. I sue the government for violating people's civil rights."

"Oh, I'd say you're in the right field."

"Thank you. I feel very fortunate to do what I do. And you? What do you do?"

"I'm an ER nurse."

"I feel sorry for you. You can have it. I hate seeing blood and hearing people scream."

"It does get old. If you don't mind my changing the subject, what did you really tell the judge in French?"

"I told him that I have never met such an unbelievably insufferable, arrogant asshole in my life. I asked him if all the judges out here were like him."

Darryl turned his attention to Millicent.

"May I pour you more wine?"

"You're such a dear. Yes, please."

She offers her glass. He pours.

"Oh, that's plenty for an old lady. Thank you."

"My pleasure."

"And your husband?"

"He's a government lawyer. He handles nuisance abatement cases. But he's very interested in becoming a judge."

"I see." She leans forward to look at me. "Good luck to you."

"Thank you."

"Ha! He'll need more than luck, by God! Luck does not make judges. Experience makes judges. He needs a broader depth of experience, and so do you. You would do well to remember that, young lady."

Chrome Dome slumps into his seat. His shirt is soaking wet and he's rubbing it with a towel.

Janisha watches Chrome Dome intently.

"I believe I now understand the need for the robe. Obviously, a tie or even a napkin isn't always enough."

Chrome Dome is processing Janisha's comment.

"Experience tempered with discretion. Mr. Cooper lacks something of the former, and you lack both, I'm afraid. Obviously."

"Now don't be so quick to count my boy out, Your Honor. I think he's got game. I've got some plans for him. He'll gain broader experience, I assure you. I'm going to make a litigator out of him yet."

Chrome Dome nods.

"Excellent. He does have potential. I have told him as much."

"I do not lack discretion at all," snapped Janisha. "I prefer honesty to discretion. Discretion hides so many evils. You are a slob and an ass."

Yeah, you go, girl! Just loud enough to perk a few ears over this way.

Chrome Dome's chest swells, and he leans back in his chair.

"You are immature, impertinent, and disrespectful. You're too damn young to know a damn thing!"

Now I can see the wisdom of Tami's prodding. She's right. I need to start talking to people more, and now is as good a time as any.

"Apparently, she knows enough to make a respectful living, suing the government."

Chrome Dome's mouth falls open.

"What? Oh, good lord! You would bite the hand that feeds you? Make no mistake. I am as libertarian as they come, but there are limits. They are called immunities, and they exist for a reason."

"So true," I say.

I'm feeling judicial now, by God.

"But when has that ever stopped anyone? Go for the money—the deep pocket. Isn't that the point? Government's the only deep pocket left in our society."

I'm on a roll.

"Indeed," Darryl chimes in. "Our civil rights bar has taken a page right out of the personal injury playbook. Granted, they get a bit too fanatical at times, but I say, good for them. She's learned well. Frankly, I love suing the government. There's always a way to convince a jury of liability. It's easy money."

"It is not about the money! It's about vindication of a right the government has violated after having guaranteed it in the first place."

"Ms. Ganuptha," Chrome Dome announces, "if you are getting paid, then, yes, it is all about the money."

"My name is Gupta."

"Fine. My point—"

"You're drunk!" Janisha says, loudly interrupting him.

Chrome Dome hesitates. People seated at nearby tables are staring at us.

"My point . . . is . . ." His voice trails off.

"That a little discretion goes a long way," Darryl says with a lower volume.

He winks at Janisha who rolls her eyes.

"That is exactly correct," Chrome Dome announces as his head tips forward.

"Ah! Perfect timing," Darryl says. "Dinner is served."

"Thank God!" Millicent blurts out.

I chow down on my tasty but lukewarm salmon smothered with the cold but thick mystery sauce. It's a heavy sauce, equal parts white, pasty, bland, and cold.

Out of sheer necessity, I carefully manage to kill off another glass of the delicious and decently chilled Chardonnay, sipping between bites.

Janisha seems displeased with her vegetarian plate. Tami moves the wine bottle a little farther away from me and gives me a smile. I smile lovingly in return and drain my water glass, which is refilled immediately by the young man who came out of nowhere.

Thanks! Why couldn't you be as efficient with the wine?

A waiter reaches around Chrome Dome and sets down a filet mignon platter and then turns and receives a bowl of baked beans and another salad from a coworker and places them in front of Chrome Dome. He is obviously pleased, as is Darryl who motions for the waiter, whose eyes widen; and upon his arrival, Darryl ever so smoothly passes off some crisp bills with such polished skill, I don't think anyone else has caught on.

"Tell me, Paul, when did you connect the dots aiming you toward the bench?" Darryl asks.

"It's been on the back of my mind for a while now."

"Indeed." He flashes that great white grin of his, and I wonder what he's up to.

"Young man," Millicent whispers my way, putting her hand on my forearm, "you're such an honest young man, promise me that you won't let it go to your head when you get there."

I can't help but smile at Millicent's comments, even though I'm not young and have forgotten how "young" even feels anymore. Why does everybody think I'm so young?

"You have my word on that, ma'am."

"Oh, of course, dear, they all say that. You have such an honest face. I do believe you will."

"Thank you."

I feel Tami's hand on my other arm. I smile and slowly inhale. God help me. I feel good. For the first time in a long time, I feel good. It's probably the wine. Okay, it's the wine. Too bad the feeling won't last. I'm also starting to feel a bit phony, and why the hell not? I'm in a room full of phonies. But, hey, fake it till you make it, right? Isn't that what everybody believes, what everybody says you're supposed to do?

Maybe this judge thing could really work. Like killing two birds with one stone. Eww, gross! Why would I even think of that? There must be a better way to describe multitasking. . .

Something more . . . win-win . . . Something more win-win . . . win-win. . . what else is win-win? Have your cake and eat it too! Of course! Win-win!

I begin savoring what may be the last of my wine, thinking maybe I've got this thing all wrong, maybe a multitask approach is the answer. Images of beautiful and gorgeous-sounding acoustic guitars adorn the walls of my very own judicial chambers.

It's good to be the judge!

How many times have I heard that one before? What's Tami going to say? No?

No. I don't think so! Not if I'm the judge, she's not. Oh, such sweet cakes! Tami gets me, the judge, and I, the judge, get my guitars and keep Tami! Oh! This is big-time win-win! Let's do this! And this whole judge thing? Seriously, how hard could it be, really?

I steal a quick glance at Tami. She's stunning. I imagine how easily she might have been a singer or maybe an actress. She's certainly got the diva part down. Probably a good fit for the whole judge thing, now that I think about it.

I lean forward, and she shushes me like I'm about to say something. How does she know if I'm going to say something or not? Most of the time, I don't even know if I'm going to say something. It's different this time because, yes, I wanted to say something— something she'd be only too happy to hear. Throwing my hat in the ring and all that. If only I could just have a little more wine to fuel this happy dream.

I realize somebody from Somebody, Somebody, and Somebody has just introduced the evening's speaker; and Tami seems acutely interested in the guy. I don't know why. He's not exactly killer in the looks department. She's staring at him though and rather intently.

Women.

He's bald too. I scan the room. Maybe half the men here are bald. Wait. Not just bald—this guy has shaved his head. He shaved his head.

What the fuck is that all about?

I guess a lot of men do that too, but for the life of me, I can't understand why. My hair is thinning, but it's still almost hippie long. Maybe that's why everyone thinks I'm so much younger than I am. There was this cute court reporter that said something like that to me a while back. I think. Maybe she was joking. I can never tell.

Women.

Tami is really interested in L. Michael Taylor, associate justice for the Ninth Circus. I don't know what the hell for. He's a liberal jackass who gets overturned a lot. He's never met a drug crook who, in his twisted little mind, wasn't innocent or a cop or PO who wasn't a liar. This guy's reality meter is pegged at zero.

He starts off with a recap of his bio. Big effin' deal. Teenage addictions.

Duh.

Pointy little crackhead. He thinks he was a musician? He says he can't remember. Something about electric shock treatments. Okay, that's creepy. He says his pedigreed Bay Area family swears he's never picked up a musical instrument in his life. Still, he has these weird dreams about electric guitars, one black-and-white electric guitar in particular. Fascinating. The family moved him around a lot. They changed his name.

He moves on to describing his many déjà vu trips in and out of drug rehab, getting clean, and going to "Berzerkley" for his undergrad and master's degrees. Of course, that's not what he calls the place. Then he's on to that quaint law school in neighboring Palo Alto where he was the one, the only, all-law, law review guy, naturally; and then, just as naturally, he had to clerk for a handful of federal judges after graduating. After all, how could he pass up all those offers? Titter. Titter. Titter.

Yes, he passed the bar in three states and the District of Columbia—all on the first try, of course. Cocky, pointy-headed little prick. Then, just to give back, because that's just what you do when you hail from Bay Area old money, he went to the federal public defender's office and almost immediately from there to the federal bench, and then to the Ninth Circuit, which so many of us less stellar, less idealistic, less accomplished practitioners stuck in the gutters of the real world, like to call the "Ninth Circus."

After some time, I realize this is a good thing. This is a very good thing. Hell, this is a wonderful thing because Tami is so focused on Taylor that she is not paying any attention to me whatsoever. This is righteous!

I can freely move my chair, and I do. I back up, I shift it a little more to my right, and though she has turned to face more towards the speaker, I have an excellent view of her back, very enticing in the low-cut dress and the calves of her crossed legs and her beautifully turned ankles supported by the cant of those three-inch heels.

This is a very good thing, and I can stare at my goddess of a trophy wife as intently as I want, and anyone who notices me will mistakenly assume that I am worshipping at the altar of the almighty Justice Taylor instead and, good lord, may they do so!

I can even reach my wine glass unnoticed, and I do; and Darryl fills it. Damn. Amazing how the devil's always near and always with such impeccable timing. What the hell. Why I am complaining? A minute ago, I didn't have any wine left! Drink up. A nice little buzz. A genteel buzz. A lawyerly, legal buzz. It dawns on me—perhaps a prospectively judicial buzz. I like such buzzes. I could get used to all this buzziness.

I hear some groans from nearby tables; and either they are enjoying the same or better view of Tami or, in the alternative, Taylor is pontificating on the sheer stupidity of state sentencing laws for repeat drug offenders.

I hear gentle snoring, and I notice that Chrome Dome's chin is resting on his chest. Janisha wastes a perfectly good sneer, she's so young, and nobody else lets on they even notice. Maybe it's not so bad, maybe it's genuinely good, to be the judge. I can come to these stupid soirees, get good and buzzed, and get to look at Tami dressed to the nines. *Regularly.*

There's another round of groans, and I join in, ever so softly. Only mine has nothing to do with legalizing pot, I groan because my trousers are too tight. And there are more groans, and I groan with them, only louder, because a lot of people are getting up and he's done; and he finishes with "I'm afraid my time is up. My apologies, I was just getting started."

No! You can't stop now! People are clapping. No, don't clap. Can't you see he's just getting started?

"Wait! Cut him some slack, people! He's just getting started, let him finish!" I say, okay, maybe a little too loudly, getting up for relief and garnering surprised looks and a mixture of jeers and cheers.

"Seriously, this is important, no matter whose side you're on," I say, and I'm on Tami's side and her lickably delicious backside, and I want to see more of every side of her.

She even turns and smiles at me.

That's it! I'm getting that stupid application done tomorrow!

I mean, how hard can it be to become a judge?

The conservative crowd has begun to bail, and the liberal crowd has Taylor penned in at the podium. He's not going anywhere soon. Janisha is elbowing her way toward him. She won't let him get anywhere either, and I imagine her imagining herself giving Taylor the boning of a lifetime. Okay, maybe I've had enough wine.

People I've never met are introducing themselves to me and shaking my hand. I smile and share my newfound enthusiasm for bench and bar, God, and country. Tami beams. I like it when she beams. I could get used to this.

It's been a wonderful night, and I'm buzzed as hell and don't want to screw this up. So I stay put and wait. Tami frowns at the immense crowd hugging Taylor. He appears delighted at the attention, and no one is moving. I stand still and attempt to look—I don't know—judicial.

Fake it till you make it!

In her heels, Tami can see me eye to eye. I like that. Her eyes are radiant, and they suck me in, and she smiles.

"Thank you," she says.

I just smile.

She puts her arm around me.

"Let's go."

We fall in with the last of the crowd that's leaving.

"Maybe this judge thing won't be so bad," I mumble, more like thinking out loud.

Tami pulls me closer.

"I wonder if it's too late for room service," she whispers, turning her head and giving me a little wink.

"We . . . can ask, if you like," I reply, desperately resisting the nearly irresistible urge to adjust my pants.

"Why not?" She gives up the slightest of giggles.

I love the sound of her giggles, knowing how rare they are and how this night is so strangely different—Halley's Comet different—

and will likely never, ever happen again. The chances of all I secretly yearn for ever occurring are as rarefied as the air atop Everest. I focus on and savor the sound of her giggles. I tell myself it's all I'm likely to get.

Relax, ace. Nothing's gonna happen. It's okay. It's all been a sweet gift. It's enough.

Then I find myself with her in a room of the inn overlooking the hotel's garden and the open-air restaurant, two floors below. We're in a room with champagne and chocolates, and I am oh, so grateful, on my knees, begging "Darling, please," so grateful that I get to hear more of her giggles.

Oh my god, I get to see her—all of her—for as long as I want, in and out of a white terrycloth robe that comes with the room.

And as she tugs playfully at my belt, I swear I hear that crashing chord, once rumored to be a G7 or an Fadd9 or something—the unmistakable one that starts one of the greatest rock and roll songs of the '60s, hell, of all time—and we have the greatest sex of my life.

Please, God. If I'm just dreaming, then have mercy and kill me now. Or at least give me the DVD.

God doesn't give me the DVD.

He doesn't kill me either.

Damn it.

◆ ◆ ◆ ◆ ◆

He doesn't harm me at all. In fact, nobody says anything when I show up two hours late for work this morning. There are no emails. No voice mails. Nothing.

So I'm startled when my phone rings.

The LED says "Reception."

"Paul Cooper," I answer in dull monotone.

"Dr. Newell's on the line. Do you want to speak to him?"

"Who's Dr. Newell?"

"I don't know. He's on the line. Do you want to talk to him or not?"

"Sure."

I talk to him—only it's not him it's a her, and I didn't get her name and she's bitching about something. I take her number and promise to look into whatever it is that she's bitching about. I'm preoccupied with the manila folder on my desk, the one I stuffed all the judicial application paperwork into.

I open the folder. I stare at the application it stares back. My pulse quickens. I start reading. I notice something about not embarrassing the governor. Really? Like that could even be possible with the moonbeam guy? This isn't right. I can't do this.

No, I *can* do this. I *need* to do this.

Fuck it. I don't want to do this.

I reach for a pad and pen. I'll read through the rest of it. Take notes. Do the groundwork. Tami's been waiting for this a long time.

"Dude!"

I jump.

"What the hell, Ryan!"

"Dude, I've been looking all over for you! Where the hell have you been?"

"Right here."

Chapter 23

"Get up! Get up, Paul! We gotta jet!"

I get up.

"Why? What's wrong?"

"Not now. We gotta go!"

"Go where?"

"I'll explain on the way."

He pushes me out the door and into the stairway and halfway down the stairs. He passes me, hurls himself against the door's crash bar. I follow as he bursts outside, and we run to the parking lot.

I stop and stare at the limo where Danny is waiting by the open door.

"Where the fuck did you find him?"

"He was in his office after all," Ryan says, out of breath.

I stop. I'm out of breath.

"This is a joke, right?" I finally manage to speak.

I can hear AJ and Robby laughing inside the limo.

"Get in. We're on a tight schedule," Danny says.

He uncorks a bottle of champagne.

"C'mon, guys. What's this all about?"

"Ah, to hell with him," Robby says, slurring his words, before he laughs at whatever has struck him as funny. "Jus' leave him here if he wants to play twenty quessions!"

I look back at the government center and instinctively reach for my wallet and pat the rear pocket of my suit pants.

"Dude! Will you just relax? You're fine. Trust me."

Everybody's laughing, and Danny's leaning down and pouring champagne into glasses held in the hands of outstretched arms.

"Please!" Ryan pleads. "For the love of God, will you just get in the limo?"

I get in the limo. Everybody cheers.

Danny hoists the bottle.

"To the bubbleheads!"

"To the bubbleheads!" multiple voices ring out in unison,

"Bubbleheads? Wh-what is going on?"

Robby leans forward, waving one hand and pressing the other against his cheek, trying to press his index finger to his lips.

"Shhhhh! Issa secret."

"Okay, Lightnin' Man, that's enough for you." Danny turns to AJ. "Seriously, is he gonna be okay?"

AJ hugs Robby.

"No worries, mate. It's an easy two-hour drive, maybe longer with traffic. It's a gig. He'll be sober enough."

"Bingo! No wor-reez, Mate," Robby says, wagging his index finger, his voice fading in a mumble. "Vibe-bussin' asshole."

AJ pulls Robby closer.

"Hey now, rocker. We're pros. Time to go pro mode, my brother," he smiles.

Robby nods, grinning now.

"Pro mode. Goin' pro mode with my brother."

"Here," Danny, says, handing me a chilled glass of the bubbly. "Here. You're the one who actually needs this. Drink up, Paul."

I drink up. I can feel the limo pick up speed. I try to look out, but my view is blocked. I'm sandwiched between Danny and Ryan like they're my bodyguards. The two wild men, the pros, are across from me. Robby's sort of sprawled out with AJ who's more or less holding him like a soldier carrying a wounded comrade in arms.

I think we're on a freeway—we're really flying now.

"So there's a plan to all this?"

Everybody laughs.

"Yeah, dude, there's a plan."

"And I get to know about it, right?"

"No!" chimes the chorus.

"Not until the magic moment, O Bard of Bards. Not until the magic moment. It's all part of the plan," Danny says, reaching to refill my glass. "Here, you really, really need this."

"Uh, guys, I haven't eaten anything yet this morning."

Danny nods.

"We know. Relax, I got this. Finish that. Next one's polluted."

"Polluted? No, wait. I don't think—"

"Actually, Paul, you think too much. That's a major part of your overall fucking problem. 'Polluted' means we add something to the champagne. In your case, it means we added orange juice."

"You mean a mimosa. Why not just say so?"

"And they call me the vibe-bustin' asshole. I mean stop being so fucking precise all the time. Geez, Paul, what are you, a friggin' lawyer now? Lighten your ass up. Try going with the vibe once in a while in your overly anal-retentive life."

"Yeah, a-null."

I don't need any shit from a drunk.

"Yo, Robby! You're in pro mode."

So there.

He blinks. He blinks again. I'm not blinking.

"Okay, okay," Danny says. "You amateurs drink up."

He hands me a polluted champagne.

"Okay, okay, my ass. Will somebody please tell me where we are going?"

"No!" chimes the chorus.

There's another round of laughs.

"A toast!" says Danny. "To Paul, the noble bard!"

"To Paul!"

"He dussin have a clue, duss he?" Robby asks.

"No, mate. Our bard is clueless."

"Thass funny."

"What the hell. Gimme another." I hand the glass back to Danny.

I like polluted champagne. I look around. I see how chummy everyone is and realize I'm in the middle, like I might even belong. Okay, that's gotta be the champagne hitting my empty stomach. A long exhale. This is ain't so bad. This ain't bad at all and sure as hell beats working.

"Sure as hell beats working," I tell Danny.

"Now, you're catching on," Danny says, handing me a cold glass.

"I like this vibe. Whatever the hell it is. Any chance we can have some music?"

"Music for the Bard!"

"Music for the Bard!" chimes the chorus.

"I'm on it," Ryan says, producing a CD. "Road mix one coming up."

He opens a hidden console and does his thing, and we have music—something acoustic upbeat yet mellow. I close my eyes and enjoy the ride.

I hear someone snapping fingers.

"Almost forgot," Danny says.

I open my eyes.

He pulls a sheaf of papers out from behind his back.

"Here," he says, thrusting them at me. "Sign these."

"Yeah, right. What are they?" I ask as I start looking them over.

"You—actually, all of us—are joining the Society of Independent American Songwriters Association. It's an artists' rights organization. You wrote lyrics of a song that's getting attention on the internet. We came up with the melody, the music. This is one of the steps necessary to further protect your and our rights to future royalties as much as we can. The world's changing, and only the artists are losing."

AJ chimes in—and that's rare—so I listen.

"The way I figure it, Paul, we're hotter than hell right now for maybe the next thirteen minutes. We gotta cash in while we can."

"Fair enough."

AJ takes the pen from Danny's hand and gives the pen to me.

I sign.

"Good man," says Danny.

Everybody cheers.

"Oh, there's more. You need to sign those too," Danny adds. "We're forming a limited liability company for music publishing. We're publishing our own stuff. It's another layer of protection and creative freedom. We're calling it The Bard, LLC. I think you will find that self-evident."

I look up. He's grinning.

"Fair enough."

I flip through all the pages and sign everywhere my name appears. Everyone else has already signed them all. I give him back the pen and the papers. He has his phone waiting. He lays the pages across the portfolio on his lap and starts taking pictures.

"I'm sending these on to our entertainment lawyer."

"Makes sense."

"Oh will it ever. And, hopefully, then some." He's still grinning. "It's official. We're in this thing together."

"Even him?" I nod toward Robby who's snoring in AJ's lap."

Danny nods. "Yep. Even him."

I take a deep breath. "Fair enough."

Ryan pours us all another round, except for Robby. He's out.

I raise my glass.

"What the hell. To us!"

"To us!" they all reply, except Robby. He's out.

The ride is over. I have no idea where we are as we get out.

An attractive young twentysomething in a very short skirt, peach-colored blouse, and bright yellow pumps greets us. She's friendly and vivacious but all business, talking quietly into some kind of headset that's connected to what looks like a walkie-talkie on her hip; and she's got a clipboard in one hand and a lanyard with several laminated cards hanging from her neck.

"Danny and friends?"

"That's us," Danny says. "I hope we're not late."

He turns and looks at AJ and at Robby who is awake and staggering out of the limo. What a rock star.

Chapter 24

She checks her watch.

"No, you're good. Okay, welcome to the *Jenny Curtis Show*! I'm Summer! I'm from guest relations. If you'll follow me, I can get you set up and comfy, 'kay?"

We follow her through huge doors and pass thick black cables snaking all over the concrete floor. In the darkened distance, I can hear faint laughter.

I'm looking around.

"Is this a movie studio or like a TV show or something?"

She looks at me and smiles.

"Well, yeah! It sure is."

"Are we going to like a green room or something?" I ask.

I can hear snickers.

She smiles again.

"Yes, we are. Only it's not green."

"Oh, okay."

"I hope you won't be disappointed."

"Oh, no. Not at all. I've never been in one, actually."

She smiles.

"Then I'm sure you'll like it."

She stops partway along a narrowing corridor. There's a small placard on the wall identifying room 111, and a label below it that says "Danny & Friends." She opens a door.

"Here we are. Fresh, hot coffee and tea are over there, bottled water is in the fridge." She points to a table of fruit platters and veggie trays. "And plenty of snacks. Please, help yourself. Tony, our assistant stage manager, and Leif, our musician's coordinator, will be in shortly to go over everything and get you ready. Make yourself comfortable and enjoy the show."

"That's awesome, thanks so much," says Danny.

I make my way to the couch. It's super cushy, despite being a gross-looking gray color, and I enjoy sinking deeper into it—keep sinking until I disappear completely. Only I don't.

I notice several large-screen TVs on every wall, and Jenny Ellen Curtis is interviewing some movie star whose face I recognize but whose name I can't remember.

Oh god, please don't let them put me on television.

"Dude, will you just breathe? It's fine."

"I can't do this."

My neck feels hot as I hear Robby's snort. So help me God, I'm gonna kick his ass if I can ever get off this couch before I pass out, and I turn and I see he's just snoring. He's not giving me shit. He's asleep again. Thank God for ugly furniture that sucks you in and puts you under. I want to go six feet under. I feel it's getting dark. It's almost too dark for me to see.

"Dude, don't go all morbid on me. You're gonna be fine. We got you covered. Trust me."

Danny steps directly in front of me and sits on the coffee table.

"Paul, look at me."

I look at him.

"This is why we didn't say where we were going. I need you to be more like him," he says, pointing at Robby. "Only not asleep."

Danny looks at me.

"Ryan's right. We got this. Enjoy the ride, man. It's all good. Just good, clean fun. Our moment in the sun. You won't be miked up, and your guitar won't be hooked up to a live amp. Just strum C and D or an A and D or P and Q for all I fuckin' care. It doesn't matter. Nobody's gonna know or care. Have fun with this, Paul, and fake it if you have too. Just strum whatever, however, and whenever you want.

"But don't get stupid and draw attention to yourself. You'll be fine. We're doing 'Bubblehead' and you get to watch as one of us because you are one of us. You hear me? You're part of the band now. 'Bubblehead' is all you, man. Robby's solo didn't get us here—your lyrics did. Remember that. Be proud of that. Those are your lyrics, man, and your lyrics made that song viral on the internet. You got us here, Paul Cooper."

He stops and leans forward.

"Paul, look at me! Is any of this getting through to you?"

I hear him, sort of.

"I'm viral? I'm fine?"

"Is he okay? He looks really pale," offers Summer.

She doesn't wait for an answer. She steps back and talks quietly into her headset.

"He'll be fine." Danny pauses and looks at Robby then AJ.

"Right now, our problem is Robby. We can't fake his solo."

"He'll be fine. I told you that already. Leave him alone," AJ says.

A tall, dark-haired woman wearing green scrubs and a white lab coat enters the room and comes straight to me. She kneels next to me and opens a backpack and removes a blood pressure cuff.

"Hello. My name is Paula, and I'm a staff nurse for the show. You do look a little pale. Is this your first time on television?"

"Yes. No. I mean, I'm not really going on television, am I?"

"That's not up to me. May I check your blood pressure? I just want to make sure you're all right. Is that okay?"

"Okay."

"Okay," she says with enthusiasm.

Maybe she's trying to cheer me up.

I hear the zip of the Velcro and then feel the squeeze on my arm. Then a release of the pressure.

"Okay. We have 138 over 82. That's decent. Let me have your hand, Paul, please, I want to check your O2 level."

I give her my hand.

"Okay, you're a little clammy." She clips something to my fingertip. "Okay, I'd like that to be a little higher. Hold your arm a little higher. There. That's perfect. Taking your pulse now. Ooh, a little racy, ninety-four. Are you nervous, Paul?"

"I am now."

"Relax, Paul. Everything is going to be fine. How old are you?"

"50."

"Okay. Are you feeling any chest pain?"

"Not yet."

"Any pain in your jaw or along your left arm?"

"No."

"Can you breathe okay?"

"I think so."

I notice two men enter, and Danny gets up to talk to them. Ryan moves in and takes Danny's spot.

"Any history of heart problems?"

"No."

"Are you diabetic?"

"No."

AJ has roused Robby, and he's none too happy about it. AJ helps him up. Summer is opening a pink cardboard box full of donuts. I don't remember donuts. Robby picks one, looks like a jelly-filled. Must be. They're his favorites. Now he's slamming cups of black coffee, and he and Danny and AJ leave with the two men.

"Where are they going?"

Ryan looks over at them at then at me.

"Someplace to make some noise, get the drums ready, let Robby wail a bit."

"Paul? Are you taking any medications?" asks the nurse.

"No."

"Are you taking any sexual enhancement drugs?"

I blink and look at her.

"No. Not even that."

"Nothing personal. Just checking. It's important, and it relates to blood pressure." She slips a plastic tube over my head and positions it just beneath my nose. "A little oxygen for you. Do you tend to hold your breath whenever you're nervous?"

"Yes."

"Okay, that's a habit I want to suggest that you change. Hyperventilation is not good. Breathing is very good. Do you practice yoga or meditation at all?"

"No."

"Okay. Something in the way of good habits for you to consider. Have you taken any drugs in the last three days?"

"No."

"Any alcoholic beverages in the last 24 hours?"

"Yes."

"What, when, and how much?"

"Polluted champagne. On the limo ride here. Within the last two hours."

"Polluted champagne? That's a new one. How much?"

"Three or four glasses."

"I see. And what is polluted champagne?"

"A mimosa."

"I see."

"I'm sorry."

"You don't have to be sorry," she smiles. "You're fine. You're being a perfect gentleman and a good patient. I'm used to working with all kinds of rock stars. You are one of the nicer ones."

"Oh, I'm not really a rock star."

"That's not what I hear," she smiles again. "I hear you are quite talented and create killer lyrics to very catchy songs."

She has a pleasant smile, and I'm feeling calmer.

"Paul, I want you to lean back and rest. Close your eyes. Think happy thoughts, okay?"

"Okay."

"One more thing. When have you eaten last?"

"Probably last night."

"Okay, then I'm going to ask that you eat a banana, slowly, and drink a cup of orange juice now. Will you do that for me?"

"Sure."

"Super."

She brings me a banana and a cup of juice.

"After this, just water for a while, okay?"

"Okay."

"After you come off stage, eat a little bit. Pace yourself and hold off the booze until after you've had a good dinner and only if you're feeling okay. Okay?"

"Okay."

"Okay."

I hand her the peel and the empty cup and lean back into this really comfy couch.

Closing my eyes is easy, and Tami's there in terry cloth and she's my happy thought. And all too soon, there's noise, and I open my eyes. Ryan's there.

"C'mon, dude. Showtime."

"No. Seriously? Do I have to do this?"

"Yes. Now suck it up. C'mon, I got a surprise for you."

I get up.

"Okay, what's the surprise?"

"Look what you get to borrow."

I look at a beautiful acoustic guitar, a dream of a dreadnought.

"Is this a—"

"It sure is."

I'm amazed how light it is. The craftsmanship and the tone woods, the Adirondack red spruce top and the Brazilian rosewood sides and back, are flawless and gleaming. This babe must be damn near ancient and priceless. I slip the suede strap over my shoulder. Ryan hands me a pick. I finger and strum a D. I really hear the voice of God and He's made the trip here all the way, all the way from Nazareth to Los Angeles, California. I finger the chord shape of an A and strum. I'm still hearing the voice of God, and oh is it ever. It's Him. It's a happy, joyful, loving voice. I could listen to it forever. I want to listen to it forever.

"Wow. Oh, God. I want one, Ryan."

Ryan grins.

"I'll tell Santa. C'mon, let's do this and get you on his nice list."

"Okay."

I follow Ryan as we're led down a dark hall around a curve to a staging area, and then on to I'm guessing the part of the stage that's off camera. I can see the audience, and over to my right, I see the back of Jenny's head above the back of her chair on her set at center stage. I hear her through a monitor somewhere.

"My next guests are living proof of what happens when baby boomers get bored. They try to become rock stars. Imagine that. Sometimes they succeed. Most times, of course, they don't. But if the reaction on the internet to the song these guys have about careers being frozen is any clue, they'll soon have a new career—and it'll be anything but frozen! I know you all know what song I'm talking about. That's right, loud guy in the fourth row, it is 'Bubblehead,' and I thought, you know, what a treat it would be to have it performed live for you here on this show."

To loud cheers that surprise me, Jenny announces us.

"Making their first and certainly not their last appearance on national television, please welcome my new friends and yours too, Danny & Friends!"

Ryan breaks out with the driving bass line, AJ's poppin' his toms, and Robby, well, Robby's doing it all. Functioning alcoholics rule. Who knew? I almost forget to pretend to play. I see the camera swing. Oh shit! I fumble for an A, get it, and strum. I can hear it, not quite clean but not bad. There's no microphone near me, thank God. I realize my tongue's sticking out. I correct the situation and strum away, searching for the chord of God's voice.

The crowd really loves the song. I'm in awe. I'm agog. It's just a song. But songs can move people. Maybe the part that's so hard for me to get my head around is the part that says it's my song that's moving these people. I mean, how can it be me who's doing that? All I've ever been my whole life is a worthless failure, a POS failure.

But the crowd's moving with the band, and these guys are white hot like the studio lights burning down on us. They're cranked up all the way to eleven and groovin' on, making full-color sound, every note pristine and pure.

And Danny, damn! Danny is in his element! He's nailing the lyrics and making my words live—and I mean *live*—and I can see that every woman in the audience from eight to eighty wants to rip his clothes off, even if the youngest ones don't yet know why and the oldest ones can't remember why. They only know they wanna, and they wanna really, really bad. And that's all there is to it. He is the luckiest son of a bitch ever.

I just keep strumming an A, looking around, and taking it all in. This is so cool. I have no delusions of ever doing this again, but I admire and respect those who do and how they can do whatever it takes to pull it off. How amazing it must be for the chosen few who know what they're good at and make their living do it.

I realize I'm strumming a G. I don't even remember making the transition. But I did it, obviously, and I must have done it without screwing it up. I would have noticed that. I always notice when I screw up. This is different. I feel good for a change.

Not screwing up feels really nice.

The crowd is going absolutely bat-shit crazy. They love it, and this is so weird; but I feel all this energy and the four of them, my bandmates—I can't believe I'm thinking that—are feeding off it like, like, I don't know, sharks. It's a feeding frenzy for the four of them, and their performance is becoming phenomenal. It's like they're all instantly twenty-five years younger, and whatever this vibe is, it's intoxicating.

Jenny is up and dancing. Shit, half the audience is up and dancing. Now Danny's over there dancing with her as he's singing, and everybody loves it, and I love it because I'm invisible, and there's nothing I like more. Well, except being with Tami when she's wearing a terry cloth robe and then nothing at all, and we're having the greatest sex of my life.

Robby hits the last chord, and the tone trails off. I mute my strings.

Jenny takes a cue and says, "That's our show! Thank you, everybody, for being here. I know you have your choice of airlines, thanking for choosing to fly mine. Thank you to all my guests, thank you to our new friends, Danny & Friends. And if you're wondering why you were given wristbands at the beginning of the show, now you know—those wristbands are your e-ticket ride to the recording of the live performance of 'Bubblehead' you just heard on this show."

She's applauding, everyone's applauding, and someone is taking this babe of a guitar away from me.

Jenny is walking toward us.

She turns to the audience and says, "Of course I'm kidding about the show being over."

There's an outbreak of cheers.

"But you knew that."

Oh, crap. I thought we were done.

She hugs Danny.

"Okay, hunk, so which one are you?"

"I'm Danny."

"Well of course you are. And you guys were great. I mean that. Just fantastic. You're even better in person. I thought you'd be good, but wow! That's all I can say. That's quite a retirement plan you've come up with and probably in the nick of time too."

The audience laughs.

"I think it's time to meet the band. So who's this bad boy with the screaming axe?"

"That's Robby Sherwood."

"Robby, hi, how are you? I'm forever deaf now, you know that, right? But in a good way."

Robby grins and rests his arms on his guitar. He knows he's a guitar god, and now everybody in the world knows it too.

"And who do we have on the drums?"

"That's AJ Goldman."

"Thank you, AJ. You totally rock! You can beat skins for me anytime."

AJ smiles broadly and reaches up with both hands and twirls his sticks.

"And who is the silent one on bass? And why are the bass players always the silent ones? Must me a musician's union rule or something."

"That's Ryan O'Byrne."

"Ah, there's a charm of a lucky man! Way to go, Ryan. Thank you. Thank you so much."

"And last, who do we have here? Who's this guy? The one who's not sure if he's in the right band. Who are you really?" she asks me directly with this look of surprise on her face as she steals a few peeks at the monitor overhead.

"I'm Paul."

"Are you sure? I'm just, I, well, let's take a look at the monitor." She points.

I do and see myself with a look of shock. The audience laughs.

"Okay, I see this, and I see the look on your face, the 'I don't know these people, how the hell did I ever get here?' look, and the 'oh, maybe I should start playing something' look. Am I missing something? I'm just saying. Then we see the light go on. Right . . . there. Too cute. It's almost like you're telling yourself, 'Oh! I need to play something. Yeah, let's do that.' Oh, wait, back up. Show the tongue again. Okay, that's precious."

The audience is howling.

"You guys do practice together, right?" she asks.

"Absolutely," Danny says.

"And you let Paul in too? Right? He gets to practice too?"

"Absolutely," says Danny again.

"Wait," she says, looking at a small index card she's holding. "It says here you're a lawyer. First off, I'm not sure I should even trust you."

Danny laughs. The audience laughs.

"Okay, it says here you're all lawyers except for AJ who is an accountant." She looks at AJ. "AJ, how did you ever get mixed up with a bunch of geezer lawyers?"

"Poker."

"Poker? Okay! I see somebody lost a bet somewhere. I see that. That makes sense. Now back to Paul. I get it. Danny sings and, Lord, have mercy, can he sing. Robby rips on lead guitar, that's obvious. Even a blind person would know AJ on drums. Ryan, the strong, silent type on bass, steady and dependable—okay, I get that. But I'm curious about you, Paul. What exactly do you do again? You're the occasional guitarist, is that it?"

"Pretty much," I say.

What the hell can I say? I was right, I don't belong. It's too much to hope for. I saw it on the monitor. Everybody in the world saw it too.

"Paul writes the lyrics," Danny interjects. "AJ, Robby, and Ryan come up with the music. I just sing it like they make me do."

"Oh, well then. That makes perfect sense. In the middle of a song, Paul gets a flash of inspiration, starts thinking of lyrics to a new song and forgets to play the one he's playing. Of course. Sounds like pure genius to me."

<h1 style="text-align:center">Chapter 25</h1>

"Yeah, there's that," Danny says.

"Is he always preoccupied like that?"

"Oh, even more so now. His wife is pushing him to be a judge," Robby adds.

"Really? Is that true, Paul?"

"Yes. No. I mean, not really. It's . . . actually, it's a mutual decision."

"Of course, it is. You're married. Say no more. Does she know how talented you are?"

"Uh, no. Not exactly."

"Do you even know how talented you are?"

"Uh, no. Not exactly."

The audience and the band all laugh.

"Oh, I think someone needs to tell both of you. Those are some killer lyrics as they say. And I gotta tell ya, my audience knows killer lyrics when they hear them. Am I right, audience?"

The audience erupts in cheers.

"So what do you think?" she asks them. "Killer lyrics?"

Cheers and screams of "yes," "yeah," and from the back a shrill, "oh, baby!"

"Yeah, oh, baby! There it is. My audience is never wrong. Tell me, just between us girls, where do you get your inspiration?"

I shrug.

"In the quiet moments, I guess."

"Works for me. Who do you listen to? Not your wife, I mean musically?"

"Oh, uh, I like Duggie Meadows. I listen to his stuff."

"Ah! There you have it, the maestro of mellow. The beatnik for beachcombers. The soul of surfers. I'm so with you on that."

She moves.

"Now, let's talk about this judge thing. Is this something new or has it been in the works for a while?"

"It's new."

"And your wife, what's her name?"

"Tami."

"Tami. She wants you to become a judge. I get that. What does Paul want?"

"Oh, I want it too."

"But she wants it more, obviously. What does she do, if I may ask?"

"She's an ER nurse."

"Wow. That's outstanding. How long has she been doing that?"

"About nineteen or twenty years."

"Ouch. No wonder she wants you to become a judge. I'm surprised she's not shoving you from behind. Giving you injections."

More laughter.

"Well, I certainly wish you all the best. Let me ask you, how do you become a judge?"

"Usually you apply for an appointment by the governor. There's an application and review process. There's uh, an extensive vetting process that takes into account the candidate's background and experience. Then, if you're good enough and fortunate enough, you get a phone call from the governor."

"Okay, I'm hearing politics and money. Lots of money. Are you active in politics?"

"No. Not really."

Everybody laughs.

"Do you have a lot of money?"

"No. Not really."

Everybody laughs louder.

"Okay, I can see where this is going."

More laughter.

"I'm thinking this retirement plan you and the band have going may be your best option. I don't know. I'm just saying. Wait, I know who can tell us. They're never wrong, and they're very democratic, which as everyone knows means everything in this state."

More laughter.

"How about it, audience? By your applause, all those in favor of Paul writing songs?"

Loud applause.

"All those in favor of Paul becoming a judge?"

Silence.

Then a few people clap and then more silence. Then laughter. Then everybody in the place, even the crew, starts cracking up.

"Paul, I think it's pretty clear. I mean, the audience knows these things. They're like this really humongous jury pool of your peers. Even they can tell this judge thing might be a huge mistake for you. So, let me ask you this, after you become a judge, what happens, I mean do you stay a judge forever?"

"No. You have to run for reelection."

More laughter.

"I see. More politics and even more money. Okay, now this is really starting to sound like a really bad idea, Paul. The audience knows these things. Now, granted it's not easy being a songwriter either and who knows maybe you're only good enough to write the one song."

She pauses to let the laughter die down.

"But then again, sometimes one song is all it takes." She looks at the audience. "Right?"

The audience cheers.

"See? There you go. And I think you may have hit on the one hit song you need. I also think somebody needs to break the news to your wife."

Jenny looks at one of the index cards in her hand.

"Let's see, emergency contact numbers, Tami, here it is. I'll just have a seat and let my staff dial the number. Is it ringing? It is? Oh, goody."

She picks up the phone by her chair.

"I love this part of my show. Reaching out and touching people. I just love it."

The audience goes bat-shit crazy again.

"I love it. My audience loves it."

This can't be good. There's nothing I can do that won't make it worse.

"Hello?"

"Hello, Tami? This is Jenny. Jenny Curtis. Hello?" She looks around. "Did we lose the connection? We did? No? We're okay?"

"Hello? Did you say Jenny . . ." Tami's voice fades.

"Hello, Tami? Can you hear me now?"

"Yes. Now I can."

"Oh, good. I thought I lost you for a minute. Listen, we're on the air, and I have a couple of questions for you about your husband, Paul. I understand he's applied to become a judge."

"Oh yes!"

The audience laughs.

"Hello? Is that static?"

"Yes! Yes, there seems to a lot of static on the line or maybe just applause from a rambunctious audience," Jenny says with a grin, waving frantically at the audience, trying to quiet them down, without much success.

"What?"

"Anyway, as I say, we'll just have to make do, I suppose. I don't have a lot of time."

"Oh, I understand. I understand completely. I was expecting your call. I just didn't think you'd be calling so soon. I guess this is a bit unusual."

Jenny mugs a surprised look.

"Oh, you have no idea. Yes, well, I understand Paul is in a band?"

"No, he is not. Oh dear god! I hope that's not a problem. I can explain! It was just an office party. Some of the attorneys had formed a house band. They do it every year."

"I see."

"It's nothing, really. He was considering taking up the guitar as a hobby, and he had to play at the party. Everybody had some laughs. That's all. He's not pursuing it. He's really focusing on his legal career."

"I see. Well, what about the video?"

"Oh my god! What video?"

"Well, there is a video on the internet of the band he's with playing a song. It's a very catchy song."

"What song? Are you asking about 'Three Blind Mice'? Is there's a video of him playing 'Three Blind Mice'?"

Jenny mugs to the camera.

"No. No, the song is called 'Bubblehead.' I understand it's quite popular."

She looks at the audience, and the audience cheers.

"Yes, my understanding is correct. The song is quite popular."

"Is that static? There's too much static on the line. I can barely hear you."

"Something like that." Jenny gestures at the audience. "Tami, I understand Paul wrote the lyrics for the song. The video had gotten several thousand hits, and the song is gaining in popularity. What do you think of Paul's songwriting?"

"What? Did you say 'songwriting'? Paul's not a songwriter. He is not a guitarist. He is not a musician of any kind. He has no musical talent whatsoever! I told you, he's not in any band. That's . . . that was just some coworkers getting together for an office party. That's all. I told you. It's nothing, really."

"I get that. Now about the band."

"Forget the band! Okay? There is no band! Well, there is, I'm sorry, but Paul is not in it. He's not! He's not in any band. Paul is a very good lawyer. An excellent lawyer. I believe he will be an even better judge. He is fair. He is honest. He is compassionate. He listens to people, and he goes out of his way to understand their needs. He is very smart, patient, and conscientious. He's extremely diligent. Very hardworking. Anyone who knows him will tell you that. It isn't just me talking."

"I, okay, I get that, really. But what about his songwriting? Will he even have time to be a judge?"

"Of course he'll have time. He is not a songwriter, and no one song has ever made anyone a songwriter, and it certainly won't happen to Paul. I already told you! He has no talent! No musical talent. None whatsoever! Please understand this, Paul is totally committed to his legal career—100 percent."

"Well, if he's not a songwriter, then what does he do for a hobby? The governor is quite concerned that judges be well-rounded individuals. I mean, all work and no play—where's the justice in that? The governor does not want overworked sourpusses on the bench."

Jenny makes a "so there" face to the audience. They love it. They laugh and cheer.

I don't love it. I feel a crash and burn coming on.

"No, you're right. Absolutely! You're absolutely, right," Tami says, backpedaling like a pro. "Paul has interests in photography and art. He's had those interests for years. I'm sure he will be renewing those interests, but he has been focused on his work this past year developing a new legal program for the county. That's finished now, so he has more time to pursue those interests, and he's attending more county bar functions as well."

"Okay, well, that certainly sounds good. Paul seems quite the guy. I definitely see potential here."

"Oh, yes! Yes! Paul has so much potential!"

"Yes, he certainly does. And again, like I said, I'm inquiring about his songwriting and the guitar thing as there seems to be considerable interest in that. You say he has no talent. I disagree! My audience certainly disagrees. They think he has plenty of talent. They love his song."

"What? What audience? Who is this?"

"Jenny Curtis."

"You're from the Jenny Commission, right? The state commission that evaluates judicial candidates?"

"No, I'm sorry. I thought I had made that clear at the beginning. I'm Jenny Curtis from the *Jenny Curtis Show*."

"The what?"

"The *Jenny Curtis Show*. Do you watch television? I'm on every weekday at four."

"No, I don't watch television."

"Oh, well, see. That's your problem right there."

The audience erupts into more, raucous laughter.

"My problem?"

"Anyway, your husband Paul and his band, Danny & Friends—"

"Jenny, we don't really have a name yet," Danny says.

Jenny turns to face Danny and, in a lowered voice, replies to him, "Oh, now you tell me."

She turns back, faces the camera, and speaks into the telephone, "As I was saying, Paul and the band you say he's not in are here with me now. They're on my show, and they just performed the internet song we've been talking about—it's called 'Bubblehead.' I don't remember if I told you that. It's really quite good. The studio audience loved it. That's my always dependable, always reliable studio audience cheering in the background. It's not static you hear but the cheers and applause of my loyal studio audience. You're probably hearing it as static, which is a shame because it's a wonderful thing to hear people cheering for your husband."

"My husband's on television?"

"Yes."

"Right now?"

"Yes."

"And the audience is cheering for him?"

"Yes. Well, they were. Now they're laughing."

"Oh my god! They're laughing at him?"

"No. They are not laughing at him. Definitely not at him. I think they're laughing at me. Maybe at you and me. Us. They're laughing at us."

"I don't believe you!"

"Okay. Well now, that's certainly fair, I think. I think it's a little myopic, frankly. Are you near a television set or somebody's laptop, tablet, anything remotely twenty-first century?"

"Wait a minute, please. Someone here is talking to me."

There's muffled noises. Tami's audible in the background, saying, "I said, just a minute! Please!"

"Make it quick! My show's almost over. Paul? Why don't you come over here, sit in that chair, and, guys, you can all gather round behind him. Hurry. That's it. Everybody look into that camera, smile, and wave for Tami. Tami? Are you there?"

"I can't believe this! My husband is on television. Oh my god! No! No! No! This cannot be happening!"

"Yes he is, Tami. It's so happening! Paul and his band have been delightful guests on my show today. They sound wonderful together. Paul even plays guitar, a little bit. Okay. He plays, sort of—I mean, a little bit. I'm sure you'll see that part later. It'll be viral any minute now. He's written some great lyrics, and the rest of the band put them to music, and the combination is a killer song, totally killer, and I do wish you had been here to see it in person."

The audience applauds.

"Tami? Are you there?"

Silence.

"Tami?"

One of the crew catches her attention and moves his hand across his throat.

"Oh? Okay. I've lost the connection."

Crash and burn.

Jenny stands up and looks into the camera.

"Tami, if you're still watching—and I hope you are—I want you to know that I think Paul is a great guy, and I apologize for any confusion that occurred during our conversation. Jenny Curtis. Jenny Commission. Potato, po-tah-to. Certainly understandable. If anyone from the Jenny Commission is watching, I want you to know that Paul is a great guy. He's written the lyrics to a very popular pop song that my producer has just let me know is going viral as I speak, and Paul's about to become famous. More like, uber famous."

She quickly turns and snaps a photo of me with her phone.

"Okay, he is famous. I'm tweeting about him now to my 26.4 million forever best friends, so there. It's official. Paul is now officially, uberly uber famous. I can't think of anyone more deserving right about now. I certainly can't think of any reason why a little something like fame should ever disqualify someone from being a judge. After all, Ronnie Reagan was famous, and look where he landed. Not to mention Paul's wife gave him a really, really good plug. So there you have it!"

The audience applauds and cheers.

I look around. I think the show is over. I'm exhausted, sick, and starving. I want to eat, and I can't eat. I find a men's room. Whatever's been in me the last week is leaving in a hurry.

I check my cell phone. Nothing. I call her. It goes to voice mail. I need words—words to take her heart away—but I have no words. I press Cancel.

I finish my business and emerge.

"There he is! The Bard! C'mon, man. Lighten up," Danny says, putting his arm around me. "Nothing bad is gonna happen, man. Relax! You're famous. Anything that anybody does just draws all the attention on to them, and they'll look ridiculous. Ridiculous and stupid. Trust me, Paul. You're golden! You are so fucking golden right now! Take a breath and enjoy it!"

"Okay," I manage to mumble. "Fair enough."

"That's the spirit! C'mon, we need to eat something."

"Okay," I hear myself say in a voice that feels not quite like mine.

I'm struggling to hear Tami's giggles—only I can't—and it hurts and I'm desperate. I fear what I'll hear, when the time comes, is her screaming instead.

Chapter 26

I don't hear that either. Just her voice—no less pained but now flat, lifeless. Even the anger's gone when I see her. Or so I think. All I see is a blank stare. She'd kill at poker.

"Seriously," she speaks, "the *Jenny Curtis Show*?"

She makes quotation marks in the air with her fingers.

"I don't even know you anymore. What the hell were you thinking?"

I try to remember the night before and what I was thinking.

"It wasn't me."

"No, Paul. It was totally you. You stood on her stage with a guitar, and the whole time you looked lost and totally stupid. No. Totally beyond stupid. Totally guitarded! How can you possibly look at me and say it wasn't you?"

"I meant it wasn't my idea."

"Then whose idea was it, Paul? Do you ever stop to listen to yourself? You sound like some twelve-year old kid. Stop acting like a child!"

"I'm not."

Another sigh.

"Oh! You are so stubborn! Fine. Then how come I didn't see you kicking and screaming to get off the stage? Huh? Obviously, nobody forced you into that ridiculous fantasy charade that's all over the internet. I had to unplug the house phone! And you can forget the answering machine."

"What about it?"

"Whatever. It doesn't matter. I threw it away."

"You threw the answering machine away?"

"Are you as deaf as you are stupid? Didn't you just hear me tell you that?"

"Yes."

"Paul, I have never been so embarrassed in my life! A complete stranger grabs my arm and practically drags me down a hall where a crowd has gathered at the TV in the hotel bar."

"What hotel bar?"

"The one we were at last night."

"Why were you there? Who's *we*?"

"Trying to help you. I was meeting with"—she checks herself—"some people and hoping to help your cause in becoming a judge, only to have you totally screw me over in front of them, in front of everyone the world over, on national television. I looked the fool as much as you did. I can't believe you did this to me! You! Of all people claiming to love me. This is just so wrong and on so many levels, Paul!"

"I didn't *do* anything."

"Oh, that's right, guitard. You didn't do anything, and you certainly didn't do anything worthy of convincing anyone that you were serious about being a judge or even qualified to be one. The part that hurt the most was watching . . . everyone there laugh at you and then see them . . . laughing at me. Just rip my guts out, why don't you! Go ahead. Oh, wait. They're ripped out already! Thank you for that, Paul!"

"Look, I'm sorry. Okay? I mean it. I'm really, very, very sorry. This is isn't what I wanted."

"Oh, really? Since when? It's not what I want either, but you don't care about that. Why are you doing this? What are you hoping to gain from this pediatric phase of yours, Paul? Why now, after all these years, why now? Tell me, Paul. Tell me!"

"Okay, fine. Fair enough. Truth?"

"Truth? What the hell are you talking about?"

"My job? Work? Total lie. Our marriage? Another all-out lie."

"Our marriage? Our marriage is a lie to you? Then what the hell is the truth, Paul?"

"I'd like to show you, but I can't."

"Oh, that's just great. You're so full of shit right now!"

"I'd show you, but you busted my guitar all to hell. Truth? Truth is a C major chord. Whether you buzz it or nail it, doesn't matter—it's there, undeniably there. Can't twist it, change it, hide it, sweet-talk it, spin it, or cover it up with an excuse. It is what it is for all the world to see. You either played the chord clean or you didn't. All can tell. Immediately. Truth. The guitar—and the sound it makes—is truth. The guitar doesn't lie."

"Oh! This is such bullshit."

"No, it's not. The guitar doesn't lie. It's the only truth in my life, and right now, I don't want anything else."

Tami's face flushes.

"And two nights ago, that night at the inn, you don't want that? You certainly didn't want anything else that night, sailor!"

Now I feel my face burn.

"Of course I do! I want it more than anything."

"Then make up your goddamn mind, Paul, and grow up! All this guitarded shit stops right fucking now! You hear me?"

"Okay."

"Okay? Shit, Paul, you say that like you're agreeing to go to the dentist. Unbelievable! I'm so sick of all your pediatric phases, all your midlife crises! I'm sick of you never finishing anything!"

She moves down the hall toward the bedroom. I follow. She stops, and I bump into her. She pushes me away.

"You spent what, two grand on flight lessons?"

"C'mon, that was a long time ago."

"And a computer and a home-model flight simulator so you could practice, those whataya call 'ems, those on and offs?"

"Touch and goes."

"Whatever! All that, and you're still not a pilot!"

"I ran out of money."

"No shit! God knows what you spent trying to add on a darkroom to the garage. Oh, and that stupid glamour photography course at the community college! What the hell was that? Tell me it wasn't just a lame-ass excuse for middle-aged men to photograph half-naked teenage nymphs. Go ahead, you fucktard! Tell me!"

"What does that have to do with anything? Besides, they were taking a fashion and modeling class at the same time and there were several joint sessions and the girls were all over eighteen. Everyone was working on putting a portfolio together, on both sides of the camera. Besides, that was ages ago. You never bitched about it then. Why is this a problem now?"

"Oh, give me a break! What portfolio? What skin rag hired any of them or ever hired you? When was the last time you even used a camera other than the digital one I bought? What's next on your list, Paul? A recording studio in the garage?"

"No, of course not."

She's in the bedroom now, and she pulls a travel bag off the bed.

"I'm sick of this shit, Paul. Whatever your midlife crisis is this week, get over it and grow up. For once in your pathetic life, just grow up for me."

"How long will you be gone?"

"A couple of days. The weekend." She glares at me. "One of us still has to work."

I follow her to the front door.

"See you soon then?"

She ignores me and puts the bag in the car. She walks around to the driver's side, gets in, and starts the car. She looks up into the rear-view mirror, touches her lip, and then turns to look behind her as she shifts into reverse and backs out.

"Drive safe."

She turns the car into the street, revs the engine, and peels out.

"Or not."

In the distance, brake lights gleam for an instant. Then she's gone.

I close the door and go back inside. I feel my phone vibrate and wonder why the stupid thing doesn't ring. I answer thinking it's got to be Tami. It's not.

"Hey, Papa. Wazzup?"

I stand there for a second wondering how to be cool and nonchalant and remember the NASA joke.

"Fifty miles," I say.

"What?"

"Fifty miles. Anything past that is out and no longer up. That's what NASA says anyway. It's their definition of *up*."

"That's cute, Papa."

"You're up late. What's on your mind?"

"You know I'm coming home for Thanksgiving for sure now, right?"

"I do now."

"Mother didn't tell you?"

I take a breath.

"No."

"Is she not talking to you?"

"Something like that."

"I guess that means your appearance on the *Jenny Show* was a hit."

I can't help but chuckle and get a little teary-eyed.

"Oh, yeah. Big time. Like a fart in church."

"Papa?"

"Yeah?"

"Save Friday for me, okay?"

"Friday?"

"Of Thanksgiving week. That Friday, don't make any plans."

"Fair enough. The day is yours."

"Thank you, Papa. I'll talk to you later. I've got a paper to finish."

"Okay. Love you. Bye-bye."

"Love you, too, Papa."

I press End Call on my phone.

◆◆◆◆◆

The weekend is quiet. I go into the office and practice and make up for the couple of days I've missed. I suck so badly. I try not to think about it. I try not to think about anything for the next few weeks. I go through the motions at work. Darryl's not around much. Probably a good thing. No news on the discipline front. Probably a good thing. I keep my appointments with Sasquatch; they're monthly now, and there's not as much ice time.

Thank God.

Tami's working nights as much as possible and disappears on the weekends. I leave judicial application paperwork on the kitchen table, a prolonged work in progress for her to see, but she says nothing. Except for passing in silence around the driveway a few times, I haven't seen her in maybe ten or twelve days now.

I decide to get serious about the DVD. I go to the office and repeat the last three sections that I've been working on. I practice until my fingers are so sore that I can't stop buzzing the strings. I tell myself I am getting better. I am getting good. I am making progress. I am kidding myself.

I tell myself I might see Tami today. It's Thanksgiving at her folks' place. Time for the annual bitch-and-blame fest. I only go because Shelley Lynne's there, and she's there because she's close to her grandparents and they really dote on her. Shelley Lynne would be close to them even if they didn't. But they do, and that just pisses Tami off to no end. Every year is worse than the year before. Pretty much a toss-up as to who hates whom more—Tami or her father.

This year will be especially bad because there's a godawful pink Ford Mustang convertible in the driveway, one of those haul-ass, street custom jobs—an early Christmas present from Grampa to Shelley Lynne because he "goddamn feels like giving it to her early" and because pink is still Tami's favorite color, though she never admits it anymore.

I hear the front door slam and then the squeak of worn running shoes.

From the kitchen, I hear Shelley Lynne's voice, "Mom's here."

Followed by Nana's, "And late as usual, I might add. I do hope she remembered to bring the Brown 'n Serves."

And I hear the clink of a wine glass, which means my mother-in-law is fortifying herself. I'm in the hallway trying to figure which way to run—and I can't—so I'm just frozen here.

Tami blows past me into the kitchen and tosses the package of rolls onto the counter.

"Where's Daddy?" she demands.

"Well, Happy Thanksgiving to you too, dear. Thank you for remembering the Brown 'n Serves. I wasn't sure you got my text. Your father is in the study."

"Fine. Yes, I got your stupid text."

"Well, you don't have to take my head off, dear."

My bespectacled white-haired father-in-law looks like a railroad tycoon of the twenties in his plush burgundy smoking jacket. He is tapping his pipe and strolls by me like I'm not even here—and in his view of the world, I'm not—and into the kitchen without a word. What the hell. I'm invisible. I follow him.

Tami is wearing a light gray jogging suit, trimmed in pink, with a hoodie.

"Oh, please don't smoke that thing in here while I'm cooking."

My mother-in-law's hand trembles as she reaches for her glass. I see it flinch as he barks at her.

"Oh, don't be silly, Barbara, I'm stepping outside to smoke. That should be obvious, even to you. An altogether lovely day. Splendid chill in the air, don't you think?"

He looks directly at Tami and gives her a broad smile.

"Speaking of outside, that reminds me."

"No! Oh, Daddy, how could you? Tell me you didn't!"

"Didn't what? Frankly, Tami, your question is vague and ambiguous, unintelligible, and utterly annoying as usual."

"Don't pull that interrogatory objections shit with me, Daddy! It's *pink*!"

"Of course it's pink. And that reminds me," he says, pulling the keys from his smoking jacket pocket and handing them to Shelley Lynne. "As I recall one joyful afternoon long ago, teasing you about orange pumpkins and you telling me how much you liked pink and wanted a pony, your little pigtails bobbing every which way like your mother—I believe pink was your favorite color as a child."

He chuckles.

"Alas, look at you. You are a child no more, and doing so well in college, I couldn't resist. The pink is a special order, of course. So now you have it, finally," he says with a grand wave of his pipe. "Your very own little, pink pony. Yes, indeed, a little, pink pony for our princess—550 ponies, to be exact. So do drive it carefully, and I do hope you like it and pray you forgive me for my indulgence."

Shelley Lynne is blushing.

"Ha! Barbara, I believe our little princess is speechless!"

"Or maybe she's just feeling guilty."

The old man's face reddens.

"Oh, for God's sake, Tami!" He rips into her. "What the hell is your problem?"

Tami tears up immediately. She's gone pale.

"My problem? Oh, no! Don't put this on me! Go ahead, princess, tell them! Tell your grandparents your dirty little secret! Break their hearts like I did!"

"Tell us what, dear?" Barbara says, feebly, fumbling for a chair.

"Oh, for the love of God, Barbara! Do I have to spell out everything for you? She's pregnant! Like mother, like daughter! This shit just never ends! It just never ends!"

"Oh my god. It can't be. Please tell us it can't be, dear."

"It's all 'it can be,' Barbara! It's all it ever is in this cursed family!"

"*What?* No!" Shelley Lynne interrupts. "What are you talking about? I'm not pregnant. Everybody just stop! I am *not* pregnant! Seriously, people, get a grip! Nobody is pregnant here! I am definitely not pregnant!"

"You're not?" asks Barbara, as if she thinks Shelley Lynne really is.

"No I'm not! Nana, please! Everybody shut up and just listen to me!"

"Son of a bitch," Tami says. "I think I'm gonna hurl."

"Actually, Tami, I don't believe that's an issue now, but thank you," I say, throwing in my two cents for whatever they're worth.

"Please use the guest bathroom in the foyer, dear, if you're feeling ill," her mother offers. "Perhaps wash your mouth out when you're done. Such language."

Her voice trails off as she speaks as if needing to speak but fearing being heard and gulps down a full glass of wine.

The old man's holding up his hands like he's calling time.

"Everybody just stop!" Shelley Lynne yells.

She breaks down and sobs and screams.

"Shut up! I am not pregnant, all right? I'm gay! All right? There, I've said it! I'm gay! I've come out!"

Dead "you can hear a pin drop" fucking silence.

"Oh, thank God!" bellows my father-in-law.

He looks down at Shelley Lynne. We all do. She's crumpled on the floor in the fetal position.

Before I can move, the old man has dumped the pipe and is on the floor next to her.

"There, there. My poor child. It's all right. My God, how you must have suffered. How I wish you had told me sooner. Such needless pain. There, there. There now. It's all right. It's perfectly all right."

He rocks her gently and strokes her hair and begins to sing to her. He's singing her a lullaby.

"No fucking way. I don't fucking believe this shit," Tami mumbles.

"Oh, Tami, how could you put your child through this torment?"

"Me? Mother!"

"Don't 'Mother' me, dear. This is just cruel. Even for you."

"Me?"

I hear Shelley Lynne's muffled voice.

"You're not just saying this? You don't hate me?"

"No! For the love of God, no, princess. I am most certainly not just saying this. I mean every word. Your grandmother and I love you without question. We always have. We always will. I have brought many a lawsuit on behalf of the LGBTQ community in my day, of course, it wasn't always known by such acronyms as are so popular now. That's beside the point. Society takes forever to change. Hopefully, such days are behind us."

"Thank you."

"Let's get up, shall we? I'm too old to do floors."

They get up. He tenderly kisses her forehead.

"I'm going outside for my smoke."

He sees his wife's hands shaking. She can barely hold the glass. He gently cradles her hand with both of his.

"There, there, Barbara. It's all right. Everything is all right now."

"Yes, dear."

She begins to cry as he leaves.

Tami looks at her watch.

"I'm late for work."

She walks out.

"That's fine, dear. I think I will sit down."

Silence.

Even with Tami gone, dinner is subdued.

I even get invited to stay for the night. Pumpkin pie on the back-porch swing with Shelley Lynne. Her grandparents are quite jovial. Her grandmother floats about as if freed from some horrendous burden.

Chapter 27

Morning arrives all too soon, but even it is pleasant.

"Oh, good, Papa. You're dressed."

"Yeah."

"Okay then. Let's go. Wait. Get your jacket."

"Where're we going?"

"For a drive. I need some time with you, remember?"

"I do," I say, smiling.

I'm settled in the new Mustang with Shelley Lynne at the wheel, and the sports car rumbles down the long, curving drive to the road and the winding streets of her grandparents' wooded and ritzy neighborhood. A stop for coffee, an adjustment to the MP3 player, and some Duggie road trip tunes and we barrel on down the freeway. We're rumbling off the freeway now and down the Laguna Canyon Highway.

"We're going to Laguna Beach?" I notice a bit of rain on the windshield.

"Well, not the beach, exactly. Laguna, yes. Close enough. It's a surprise."

She's hunched forward toward the steering wheel. Her hair is pulled back in a ponytail.

"I'm looking for—there it is," she says as we pass the Canyon Arts Festival grounds.

She turns onto a narrow wooded drive and then into an enclave of small Spanish-tile-roofed buildings of various arts-and-crafts shops. She finds a spot that doesn't have a No Parking sign hovering over it and parks her car.

"We're here!"

I get out and stretch. The air is drizzly and cold. The clouds hang low, hiding the canyon's hilltops.

She takes my hand.

"C'mon, Papa!"

I can hear the feint sounds of finger picking on a guitar as we approach one of the buildings. Two large clay pots rest on the stone walkway. Each one is a brilliant blue and filled with some broad-leafed plant. They adorn the sides of a wooden door that's reddish-brown and curved at the top. From just above my head hang chimes of metal tubes and pieces of stained glass. I like this place already. On the stucco wall, almost a pale pink, is an unpretentious small wooden sign. Carved into the wood in relief is the name of the business, Calypso Guitars.

"What do you think, Papa?"

"Sweet."

"Let's go!"

We go inside. There is a small counter to our left, near a gift area with racks for ceramic coffee mugs and leather guitar straps. There are some shelves for tee shirts, sweatshirts, and hoodies. On the wall to my right, above the shelves, five acoustic guitars hang from their headstocks. I'm drawn to them for a closer look.

I hear a door swing and turn to see a very pretty young woman—I'm guessing in her twenties—come in from the next room and walk around the counter to greet us. She's quite short and very athletic looking in her skimpy denim cut-offs with well-muscled thighs and calves. Her skin is deeply tanned. Her long, wavy, black hair is bushy and gathered tightly at the back of her neck with a scrunchie and fans out across and down to her lower back. She's wearing the same kind of tan boots I remember Shelley Lynne's friends from the swim team like wearing. She pushes the sleeves of her oversized sweatshirt up to the elbows. The silk-screened logo for Calypso Guitars set in a surfboard design of yellow and light gray stands out from the dark blue fabric.

"Aloha," she says, smiling with teeth perfect for any toothpaste commercial. "I'm Lani. Welcome to Calypso Guitars."

"Hi. I'm Shelley Lynne, and this is my dad, Paul. I think I talked to you on the phone a couple of weeks ago about a tour for today."

She smiles. "Oh, right. For the tour."

"Yeah, I wrote it all down," Shelley Lynne says, pulling a folded piece of paper from her jeans pocket.

"It's okay. I believe you," Lani smiles. "Let's get started."

She heads for the door we came in. We follow. Shelley Lynne catches up, and I trail behind them. We walk downhill on the stone walkway. At times, I duck various cloth banners shaped and painted like fish and bunches of chimes made of bamboo and metal tubes, and I move around the fired clay pots with their glazes of bright colors—red, purple, orange, and occasionally a brown one. I take it all in because Sasquatch says I need to be more mindful. I'd take it all in, even if I wasn't supposed to be more mindful. That's how beautiful and charming this place is. Even more so on a cool, rainy November day. My favorite kind of day.

"How did you get interested in our guitars?"

"I have one! There's a music shop near campus, and they had a few when I went in at the beginning of the semester. I went with my roommate. She was looking for, I don't remember now, but I saw them and started strumming them. I fell in love with one, and I bought it on the spot. I don't think my roommate bought anything. I started taking some lessons on campus, and I'm still playing."

"That is just so awesome! Thank you."

"Now I'm trying to get my dad interested. Then we can have a hobby we can share."

Lani hugs Shelley Lynne.

"Ahh! That's so cute!"

She looks back at me and smiles.

"I'm glad you're open today. I would have thought with the holiday you'd be closed," I say.

"Well, we are and we aren't," she says.

"Oh."

"My husband wanted to work today, and your daughter wanted a tour."

"Fair enough."

"We're always happy to give tours to our owners," she laughs. "We don't give public tours yet."

"I see."

She turns to Shelley Lynne.

"Where do you go to school?"

"Davis."

"Oh, yeah, I know that shop. I haven't been there yet. But I do all the paperwork. Norse God's gonna be thrilled."

"Norse God?" Shelley Lynne asks.

Lani laughs.

"Yeah, that's my nickname for my husband, Eric Gregersen. He makes all of our guitars."

She rounds the corner at the end of the building.

"Here's where it all begins," she says, and we step inside.

"Okay, this is our wood storage area. We take deliveries through the big roll-up door over there. The chunks of logs stacked like firewood are what my husband calls bolts, like in a fabric shop. I have no idea why. These chunks or bolts are all walnut. We get most of our walnut from central California. We get some from Walnut Creek, of course, up near San Francisco. Typically, it's Claro Walnut."

Lani smiles as she continues, "Right now, Norse God makes two guitar models—the Spirit and the Muse. Both models use this walnut for their backs and sides and headstocks. Sometimes the necks are walnut, sometimes they're maple. Usually walnut. Walnut is a strong hardwood with good bending properties and is easy to work with."

Lani gestures with her hands.

"Walnut is also a popular choice for furniture, given its strength, beauty, and good woodworking properties. And as Norse God got his start as a furniture maker, it's the perfect choice for his transition to guitar making.

"In terms of sound—what he calls tone—walnut is between mahogany and rosewood, so it's a good choice for a tone wood. It's also more readily available and not nearly expensive, so for a very small company on a shoestring budget like ours, it's a remarkably wise choice. That and the colors and grain patterns can be incredibly beautiful with distinctive variations from one guitar to the next. Each one looks different."

She moves over to a series of orange-colored metal racks and shelves.

"Over here, these are all neck blanks. Eric will carve these into the guitar necks. Over here, this stack of flat sheets is spruce—Sitka spruce from the Pacific Northwest and Alaska, to be exact. Spruce is generally regarded as the standard tone wood for guitar tops also known as soundboards. Over here," she says, pointing, "are shelves of western red cedar. This wood is also a good choice for tops. It's less dense than spruce, and we use it on the smaller of our two models, the Muse."

She takes another step.

"Finally, over here we have maple. Some of it has been cut into long narrow strips that Eric uses for binding. That's where the top meets the sides and the sides meet the back of the guitar. Some are in the long blocks that are precut for later carving into necks, and then we have a shelf or two of maple tops. Oh, and I forgot, that shelf has rosewood pieces that will be used for all of the fretboards on our guitars. We buy the rosewood from other guitar manufacturers. We subpool our orders with other small-lot buyers around the country to keep the wood affordable."

"Whataya think, Papa?"

"Very cool. I love all this wood stuff."

"Yeah?"

"Oh, yeah. Very much so."

"Awesome! Norse God will love you for sure. I'll definitely tell him. He's a fanatic about wood and making sound with it. He grew up here in Laguna, hanging around his father's cabinetry shop, which is just about a mile or so up the highway from here. I grew up surfing on the North Shore of Oahu. I have six brothers and they talk about water the way Norse God talks about wood. I grew up around water, so I understand them more. What can I say? Ready for the next room?"

"Lead on."

She opens another door and we follow.

"Okay, this is the milling room because that's what Norse God calls it. I call it the shit-scary *Saw* room because this is where he keeps these band saws and table saws that scare me to death. That one's Bruce, that one's the Great White Death, and that one is Mako."

"You named them after sharks."

"Oh, you noticed!" she says, smiling at me. "Yes, because they remind me of sharks. All those thrashing teeth. Dangerous as hell in here. This is the one place I fear for my Norse God more than the ocean. Okay enough of this room."

"No arguments from us."

"All right," she says and looks at Shelley Lynne. "You have a Muse, right?"

"Yes."

"Okay, be honest. How do you like it?"

"I love it! It's easy to play, and I really love the sound!"

"Awesome! Be sure to tell my husband. That will make his day. Definitely."

"Okay, I will."

"How 'bout Dad?" she asks, looking at me. "You have a Spirit, right?"

"Uh, no. I don't."

"Okay. A challenge. Well, let's see if we can make you a Spirit owner by the end of the tour, huh?" she laughs. "No pressure."

"We'll see," I smile.

"You do play, right?"

"I wouldn't call it that exactly. I'm just getting started. So, no. Not really."

"That's okay. Do you prefer finger picking or flat picking?"

"More like just, you know, strumming. Down strums mostly, so I can make very simple, very slow, chord changes every time I count to four so I can start a new chord on one."

"Okay. That reminds me, thank you. We have a five-step process. We start with wood selection, you've seen that. The next step is milling, and you've seen the shark tank. Norse God doesn't like it when I say that. He prefers to call it the milling room or just the mill. Next is assembly, and that breaks down into three major stages. The first one focuses on the neck, fretboard, and headstock. The second one focuses on the body. And the third one on joining the neck to the body. And all that starts in here."

We follow her into the next room.

"Okay, this contraption that looks like a mini paddlewheel from a riverboat is what we call the Huck Finn jig. Each top or soundboard is actually two matching pieces of wood glued together edge to edge. Then the glued piece is clamped and pressed into this rolling frame. It's almost like a paddle. See?" she says, giving it a spin.

"This jig was in the milling room, but we had to move it to make room for Bruce. Now when the tops are dried, they go back into milling, and Norse God will use a jig saw to cut out the top in the proper shape for the guitar he's making. Then the cut tops go on those shelves on the other side of this room. Next up is the steam room. It really isn't, but it's where the tables that have the side-bending jigs are set up. The wood strips used for the sides are bent over these steam pipes and then put into these molds to dry and keep their new shape."

Lani leads us around a corner where a well-muscled tall man in his late twenties stands, leaning over a belt sander, holding a guitar body in his hands and slowly moving it around. The sanding belt sends a faint spray of wood dust into the air. His shoulder-length, blond hair has a golden hue. His bushy mustache is a shade or two darker.

"Aloha, Norse God!" Lani calls out.

He pulls the guitar away from the sander and looks up. He grins. He lets go of the body with one hand and turns off the sander.

"Hey, there, Hula Babe. Who are your friends?"

"A very happy owner of one of our Muse models and her father. I'm giving them a tour. Sort of," she says, giggling.

His grin gets big.

"That's cool."

Lani nudges Shelley Lynne.

"Now would be a good time," she laughs.

"Yes. I have a Muse. I really love it a lot. I got it at Bo Jangles in Davis where I go to school. Lani said telling you that would make your day."

"Oh, most definitely."

"See? Told ya!" Lani giggles.

"And I'm fascinated by the whole woodworking thing you got going here."

He turns my way and cradles the body under his left arm.

"Yeah? Well, that's good to hear as well. I'm Eric by the way," he says, offering his hand.

I shake hands with him.

"The Norse God."

"That too."

"I'm Paul."

"Good to meet you."

"I'm Shelley Lynne."

"Good to meet you too. What do you like about your Muse?"

"It sounds good, really good. It's bright and woody, and it's so easy to play."

He nods, still grinning.

"Yeah? Good. Don't stop there. Keep going."

"That's it. That's all I got."

"Hey, I'm just joking with ya. That's great to hear. Thanks."

"You're welcome. What are you working on?" Shelley Lynne asks. "It looks smaller than a Muse."

"Oh, good eye. Yeah. I'm experimenting. This may be a new model. Thinking of calling it the Gypsy," he says as he takes it from under his arm, holds it up, and looks it over. "Not sure yet."

"Yeah? Who's it for?"

"Backpackers, beachcombers, barbecuers. Basically, I want to see if I can make the Muse into a travel guitar. This body is all walnut with a cedar top and maple binding like the Muse but about three-quarters in size. I might have something, or it might be a bust. I don't know yet."

"Sounds exciting."

"Yeah, I think so."

"Can I ask a question?" I ask.

He looks at me. "Without a doubt."

"What is binding?"

He shows me the body.

"On a guitar, binding is typically a strip of plastic or ivoroid. That's a kind of simulated ivory or a strip of wood that masks the area where the tops and backs meet the sides. Like here, see?" He runs a finger along the edge of the top. "See this edge?"

"I do."

"I'm gonna take a router and cut this edge back a bit, like making a little shelf right here, and then I'm gonna glue a strip of maple there. Then I'll sand it down till it's flush and smooth. When I'm done, I'll have this beautifully darkened chocolate hue of the walnut highlighted by the bright, creamy color of the maple. The body will look like a chocolate cake trimmed with vanilla frosting."

He looks up and shakes his head. "Okay, maybe I'm hungrier than I thought."

"Hey! You promised me you'd eat breakfast."

"I know. Sorry. I meant too, though. It's just, you know, the rain, getting busy in our shop . . ."

"Your shop. I don't do this work. I surf and throw pots. And yes, baby, I know."

She smiles, moves next to him, and leans up for a kiss and he bends down and gives her one.

Feeling lonely, I look away.

There's a loud grumbling.

"My Norse God! Is that your stomach?"

"Listen, maybe we should go and let you guys get some lunch or something."

"Oh, no way, man. I'm good. Trust me, I'll last."

"Okay."

"Besides," he says, "you gotta try this for yourself. Here."

He holds the body out for me.

I hesitate. "Wait."

"What's the matter?"

"Well, isn't there a book for this? You know, like a manual I can look at?"

There's a puzzled look on Norse God's face.

"What are you talking about, man?"

My pulse quickens.

"You know. A manual, a treatise, practice guide—something that lays out the procedural steps of the process. Is there anything like that?"

"Yeah, I suppose. Why?"

"Well, shouldn't I look at it first?"

"What for?"

"I-I'm just saying . . . look, I don't want to make a mistake, okay?"

"Why not, man? How you ever gonna know you got it right if you haven't messed it up first somewhere along the way? Besides, you been watching me, right?"

"Well, yes, but . . . you know."

"Then you've already seen all you need to know. The rest is just feel. You're never getting that out of a book."

I take a breath, reach out, and accept the body. I look at it as I hold it and run my fingers across the space near the sound hole where the bridge will go. I can feel the grain and that feels good.

"Okay." I move closer to the sander. "Are you sure?"

"Sure, I'm sure."

Chapter 28

"Okay."

Heavy sigh.

Got to remember to stop holding my breath. I try to copy what I think I remember him doing. I feel like an idiot. He's all excited about his work, his effort, and just like that he hands it to me like I'm his twin or something. I don't want to damage this work of art, and my head's flooding with thoughts of all the horrible ways I can screw this up. I pull back.

"I-I can't."

"No problem, man. It's okay. Here," he says, "hand it back to me."

I do. He sets it down.

"I'm sorry."

He waves me off.

"Oh, man, relax. No big deal."

He looks around and then reaches down into a bin on the floor and picks up a small block and then swaps it for another.

"Here. Try this. This is a tail block. See this side here?"

I look at it. The solid block is a slender sandwich of three different pieces of wood. The grain of each block runs a different direction.

"Yes."

"Good. Feel how rough that side is."

I do.

"Feel that?"

"Yes."

"Okay. Put it lightly against the belt like this." He demonstrates. "Do that a few times and get it smooth. Here. Give it a try."

Shit. Okay. Suck it up and just do this thing.

I give it a try, feeling like a total klutz-butt dipshit. I feel the vibrations of the belt through the block. The sensation is weird at first. Then it becomes damn near intoxicating. I lift and look and feel and put it back down, two, three—I don't know how many times, always checking.

"Ain't so bad now, is it?"

I can't help but grin.

"No. It's kinda fun in a way."

"Feels good, right?"

"It feels great, actually."

I'm embarrassed to admit it. My neck feels hot.

"Right on. I knew right off you're a woodworker."

I feel like I'm shrinking.

"Naw, I wouldn't go that far."

He grins.

"Give it time, man. Give it time."

I just nod. I check the tail block. The burred side is much smoother. I think I'm close to getting the proper curve. I hand it back to him, and he looks it over.

He puts two bent pieces that must be a pair of sides to a guitar into a wooden frame, and sure enough, they form the sides; only the top and back and the neck, of course, are missing. He holds the tail block on the inside of the form against the sides where they meet at what will become the bottom of the guitar.

"Nice work. Knew you could do it."

I'm pretty sure he's just saying that to be kind. Still, I can't help but smile. I bite my lower lip to stop smiling and to keep from saying anything stupid out loud.

He removes the sides from the frame. He holds one of them up.

"Walnut's a great wood to work with. Hand tools, power tools, whatever. Doesn't matter. I love this wood."

I nod.

"You will too. Anyway, there it is, man. The secret of happiness. Nothing's better than working wood."

Lani's eyebrows rise.

"Oh, is that so?"

Eric turns to her.

"Baby, that's a whole 'nother kind of happiness." He looks her over fondly. "I can easily talk about that kind of happiness if you'd rather. I don't mind at all."

She waves him off with a giggle.

"That's okay. No need to share. You can tell me later."

She looks up to him. They're lost in each other's eyes, and it's great.

I'm trying not to stare, and I'm trying not to be jealous. These kids are totally hot for each other, and I can't see how they have anything else in common except the ocean that brought them together.

"That's a promise," he says.

He looks at me and starts telling me how he assembles the bodies and how he shapes the necks and headstocks. He takes over the tour and shows me how he makes dovetail joints for putting the neck into the body, how he cuts the fretboards and how he cuts the frets from a grade of wire, and then shows me how he cuts the slots in the fretboard where the frets will go. We move on, and he frets a neck.

I'm getting a crash course in all things guitar making and everything he says and everything I see flows through my head like music, and I wish I could record it all without losing the spontaneity. He's on a roll—I don't know how else to describe it—and I'm rolling along with him and it's awesome.

I learn about varnish and lacquer and using them as a finish on the guitar. I learn about setting the bridge, about installing the tuners, stringing the guitar, and all the little finishing touches that go into the process, right down to a kiss before he packs each one into a shipping carton.

"Seriously?"

He grins.

"C'mon, man. I'm just messing with ya."

"Okay, right. You got me."

Christ! Am I wearing some kind of sign that's only invisible to me?

He grins.

"Well, you get the idea. I love making these instruments, man. Furniture's okay, I mean, it still pays most of the bills and that's what makes all of this over here happen." He picks up another one. "But this is where I put my heart."

All I can do is nod and hope for a place to put my own heart someday.

"Feel free to come around some weekend. I'll set you up with something easy to get your feet wet, if you want. I know you can hear the chisel calling."

"Yeah?"

"Sure. Why not?"

"Okay. I think I'd might like that. Maybe"

"Done, man, done."

We emerge into the office and store where we had started. Lani and Shelley Lynne are waiting and giggling over a box of hot pizza on the counter. I thought I had been smelling pizza.

Eric pointed at the box.

"Where'd this come from?"

"Our Muse owner insisted. She didn't think you guys were ever coming out."

"Oh, no way! You didn't have to do that."

"No worries, really," Shelley Lynne says, picking up another slice. "Please, have some, there's plenty."

"Okay. You won't have to twist my arm."

Lani hands him a cold beer, a Danish import.

"We also stopped at the liquor store."

"Oh, nice touch, Hula Babe! Thanks!"

I watch him devour a slice and knock back half a bottle of beer and sense an insight into his Viking ancestry, and words start coming out of my mouth.

"So how'd you get into the guitar-making business?"

"Fight with the ol' man."

I think I know where this is going and it's no journey I want to take, and I hold up a hand.

"Got it. Say no more. I'm good."

Then I blurt out, "How long you been in business?"

"Three years."

"That's pretty good."

"I think so. Okay, it's tough sometimes. I still need to work for him a couple days a week on average. Sometimes a little more. I just spend every free hour I can here."

I nod again.

"You do what you gotta do."

"That's it, man. I know I can't compete with the big guns. I'm aiming to find the right niche for me, a little sweet spot of my own where no one else can fit as well as I can. And that's the beauty of it, man. I mean, we're all struggling in this business. Even the big guns. We're all struggling to build, to craft, a guitar that sounds so good, with that perfect balance in the resonance of tones that ring pure and clean and plays so easy, and looks gorgeous, and does all of that without breaking the player's bank. The smaller the bank, the tougher it gets. Everybody's hungry for an edge. We're all searching for the right mix, for that perfect balance."

"Makes sense."

He grins.

"Yeah. And I live for that struggle every day. I love this, man. I love making wood sing."

"Like that sign I saw? The one in Latin hanging over the door way back there somewhere?"

"Yeah, man, you got it! *Viva fui silvis, sum dura occisa, securi dum vixi tauci, mortua dulce cano*—'I was alive in the forest, I was cut by the cruel axe, in life I was silent, in death I sweetly sing.' Yeah, man! That's what it is all about."

He devours more pizza and beer and looks at Shelley Lynne.

"Thank you for the pizza. Let's see, you look like—no. I want you to be comfortable."

He pulls a men's large hooded sweatshirt off the shelf and hands it to her.

"Here. Thanks for the pizza."

Shelley Lynne wipes her hands with a napkin and slips into the hoodie.

"Thank you too, Eric!"

"My pleasure. You'll have to come back when the Gypsy's done and test play it for me. Tell me what you think."

"Absolutely."

"You too, man."

He smacks me on the shoulder.

I catch Lani giving him a look.

But it doesn't stop me from raising my bottle of beer and saying, "Deal."

I put the bottle down, stand up, and walk over to the wall where the five guitars are hanging.

"Hey, Eric?"

"Yeah, man?"

"What do you call this cut out area, this style of cutaway that curves into a sharp point?"

"That's a Florentine-style cutaway. The rounder ones are called Venetian. Don't ask me why."

"Very cool. I like this feature. Is this guitar a Muse?"

"No. That one's a Spirit."

I nod. I turn around, thumbing over my shoulder at it.

"With walnut body and neck, maple binding, and the soundboard is?" I ask.

"Sitka spruce."

"Right." I say, looking at Shelley Lynne for a moment. "Your mother's gonna shit."

She looks at me for a moment. "Then let her shit."

"Eric, Lani," I say. "I want to buy one of these."

"Have you tried playing any of them yet?" Eric asks.

"Well, no."

"You might want to do that. In fact, I insist you play them all. That's why they're up there. Try all of them. Then pick the one in the style that sounds best to you, that feels most comfortable for you to hold, and that's the easiest for you to play. Don't just go for how it looks. That's secondary."

"And if the one that does doesn't have the cutaway, then what?"

"Then you get that style with the cutaway."

"Fair enough."

I sit on the stool and try them one at a time. I try them strumming my lifeline chords, slowly tapping my foot to keep a four-count beat and changing chords on the four count. Nobody criticizes me. Nobody laughs. Nobody says anything. A few minutes pass, and I'm lost in sound and forget they are there.

I don't tell them the guitars all sound almost the same to me. Except the bigger model, the Spirit, sounds fuller to me if that makes any sense. I'm not buzzing strings, and that feels so really, really good. I still end up choosing the Spirit with the Florentine cutaway.

Eric brings out two cardboard shipping boxes, removes the hard shell case from each, opens them, and has me play all three. They are all very close. I can't really tell them apart.

Finally, I just pick one at random, strum it a few times, and say, "It's this one."

"Then that's the one," Eric says.

"I put it back into the case, close the snaps, and, a moment later, pocket the credit card receipt for $817.50 and a cash receipt for

$67.13 for a strap, a men's extra-large hoodie with embroidered logo, and a baseball-style oil-skin cap with logo.

This is how I roll on Black Friday. I think today is Friday.

"Thank you, Lani," I say.

"Thank you!" We shake hands, and she hugs Shelley Lynne. "Please come back and see us, you guys."

"Definitely," says Shelley Lynne.

"Thanks, Eric," I say.

"Oh, you bet. Enjoy. And c'mon back when you're ready to start making sawdust."

"Deal."

Shelley Lynne and I walk out to the car. A light mist is falling from the low overcast. Before I can say anything, I hear the trunk lid pop open. Okay. I put my treasures in the trunk. I feel content, almost free. Shelley Lynne's already behind the wheel.

I want a moment to take it all in. I look around and start snapping pictures with my phone. I don't know if it's the weather, this place, or both or something else; but there's a feeling here— okay, as dumb as the word sounds to me—a vibe. It's real, and I have no words for it. I know Ryan would understand this place. I hope that if I take enough pictures, then I can hang on to it forever or at least remember something of what it's like here. I know I don't want to leave.

I stare up at the sky. I breathe in the cold mist. Reluctantly, I get into the car.

"You really like this place, huh, Papa?"

"Princess, I love this place."

I look past her and out the driver's door window at the enclave of little artists' studios and workshops, the row of little storefronts with walls of orange and yellow and pink stucco and red-tile roofs at the foot of a steep hill.

"I am so glad you brought me here."

"Oh, me too, Papa!"

She hesitates to start the car.

"We can sit here a while if you want. I'm okay with that."

"Papa?" she asks, looking straight ahead. "Do you love me?"

"Of course, I do!" I smile. "Why do you . . . feel the need to ask?"

She turns her head away and reaches up to her face. I notice the delicateness of her fingers as she wipes her eyes.

"I just really need to know."

"Okay." I wait a moment, take another breath, then another, and finally break the silence. "Why didn't you tell me?"

"I was afraid of losing the only father I have."

The words feel like a gut punch, and my eyes tear up. I take her hand and feel it squeeze in return.

"Princess, I love you always. You are mine. Forever."

She nods vigorously. Too choked up to speak.

I just breathe and feel the squeeze of her hand. I close my eyes and listen to the patter of the rain on the windshield. It's been an awesome morning. I want to hang on to this . . . this awesomeness for as long as I can because moments like these are so rare. Rare? Hell, I've never known a moment like this.

I feel her let go of my hand and hear the car start with a powerful rumble. I open my eyes, hoping I've made a good memory.

"You okay?" I ask.

She nods. The car starts moving. I take one last look as we leave and turn to get on the highway.

"Papa?"

"Yeah?"

"Do you really love my mother?"

"Always have. Why?"

"I don't think she loves you."

"And why do say that?"

"I think she's just using you to get back at my grampa."

"And how do you know this?"

"From Nana. She drinks. Then she talks."

"I see."

"I think it has something to do with my biological father. Eww. I hate those words."

"I don't know anything about him," I say, treading lightly.

"Me neither. Except what little I get from Nana. Apparently, Mom and Grampa had this big fight when they found out she was pregnant. Apparently, she was trying to hide it while deciding whether or not to abort me."

"I for one am certainly glad she didn't."

"Oh, Papa!"

I watch her wipe her eyes.

"Are you okay to drive? This is some heavy stuff here."

"I'll be okay. Anyway, last night, Nana's on a roll and she tells me that Grampa called my mother a tramp and said she probably didn't know who the father was."

"Ouch."

"Nana said my mother got in his face and yelled back and said, 'That's right, Daddy! I don't!' and then he slapped her hard."

"That hurt."

"Nana said it broke his heart."

"And hers too, no doubt. That's probably why she said it."

"You think so?"

"I know so. Let's just say your mother can be very, um, vengeful."

"You mean, like, get even?"

"That's what I mean."

"I think so too. I wish she didn't hate me so much."

"I don't know if I'd call it hate."

"Well, whatever you call it, that's how it feels."

"I know. Easier said than done, obviously. But find a way to forgive her. It will work out. She knows who it is. She won't say so she can continue punishing your grandfather as long as he keeps punishing her. Jesus. What a way to live all these years."

"I don't want to know who it is. He's not in my life. You are, Papa, and I don't want to lose you."

"Oh, Princess, you can never lose me, okay? You're safe. Olly olly oxen free. You're safe."

I hear her exhale and see her shoulders drop. What an anvil that thought must have been for her to carry around all this time.

"Nana said that was the night Grandpa cut Mother off and told her to get a job. Nana says he hasn't given her a dime since. It was Nana who secretly paid for nursing school. Though I have a hunch Grandpa knew all along. He even tried to throw her out, but Nana fought back. He finally gave in but then made their lives hell. I think that's when Nana started drinking. She's been pretty good at hiding it. Not so much anymore, though. I didn't really catch on till high school. I think the rest of the family history you already know."

"Yeah, but it can't hurt to tie up a few loose ends, though I've never really tried to find out either."

"I don't think she loves either of us, Papa. I think she just pretends. Maybe not even so much of that anymore."

"Well, let's hope not. Let's love her anyway and hope maybe that's just her way of dealing with the pain."

"Pretty sucky way of doing it. Making others suffer too."

Deep breath time.

"Yes. You're right, of course. It is. I don't have an answer for that."

"It's okay, Papa. I'm not asking for one."

Too much information, and my gut burns. I turn and look back over my shoulder at the traffic behind us. It's official. The morning's now a memory. Damn, I really hope it's a good one. Glad I took pictures.

I think I'd give almost anything to go back to Laguna Canyon and Calypso Guitars.

Chapter 29

The rest of the drive is quiet. Shelley Lynne seems relieved, almost happy. She's playing some Duggie through her MP3. That's good.

I'm torn over having it out with Tami, once and for all. I'm stewing over the shrink sessions and stuff I need to do, and God knows what else I don't want to deal with. Even Duggie sounds annoying to me now. That's bad.

I close my eyes and see the Norse God totally absorbed in making sawdust as he cuts, sands, and shapes, and glues all these different pieces of wood into a guitar. I need something like that in my life. I need a place like that in my life. I'm vaguely aware of music in the background. Not so annoying now.

She turns the car into Nana's driveway and drives on to where my car is parked and parks next to it. We get out. She hugs me.

"Super squeeze," she says. "Love you, Papa. Love you so much."

"Love you too, Princess." I retrieve my new treasures from her trunk and put them in the trunk of my car.

The air is chilly with a damp breeze. The skies are overcast. In the distance, orange leaves are swirling in the air.

"I'm ready for some hot chocolate. Are you?" she asks.

"Sure."

We have the kitchen to ourselves and make hot chocolate which we enjoy on a porch swing at the back of the house, staring off into the woods and watching the trees shed leave their leaves. Autumn is awesome.

"This is a great way to end our day, Princess. Thank you."

She beams. "You're welcome, Papa."

"Heading up to Sac tomorrow?"

"Yep."

"I'm gonna miss you."

"I'm gonna miss you too, Papa."

My phone buzzes. I check it and see a text from Ryan.

It says, "All quiet here. Let me know if you need a place to crash."

"From Mom?"

"No. A friend from work, Ryan."

I show her the text.

"You should go, Papa," she sighs. "Mom won't be any fun this weekend. Not after yesterday. No point in you beating yourself up trying to fix it."

"Yeah. Maybe you're right."

Chapter 30

I look at my phone and thumb a reply, "What time is check-in?"

Within seconds, he answers, "Whenever you get here. Door's open."

"This is a good idea, Papa. I'll have a quiet dinner with my grandparents and spend the evening with them. It means a lot to them."

"Shelley Lynne, my Princess, you are wise beyond your years."

"Thank you, Papa."

It's almost dark when I arrive. A thick blanket of blue-gray clouds obscure the peaks of the near-black mountains. As I get out of the car, I feel how much colder the air is up here. Even in my jacket, I shiver. I pop the trunk and take out the guitar case. I hear boots crunching in the gravel. The sound's coming this way.

"Hey, dude, you made it. Welcome!"

"Thanks."

"Hope you're all turkey-ed out, dude. Got us some pizzas from this killer little shop down the in the village. Glad they were open. Turkey's so overrated anyway."

"Love pizza."

"Right on. Whatcha packin' there?"

"Oh, my daughter and I had a great day and we got a tour of Calypso Guitars. They're in Laguna Beach, and I bought one. Love to show ya."

"Love to see it. C'mon in."

I follow Ryan into the barn. Despite the cold, I take another look around, but it's too dark to see.

"I gotta tell ya, man, your place is so cool. I love it up here. Your place and Calypso have got to be my two all-time favorite places. It's a shame they're not closer together. I hate driving."

"Well, you're done driving for now. C'mon in. Okay if we eat first?"

"Sure. So peaceful here, so idyllic. Though I think traffic sucks sometimes with everybody using the same road to get in and out. You take that into account and stock up so you don't have to leave, right?"

"Mostly. Traffic doesn't bother me, dude."

"I was in a bookstore the other day. I saw this book about the musicians living up in Laurel Canyon in the '60s. I almost bought it. Now I wished I had."

"No need to. I got it. Borrow it anytime."

"Cool. Thanks. I mentioned it because I think of that place every time I'm up here. It's like this place is Laurel Canyon East."

"That's funny, dude. It's much nicer here. But my guess is we're a little short on musicians. Not many budding rock stars fan out this far."

"Oh, I don't know. Seemed like you had a few the last time I was here."

"That's nice of you to say, dude. Grab a chair."

I grab a chair. Ryan sets the pizza boxes down on the table and walks over to the potbelly stove, opens it, and tosses in another chunk of wood from the stack on the brick floor.

"Beer or soda?"

I think for a moment. Oh, what the hell.

"Beer," I say.

He points to a metal tub full of ice.

"Help yourself," he says as he sits down at the table.

"Okay." I get up and go to the tub, bend down, and reach in. "You want one?"

"Please."

I fish through the ice and pull out two beers. I come back, hand him one, and sit down. He opens his and slides the opener across the table. I open mine, set it down, and grab a slice of pizza.

"Damn! That's hot." I drop it onto a paper plate and grab the icy bottle.

"There it is. That's the story of your life, dude—this chapter of it, anyway."

I blink. I blink again. I have to think about this. Another one of Ryan's riddles.

"You mean like, slow down?"

"Duh."

"I don't know, man. Maybe I'm just not wired that way."

"Your choice, dude. You might wanna give some thought to rewiring yourself. Speaking of which, how's the practicing coming?"

"That, I'll have you know, is the one part of my life that is going slow," I smile. "Quite slow, actually."

"But it's still going, right?"

"Yeah. It's still going."

I drink some beer and eat a slice of pizza.

"That's good. I haven't seen you much at the office lately. I've been crazy busy. And you don't need anyone checking up on you. How's life on the home front?"

I take another slice of pizza.

"Right now, let's just say we sort of have an uneasy truce. It's like the Cold War I always heard about in the news growing up. Each side's waiting for the other to blink or go nuclear."

"That's too bad, dude."

We chow down the pizzas. They're good.

"I think these are maybe better than at Lil' Italy's, you know? I feel guilty just thinking that."

"No need to. It's the same family. It's the grandson. He's in construction and that's seasonal, so they set him up with this as a backup."

"Nice!"

"I'll say. Here."

He tosses me some wet wipes. I clean my hands. He throws more wood into the stove.

"It's getting a little cold for beer. Any chance you got some hot chocolate?"

"Sorry, dude. This is apple country. All I got is cider."

"Oh yeah! Can you make it like last time? That was really good."

"Yeah, dude," Ryan says, grinning and laughing. "Yeah, I can make it like last time."

"What?"

"Nothing, dude. It's good to see you excited for a change."

"Okay."

"Lemme use the john first. Then give me a minute. I'll be back in a few."

"Sure."

"It'll also give you a chance to break in your new guitar."

"Oh yeah!"

I reach for the case and open it. I take out the guitar and rest it on my right thigh. I form a D chord and strum it. I release my fretting fingers and strum it again. I do this a few times then release my middle and ring fingers slide down my index finger down one fret and put the tips of the middle and ring fingers on their strings, press down, and strum an A.

I release them all slightly as my strumming hand comes up and then press down on the strings again as I strum down on the strings, sounding another A. I do this a few times, each time to one beat of a four-beat count, and then switch back to D for four beats, and then back to D for four beats. All the while, I tap the floor with my left foot.

"Hey! Look at you! You're coming along! You've been practicing. Can you see how relaxed you are? Dude, this is awesome! I'm happy for you."

I feel my goofy grin.

"And this is the Calypso?"

"Yeah, this is it. A Calypso Spirit. Soundboard's Sitka spruce. Back and sides are some kind of walnut—Claro, I think. So's the neck and head stock. Fretboard and bridge are, I want to say, rosewood. Not sure."

"Walnut? Interesting. Hey, now. That's some beautiful wood," he says, admiring the walnut back and sides. "That's a nice little axe you got there, dude. Pretty."

He strums a few chords.

"That's good sound. Righteously good sound. Dude, you got a lot of value for the money on this," he smiles and hands it back to me. "I'm proud of you, dude! You done good. Real good."

I feel my goofy grin getting bigger.

"Thanks. I met the kid who makes 'em. He's like this super buff, twentysomething, Viking guy. Swear to God he looks like Thor hanging out in a woodshop. He's got sawdust in his beard, you know, he's got the whole thing."

"Right on."

"Yeah, and he loves—I mean, *he absolutely loves*—what he's doing." I take another hit on my beer. "I have no fucking idea what that must be like. Anyway, he's all about the wood and crafting guitars from it. But he's scared too, I think, and yet he's fearless at the same time. Damn. I'm not making any sense, am I?"

"Dunno yet. Keep talking."

"It's like this. His old man runs a furniture business, really successful, and the kid works there too. And the old man really wants him in that business, but the kid's also got his own shop. And he's making these really decent guitars, and he knows everything he's up against, but he does it anyway. Like, fearless, you know?"

"I do."

"And he's married to this sweet little hottie of a Hawaiian doll, a drop-dead gorgeous little surfer chick who does pottery. She's got this bronze body, all muscle but so beautiful and graceful, like a dancer. She's got long, black hair, dark eyes, and this brilliant snow-white smile. Ryan, did I tell you she is drop-dead gorgeous? Man, I really struggled to keep from staring at her."

"I bet."

"Anyway, she calls him Norse God, and he calls her Hula Babe, and they are happy as clams and so in love. And I have never in my whole life ever seen a couple like that, and I'm so jealous I could cry, and why am I even telling you this?"

"I dunno. Anyway, relax, dude. No one's gonna know."

"Fair enough."

Another sigh escapes.

"You shoulda seen 'em, man. Oh, and get this! So Hula Babe, her name's Leilani Tonono—okay, it's Gregersen now. She goes by Lani, and she's giving my daughter and me a tour of the place. And we meet Norse God, his name's Eric Gregersen, right? And he's buff-sanding some guitar body. It's something experimental, and he hands it to me and tells me to do it, and of course, I chicken out cuz I'm scared shitless I'll ruin it. So he takes it back and then he pulls a tail block out of a bin and gets me sanding it into the proper shape and says I'm a woodworker. That he could tell I'm a woodworker."

I'm shaking my head. "Can you believe that? I mean, it was fun and all. Hell, it was a blast. But woodworker? I wouldn't go that far. Not yet, anyway. Then get this, he tells me that I've got an open invitation to come down anytime and start learning to build guitars. How insanely cool is that?"

"I'd say that's insanely cool, dude. How soon do you start?"

"Oh, I don't know. But if I do, you'll have to come down and meet these kids. They're amazing."

"Okay."

"Yeah, I think he's got a system going, and it seems to be working for him, and she totally believes in him, and they're taking on the big-ass scary world, and they're just so happy together." I reach for my mug. "How do you do that?"

"You go with your gut."

"Yeah, but that ain't me, man."

"I know."

"Yeah, he told me to come on down and he'd start me off making tail blocks and that we'd go from there. He said I could learn something and that he could get some free help in the bargain."

"Sounds like a fair trade to me, dude. You oughta do it."

"Think so?"

"Yes."

"Okay. Maybe I should."

"Yeah, dude. You definitely should."

I put my mug down and look at my new guitar.

"I mean, it's amazing! Look at this thing, Ryan. He built this"—I pick the Calypso Spirit up—"this instrument, this guitar, all by himself. I've never built anything by myself in my entire life. Well, except for a few plastic model airplanes at my grandparents' place. But I don't think that counts all that much."

I can't help it. My eyes tear up.

"I hear ya."

"I'm talking to him, you know, and we come out into the store area of the shop, and Lani and Shelley Lynne are waiting for us with beer and pizza, and I see some of his guitars hanging on the wall, and I wanted to play them."

"That's why they were on the wall, dude."

"Yeah, right? Duh! I know now. I asked if I could play one, and he laughed and said, 'Yeah, play 'em all,' and I did, only, you know? But, it's not like I'm really playing, right? I'm just strumming some of my lifeline chords and nobody's giving me any shit about it."

"They wouldn't do that, but you're right. I know what you mean, dude."

"So I do and, of course, they all sound pretty much the same to me. They all sound amazing actually, and I really liked this one." I pick it up again. "Mainly cuz of this cutaway thing."

"The Florentine."

"Yeah! How'd you know?"

"Dude."

"Oh, right. Sorry. So I pick this one, right? And then he brings out three more just like this one, and I play 'em all, and of course, they all sound the same to me. But I can't tell them that, you know?"

"I understand."

"So I say, it's this one, and I hold it up, and it's the one I saw on the wall the first time. And he smiles at me and says, then that's the one, and I buy it. Along with a hat and a hoodie."

"Good for you, dude. I'm really proud of you. How about your daughter?"

"You mean did she get one?"

"Did she?"

"No, she already has one of their guitars. It's little smaller than this. She has a Muse model. Pretty sure it's a '00' body size. She got it in a shop up in Davis at school. That's how she knew about Calypso and arranged the tour. It was a surprise trip for me she had planned."

"Very cool, dude. Very cool."

"Yeah, so very cool. I mean, I got to watch this guy work. Amazing. He's so skilled, so methodical, so focused. And so much of it is just feel, and that part just kills me. And then, on top of it all, he's just so damn nonchalant about the whole thing, like it's no big deal, just an everyday thing. Holy Christ! I couldn't be nonchalant folding a paper airplane."

Ryan laughs. "I know. The paper would be as creased as your forehead."

I shrug. "I know. Right?"

"Ease up. Don't go south on me, dude. Drink up. You're doing great. I'm lovin' the story."

"You're right."

I grab my mug and drink up. The cider's cold, but I down it anyway. Ryan probably knows.

"Anyway, knowing he made this, I had to have it." I shrug again. "Besides, I need my own anyway, and borrowing yours makes me nervous. But it's not so bad, keeping it at the office like you said."

"And if you'll allow me to make a suggestion, I'd keep this one in your office too, along with my loaner, if I were you. Don't you dare let your ice queen anywhere near it. I'm serious, dude."

"Oh, I know. I get it. And I will too."

Ryan gets up and puts another piece of wood in the stove.

"You're gonna do it, right?"

"You mean work for the Norse God?"

"Exactly."

"Man, I don't know. I want to think about it. I mean, it sounds great and all that, but it's gotta be too good to be true. He's a great guy, I'm sure he's . . . he's just being nice."

"Try *honest*. Dude, if he didn't mean it, he wouldn't have made the offer. Take him up on it. Go learn to make guitars and do happy shit for a change."

Chapter 31

I catch myself holding my breath again and, this time, nicely remind myself to keep breathing. It's all good, and I don't beat myself up over it.

"So you think I could do it?"

"Damn it, dude! It doesn't friggin' matter what I think or what Tami thinks or what Woo or Darryl or any other sorry-ass motherfucker thinks. All that ever matters is what you think, and dude, you think way too damn much! Go with your gut once in a while and stop living in your fucking head all the time. Shit, dude, hasn't your shrink made that clear enough yet?"

We just look at each other. I blink first.

"Okay, I apologize. I'm way out of line here. Let me try this again."

He rubs his neck and wipes his hand across his mouth.

"Hell yeah, dude! I think you can do it. I think you are tailor-made to do it. I shit you not. Now listen to yourself for a minute when you're not overthinking everything and second-guessing yourself into some friggin' pit. You were alive in that dude's shop."

Ryan uncurls his index finger from his mug hand and points at me.

"Alive! You were happy and alive down there, dude! You hear me? You had a say in the process of doing something that obviously matters to you! Are you getting me? You were taking part in making a musical instrument, dude, and if even if you don't know it, your insides and your unconscious and wherever the fuck you've managed to bury the real you, all them dudes know about it. I am righteously excited for you!"

"I-I know what you're saying, and I actually thought about the part about kinda making a piece—okay, a little piece of a guitar—and I agree that's pretty cool. But I can't tell anyone that stuff."

"Well, you can tell me! Seriously, I am here for you, dude. There it is. Go work for that dude and make happy shit that matters, but only for as long as it matters to you! And I'll tell you what. I'll help you out this one time on one condition. Okay, two conditions."

"Okay. What conditions?"

"First, stop judging yourself. I mean it, dude. Just go for it. Just learn from the dude, have fun, and don't get all hung up thinking about it. Second, keep playing, keep practicing. Stick with something and see it through, just for yourself and nobody else."

He runs a hand through his hair.

"I can see now that, for you, learning to play the guitar and learning to build a guitar go hand in hand. Okay. Each skill set inspires and develops the other. I can feel that. That is awesome. That in and of itself is a gift, dude. A great gift! If this is working for you, then just go for it. Learn from the dude and keep playing. Will you do that?"

"Yeah. I can—I mean, I will."

"Okay then. I'm gonna help you out. Here we go. You've got my permission and my blessing to do this. I'm your second, dude. Like that French novel, I'm Athos to your d'Artagnan. I am with you all the way."

I feel a smile spread like wildfire across my face.

"Yeah, dude, that's more like it. That's the face you need to be seein' in the mirror every day. I want to see that look from now on. That one, right there. That happy face."

⸻ ✦✦✦✦ ⸻

I wear my happy face to the office Monday morning, and I'm still wearing it right up to the moment I absentmindedly answer my buzzing cell phone and hear Tami's voice.

"What the hell did you do, Paul?"

"I'm not sure. Care to give me a hint?"

"Black Friday, you idiot! You went shopping!"

"Black Friday? No I didn't. I hate malls."

"I'm not talking about a stupid mall! Think, Paul! Where did you go last Friday?"

"I went with Shelley Lynne to Laguna. Why, what happened?"

"You went shopping in Laguna, Paul!"

"No I didn't. We toured this really cool, kind-of-bohemian guitar shop where they make guitars. Okay, this one guy, the one who owns it, he makes guitars. I think he has some help, but mainly it's him."

"Damn it, Paul! Will you just shut up and focus for a minute? What did you buy there?"

"I didn't buy anything. Wait! Oops, my bad. Yeah, I did buy some stuff."

"That's right, Paul! You did! You put $817.50 on our credit card, Paul! *Our* credit card! That's almost a thousand dollars! Did it ever occur to you to ask me first?"

"No, not really."

"What do you mean *no*? You went and spent nine hundred dollars on a something Calypso. Whatever the hell that is. You put it on our credit card. You didn't even have the courtesy to ask me first. That's almost a thousand dollars, Paul! What the fuck did you buy, Paul? Spending that much money needs to be a joint decision! We are a partnership, Paul! That's what a marriage is all about, remember? Partnership! Are you telling me it never occurred to you to at least discuss it with me?"

"Yeah. Pretty much."

"Tell me why, Paul! Enlighten me!"

"Honestly, I didn't think it would be big a deal. Besides, I'm a grown man. I'm a professional. I don't need your permission for this. It's not like I bought a car or a house. Something like that, sure, of course, I'd talk to you first. This is different, and I don't spend this much every month. In fact, I don't remember having spent anywhere near this much at any time over the last six or seven years. So what's the big deal now?"

"That's not the point, Paul! This hurts me! Deeply! What about trust? And what the hell is a Calypso anyway?"

"It's an acoustic guitar."

"*What?*"

"All wood. No laminates or ply veneers. It has a Pacific Northwest Sitka spruce top. Nice pale color."

"Paul!"

"That's the soundboard. Claro walnut back and sides. Deep browns and purples."

"Paul!"

"Rosewood fretboard and bridge. Florentine cutaway. Easy and comfortable to play. There's a lot of value there for the money. Easily double that with any of the major manufacturers out there."

"You bought a guitar? No! Don't you dare tell me you're a grown man and then in the next breath tell me you bought a guitar! Grown men—professional men—do not buy themselves guitars! *Ever*! No, Paul! You had no right to go against me like this!"

"I didn't go against anybody. We agreed this would be my hobby that I'd share with our daughter and that, yes, I'd do the judge thing just like you asked. Okay. *Demanded*. Whatever."

"First of all, whatever the agreement for a hobby you can share with our little Barbie did not ever include you buying any guitars! Secondly, you dare call it a *demand*? The only demand is that you take it back!"

"Nope."

"Paul!"

"Tami!"

Click.

That went well. Or maybe not . . .

So much for my happy face today.

So much for my happy face the Monday after that, and for several more Mondays after that, I've tried. I'm pretty much faking it.

Christmas was no different than any other day of the week, except I was off and pretty much had the day to myself. Tami made sure she had lots of extra shifts to work through the holidays or so she said. Shelley Lynne got invited to go skiing with friends. I'm glad she went with them.

Just like it was with her birthday, Tami didn't want anything—or, rather, insisted I not get her anything—unless and until I had checked with her first and gave up the guitar for good. But I couldn't bring myself to do that. Tami hasn't been around much since.

She gave me a T-shirt for Christmas. It's a black T-shirt with "Guitarded" silk-screened in big, bold, white letters across the front and a rather snide definition under it, also in white dictionary-style letters.

It came with a generic holiday greeting card that included a slip of paper with a computer pass code to an online porn site, one specializing in romantic erotica for couples. Touché. I watched a couple of them. Decent-enough-looking young people having fun, having fun sex—I get it. No need to see any more. Too depressing.

I keep practicing, but it's getting harder. I've hit a plateau. I've also had some great Saturdays at Calypso and several not-so-great Saturdays when Eric had to do furniture work so I wasn't needed. It's been a frustrating time of hit and miss.

I realize that's pretty much what my whole life has been up to now—just hits and misses. A few hits now and then but mostly misses. Still, I want it to go on. There's so much to learn and trying to learn it as I go. One day a week here and there probably isn't the best way, but it's all I have for now.

Whatever happy face I had, real or fake, is pretty much gone by lunchtime the Friday after St. Patrick's Day when I look up from my desk and see Darryl standing in my office.

"How long you been standing there?"

"Not long. You seem lost in thought. That's good. Got a minute?"

Let's see . . . Hmm, how do I tell you, no?

"Sure."

"Got something else for you to think about."

He takes a folded piece of paper from his pocket and holds it up.

"You have skills, slugger. Your big problem, as I see it, is your total lack of self-confidence. Been there, done that, got the licensing rights. In short, I can help you with that. These eggheads you're working for push you for solutions and then back down when you deliver. You have no future here. None. I can help you with that too. Face facts, Paul. This ship's sinking. I think it's time you abandon it. Here's my offer."

He hands me the folded slip of paper.

"Think about it. Make sure you understand what you're getting into. Slaves have more freedom. You need to know that up front. On the other hand, I'm talking real money here, so don't take it if you can't commit to me 100 percent. An opportunity like this comes at a very high price—and for a very good reason—so this isn't for everyone, even if they do have the skills I'm looking for."

I look at the little white square under my thumb.

"You're trying to decide whether or not to open it. Got you pegged," he grins. "Anyway, I'll expect your answer on Monday morning and not before. Understand? Not before."

I look up. "I understand."

"Excellent. Send a text to my cell number. A simple *yes* or *no* will do. My offer lapses Monday at 9:00 a.m. sharp." He reaches for his phone. "And speaking of phones, there's one more piece of information I want you to think about. I believe it's relevant to your decision."

Darryl holds the phone out, so I can see the image.

"Recognize this guy?"

"Isn't he that appellate court justice? What's his name? He spoke at the last dinner thing we went to."

"Correct. Lynne Michael Taylor, associate justice, Ninth Circuit."

He selects another image.

"I believe you recognize this woman."

He shows me a picture of Tami with the same background as the one with Taylor.

My heart starts pounding.

"Of course you do. And now, the moment you've been waiting for. Drumroll please."

He shows me the phone again. This time, it's a photo of Taylor and Tami in a deep lip-locked embrace, and the palm of her hand is on the back of his bald head.

"This was taken yesterday afternoon. Treasure Island is lovely this time of year. It's so popular with lovers."

I can hardly breathe. If ever I needed a poker face, it's now. And I just don't have it. I blink. I swallow hard. I'm losing it.

"I know just what you're thinking. It's good to be the judge. What can I say, slugger? The truth hurts. You know what else they say about the truth, right?"

I look down toward my desk. "It will set you free."

"Exactly correct. Consider this image for perspective and motivation. Nothing more. Trust me, Paul. Your life's at the crossroads. I'm offering you a new path. Think it over. You'll thank me later."

He puts the phone away.

"Think about it. Let me know on Monday."

I look up. He's gone. I stare at the blank screen of my computer. *This isn't working.*

I get up and move to the doorway of my office. The whole floor looks different now. Like the whole bureaucratic veil has been lifted from this place. I understand I've been ignoring the crap that's been going on here for probably forever, stuff I don't remember seeing in private practice. Secretaries with unwashed hair and moping about in their yoga pants pretending to work. Tired bitches using their workspace computers for their shopping needs and social media bullshit. A couple of supervisors use theirs to book golf trips and travel.

Fuck this place.

I walk away from my office. There's three loud women congregating en masse in the only doorway that leads to the restrooms, milling about, discussing their various health issues in intimate detail, oblivious to anyone trying to get through, like me, to get into the men's room and do my own business.

Wouldn't it be nice if they just hung out together in one of their own cubicles instead of the only public space that should remain open and accessible so that others can use the restrooms without having to delicately maneuver around and between them, standing there arrogantly, oblivious to anyone else's presence?

Selfish bastards.

"Excuse me," I say politely and navigate my way in and, when I'm done, again on my way back out.

I shouldn't have bothered. They ignored me anyway. It's like I'm suddenly invisible as well as irrelevant.

That's fine. I could use some invisibility about now. That and some brass knuckles.

I don't want to see any more of this world. I need some other world.

I want to hear. I want to listen. I want to know that what I hear is an A minor just from the sound of the strum of the strings. Same thing goes for the B minor and the F# major and all the chords. I want to know them all, hear them all, play them all.

I still can't muster a poker face, and I'm pretty sure the best face I can do is more like the thousand-yard stare. I'm probably still wearing it when I wander back into my office sometime later. Ryan and Danny are there, waiting.

"Hey, man. How you holding up?" Danny asks, closing the door.

"I'm okay," I flat out lie to him and sit down.

I turn in my chair and glance at the guitar case in the corner behind me.

"Why?" I ask.

"Nothing in particular. Heard it's been a rough week for you."

"I don't know. I've kept on top of things. Why, have you heard something, anything?"

"Naw, same old crap. Your wife still on her hiatus?"

"Something like that. Not a big deal." I'm staring at my desk now.

"Good. That's good to know. Paul, listen, Ryan here's been burning the midnight oil a bit heavy these past few weeks, so I am dragging him off to Vegas for a guy's getaway weekend. and frankly, he's reluctant about leaving you behind. I agree. We want you to tag along. Whataya say?"

"No. I don't think I can. I can't."

"Paul, you need a break from this place."

"What about Robby?" I ask, having nothing else to say and wanting nothing more than for them to leave.

"Naw, I prefer to leave it a threesome," Danny says.

"Sounds good. I suppose."

I'll just wait for them to leave.

"Then it's a deal. Good man. I'll meet up with you guys at Ryan's place at four. I want to head out before it gets dark. Oh, I already cleared it with Woo and Huntington. You're good."

"Okay."

I can't think. I need to think.

"That means the three of us are getting off at three today." He checks his watch. "All right. I'll see you gents at four."

"Okay."

Danny gives me a pat on the shoulder, turns, opens the door, and leaves. Ryan lingers.

"Lunch plans or are you waiting to tell me something?" I ask him.

"I'm down for lunch if you are, dude. You still need to practice when we get back though."

"Fair enough. Maybe something quick then."

"That works. Tell you what, dude. You get started, and I'll make a taco run."

"Okay."

He leaves, closing the door behind him, and I reach for the case. I lower it to the floor, release the snaps, open it, and take out my Spirit guitar. The arms of my chair get in the way, so I make room on my desk and sit there. I fumble a bit framing a G chord and remind myself not to beat myself up about it still not being automatic. And besides, as my daughter would say, "I've got a totally bitchin' excuse" now.

I just accept that all the clutter in my head is getting in the way. I can't think. Maybe I need to let go and listen to the strings and adjust to the sound, if I can find the will and the way.

I try a C next, and the same thing happens. I remember I usually start with an A or D, so I choose to work on G and C today. I tell myself it's okay to go slow. What the hell, my life ain't going nowhere any time soon. Hell, I'm probably already there.

I start with G, taking my time and getting my fingers on the strings over the fret spaces just right, press down, strum, and then just ease up a bit, maintaining touch on the strings and press down again. I do this slowly and repeatedly to help build the muscle memory of this chord shape and convince the fretting fingers to move together as one. They never want to do that, so that's still hard for me, and I often get frustrated and think I can't do it. I keep at it, fighting through the growing impatience.

"You're just wasting your time, Paul."

I mute the strings and look up.

Robby's all glassy-eyed and staring at me from the doorway, leaning against the doorjamb.

"I didn't ask you."

He waves an arm. "No matter. I'm telling you anyway, as a friend."

Friend? I've got enemies who'd make better friends. Must be Dump on Paul Day. First Darryl, now Robby.

"Darryl sent you, right?"

He waves me off.

"He's an ass. I don't listen to him."

He slides along the door, takes out his phone, taps the screen, and then shows me an image of a gorgeous young brunette. The image looks like a photo of a photo. But an old one. I'm confused.

"Okay. She's gorgeous. Your daughter?"

"My wife. A few weeks before we married. About a year before she died."

Ouch. My mouth is going dry.

"I'm sorry."

"Me too. Every day. Every fucking day." He puts the phone away. "Your wife is to absolutely die for, you know that, right?"

He doesn't wait for an answer.

"She's still alive. She's still yours. Why do you want to throw all that away? For what?"

He points at my guitar.

"For that? Listen to me, Paul. Don't fuck this up. She's your dream girl. You've said so yourself. I heard she calls you 'guitarded,' and that means even she gets it. She knows you got no chance at this."

Robby catches his breath.

"Look, I was eleven when I started, okay? My brother played. My dad played professionally. He was a studio musician. Feast and famine. Half the kids in my neighborhood played. In two months' time, I was skipping homework and practicing two hours a night. All summer long, I couldn't get enough. I was playing six, sometimes eight, hours a day, every day. Every day, Paul."

He does his arm wave again.

"Be smart for once, Paul, you hear me? For God's sake, be smart here. Choose your trophy wife and give her whatever the hell she wants while you still can. Don't be a dumb shit. I'd give anything, Paul—anything to have mine back," he sighs. "Remember this. Only champions get the trophies, Paul. You are never going to be a champion. Think about that."

He leaves.

"Okay."

I wait. I make sure he's gone. I get up and close the door. I pick up my guitar and play, sitting on my desk with my back to the door. Just like I did yesterday. I practice lifting my fretting fingers off the strings completely but staying very close to them and then pressing down again. I do a series of simple down strums using my right thumb. As it swings up, I lift my fretting fingers slightly off the strings. As my right thumb swings down, I fret the strings, staying in time with the movement of my thumb for the next strum, just like yesterday.

It's become so hard to concentrate. The sound is still pleasant enough, thank God, not much buzzing fortunately, and the sound helps me fight all the heavy thoughts weighing me down.

Thoughts of Tami and Treasure Island and that other guy. Then there's the thought that I am forever wasting my time doing something that's only for kids who get awesome in their teens and then famous in their twenties and no one in their right mind, and certainly not a professional, ever tries to do in their fifties.

I don't need Robby's advice. Hell, I've got plenty of my own head voices telling me that stuff. Then there's the thought I can't bear to think anymore. I think chicks dig licks instead of only champions getting the trophies, and I try harder; but it's so hard to concentrate. I end up just going through the motions, and my mind wanders to Tami. I can't lose her.

It's no use. I've had enough. I can't do this right now. I just sit there, hunched over my guitar. My mind wanders off, and in my head somewhere, I hear Tim telling me, "See? Like that. Told ya you could do it," and I remember him smiling as I'm strumming his acoustic—the same one he would leave for me when he moved away.

I remember getting the hang of it, little by little, and switching between a couple of chords just fine. I feel awesome. He's tapping me on the shoulder and telling me I've finally got it, and I'm feeling my shoulder really moving, and I blink and look up at Ryan. That feeling lingers for a moment, and I manage a smile before it fades.

"Good for you, dude."

I put the guitar in its case and pay Ryan for the tacos and large cola. Except for the loud, crunching noise, we eat in silence. I'm too numb to care. But that feeling of goodness from that memory of Tim keeps coming back, just enough for me to notice. It was a happy day, and I want it back.

I think about it, and I remember other happy days with my grandparents. I want them back too, but they're long gone, so I'll settle for the memories. As many as the Lord will let me have. Feelings of goodness and sadness, my life then, my life now, advance and recede like waves on a beach. I reach for the case and open it again and take the guitar out. I look at it—really look at it. There's a voice in my head that says I'm being silly, that I should just grow up and stop acting stupid.

"No. Go away."

I hold my guitar gingerly by the neck and run my right hand along the side, following the curve from upper bout to lower bout, feeling the silky feel of the wood and admiring Norse God's craftsmanship.

I imagine Tim's voice again. I listen for it. It's there, I know it's there; even if I can't hear it, I decide that's okay. It's okay. I rest the guitar on my leg so its waist curves over my right thigh. I close my eyes and try to remember the chords Tim had shown me that day. But I can't. I decide that's okay.

It's okay. From habit, I form the D chord shape; and in the silence, I remember Shelley Lynne helping me learn how to switch between D and A with that "slide, hop, strum, and let-'er-ring" technique. I can't help but smile, even with all the crap I'm dealing with. I remember her telling me that if I add a G after the A, then I'd have the chords to my favorite Duggie song.

I close my eyes and softly strum the D. It's clean, and it's good. I slide and hop to the A and strum, and it's good and it's clean. I slide back to D and I do it all again, and it's good and it's clean. And I think I'm gonna be okay. This will do. I'm not spoiling it trying for the G. This'll do for now.

I'm not giving it up. I can do this. Yes, I suck now, but it won't always be like it is now. I don't need anybody telling me I'm too old and too slow and I suck or that I have no talent or that I'm wasting my time. I know all that, and I don't care.

I believe I can do this. I just need to find the right way of learning how. The DVD Ryan got me is a good one. I play the rhythm, clapping, and finger-snapping games when I'm in the courthouse hallways waiting for the departments to open up. Definitely, this has been the right step. I'm starting to get the hang of simple chord changes in time to a four-fourths beat, even with a couple upstrokes on the "and" count. This is especially huge.

My time spent practicing with Shelley Lynne about playing guitar makes the future inescapable. I decide this means real lessons. That means I'll have to deal with all that other stuff all over again. Already I'm tensing up. Okay. I have to go to Sasquatch on this one.

And all that Robby crap? Forget him. He'll never understand what I'm going through.

I have no idea how long Ryan's been gone, so it's a surprise when I look up to see him poke his head in my doorway and tells me it's three o'clock and time to go and he'll see me at his place. I tell him I will, and just shy of an hour later, I do.

❖❖❖❖❖

A few hours of endless desert and freeway, a bad burger somewhere, and a foul-smelling potty stop at a gas station only God and Danny's limo driver could find—hey, whataya know, we're strolling the balmy Strip, taking in the neon nightlife of Vegas. And I'm still just as numb.

We make our way back to our hotel—a swanky place, naturally—all lavish with flashing lights and glass and chrome and palmy plants. And there's, what is that, jazz? And it's coming from everywhere and nowhere, man, and this cool place is probably way too expensive for me.

I swear Danny and Darryl must be the devil's own twins, and I wonder where Danny's money comes from. I know where Darryl's money comes from. I begin to feel uneasy and my arms itch and my vision's fuzzy, and I wish they'd let me bring my guitar. At least I'd have something to do. Then again, maybe I'm too numb to do anything.

I feel a sharp jolt to my ribs. I gasp.

"Breathe!" Danny says. "What the hell is wrong with you?"

He looks at Ryan.

"What the hell is wrong with him? Why does he keep holding his breath like that?"

"Beats me, dude."

"I'm fine."

"Fine? Get a life, Paul. You're fine? Right."

Danny takes a deep breath.

"Like that, Paul. Give me one of those. Show me one of those right now."

I take a deep breath.

"Deeper, Paul. One time."

I breathe deeper.

"Attaboy! Like that. Relax. Get loose."

He stands there, looking at me.

"What?"

"What do you mean 'what'? I tell you to loosen up, and nothing happens." He keeps staring at me. "Who are you, Paul?"

Shit. Like I would know?

I shrug.

"Look, Danny, I'm just trying to go along with the program here, you know? Like you said. You're paying for everything. I feel like I am walking on eggs here, man. I don't want to screw this up. I sure as shit do not want to spoil your party, so you know, no heartburn if you'd rather I'd go. But I got nowhere to go. I don't want trouble. Honest. Swear to God. I'm not a dick, and I'm not trying to be one here. I'm not making waves. Really, I just want to fit in. So please, just . . . for the love of God, just tell me what the fuck to do. Tell me how to do it so I can pass the audition, get accepted, and then become, you know, like an invisible part of the wallpaper. I'm serious, man. Whatever it fuckin' takes."

Danny looks away. He rubs his chin. He's nodding. He starts looking me over. He's got a weird look on his face, like a squint but not quite, and I have to turn away for a moment to escape those judging eyes.

"Okay. Okay," Danny says. "I think I'm getting the picture here."

He looks at me. His eyes are softer, and there's a bit of a smile on his face.

"Okay. First off, Paulie my boy, you're golden. Look at me. Rock-solid golden. Okay?"

I'm not all that convinced, but I feel the need to nod anyway.

"You're in. All in. You belong here with me and Ryan. Okay? That's number one. Let that sink in for a minute."

He keeps looking at me.

"Second, you don't need to do anything. You're fine. Just be. Just be, Paul. Third, third is, it's okay if you're not too sure who Paul is right now. Okay? Just be. That means breathe. That's okay. Whatever you feel, you go with that. Okay? Just go with that, Paul, whatever it is. Whatever pops into your head, whatever's the first thought to arrive without you first thinking of me or anybody else, it's okay. That thought rules. You go with that. It will be the right choice."

So far so good.

I nod again.

"If that troubles you or if you feel like you need permission, okay then, here it is, Paul. I'm giving you my permission. Ryan is giving you his permission. Whatever permission you think you need from anyone—and I mean *anyone*—as far as this weekend goes, you've already got it. It's a done deal. Most important of all is you're giving yourself permission."

He takes me and Ryan by the arms.

"Fellas, Ryan's got the right idea. This weekend, come hell or high water, we are the three musket-fuckin'-teers! We are all for one and one for all!"

Danny claps his hands.

"C'mon, boys! This is our time now. Fun time. We're off the grid, off the clock, and off the radar. Also, one other thing—and, yes, I'm talking to you, Paul—don't worry about the money. Understand? It's on me. That's all you need to know in a nutshell. The weekend is on me. Period. The room, the food, all the drinks, the shows—that's all on me. No arguments, boys. You want to buy a souvenir, some artwork, a shotgun, knock yourself out. It's on me. Okay?"

"Yeah, okay. Sounds good." I remember to breathe.

"Good! We're gonna have some drinks. We're gonna roll some dice, and we're gonna flip some chips. We're gonna flirt with Lady Luck, and we're gonna spank her sweet little ass just the way she likes it, and she—I promise you, boys—she is going to take very, very good care of us," Danny smiles. "Trust me on this."

Chapter 32

As if to make a point, he raises his hand.

A lovely lass comes over, gives Danny a wink, and whispers at him, "What'll you have, boys?"

She has bobbed black hair wrapped with what looks like some kind of crown, and she's dressed—oh, I get it now—like a flapper from the roaring twenties. Only seconds before, she looked like a mannequin in her flimsy, lovely low-cut, lovely shade of rose lacy, satiny dress that's shredded at the hem into long strings, as she had leaned invitingly against some kind of fancy long automobile. And there are several of them, motionless lasses and limos, scattered about this lobby.

"Hey, baby doll, start us off right with a bottle of Chantalle Savoy Brut '26, please."

He swipes two fingers over the face of his phone and holds it out for her, and she pulls a slim, silver cigarette case from a dainty sparkly little purse dangling from her shoulder and waves it over his phone.

"Anything for you, sugar boy," she smiles and gives a little eye flutter and sashays away.

He's grinning broadly watching her glide away.

"Trust me," he says.

I hate it when he says that.

I catch him catching me looking at him. He chuckles.

"Yes. We are all checked in." He looks at his phone.

"Rooms 422, 424, and 426. Won't be much of a view, but we're not here to be looking out of windows. Trust me," he says again and laughs, giving us a showman's wave with his hand. "Gentlemen, our weekend awaits."

He leads us poolside now. Seriously? Oh, what the hell. We're not alone. We're just not in swim trunks or wandering around more or less naked like everybody else who's here. Who knows? Maybe a couple sips of that something '26, and I might even like this place. Just keep me numb. Comfortably numb.

The champagne catches up to us on a silver tray carried swiftly by some buff kid with slicked-back hair. I find myself longing for the flapper.

"Gentlemen," he says, wasting no time cracking that bubbly and generously pouring us liberating libation.

I chuckle to myself at my own version of Danny-speak.

"Gentlemen, I offer you a toast," Danny says. "To the sacrifice of youth on the altars of power, prestige, and privilege."

We clink our glasses to the weird toast and take our places on some chaise lounges. The champagne is quite cold and quite delicious. Not as sweet as I like would it, but then I'm a soda pop drunk.

Three sips or so later, a little, petite honey, whom I realize has been watching us, gets out of the shallow end of the pool and ambles on over. She giggles, looking at each of us, and then focuses on Danny.

"Are these two taken?"

She points to the lounge chairs on his right.

He sits up, showing interest.

"Why no, little darlin'. I've been saving them for you. Wherever have you been?"

She giggles again and sits down, facing him.

"Looking."

All I see is the back of his head, and she's slightly off to one side, all bubbly and curvy and coy and mostly hidden from view.

Damn.

I want to sit up and watch, but a little voice tells me I'll live longer if I don't look at them so much, stay back on the lounge, and just sip the champagne instead.

I need numbness. Lots of numbness. I wonder what the hell Ryan's thinking. He's laid back on his lounge, between me and Danny, sipping his champagne and staring up at the stars that are staring down at us all.

"Looking for whom, my little darlin'?" asks Danny.

She giggles, and her knees wiggle.

"For my sugar daddy."

Ryan spits up and grabs a towel. I don't feel so bad. I wanna hurl, but at least I didn't spit up champagne all over myself.

Danny doesn't flinch.

"Well, as Lady Luck would have it, I too am looking. Seems I have lost my little lovey bunny. Oh where, oh where, could she be?"

"I don't know," she says, giggling. "What does she look like?"

"Well, let's see. Oh, I remember! She's about five feet two, eyes of blue, blonde hair—in the cutest little pixie cut, ever—and she's wearing the most adorable blue bikini."

"Oh, I'm right here! You found me!"

"I must have!"

I see his arm move, and she gets up and sits next to him.

"Tell me again, what does your sugar daddy do?"

"Oh, he takes care of my room charges and expenses. Umm, what does your lovey bunny do?"

He whispers in her ear. She giggles.

"That sounds like fun. But no anal, okay?"

Ryan chokes and starts a spasm of coughing.

Danny doesn't flinch.

"Wouldn't think of it. You know, let's go to my room and get you out of this cold, wet bikini and into a nice, hot, steamy shower. I know, I'll order room service. Would you like that?"

"Okay!"

They get up. He turns, points at Ryan, "424," then at me, "426." He swipes and taps his phone.

"Okay, boys, you're all set. Check your emails on your phone. You should each have one from the hotel by now. Open it and hold it up to your door scanner. You should be good to go. Backup key cards will be in the rooms. Be good. Stay out of trouble. I'll check back with you in about an hour or so for dinner."

Ryan checks his phone.

"Got it. No worries, dude. Have fun."

I check my phone.

"I've got nothing."

"Lemme see it, dude."

I give my phone to Ryan.

"Interesting. Okay."

He looks at Danny.

"Go on. We'll figure it out. No worries."

"My man!" Danny turns and looks at me. "Relax. It's all good. Trust me."

I hate it when he says that. I hate how watching them—how watching her—makes me long all the more for Tami, and I hate the sinking feeling that leaves me with. I want champagne. A lot of champagne. Icy cold. Sweet. Numbing.

Apparently so does Ryan, who has upended the bottle over his glass until there's nothing left and then drains his glass.

He stops and looks over at me.

"What?"

"Whataya mean 'what'? You drank it all. Some of us might actually need that stuff. Shit, Ryan. Muffin-fusskin-teers my ass."

And I'm thinking I'm still sober.

"Sorry, dude. You're right."

I shrug it off.

"No matter."

I stare at the pool deck.

"Maybe I should have stayed home. Might've had a chance to work with Norse God tomorrow."

"Bad idea, dude. You're too distracted."

"No I'm not."

"Dude."

I can't tell him that he's probably right.

I send a lame text to Norse God instead. He replies that the door is always open and that if I win any money to share the love. Me winning? Yeah, right. That brings me a chuckle. I'm not likely to win anything. I don't have that kind of luck. It's more likely I lose everything. But hey, if it ever changes, then yeah, I'm not greedy. I decide then and there to keep working with him and learning from him as long as he'll let me and see where it leads.

As numb as I feel, my stomach still hurts—maybe this time, for other reasons.

"I think I'm hungry. You hungry?"

"Yeah, dude. Let's eat. We're gonna be on our own a while as it is."

"What goes with a bloody Mary?"

"I don't know. Swap out the vodka for tequila, make it a bloody Maria instead, and then I'd say, Mexican food."

"Then let's do that."

"Excuse me," a woman's voice says.

I look up as Ryan says hello to what I'm guessing is the older brunette version of the lovey bunny.

"Is the gentleman who left with my niece with you?"

"He was. However, he left with his lovey bunny. Why? Whataya you care? What is she, like, your niece or something?"

"Hey, c'mon, dude! Where are your manners?"

The woman glares at me.

"Well, aren't you prince charming." She squints. "Or do you save the charm for the handicapped?"

"Say what?"

"You heard me, asshole." She looks at Ryan. "What's he's ranting about?"

"Uh, what he's trying to say, uh, is that your niece and our friend, the babe magnet, have hit it off—that would be our friend the babe magnet dude and your niece the babe—and it looks they'll be spending a good part of the evening together."

"Oh, is that right?"

My turn.

"Yeah, she just sashayed her cute little wet ass on over here and told our friend she was looking for her sugar daddy and she asked him if he'd seen her, and he said, 'imagine that,' that he was looking for his lovey bunny, and then she asked him what did she look like, and he described her eyes of blue, and then oh my god, that was her and then they leave, and then you show up. Your timing is like impeccable."

"Dude! What the hell is wrong with you?" Ryan stands up. "Look, Miss, I'm really, very, sorry about this whole thing, and I apologize for the dude. His wife's leaving him, and he's not handling it real well. It's a long story."

"Hey, moron! She's not—you don't know a damn thing about any of that! Nobody knows that but me! Wait! No! That didn't come out right."

"Oh, dude! The whole world knows. Deep down, you know it too, hence the Freudian slip. You just won't admit it yet. Let it go. It's normal."

Ryan turns back to the woman.

"Miss, I'm really sorry. He's really sorry. We're sorry. We're all really sorry here."

"No, Ryan! You got this all wrong! She's not leaving me, okay? She's not."

I hold up my hands.

"And yes, I'm sorry. I apologize. I was out of line. Please, just forget you ever saw me."

I get up to leave.

"Miss—"

"It's Maria. You can stop calling me *miss*. You don't have to make brownie points with me. Hell, I'm almost as old as you are. On second thought, though, it is Vegas. I'll give you points for trying."

"Maria! Love that name. Hey, I'm Ryan. The rude dude you want to forget you ever saw is my good friend, Paul. Forgetting him is probably a good idea because he's decided to be a buzzkill tonight. But you gotta forgive him because he's still madly in love with his wife. Only she doesn't deserve him, and he's all jacked up about it. I don't know what else to tell you."

"Then shut up, Ryan."

"Oh, what am I thinking? Our other friend is Danny, and he's really a cool dude too. He's with your niece. And they're in room 422. Oh, and just so you know, he's a total babe magnet. Did I mention that? I mean, just so you know."

"Yeah. Total babe magnet," I say, picking up the empty champagne bottle and shaking it. "A few minutes sooner, and that could have been you sailing Danny's single-masted schooner. Anyway, he's ordering room service. He's a gentleman. Absolute gentleman."

"At least one of you—okay, maybe two of you are."

"What the hell. I'm trying to be helpful. Truly."

Maria glares at me, yanks the towel from her hips—*whoa*, and they're really nice hips too—and begins toweling her hair.

"Sugar daddy, huh? She said that? 'Sugar daddy'?"

"Yep."

"Well, ain't that peachy. Damn it. She said she was going to do it too. I thought it was the Cosmo talking. She said this was the place for it. I didn't believe her. I thought it was a joke. Then again, what the hell do I know, right? It's a bit slutty, if you ask me. And here I thought I was being nice meeting her out here for her twenty-first birthday an' all. She never told me she was gonna get herself a sugar daddy for a present. Well, if that just don't beat all. I guess that makes Connie a hell of a lot older than I give her credit for, the little mink. Okay then. I guess she's safe enough. None of y'all seem the least bit evil."

My turn.

"No, ma'am. We are not evil."

She gives me a familiar look. So much for trying to be polite. She's well, curvy, really cute, and so different from Tami—shorter, curvier, maybe bustier, probably a close call on that one. Though her muscles are toned like Tami, so she probably works out too. Maybe she's a dancer. Maybe she plays softball. Maybe she's into martial arts and will kick my ass into the desert and a shallow grave if I don't look away. Now. While I still can. I can't look away. Lord, please make me numb. I'm pathetically trying not to stare, which means I'm locked on her like radar, and I catch a glimpse of her catching a glimpse of me staring at her in radar lock mode.

She's gonna fry me like toast.

She has this funny smile—beautiful smile—as she shakes her head and puts her hands on her hips, the towel dangling from one hand.

"Well, hey there, cowboy. See something you like?"

"Oh, no, ma'am."

Her eyebrows peak. "Excuse me?"

"I'm sorry. I didn't mean it that way. I mean, you don't look anything like my wife."

"Wow. Still pouring on the charm, aren't ya? That'll do wonders for my confidence. Why'd your wife leave you anyway? You beat her? I know all about that. Are you cheating on her? I know all about that too."

She leans back, keeping one hand on that curvy hip, and gives me a once-over.

"You don't look like a cheater. More like a boy scout—a really, really old boy scout. 'Course they're the worst ones by far, pretending to help those in need. That would make you the lowest of the lowest, sand-poundin' scum then now, wouldn't it?"

"Uh, actually, truth be told, it's for playing a guitar. Okay, wanting—well, *trying*—to learn how to play. I really . . . I can't play for shit, okay? Not yet anyway. Okay, never. Oh, and apparently, not becoming a judge fast enough to suit her wishes."

She does a double take and crosses her arms.

"Huh. Well, don't that beat all. Here I'm thinking it's all about the money. That's the craziest damn thing I've ever heard. A few more drinks, and I'd be almost drunk enough to believe you."

"Believe him! He's too straight an arrow to even think of making up crazy stuff like that." Ryan shows her his phone. "Here. I can prove it."

"What's this? What am I looking at?"

"This is his wife." He swipes the screen. "This is the bald dude she's with. This is his wife lip-lockin' this bald dude. Any questions? Sure. You gotta have questions. Lots of questions. It's only natural you'd have questions under the circumstances. See, the bald dude's a wealthy, federal court of appeals justice. Paul here, he's just your average, everyday lawyer, and he's actually a super nice guy once you get to know him."

"Hey!" I grab his arm. "Where the hell did you get this? Who else knows about this?"

I feel faint, and my eyes well up.

"I told you! The whole world, dude. Okay, the whole world except for you."

"Damn. What is she, a supermodel?"

"No. She's a nurse. A diva nurse."

"And she's married to him?"

"Yes she is. Go figure."

"Damn. If that don't beat all. Must be the money. That bald guy's rich, ain't he?"

"Dude's loaded like a gun."

"Well, there ya go."

"Well, shit, Ryan!"

I stumble and fall onto the lounge chair but at the wrong angle or on the wrong spot, and I tumble to the pool deck, flipping the chair onto my back.

"This looks vaguely familiar," she says.

I feel like I've been kicked in the gut, and I try to curl up.

"Shit, Ryan. I thought you were my friend. Shit!"

"I am, dude. I am. Me and Danny. The rest of the world's all against you, but we're not."

He pulls the chair away.

"C'mon, dude. Get up."

He offers a hand, and I slap it away.

"Get away from me!"

"C'mon, dude. Don't make a scene. Security's coming."

"I'm not against you either, Prince Charming," Maria says. "Please, just get up. We'll call it even."

I get up and stand almost face to face with some buff-ass, FBI-looking guy.

He's a tall guy, obviously buff as hell beneath a fine suit, like all FBI guys. Earpiece in his left ear, a clear coil spiraling down from the earpiece and disappearing into the charcoal gray lapel.

"Are you all right, sir?"

Shit.

"I am now. My apologies. I slipped, and then I tripped on the chair thing. My fault, my fault, my most grievous fault. Won't happen again, promise. Scout's honor. Would it be okay if I just go to my room now?"

I'd like to order room service, some drinks, some pills, and then die.

"That's an excellent idea. Your name, please?"

"Paul. Paul Edward Cooper."

"What room are you in, Mr. Cooper?"

"Oh, crap. Ryan?"

"He's in 426, officer. I'm in 424."

"I see. Your name, please?"

"Ryan O'Byrne. That's O-apostrophe-b-y-r-n-e."

Thank you, Mr. O'Byrne."

"Excuse me, Officer. I'm Maria Templeton. I'm in Room 383. We were just discussing maybe getting something to eat and maybe having a few drinks."

"That's fair. In that case, we have several, excellent restaurants in the hotel. You will need to change into clothes, of course, Ms. Templeton. Otherwise, we also offer excellent room service."

I'm ready to leave.

"Fair enough," I say. "How do I get to my room?"

They all look at me.

Chapter 33

"Go to the end of the pool deck behind me," says the FBI guy. "Elevator is on the right. Get out on the fourth floor, turn right. Your room is on the right, about halfway down the hall. Will you need any further assistance?"

"No, officer. I'm fine. Thank you. I've had enough excitement for one day."

"Enjoy your stay, Mr. Cooper."

I head for the elevator, leaving the others behind. Their conversation sounds like mumbling, and I don't care. I just want to hole up in my room. A man should drop dead and die in his own room. No matter who's paying for it.

I start to worry about the money.

Should I get room service and try and eat something? What's a milkshake cost in a place like this? Twenty bucks? This is Vegas, for God's sake. Aren't they supposed to have cheap buffets here?

Too much booze probably isn't a good idea, although passing out from too much booze wouldn't be so bad, if I could skip the booze part. I could do without the puking.

I wave my phone in front of the wall pad thing by my room door. Nothing happens. I remember to open the email and try it again. Nothing happens. I'm missing a step, obviously. I hate technology.

What's wrong with the old-fashioned key card? Or even better, an actual key for this hotel with its glitzy roaring twenties motif?

Real keys for real people. Is that so much to ask? I look around. I look up. There's a little black dome on the ceiling. Ah! The FBI. I look up and wave at it.

"Yo! Efram! Down here!"

I point to my phone. I point to the door of my room. I hold up both hands.

Then I go to my room and sit cross-legged on the floor in front of the door and close my eyes. I figure I've got about five minutes. I hope they send somebody else.

Wrong.

"It seems you're having a run of bad luck, Mr. Cooper."

You think?

I open my eyes and look up at the FBI giant. I get up.

"You have no idea."

I give him my phone. He checks it. He taps the screen twice. I hear a clicking sound at the door. He opens it.

"You are all set, Mr. Cooper."

Then he steps back and lets the door close before I can get in.

What the hell did you do that for?

He shows me an icon that is the FSF logo for the Hotel Fitzgerald appearing on the screen of my phone. He touches the icon. There's a menu showing more icons with brief, descriptive labels. He touches another icon, and a barcode appears. He holds it near the wall pad where I see a glowing dot for a second and hear the door unlock. He hands me back my phone.

"If you need any further assistance, touch the front desk icon. You'll see a smartly dressed gentleman. At the prompt when he speaks to you and says, 'How may I help you, Mr. Cooper?' that's your cue to ask away."

"Thank you."

"Enjoy your stay, Mr. Cooper."

The room lights are on. I see my bag's already sitting on a suitcase stand. I lay down on the bed. I roll over and futz with my phone. Finally, this dapper guy appears on the screen. He's got short, almost wavy, slicked-back, blond hair. He's wearing a navy, pinstripe suit. He looks at me and smiles.

"Good evening, Mr. Cooper. My name is Winston. How may I help you?"

"What does a chocolate milk shake cost, Winston?"

Dapper Winston smiles.

"Certainly. Let me find out for you. One moment please."

He looks down into some book and starts turning pages. He stops. He reads. He looks up and smiles.

"You're in luck, Mr. Cooper. A delicious, forty-ounce chocolate shake, made deliciously thick and creamy with vanilla bean and chocolate ice creams churned from the finest milk and cream from Vermont and delectable chocolate imported from Switzerland, is available from the room service kitchen for only $18.95, gratuity included, and charged to your room. I will have one delivered, frosty cold, directly to your room, 426, in twenty minutes, tops. Believe me, old sport, it's well worth the wait. Please say *yes*, and I will place your order with the kitchen."

"Yeah, sure. What the hell. Why not."

"I'm sorry. Did you say 'yes,' Mr. Cooper?"

"Okay. I'll play along. *Yes*," I say, with emphasis on the *yes*. Winston must be a new man.

Winston winks and flashes me the all-American okay sign.

"Excellent, Mr. Cooper. I am placing your order at 9:48, p.m. Now, is there anything else I can do to make your stay at the Hotel Fitzgerald more enjoyable?"

"No."

"Thank you, Mr. Cooper. Enjoy your stay."

Winston goes back to his desk book, and the screen returns to the hotel menu.

I clear the screen and put the phone down. I ignore the hunger. A thick and frosty shake is on the way. I'm thinking it'd be nice to have a guitar about now. Yeah, right. I knew I should have brought mine.

I decide I'll never be without one again.

But now? Wonder what that costs. No doubt Winston would know. Were guitars even popular in the roaring twenties? The jazz age? No doubt Winston would know that too. Wonder if he knows what Tami's doing about now. I can only imagine what she's doing about now, and I don't want to know if Winston knows what she's doing right about now at this very fuckin' moment and whom she's doing it to or with, and I need to stop imagining that because it's making me sick to my stomach.

I futz with my phone.

"Winston!"

"Good evening, Mr. Cooper. So very good to see you again, old sport. How may I be of assistance?"

"Winston, old sport, this is quite the jazzy hotel you got here! Smashing first rate and all that. But now I'm wondering. I haven't seen any guitars around here anywhere. So my question to you, my dear Winston, is whether or not the guitar was a popular musical instrument during the jazz age of the roaring twenties. That is the issue. Answer me that, old sport!"

Winston smiles.

"Well, certainly, Mr. Cooper. Let me look into that for you. One moment, please."

He directs his attention to his desk book.

"No worries, Winston. Take your time."

Winston looks up, nods, smiles politely, and turns a few pages.

"Ah! Here we are!"

He reads a bit and then looks up.

"Oh, my. Well, so sorry, old sport. It seems the guitar was not a key instrument at the dawn of the jazz age. The string instrument of choice, aside from the stand-up bass, was the banjo. However, that did appear to change in the '30s with the advent of the archtop guitar. By the late '30s, archtop guitars had all but replaced banjos in the rhythm sections, typically comprised of drums, a bass, or a tuba. In addition to having a rhythm section, jazz ensembles of the day usually featured a clarinet, a trumpet or coronet, trombone, and a piano."

"I simply had no idea, Winston."

"Oh, indeed, sir. It says here that that the archtop guitar, although not as loud a banjo, offered a smoother tone and a wider harmonic range that appealed to many of the bandleaders of that era. It was all the rage, as they say."

"You don't say."

"Oh, indeed, sir. One of the innovators of the use of archtop guitars in jazz was Eddie Brown. He was known for his elegant, steady rhythm. Eddie Brown's rhythmic chord accompaniment remains a popular style with jazz guitarists today. Please say *yes* if you would like to listen to a selection of Eddie Brown on your room's sound system."

Why not?

"Yes!" I confirm.

"Excellent choice, old sport, if I may say so. You may adjust the volume by turning the volume knob on the radio atop the armoire."

As he spoke, the room swelled with the sweet sound of strumming, nestled like a lush valley between high canyon walls of wailing trumpets and other horns. Hovering above like the sky came the gentle tinkling of piano keys like shimmering stars at twilight.

Nice! Kind of like the big-band sound but different. Duh! Jazzier.

A knock at the door, and a pleasant lad from room service arrives with my shake. It's in a frosty silver cylinder like an oversized shaker for making cocktails. There are other silver containers gathered on a silver tray. I open them and find cherries in one, crushed peanuts in another, whipped cream in another, and white and dark chocolate shavings in another. There are a couple of different-sized spoons on the tray and two silver linen napkins with a satiny sheen. "SFS" is embroidered on one corner of each napkin in black.

Nice!

I hear a cheerful, "Enjoy your stay, sir," and see a blur as the door closes behind him.

Okay. Shake time.

I dig in and then pause, trying to hear Eddie Brown. It's hard because he's seamlessly woven into the background, and I wonder what an archtop guitar looks like. I futz my phone searching the internet for pictures. Interesting. They don't look right. I'm not sure why.

Is that knocking? I still have the fountain glass in one hand as I open the door to a cute short woman with thick, wavy, brown hair and gorgeous brown eyes. The pool lady is in a yellow sundress and cowboy boots.

Olé!

"Is now a bad time?" she asks, crossing her arms.

"For what?" I say before mouthing another silky-smooth spoonful of chocolatey deliciousness.

Maria's eyebrows arch, and she hunches her shoulders.

"Oh, I don't know. It took you a while to come to the door."

I'm spooning away.

"It did?"

"Uh-huh. Okay. You're obviously not that hurt. I'll let your friend know you're fine." She turns, stops, and then comes back. "Okay. I have to ask, what is that you're eating?"

"This?"

"Yes. It smells sweet."

"The bestest, thickest, chocolatiest milkshake ever. Wanna taste?"

I hold out my spoon.

She looks at me like I'm nuts.

"Oh, sorry. Let me get you a clean spoon. Come on in." I turn to get her a spoon. I pick one up from the serving tray. "Here."

I hand her the glass and a clean spoon.

"Try this."

She takes a small spoonful.

"Oh, you gotta have more than that."

"You sure? I wouldn't want to deprive you."

"No, it's okay 'cause as soon as that bad boy's finished, I'm getting another one. Best twenty bucks I ever spent."

"Twenty bucks for a milk shake? It better be good." She freezes, the spoon still in her mouth.

"Mmm." She takes the spoon out. "Since you're getting one more, may I?"

"Absolutely."

She takes a bigger spoonful.

"Oh my. That is so good. What kind of booze did they put in this thing?"

"What booze? There's no booze in there. Just the finest milk and cream from Vermont and some imported Swiss chocolate."

"Oh, sweetheart, anything this good and this expensive has to have booze in it. It's a rule." She licks the spoon. "Some kind of chocolate liqueur at least. Something."

"There's no booze. Wait. I'll prove it."

I try to get Winston.

"What are you doing?"

"Proving it. Winston? Winston, old sport, I need you."

"Who's Winston?" she asks.

"He's the hotel guy. New man."

"Good evening, Mr. Cooper. How may I assist you?"

Maria grabs my hand, the one holding the phone.

"Give me that! Winston, sweetheart, just tell us what booze you put in this milkshake to make it so expensive and taste so damn good. He says there isn't any, but I'm not sure I believe him."

"I'm sorry. I do not recognize your voice."

"Oh. Well, it's me! Maria Templeton. Oh, I forgot! Room 383. I'm here with Mr. Cooper." She turns and gives me a wink. "We're in his room. We're about to get naked."

"No we're not!"

"Yes we are!"

"No we're not!"

I grab at my phone, but she commandeers the phone from my hand.

"Give me one good reason for not getting naked with me, Prince Charming."

She wanders into the bathroom and wanders back out wearing a terrycloth robe. She would have to find the ultra-small.

"Because we're not married."

"Are you kidding? That's like the best reason! If we were married, I'd be curled up on our worn-out couch eating ice cream right out of the carton and watching figure skating on TV, and you'd be curled up in your custom man cave knocking back the brewskies, surfing the internet, and watching streaming marathons of American babes spread wide open world of sports."

I have to think about that for a moment. Okay. Back to reality.

"Winston! Listen to me! Nobody's getting naked in here!" I yell at the phone. "Now give it back!"

"No!" She jumps onto the bed with a shriek of glee and throws a pillow at me.

I duck. I stand up as a sundress sails through the air, and a damp bikini top hits me in the face. She kicks off her cowboy boots and crawls under the covers.

"Oh yes, we are. We are so getting naked!" she taunts from somewhere under the mound of covers.

"No we're not!" I yell. "Winston! Winston, it's not what you think!"

"Oh my! Good evening, Mr. Cooper. One moment please. Ah, yes. Very well done, old sport. Rest assured your privacy is most important to us. Your secret is safe with me. 'What happens at the Hotel Fitzgerald stays at the Hotel Fitzgerald,' I always say. How may I assist you, Mr. Cooper?"

"Atta boy, Winston," Maria giggles. "You tell him."

She covers the phone with her hand.

"You know Winston's a computer avatar, right?"

"A what? No, he's not."

"Yes he is!"

"No he's not! He's like, you know, the concierge hotel guy."

"Oh, you are so naive," she smiles. "You need to get out more. Or maybe not. That naive thing you got going makes you cute. You may want to hang on to that at your age."

She directs her attention to my phone.

"Winston? Maria Templeton, Room 383," she begins speaking much slower. "Please tell me what is the brand of alcoholic beverage that is used to make the chocolate milkshake that was delivered by room service to Paul Cooper, Room 426, today."

"Yes, of course, Ms. Templeton. So good to hear from you. One moment please."

"Told ya."

"Told me what?"

"He's a computer, sweetheart. There's over a thousand rooms in this hotel. There are hundreds of drunk and horny guests all talking to Winston right now."

"Really?"

"You are so cute right now, you know that?"

"No."

"Yes, Ms. Templeton, I have it now. The chocolate milkshake offered at the Hotel Fitzgerald is made from delicious chocolate and vanilla bean ice creams from certified organic dairies in Vermont featuring grass-fed-only Guernsey cows and the finest, imported Swiss and Belgian chocolates. The milkshake is alcohol free. However, there is a fully stocked wet bar in Mr. Cooper's room. All items are individually priced. Do enjoy. We also offer, if you prefer, a full-service bar for room service."

"Well, don't that beat all. Winston, what do you suggest I take from the fully stocked wet bar to add to the delicious shake to give it that extra boozy kick and make a real chocolatey cocktail, huh?"

"One moment please."

'That's so cute. He's pretending to flip pages in some book. They think of everything. This place is almost a theme park."

She winks at me.

"Hey, why not? Can't hurt, right? Your supermodel wife's doing the nasty with some federal judge, so you need a drink. I'm totally with you on that. We're here together, in Vegas—Vegas, sweetheart! I'm hoping for a romantic romp with just the right guy, so I want several drinks. That's fair, right?

"Let's be honest here. We could both do a lot worse, not that I'm wanting to, not by a long shot, but neither one of us is getting any younger. I, for one, am craving a whole lot of great lovin' sex, a whole lot of it. I want it before I'm shriveled up like a Kalahari prune stuffed under a floormat in some junkyard car. Besides, we're in Vegas!"

Chapter 34

Oh, dear God.

I move as far away from the bed as I can, which isn't nearly far enough, and back to spooning my shake.

"Cheer up, sweetheart. It'll be fun. Get a little booze in my shake, and I can get a little shake in my booty for ya, we can have some fun, maybe get your mind off things. What do you say? I say it's party time, Prince Charming!"

I'm thinking the apple apparently does not fall far from the tree in her family, but I'm sure as hell not about to think out loud this time. I've got enough problems.

"Why, yes, of course, Ms. Templeton, a Brandy Alexander would be just the thing. Please say *yes*, and I will send the recipe and mixing instructions directly to your phone."

"No."

That's a relief. I thought for sure she was about to say yes.

"Is there a problem, Ms. Templeton?"

"Yes, Houston, we most certainly have a problem. There's been a change of plans. Listen to me carefully, Winston. Please send the Brandy Alexander recipe to Mr. Cooper's phone. Yes, Paul Cooper, Room 426. I do not have my phone with me, and I am not leaving this poor, lonely boy alone, if you catch my drift."

"Yes, of course. I am so sorry for this error. I do apologize. I am sending the Brandy Alexander recipe to Mr. Cooper's phone. Is there anything else I may help you with?"

"Yes. Please send three more—no, four more—four of those chocolate milkshakes to Mr. Cooper's room, Room 426, right away."

"Yes, of course, Ms. Templeton. Please say *yes*, to confirm a room service order of four chocolate milkshakes to Room 426."

"Yes!"

"Thank you for your order. I am placing your order with the room service kitchen at 10:33 p.m. One moment, please. Ah, yes. I have it now. Where are my manners? Ms. Templeton, please say *yes* if you would like two complimentary Brandy Alexanders sent from the room service bar to Room 426."

"Yes! No! Please make that *four* complimentary Brandy Alexanders to Mr. Cooper, in Room 426."

"One moment, please. Yes, of course, Ms. Templeton. I have made the correction. Thank you for allowing me the opportunity to assist you and do enjoy your stay with us this evening at the Hotel Fitzgerald."

"Oh! I will. Thank you so much, Winston! You're such a sweetheart!" she laughs and does something with the phone.

"This is gonna be so fun!" she squeals. "Oooh, here's the recipe. Where's the wet bar?"

"I have no idea."

"Well, get with it, Major Prince Charming Nice Guy! Get your party on! Let's find the wet bar. Muy pronto! Andale! Look for a refrigerator and like a little kitchen sink or something."

Fair enough. The room is big but not that big, and on the way to the bathroom there is an alcove where I find a kitchenette with a bar sink, a good-sized refrigerator under the counter, and a mirrored wall with four lighted glass shelves stocked with all kinds of liquor bottles. Look at all this booze. No wonder this place is so expensive.

I open the refrigerator. There are lots of canned soft drinks, mixers, little bottles of champagne and white wines, and assorted bottled beers. There are several sealed plastic containers of lemon, lime, and orange wedges, maraschino cherries—is that margarita salt?

"I found it!"

The cabinet next to the refrigerator has a seriously industrial-strength blender and all kinds of cool glassware. I pick one up.

"Hoo-ah!"

And little Miss Tornado slams into me, and the glass sails from my hand and bounces on the tiled bathroom floor. I flinch but it doesn't break. How 'bout them apples. It's not glass.

"It's not glass!"

I go pick it up. It's crystal-clear acrylic.

"They must have known you were coming."

"Well, of course they knew! Hello? I made reservations, you silly!"

"I'm sorry. You're right. How naive of me."

"Well, yeah! You know, for a lawyer, you're not so smart."

"You're right. Tami's always reminding me how stupid I am."

"I didn't say you were stupid. Fuck Tami."

"Oh, believe me, that's tops on my list."

"Ewww!" She gives me a pouty look. "Never mind that now. We're looking for something called cognac and oooh! What's this? Crème de cow-cow?"

"Close enough."

I peer among the bottles. I lick my fingertips and slide bottles about by their necks and tops.

"Let's see . . . cognac, cognac, looking for cognac. We've got bourbon. We've got scotch. We've got rubbing alcohol, iodine, hair tonic."

"Iodine? Hair tonic? Eww!"

"It's a joke."

"I don't get it."

"Forget about it. It's a line of dialogue from an old war movie I like."

"Never mind that. We can watch movies later. Keep looking."

"I'm looking. Ha! Here we go, right next to the brandy. Cognac it is."

I hand her a couple of bottles.

"What's brandy?"

"It's sorta like cognac."

"Then hand it over, Major Prince Charming Nice Guy!"

I hand them over.

"And all we need now is . . . yes! Here we go, crème de cacao."

I give her the bottles.

She studies the text image on my phone.

"Okay. Says here we pour this and this into a chilled cocktail glass. Do we have any of those?"

"Not yet. But I bet four are on the way."

There's a distinct knocking sound at the door.

"Betcha they're here."

"Hoo-ah!" Little Miss Tornado scampers to the door, tugging the hem of the robe below her basketball-round butt and opens the door.

"Room service."

"You brought our shakes and the Brandy Alexanders!" She starts counting. "Oooh! They're all here!"

A dapper-looking gentleman enters, pushing a cart, atop of which wiggles all the makings of our paradise of libations. He quickly offloads the cargo onto the table. There are four ice buckets, each containing a cocktail glass filled to the brim with a creamy white liquid and covered with a plastic wrap and the usual milkshake setup times four.

"Good evening, dear guests. If I may suggest," he says with a flourish of his hand, "if you have not yet enjoyed one of our signature Brandy Alexanders, peel back the shrink-wrap slightly and start with a sip to check if the temperature is to your liking. If you prefer a somewhat colder drink, reseal and refrigerate for up to five minutes, tops. After that, it's simply too cold, and you'll lose much of the richness of the cognac's bouquet and this lovely drink's sophisticated and refined flavors. The milkshakes, of course, are ready for your enjoyment, immediately."

"Can't we just pour them into the shakes?"

The dapper man gives her a look, stifling a grin.

"You could," he pauses, "after you make some room. But I do not recommend it. The flavors simply are not the same."

The little tornado makes another pouty face.

"Well, shit. You're no fun."

"On the other hand," he says, with another flourish, "if after a sip you find the taste of the Brandy Alexander is not quite your thing, then by all means, mix the drink directly into the shake. Be sure to generously add rum to taste. That should balance all the flavors quite nicely."

"Oooh! Rum! Like a rum punch!"

"And quite a punch at that," he smiles.

"Oh, I like you!"

"Thank you so much. Do enjoy your stay."

"I will, I will, I will. Um"—she points at me—"how does he tip you?"

The dapper man smiles.

It's already taken care of and charged to the room. Now, if you will excuse me, it's party time for you two. Please enjoy. Oh! For extra sweetness, you can always add some maple-flavored bourbon." He points to the alcove. "Third shelf. Far right."

"Oooh! I like sweetness! Okay! Bye-bye!"

She bounces behind him, following him to the door, opens it, and slams it shut as soon as he's clear.

"Hoo-ah! Belly up to the blender!"

"Yes, ma'am. One blender, coming up."

"Hey, don't call me that! I'm not your mother."

"You're right. Let's make some drinks, shall we?"

I dig out the blender. I no sooner set it on the counter, and she dumps in a cocktail and as much shake as it can hold. I get the cover on it just as she hits a button.

Vrooosh!

I shut it down and retrieve some tumblers from the cupboard.

She's grabbed another cocktail, peeled away some of the shrink-wrap, and gulped it, leaning her head back—way back—downing that baby in rapid swallows, boozy cream dribbling down her chin, down her neck, and under her robe.

"Not too cold then?"

"Huh?" She licks her lips.

"Cold. Was it too cold?"

"Oh, not at all."

"So how was it?"

"What? Oh! Good. It was good. Not very chocolatey enough. You try one."

I select a cocktail. In gentlemanly fashion, peel back the shrink wrap and take a sip. Not bad.

"I think I would like this a bit colder. I don't need all the fragrance of the cognac."

"Then let's try the brandy shake."

She pours some from the blender into the tumbler and guzzles.

"Hey, Maria! Take it easy with that."

She blinks, gasps, and then grabs her forehead.

"Oh, shit! Brain freeze. Ow! Ow! Son of a bitch, ow!"

She leans on the counter.

I take the tumbler and set it down.

"Whoo-wee! What a ride. Okay, Major Nice Guy. You're up. Hooh-ah?"

She points to the blender.

"Sure, why not."

A little bit of a boozy aftertaste, but it's still pretty much a chocolate shake.

"Not bad."

"I think it needs something."

"Oh, I don't know, Maria."

"No, it needs rum. You're tall and handsome for an old guy. Make yourself useful and get us some rum. I can't reach it."

I get some rum.

"This one's a banana-flavored spiced rum."

"Oh, I love babana. Like a sundae."

She pours in half the bottle.

Thank God it's a small bottle. Too bad it's a huge blender. She fires it up. We taste. *Not bad.*

"You're right, Ria. That's good babana."

"You called me Ria," she smiles.

"You're right, I'm sorry. It slipped out."

"That's okay. Slip it back in. I like it when you call me that."

Okay. I definitely need to talk less and drink more.

"Look at that!"

"Look at what?"

"We need to make another batch."

She opens the fridge and grabs the cherries.

"Here, dump these in too."

I dump. She pours in the last Brandy Alexander, more cognac, and more banana spiced rum.

"Hey! We need more sweetness."

"No we don't. Really, we don't."

"Okay! Let's get naked now!"

She starts untying the robe.

"Whoa whoa whoa whoa!"

I hug her to make her stop.

"Mmmmm, you smell so manly. I like that smell."

"Hey, Ria! Ria, honey, you know what we need?"

"Baby oil?"

"No, honey. Sweetness! I think we need more sweetness!"

"Okay!"

I grab the maple bourbon and start pouring.

"Tell me when."

I keep pouring.

"Ria, please tell me when."

I'm still pouring.

"When what, sweetheart?"

"Never mind."

Fuck it. The whole bottle is probably a good idea. I won't make it through the night if she calls me that again.

I add as much milkshake as it will hold, which is surprisingly a lot, and mix a new batch.

"Okay, try this."

She's not there. I turn around.

"Oooh! What have we here?" She opens my travel bag and starts rummaging. "We need to get you unpacked, Major Prince Charming Nice Guy."

"Hey, get out of there! There's nothing in there for you."

"You never know. What's this?" She holds up the Duggie book. "Connie loves this guy. She's always going to his concerts. She almost dragged me to the last one. Heard it was good." She tosses the book aside.

"Hey! Easy with that. I happen to like that book."

"Why?"

"I wish I could be more like him."

"Really?"

"Long story, okay?"

She retrieves the book and holds it up. "You mean like being more naked?"

"No! No, not that!"

"We'll see." She sets the book down.

"C'mon, please. There's nothing in there for you."

"Wanna bet?" She holds up one of my ratty old basketball tank tops that I like to wear after a shower.

"Oooh! I think I'll change into this."

Oh, Christ, no!

"You don't need to—whoa!"

I cover my eyes and feel the soft terry cloth draping over my head. She laughs.

"What do you think?"

I peek through my fingers, just in case. She's almost fully covered.

"Nice!"

Not sure there's anything else I can say in this situation.

"Yeah? La bamba!"

She scurries to the bathroom and checks herself out in the full-length mirror.

"Hmm. You're taller than I thought."

She rolls up the bottom of the shirt near the top of her thighs, then pulls it tight to one side, and loops it into a knot.

She bounces back.

"How about now? Better, right?"

"Much better."

Oh lord, just kill me now. I'm dying anyway.

She has curvy, well-toned legs, and I need to stop looking at them. I hope she's wearing panties.

"Hoo-ah!" She says, raising her arms in triumph.

She's not.

Oh lord.

"So how old are you really?" she asks.

"Fifty, fifty-ish."

"Oh."

I can't help but grin. I think I'm safe now.

"Oh, no! I saw that! You're not getting off that easy. Oh, no. Long hair, boyish good looks in a way—well, from a distance, anyway. Kinda." She squints. "Oh, I see 'em now. You got some wrinkles in your face. You got that turkey neck thing starting. Still, not bad. For a weekend in Vegas." She winks. "You might do after all."

"No I won't do at all. But thanks anyway."

I'm feeling pretty safe right now being an old guy. A few more drinks, and she'll get bored and leave or pass out. With any luck, I'll pass out.

"You're welcome, Prince Charming!"

"How old are you?" I ask.

"Uh-uh." She gives a bouncy little shimmy. "How'd you meet your porn queen?"

"My what?"

"Your prom queen. You know, your wife, the supermodel? How'd you meet her?"

"In a hospital."

"Okay, that's too creepy."

Just like that, she's got me spilling my guts. I give her the whole story, even the parts I don't want to give her, as I keep looking at her. God, I love cotton. I give her the whole story, right down to the part about how getting married was her idea in the first place.

"Wow. That's a little weird."

"It is what it is."

"I get it. She was out of your league and threw you a bone. You went for it, you rabid, little dog."

"Pretty much."

She shrugs. "Well, good for you, Prince Charming. You tried. I can't blame you for trying."

She thinks about it.

"Only you're lost in love, and she's, mmm, not so much."

"Something like that."

"Hey, it could be worse."

"Yeah? I'd like to know how."

"Well, since you brought it up. I married this dashing young soldier—hoo-ah! Army chopper jock. Everything was heaven. Then his deployments got longer. Then came the years of not having kids cuz turns out I can't—and now it's too late anyway—and then was there the whole Iraq thing. The drinking got worse. The violence got worse, and then, enough was enough."

"I'm sorry."

"Don't be. It's all good. Reconstructive surgery. I healed up. I'm good. Really."

She cups her breasts through the tank top and gives them a jiggle.

"Hey! Tits turned out nice. Wanna see 'em?"

I see them just fine and cover my eyes again.

"Please, no. I can see them just fine under the shirt, and that's too much awesomeness enough for me, thanks."

"You think they're awesome," she coos. "Then you gotta see 'em!"

"No, really. I'm good."

Why not? They're still me. They look good. Better even. We're grown-ups in Vegas, sweetheart, who's going to know? Besides, I don't think your wife's gonna care. Stop being such a boy scout."

"Yeah. About that."

"About that nothing." She pauses. "Ever hit her?"

"No!" I sputter.

She nods, eyeballing me.

"I believe you. You really are a nice guy. I'm not used to that. I gave up on love years ago. Then I meet you. Twice."

"Twice? How twice?"

"First time? I'm outside some stupid office building full of courtrooms. It's raining, and I'm careening out of control in a wheelchair and crash into you. I knock you on your ass and damn near run you over, and all you're worried about is if I'm hurt or not. You get me back up and give me a piggyback ride into the building. You deliver me to the courtroom I have to go to where the damn county hospital is suing me for bills I can't pay—I didn't have a job then—and you help me even though it's making you late for your own problems. A real boy scout. How far did you go anyway? Eagle, right?"

I am amazed at how she managed to say all of that on just three breaths.

"Nope. Never got past Tenderfoot."

"No, seriously."

"Tenderfoot. Seriously. Coach didn't approve of scouting. It interfered too much with his drinking and his golfing and giving me and my mother shit."

She twists the spoon in her mouth and smacks her lips when she takes it out.

"Oh." She tries spooning from her glass what little is left. "Who's Coach?"

"My old man. Only we're not going there. Hey! I'm ready for another one and your glass is empty, so I think we stop talking and start making more better drinking."

"Good idea!"

"Hoo-hah."

She laughs.

"No, sweetheart, that's down here." She points. "We'll get to that later. But you've got the right spirit. It's hoo-ah!"

"Okay. Then what's that mean anyway?"

"I don't know. It's army-speak. It's how all soldiers talk. It's a cheer. It's a confirmation. It means something is good. It means you understand. It can substitute for whole questions and answers. It means all kinds of things. It's very practical like the army. I should stop saying it, though. I'm not married to the army anymore. Still, it does come in handy at times."

She zips straight to the blender.

"Let's try this," she says, and we try it and we mix, and we taste.

She holds up a spoon for me, and I taste.

Chapter 35

"Not chocolatey enough. Too boozy."

"That's the idea, sweetheart. We're not getting any younger."

"And stop calling me sweetheart."

For the love of God stop calling me that.

She rolls her eyes. "Why?"

"Because I like how it sounds when you say it, and that just makes the hurt worse."

"Ahh." She caresses my face with her palm.

It's cold, but I don't mind.

"Okay, sweetheart. I'm sorry. I'll stop calling you sweetheart, sweetheart."

We swap spoons, and we taste some more and were getting totally chocolate-faced and everything's tasting awesome and she's looking really awesome in my tank top and more desirable with every spoonful. I need to drink up so I can fall down and pass out. My face is feeling numb so that's progress.

"Hoo-ah!" She's all high energy now.

Lord, how did that happen? She's got Winston on the phone and, between laughs, is egging him on to play music so she can dance the Charleston. Naturally, he complies, and Charleston music fills the room. Oh, that Winston. He's just full of surprises.

I keep drinking, and she keeps dancing. She's fun to watch, I'll grant her that. I vaguely remember her saying something about growing up wanting to be a ballerina; but she was too short, a bit too chunky, grew hooters, and how there's just wasn't much call for short, busty Latina babes in Ballerinaville back in the day. Apparently, chunky and busty doesn't tutu. Go figure.

Too bad. I think she can tutu with the best of them, and I love watching her dance and bounce, and I like the bouncy part—a little too much. I'm so done for.

Oh god.

I grab two ice buckets and carry them to a chair and crash. I put an ice bucket between my legs and squeeze. I pour the other one on top.

Lord, just strike me numb now.

"Hey! Don't do that!" she laughs. "I'm in a really good place right now, and I want to live! Twenty years can go in a flash, and then I'm dried up like a prune."

She keeps on dancing and bouncing and jiggling and moving closer.

I'm thinking I need more ice. My head feels like it's floating. That's a good sign. I close my eyes, and my chair begins to spin. I drift.

I drift and I see Tami, and she's smiling, and that's so unusual, and she's whispering something in my ear; and I can feel the moistness of her breath. I hug her and she doesn't pull away, and I'm savoring that as I drift on.

⋯✦✦✦⋯

A blinding flash paints the insides of my eyelids a brilliant orange, and I gasp. I blink and, in the near darkness, make out the forms of Danny and Lovey Bunny standing over me, looking down at me. Ryan's behind her. I lift my head, which is throbbing now, and Ria coos. I'm lying on the bed, and Ria's nuzzled against me. My tank top is hiked up to her waist, and my hand's resting on her bare butt.

This cannot be good.

I look around without moving my head. My clothes are still on, so that's good. Maybe it's not as bad as it looks.

"My, my, you're looking good there, lover boy," Danny whispers.

"Good afternoon, lover boy," Lovey Bunny giggles.

"Did you guys just take a picture?"

"Had to, dude. A moment like this is like Halley's Comet passing through."

"No. No pictures."

"Oh, dude, you are such a rock star."

"I'm not a rock star," I mumble. "Now get out before you wake Ria."

"Ri-Ria? Did you say, Ria?" Danny asks. "Pet names already. I see Lady Luck is taking very good care of you. Told you she would."

"Dude, you are so rockin' it right now. I am so jealous right now. I hate you. I love ya, you know that, but I hate you. They're fine, Danny. Let's jet."

"She say 'afternoon'? What time is it?"

"It's 4:48 p.m. Saturday. We have reservations for dinner at Ming's at eight. We'll be back in an hour and a half to pick you up. Go back to sleep."

I hear them leaving. Lovey Bunny is trailing giggles all the way.

Ria shifts her weight and exhales.

"Who was that?"

"The guys and Lovey Bunny."

"Oh. What they want?"

"Take our picture."

"Oh. They leave?"

"Yeah."

"How do you feel?"

"Like a train hit me. How you feelin', Ria?"

"Worse."

"Yeah, you ran out of track big time. Did we, you know?"

She shifts. I feel her move. She slips her hand between her legs.

"No tenderness. Either you're the gentlest man alive or no we didn't. No. We didn't. No way in hell I'd ever let you be that gentle."

"Okay."

That's a relief. I think.

I feel her nuzzle her face deeper into my neck. It feels wonderful until I realize Ria is not Tami, and I remember where my hand is. I try moving it, and all I can manage is a clumsy slide down her thigh. Not exactly what I have in mind.

"Mmmmm."

Apparently, it's what she has in mind. She pulls closer.

Shit. Ain't this just awesome?

And that's my problem. This shit is so awesome.

"Can we just stay like this a while?" she asks.

"Sure."

What's the harm? It's not like either one of us can move without excruciating head pain.

"You're sweet. You didn't touch me all night. I tried. I know you wanted to, but you didn't. I know it was killing you—so much, you even iced yourself. Damn. If that ain't love, I don't know what is."

"Ria?"

"Shhh. It's okay. I understand. You're a great guy. and it hurts me to say this, okay? Don't let her go. You love her that much, then get her back. Don't let anything or anyone stand in your way."

"Thank you."

"Shh. Let me have this."

I "shhh" and let her have this. This is wonderful, and I let her have it. I close my eyes. I open them when I feel someone shaking me. It's Danny.

"Your turn, lover boy."

"Don't touch me," I whisper. "I can't move without my head exploding."

"No one said being a rock star was without its consequences."

Danny tugs on my body, making it contort and do strange things. I'm praying I explode now. That'll teach him and end it for me.

"Stop! What are you doing?"

Danny helps me into the wheelchair.

"What is this thing? Where did you get this thing?"

"I went to the lobby and asked for one after I had counted your empties and checked your bar tab."

I think I mumble something. I'm not sure. I feel a cat crawl across my face.

"Stop it, go away."

I can't lift my arms.

"Chill. I put sunglasses on your face. You're going to need them."

"Oh, don't talk. Where's Ria? What'd you do to Ria?"

"She's fine. She holds her booze better than you. She's with Connie."

We meet up at the curbside limo and head out to Ming's. It's a fairly long drive by Vegas standards—like all the way down to the other end of the strip, I think. Danny rolls me up from the limo like a celebrity busted out of rehab hiding under hat and shades. I could be incognito Elvis, thank you very much, and still nobody would notice me because this is Vegas. But how could anyone in Vegas not notice Ming's?

Despite the dizziness and the pain, I flop my head about, gawking. Ming's is this totally awesome Chinese palace-like place with waterfalls and gongs going off and koi ponds everywhere. So cool here. Literally, the air-conditioning is freezing my ass off, and I think we're still outside. How does that even work? I wish I had brought a hoodie. There's a half-dozen people hovering about us in their flashy, flowing robes of orange and red with yellow dragons on them. I don't think we've gotten to the main door yet.

I have never heard so much Chinese—I'm guessing it's Chinese—spoken to me in my life.

"I have no idea, ace. Ask my driver. He's pushing this rig," I say, thumbing at Danny behind me.

And green. All these lush plants. And the water. Danny rolls me along this wooden bridge through massive oak-like doors. More people in flashy robes.

I wonder if they live here. I want to live here when my hangover is over.

Danny says something about a garden room. We roll on, and he parks me on a wooden deck like part of a floating dock in the middle of a pond. There's a waterfall behind me. I hear birds, but I can't see any. It's dim, and I reach for my shades.

"Leave 'em on."

"Okay, Danny."

Ouch.

I didn't think saying two words could take this much effort or cause this much pain.

Ria's in her wheelchair, and she's got her shades on too. She looks like hell in baggie sweats, flip-flops, and her hair wrapped in a bandana. She looks like a cancer patient. Oh lord, please don't let her have cancer.

Within seconds of getting parked on the floating dock, someone has put an orange cast-iron teapot in front of me. I can feel its heat. Even in my agony, I like this place.

Someone's arm in a red sleeve moves. Is that silk? The arm pours tea into a little cylindrical cup with no handle. I'm assuming it's tea—it sort of smells like tea, only better. I'm not sure of the fragrance, but it's awesome. I reach for the cup and wrap my hand around it. It's quite warm and feels good. I bring the cup to my lips, blow gently at the greenish liquid, and there's flecks of stuff at the bottom. I taste it, a little bit of sweetness and a lot of something else, a flowery something else. Quite good. Not exactly the supermarket stuff from home.

"Go slow. It's still hot."

"Gotcha."

Danny, sitting next to me, says something in Chinese like he's some hotshot British secret agent and then says to the rest of us, his lowly entourage, in English, "We will all use our first names and keep our voices low, very low"—he turns to me—"especially you."

I hear soft giggles.

"And giggles are allowed only on very low."

"'Kay," says his lovey bunny in a whisper.

"Just like that. Excellent," he says.

"Oh Christ," mumbles Ria, muting her objection.

I sip more tea. It is delicious. Only the heat keeps me from chugging it. Danny's noticed. He always notices.

"That's why I said go slow, Paul."

"Going slow here, boss," I say, consciously keeping my voice low.

"Good man."

Another sip, and my sinuses are clear. I'm breathing through both nostrils at the same time. I'm never able to do that. Another sip, and my headache is gone. There's no more buzzing in my ears. I'm feeling sublime goodness. I feel a goofy grin coming on. What's in this stuff?

Danny's still watching. He seems pleased.

Ria is humming over her tea. She has the same kind of cast-iron teapot in front of her.

"Thank you, Danny," she says.

Her voice is sweet, no edge to it.

"It's so peaceful here, so lovely. It's all so magical."

"It is indeed."

I agree. Another sip, and it's easier to look around. And even though it's somewhat dark, I can see the serene faces of the waitstaff. and their bodies seem to hover and glide as they move. They don't seem to walk as much as float like soap bubbles in a breeze.

Someone floats over with another tray of cups. These cups are blue, and the outer side of the cylinders are etched or ribbed. Neither Ria nor I are served. Ria doesn't seem to care. She's got her face atop her teacup. I lean forward and follow the waiter's every move.

"No. Not for you. You've had enough."

"Okay."

I'm feeling too good to argue. I content myself with the tea.

"What is it?" whispers the lovey bunny.

"Jiu."

She giggles. "What's that?"

"Tell you what. Let's agree to call it a lovely libation and let it go at that. Can we all do that?" he makes exaggerated nods with his head.

Lovey bunny and Ryan do likewise. Ria and I don't. But then we're excused.

"Excellent. Here's rule number two. The evening is on me, I insist, and that's final. Do not ask for menus, you can't read them in any event, and you do not need them. I will order for you, and I promise you, you will not be disappointed in the least."

"What's rule number three?" asks the bubbly whisperer.

"Excellent question. Rule number three is everyone will relax and enjoy. We are going to savor this experience. No need to rush. And yes, Maria, I have a special treat for you. I know you were hoping to visit a decent music shop before you leave for home in the off chance of finding an affordable violin. I've got you covered. After dinner, we are going to the Luthiers at Las Vegas, a little workshop boutique. Karl and Lago make excellent instruments and repair and sell them besides. They sell many name brands, known and unknown alike. Fun little place. They're dear friends of mine. We will be at their shop in plenty of time because I've already booked an appointment."

"This is all so overwhelming. I don't know what to say."

"You've already said thank you, and that is more than enough."

Plates and bowls arrive. All I recognize is the rice in pots. I have no idea what I'm eating, only that it is delicious; and by the time we're done, Ria and I are pushing our own wheelchairs back to the limo. We exchange glances and agree racing is probably not a good idea. Along the way out, she stops to take some pictures with her phone.

"I'll need this tomorrow to prove to myself I didn't dream it all up."

Danny smiles.

Back in the limo, we jet down the Strip, fly round a corner or two and maybe a couple more, whiz past some industrial-style concrete buildings, enter a narrow drive between two of them, and park in a small lot surrounding an atrium. The fronts of these buildings are brick and wood. Covered walkways connect them and meet in the center of the atrium about two or three stories up. The buildings' windows are small and tinted. We are let out of the limo and enter a foyer after security buzzes us in.

Another suited FBI-type guy at a desk in the dead center of the hallway is watching us. It's cool, almost cold inside.

"Good evening, sir. Name?"

"Schafer."

"ID."

Danny turns over his driver's license.

The FBI-type glances at it, at Danny, at us. He types quickly on a keyboard.

"Thank you, sir. Please enter on your left," he tells us.

I hear a familiar clicking sound. We enter on the left.

"Please use the elevator on the left. You'll be getting off on the third floor."

"Thank you," Danny says, leading the way.

The elevator automatically stops at the third floor. We get out and move along a hall of wood-paneled walls with framed poster-sized photographs of guitars, cellos, violins, mandolins, and banjos. Some are close-ups of the instruments, and some are autographed photos of various famous people playing them.

I hear Ria whisper, "Is that . . . Oh my god, that's . . ."

She touches her hair.

"I can't go in there! Danny, I can't afford anything in there!"

I don't think Danny heard her. I don't think anybody can afford whatever is in there.

We come to the front doors—carved, magnificent, I'm guessing walnut, from my time with Norse God.

"Wait. Danny, I look like hell. I can't go in there like this."

"Yes you can. Karl and Lago are very understanding. Trust me, they've seen much, much worse."

"Danny, it's not the same! Please, I'm serious, Danny! I look like shit, and I feel horrible."

"Hey, it's all good. Please, just trust me. Relax. You're fine. Trust me on this."

Danny opens the door, and we all reluctantly—except Danny, of course—file in.

We're met by a gangly, balding man whose thick eyeglasses keep sliding down his long, narrow nose. He keeps pushing the glasses back with one hand, and in the other, he's holding a half-eaten pastrami sandwich. It smells heavenly.

"Yo, Karl!" he hollers out. "Our company finally made it."

A few minutes later, a pudgy, redheaded man with a mustache and goatee and delicate gold wire-rimmed glasses comes out, wiping his hands with a cloth.

"Welcome, welcome, friends! We were afraid your plans might have changed."

"Never in a million years."

"Ahh! That's our Danny boy."

Chapter 36

"Come in, come in! I'm Lago."

"Browse around, explore, play," the one who must be Karl says, waving a hand. "Please feel free to open the cabinets and play anything you like."

I turn and notice rows of wood cabinets with glass doors mounted on the walls, two high. Violins and mandolins are in the top row, and guitars are on the bottom row. Ria is right. Danny's just showing off.

Another wall is all glass, and behind it is what must be a small factory, tools and all. Bright yellow hoses run in coils up to the ceiling. The cement floor is spotless. All kinds of hand and power tools and molding frames for guitar and mandolin bodies line the little factory's inside walls. Norse God would love this place.

"Why are they in glass cases?" asks Lovey Bunny.

"To maintain constant humidity and protect the wood," says Karl.

"Oh. Why is that?"

"The necks and bodies of the instruments are made of wood, and wood loves to absorb and release moisture. Too wet or too dry isn't good for them."

"Ohhh. I get it now."

What the hell.

"Where do I go for the archtops?"

"Oh, they're around that corner there," says Lago. "Do you play jazz?"

"No. I—we're staying at the Hotel Fitzgerald, and I heard something about them and a player named Eddie Brown."

"I see." Lago pushes his glasses back. "Yes, Eddie Brown, a legend. By all means, do give one a try. I think you will like the tone."

"Thank you. Thank you very much."

He chuckles, shakes his head, and wanders off to kill off the rest of his sandwich. I head toward the archtops and hear Danny behind me introduce Ria to the luthiers and something about violins.

I find what I guess are archtops. They look weird. I realize they don't have sound holes, the round holes cut into the soundboard like a normal guitar. They each have two *f* holes, and one of them is covered by the pickguard. Then I get it. The tops, the soundboards, they aren't flat like the pick guard; they're rounded—ahh, they're arched. Well, duh. Coach is right, I'm stupid as shit.

I hear a violin and stop. Is that Ria? Damn. She's good. I wander on until I find something more familiar.

There are no padded benches here like at Strummin' City, only what must be custom wood chairs. I sit in one. Oh lord is this comfortable. Plain wood, no padding, and I feel better sitting on it than I do sitting in my father-in-law's favorite leather-upholstered recliner. I see an acoustic—maybe, a 000 or OM body size—and it looks like it's all mahogany. What the hell, I'm only going to be here once in my lifetime.

I carefully remove it from its humidifier cabinet and sit on the chair. I finger the D chord shape and strum. The tone is warm, full. I strum it again. Nice. Encouraged by the sound, I try one of my drills. It's a little off, but I keep at it.

"What are you doing?" Ria asks me.

I look up.

"Oh, hi. Changing chords, why?"

Shit. Here it comes. I can feel it.

"Like that? Really?"

Great. Now she sounds like Tami. Without the f-bombs.

I shrug.

"Sweetheart, it's not a mechanical process."

Okay that's not Tami. Tami's never called me "sweetheart."

I remember to breathe.

"Hey, it's okay. Loosen up. You're not in the army."

She pulls up a chair like the one I'm on and reaches across the guitar with one hand and taps me ever so lightly on the chest, near my heart.

"What's in here"—she touches my temple with her other hand—"and up here flow out together here."

She cradles my hands with hers.

"Into the strings and becomes either music or noise."

She sits back.

"You're not making music, sweetheart, you're making noise, and I can't believe for a minute that you think doing this is any fun."

"Well, no, of course not," I sigh. "It's practice. I don't remember anyone ever saying practicing anything was fun."

She leans closer.

"Oh, that is so not true. May I?"

"Sure."

I give her the guitar and realize how beautiful an instrument it is and, when she plays it, how beautiful it sounds.

She stops.

"Okay. You were playing some major chords, changing from D to A to G, and you sounded like this," Ria says and she demonstrates.

I hear the stiffness, the mechanical droning, and it sounds bad. Ugly. I understand I'm so focused on making my fingers move correctly that I don't hear the true sound they make.

"You sound like this," she continues, "because you're trying to force it. You're so afraid of making a mistake that you stiffen up like you're a robot. Pretty soon that hand is going to spasm and cramp."

Yeah, guilty. Not copping out to this one either.

I lean forward on the bench, wringing my hands, trying to breathe.

"You know, on second thought, maybe this isn't your thing. Maybe you'd be a lot happier if you give it up."

I'm shaking my head.

"No. I can't."

A quiet moment.

"Wow. Okay. Whatever reason you've got for not quitting— and I'm just throwing this out there—has got to be dead wrong. Whatever's motivating you, it's bad, and it's not working. It's never going to work."

I'm still shaking my head.

"Talk to me, sweetheart."

I stop biting my lower lip.

"There are times—rare times—that I can strum a chord and it's clean and it's pretty, and I swear it sounds like the voice of God, almost. I mean, it really does that, you know, when you do it."

I look into the kindness of her eyes. She's not judging me like I thought.

"I need this. I need to . . . I have to do this. I have to prove them wrong. I just do."

"I believe you." She lowers her voice. "Look, all I'm saying is if that's all you've got, then it won't happen. It can't. For this to work, it's all gotta be for you, and that's a different thing entirely. It can't be for somebody else. What's more, it's gotta come from here." She puts her hand over my heart again.

She strums a D with down and up strokes and then fluidly changes to A and then to G.

"Is this what you want?"

"Yes!" I blink away the tears that are forming.

"Then relax. Let God's voice be wherever you hear it. Stop chasing it. Do this for the joy the sound brings you and nothing else. All that other stuff will have to take care of itself some other way. Here," she says, giving the guitar back to me. "Hold it like you want to hold it, not because somebody else is making you hold it. It's not your enemy."

I take it back, hoping I don't drop it.

"You want to succeed? Then allow yourself the freedom to fail. Stop punishing yourself when you do. Now show me a D."

I fret the strings and make the chord shape.

"Now, let up a little. A little more. A little more."

My fingers are just a bit off the strings.

"Good. Okay, for now, let the pad of your left thumb rest flat against the back of the neck at about its center or thickest part and lined up comfortably somewhere between your left index finger and your left middle finger. Now, as your left hand—your fretting hand—moves along the neck, let your thumb stay lined up with the gap between your index and middle fingers as much as possible. In other words, whatever chord shape you make with your fingers, you keep the same relationship with your thumb. Just keep your left thumb pointing up. That keeps your left hand in a comfortable position. Your left thumb rests on the back of the neck to anchor the chord shape you make with the fingers so they can move freely about the strings as you form chord shapes."

She looks at my hand.

"Yeah, like that. Now gently press your fingertips down on the strings for the D chord. No squeeze, no death grip, just firm enough to keep the strings from buzzing. Now, keeping the fingertips behind the frets, slide them as close to the frets as you can, keeping a comfortable grip."

Ria gently presses on my left shoulder.

"Relax this, let it drop, relax your elbow. No stiff arm. No rigid arm, no robot arm. There, that's it."

She strums each string lightly with her finger.

"Good! Now, keep that chord shape, that same grip, and strum the strings like I did. Use your right thumb."

I do.

"Good! That's a good, clean sound. Again."

I do it again.

"Yes. Like that. Good. Gently let your fingertips release and come off the strings just a tiny bit. Now press down. Let up a little. Press down. This is a simple exercise for building your muscle memory for this chord."

I move my fingers. It's still awkward, and I'm getting pissed. I think Shelley Lynne had showed me something like this before, and I should remember it. But I don't. I never can.

Why is that? Why can't I ever get ahead? Why must it be the same stupid shit over and over . . .

"This is not a test, Paul. Relax. I'm not judging you. Nobody's judging you. Breathe."

And how many times do I have to keep hearing that?

"Slowly move the fingers together and fret all the strings at the same time. No hurries, and like you always say, no worries. This is all new, and we want soft hands learning soft habits. We need to go slow and build up to learning good habits from the beginning because that's so much easier than unlearning bad habits. Patience is everything."

"Okay."

She smiles.

"Let your shoulder down."

I drop my shoulder.

"Are you always this tense?"

"I guess so." I look at her. "Yeah, pretty much."

"Let yourself relax, Paul." She moves closer, reaching in toward me. "Oh my god! What the hell was that?"

"What the hell was what?" I ask her weakly.

"That! Did you just flinch?"

"I-I don't know. Maybe. I mean, no. I didn't mean to."

Really deep breath. Really heavy sigh.

"Are you all right? My god, Paul! I wasn't going to hit you!"

My neck's on fire. It's hard to breathe. I feel flushed. My face must be fire engine red. There's nothing I can do. I just nod and force out the words as best I can.

"I know."

So embarrassing . . . No way out . . .

"Whatever it was, whatever you think you saw. I'm fine. Really. I apologize."

Another deep breath. Another sigh.

She steps back and looks away from me.

"I'm just trying to help you, Paul."

"I know."

"This isn't do or die, Paul."

"I know."

I look down and try to breathe. So hard to do. Do or die—yep. That's exactly what it is, but I can't say it.

"Hey! I saw that. The little head shake, how you hunched over," she sighs. "It can't be that bad. If it is, then, don't let it be. Do something about it."

"I'm trying to, actually."

She looks at me, and she blinks. She leans back, and her eyebrows arch.

"Oh! I get it. This has something to do with getting your wife back." A faint smile and a sigh.

"Well," she says as she stands up, "you work on that."

She pats my shoulder.

"I think I want to take another look at that violin. That's what I came here for."

I notice Danny and wonder how long he's been standing there. I'm relieved when he asks to join her. Off they go. I go about trying to learn habits with soft hands and building muscle memory for a chord shape without reminding myself how stupid and clumsy and worthless I am. I'm trying go easier on myself. I suck at both.

It's not like any of this is all that new. Okay, some of it, a lot of it, I'm pretty sure I've heard before. For some reason, I just can't remember it. I keep managing not to learn—or maybe even unlearn—what I've been trying to learn all along.

Okay then. Come hell or high water, that shit needs to stop.

Okay. Maybe it's time to think about real lessons after all. This wasn't all that bad. She was nice. She was helping. Maybe it can be different now. I'm not a kid anymore.

Coach is dead.

My fingers don't want to move like I want them to. Nothing new there either. Maybe lessons will help with that. Maybe I can choose to be patient and focus on that and work on getting my fingers to move like I want them to and accept however long that takes.

I feel my frustration building like nothing's changed; and I try focusing and remembering what Ria said, the sound of her voice, how gentle and soothing it was. I wish I had made a recording with my cell phone of her speaking. I would have her suggestions and guidance and the sounds of the kindness in her voice.

I keep working at shifting from D to A and back. I remind myself to breathe and drop my shoulder and relax my arm and the other stuff. My fingers hurt, and my coordination is fading again. I take a deep breath, sit back, and carefully put the guitar back in its cabinet. I catch a glimpse of the price tag—$8,599.99.

Holy shit, ouch! No fuckin' wonder it sounds so good.

I look at the headstock and recognize the logo set in a mother-of-pearl inlay of a small factory on the East Coast. This guitar is way, too good for me. I could never deserve anything like this.

I feel wiped out. I venture over to the violin section where Ria is leaning over an elegant carved table with claw legs and putting a violin back into its case. She seems out of place here in sweatpants and flip-flops, but like Danny said, the luthiers don't seem to mind.

"That's very kind of you, but really, I can't," she says. "And please, please don't be offended. I'm not asking for a sugar daddy."

"None taken. I know that you neither want nor need a sugar daddy."

He pauses, and in the distance, we can hear strings buzzing. He smiles.

"As for Connie, she was so adorably cute about it, and yes, so absolutely sexy, I couldn't resist. And please don't be offended that I went all in with her. It was well worth it for the two of us. Anyway, none of that matters. All sales are final," he says, holding up a receipt. "It was a done deal the moment you said you loved it while you were lost to your muse."

He folds the receipt and puts it in his wallet, the same kind I have. Wow. That's pretty cool.

"Well, damn if that don't beat all," she smiles. "Okay, I think you're even crazier than Paul is, but thank you. If this is for real, then thank you. Thank you."

"You're welcome. Consider it a gift of hope."

"Okay. I will. I will do that." She hesitates. "You know I can never repay you for this, right?"

Danny smiles.

"Not even an issue. Best decision I've ever made for a friend. Trust me on this. No one is ever going to ask you to, and you'll never need to. We're good here."

"A gift of hope then," she smiles. "I like that."

"Indeed. A gift of hope."

"Hope in what?" I ask, curious.

"Hope that I'll find what I'm looking for."

"What are you looking for?" I ask.

"The love of my life."

"Then I hope so too," I tell her. "And I believe you will, Tami. I had this great dream last night."

She's got this odd look on her face.

"I'm Ria, you idiot."

A funny kind of smile from her.

"It was so vivid, so real, like I could actually feel her next to me, and all the things I need to hear her say—"

"Paul!" Danny interrupts.

"She was saying to me, you know, and—"

"Paul!"

"Her lips, oh my god, the things she did, her swirling tongue—"

"Paul!"

"What?"

"You're unbelievable, man."

"Why? I'm just trying to share, you know, the whole hope thing."

"Paul, stop! We get it. Okay? Enough already! She gets it. We're good."

"I know, but—"

"Shut the fuck up, Paul!"

"Okay. Okay. Fine. I'm sorry."

Shit! Who's the vibe-bustin' asshole now?

Ria picks up the violin case.

"Maybe we should leave."

Is she crying?

"Yes," Danny says, checking his watch. "It is indeed time to go."

Fine. We go. Back to the limo and away from the luthiers in Las Vegas and back to the Hotel Fitzgerald. It's a quiet ride. I make sure to be polite, to nod, and to smile, and to pretty much keep my mouth shut. Polite goodbyes in the lobby.

Connie leans up and kisses Danny on the cheek.

"Thanks for a wonderful weekend, Sugar Daddy Danny. We'll have to do it again some time," she giggles.

"Oh, we will."

"Good night, guys," Ria says. "Thank you again, Danny. For everything."

They head to the elevator. Ria doesn't say anything to me. Probably just as well. Something inside says I need to make like a submarine, run silent and run deep.

Maybe if I just sink . . .

"Okay, dudes, it may be Sunday morning, but I got a few hours left, so I'm gonna go hit the slots. Maybe I'll get lucky. Maybe even, 'lucky' lucky."

"Give 'em hell, Ryan my man! See ya, Danny."

I head off to my room. After another chocolate shake and enjoying thinking about that awesome dream of Tami, I call it a night and crash.

✦✦✦✦✦✦

"Rise and shine, lover boy! Greet the new day! Checkout time."

I sit up, feeling like a zombie.

"Okay, Danny."

I look around.

"Relax. You're packed. Here's your wallet."

He hands me my wallet.

"Where'd this come from?"

"The floor."

"Oh, thanks, Danny."

"Don't mention it."

I follow Danny and Ryan to the elevator. I think of asking Ryan how lucky he got and decide against it.

Once more through the ostentatious lobby of glitz and glamour and out into the warm sunshine. The limo is waiting. I take one last look around. Wow. My life is still shit, and I feel so . . . awesome. Vegas! What a concept.

Chapter 37

"Danny, I gotta tell ya, man, this has been so awesome and so, you know, unbelievably, freakin' weird weekend. Thanks, man."

The driver takes my bag and puts it in the trunk.

"You know how to live, Danny."

"What do you mean?" Danny asks.

"Well, for starters, this whole thing is like, like—"

"Like something Huntington would do?"

"Okay, it's creepy you would know that, but yeah. Exactly. How'd you know?"

"Huntington and I are a lot alike."

"How is that even possible?"

"We're cousins."

Ryan peers over his shades.

"You shittin' us, dude?"

"How is that even possible?"

We pile into the limo.

"You're hung up on the name. He changed his during law school. He thought he'd make more money 'faking his way as a blue blood.' His term, not mine. My family had the department store. His didn't. Everything was so competitive between our fathers. He picked up on it, and ever since, he's been chasing the almighty dollar."

"But you? You don't?"

"Dude, you blind? Danny chases the women—or, should I say, they chase him," Ryan laughs.

Danny chuckles at that.

"Got me on the women. No, I don't need to chase the almighty dollar."

"Oh, yeah. Right. How'd I not see that one coming? And all this time, with him in the office, you two never . . . you know, talked or anything."

"Not once. No need."

"I don't get it."

"It does not matter, Paul. The point is, I knew he'd make you an offer."

"Yeah. He did." I look out the window. "Wasn't very subtle about it."

"He never is. He plays to win. Frankly, so do I."

"Then which of you is the devil?"

"Oh, that would be him. Which is one reason why I brought you here."

"There's another reason? I don't think I want to know this."

"Getting back to the first reason. You're vulnerable, Paul. He sees an opportunity in people like you. He offers you a lot of money up front with a promise of a lot more. What you need to know is that it's all a big lie. He ends up owning you because he gets you working so hard that you never get your head far enough out of the files to see that the big money is always kept—just out of your reach and never comes. The big money is always his by design."

"You had to bring me to Vegas to tell me this?

"No, I had to bring you to Vegas to get you away from Huntington, away from Woo, away from your piranha of a wife, and get you someplace where you could breathe a little, feel like a winner for a change, look in a mirror, and maybe even meet yourself."

"Oh. So Ria's in on it too, is that it?"

"No, man. Not at all. I'm telling you, man, that was pure chance. Beyond my wildest expectations. That's the sheer beauty of

Vegas, Paul. That's why I love this town. Forgive me, I love the pun, pure chance, but I'm willing to bet that, Vegas being Vegas, the odds were always in your favor. Anything can and usually does happen here. Lady Luck smiled on you fucking big time, my friend. Ria's the real deal, and you're a complete, fucking moron if you let her go."

He reaches into his shirt pocket.

"Here." He hands me a business card. "In case you don't find the one in your wallet."

It's Ria's business card for music lessons.

"Look. I know you got issues, Paul, who doesn't? I know Huntington's got you lined up with one of the county's contract shrinks, but make no mistake, you need to get over all the shit your old man did to you, once and for all, and whatever the fuck else is messing you up. First place to start is taking guitar lessons from her."

I look at the card.

"It's not that easy, man."

I put it in my pants pocket anyway.

"And it never will be until you choose to make it right. That shrink had to have told you that or something like that by now, neural linguistic programming and all that. You're facing the twilight of your life, Paul, and if you don't get the pieces right and make yourself whole, one day you're going to step in front of a bus in front of the courthouse."

"Listen to him, dude," Ryan chimes in.

"Look, Paul. I don't get the whole guitar thing. Okay? Whatever. But it doesn't matter because that whole guitar thing matters to you, and that's all that matters. Let that guitar thing lead your path to self-discovery. Ria can help you with that, even if it's not meant to be for the two of you. Let that wake your ass up to the fact that your gold-digging trophy wife is manipulating the ever-living shit out of you as she always has. She always will, if you let her. You love her more than you love yourself, and she's the type who can only love herself. Trust me on this, I know. Believe me, Paul. I *know* women."

My go-to move and a sigh.

"You are her beast of burden, her meal ticket, and you die for it because you think she's so fucking far out of your league and that someone that beautiful will never fall for you. Okay. You're probably right. So what? The truth is that you have no fucking idea what beauty—what real beauty—there is out there, real beauty like Ria. So number one, there's no 'league' *per se*, so get that through your fat head.

"Number two, she's not the only babe in the pool because there'll always be more than one pool and they're all full of babes in all sizes and shapes and colors. Again, Ria. And there's a lot more Rias out there."

I nod.

"Is there a number three?"

"Number three. Okay, so none of us are getting any younger. Big fuckin' whoop. Until you're well past seventy, maybe even eighty, it doesn't make a damn bit of difference if you're healthy. Pull your head out of your ass and get healthy."

Danny nudges me and smiles.

"Hey. Is any of this getting through?"

"Some."

"Okay. About time. For what it's worth, if I sound anything at all like Huntington, it's because I'm making a counterpoint here."

"Okay."

"Good. Last point. If you—and even Ryan, for that matter— would simply let go and stop trying so damn hard, you just might find you're each just enough of a babe magnet in your own right to attract any number of desirable women who would be right for you."

"Huh."

"Yeah, huh. Believe it or not, you did it this weekend. You did it despite having started off as a complete asshole. Once Ria understood why you were acting like an asshole, that it was because you were suffering as any real person would in those circumstances, well then, it was off to the races. Something to think about, stud."

"Yeah, it is. Thank you. Thank you for everything. Ming's, Ria—everything."

"You're welcome, Paul," Danny smiles. "Trust me. It was a pleasure to do something good for the Bard. Think about it, Paul. Tell Huntington *no* and let Tami go. Give Ria a chance. Your call. Lecture's over. Trust me. I've done all I can do for you."

"Got it."

He's all wrong, but there's no point arguing.

The limo has stopped. I look around.

"We're at the airport?"

"We're at the airport."

"We're flying back, dude?"

"You're flying back. Here are your tickets," Danny says, reaching into his rear pocket, handing them to us. "And from Ontario, you'll take the airport shuttle home to Ryan's place. Okay, gents, it's been real. Have a safe flight."

The driver opens the door for me to get out. He goes around to the other side and opens the door for Ryan.

Ryan and Danny do a fist bump.

"Thanks, dude. Righteous weekend."

"You're welcome, man. I'm glad we did it. We'll get you a Ria of your own next time."

"No worries, dude."

We wait as the driver gets our bags from the trunk.

Ryan and I exchange glances.

"I have no idea, dude."

"Fair enough."

I watch the limo pull away.

We catch a Cactus Air commuter flight on a twin turboprop. Nice plane. E-ticket ride through clear air turbulence for about ninety minutes. The bumping brings the dream back, and I enjoy it as much as I can.

The plane is loud too. I look over at Ryan. We don't talk much. Ryan's white-knuckling the arm rests, and he keeps staring out the window toward the prop at the front of the engine atop the right wing. C'mon, like it's going to stop spinning? Whatever. I guess we all have our traumas.

✦ ✦ ✦ ✦ ✦

Speaking of traumas, I enter the breech of yet another dreaded Monday and, from the tone of her voice, yet another smart-ass remark from the civil service secretary from hell. Hey, good for me, I'm not listening to her and have no idea what she said. Neither do I care.

I can take my regular happy pill, and then I can take a half of another pill and get to 120 mg of mellow that way. Hoo-ah!

As I shuffle through the stuff on my desk, hunting for the day's task list, I remember there won't be one. I left early Friday. I get up and close my door. My gut knots up, and I check my calendars for any court appearances in case I forgot. The computer calendar is clear, which means nothing, as the secretary from hell rarely gets around to updating it between her breaks and her association committee meetings. I check my weekly planner desk book where I handwrite all my appointments, and constantly check them over and over. A long sigh escapes from my chest as if it can't wait to get away from me.

"We're rethinking your assignment, Paul."

I jump at Woo's voice.

"Jeezus. How about a little warning, for God's sake? What the hell is wrong with you? Maybe send me one of your stupid little emails first, huh? A little of that 'Now hear this! Now hear this! Round Table! I repeat, Round Table!' shipboard crap you hold so dear, how 'bout it, huh?"

He has a blank, dull look on his face. He steps out of the doorway and sits down in a chair across from my desk. Too bad it ain't full of files as usual.

I'm in no mood for his shit at this hour, and my mouth is on autopilot so I let it fly off.

"Is that what this is?"

I look around, and no one else is near the door.

"A personal Round Table? Just you and me? Maybe discuss the usual trivia of all the mind-numbing, office-minutiae crap you can think of? Maybe, you know, who's not been wearing neckties tight into the collar, who's got their shirtsleeves rolled up before 3:00 p.m.?"

I'm on a roll here . . .

"Or who's not signing out for lunch and signing back in on time? God forbid we ever get the okay to discuss actual legal questions of concern. Oh, hell no. Can't have that now, can we? Might not look so good, airing the laundry of the county's doings, all rife with indifference, incompetence, and ignorance. Shit, no. We stick to more urgent matters like arranging the next diversity speaker and shit like that in this tiny little fantasy world of make-believe y'all are running here."

Rollin' on a river . . .

"Yeah. God forbid we ever discuss real questions of law here. And if anyone should dare bring it up, you immediately table it— *every time*—and defer it to the monitor and review for future action calendar where it stays buried."

I breathe.

"Now, what's all this crap about changing my assignment?"

Fuck it.

I'm out of steam.

Woo just sits there.

Eventually a bit of a sly grin—just a bit—appears on his face, then fades.

"Well now, Mr. Cooper. You think you're something of a crusader. You think you have a big heart, a good heart. Look at you! So valiant to insist on wearing it on your sleeve. Oh, how Quixotic! Such a fine hero you'll be someday too."

Woo leans forward in his chair, tilts his head, glaring at me.

"All that insufferable, pent-up idealism—all that due diligence, conscientiousness, all that meticulous study of the fine print, the finer points of the law. Talk about minutiae. Little good may it do you. Yes!"

He takes a deep breath. Tilts his head a bit the other way.

"All that running around pointing out all the flaws, 'Oh! The emperor has no clothes,' and yet, you always manage to stay stuck in the same place. Well, bully for you! Why do you suppose that is, Mister? Did it ever occur to you that we already know? That maybe we don't need to be reminded—certainly, not by the likes of some interloper like you—just how to run this little ship we've got here?"

Woo smiles and leans back in the chair.

"Not so smart now, are you, Mister? You see, Mr. Cooper, sometimes, it's much better for all concerned to let sleeping dogs lie, lest you infest everyone around you with fleas. But you didn't think of that, did you? No. You're out to shake things up a bit, are you? Well, let me tell you something, Mister. I'll let you in on a little secret. This county has been around since 1895. It's doing just fine the way it is, see. Change comes, certainly. But it comes gradually and all in good time and with consensus and long after it's been tested out by other counties—bigger ones, the donor ones, the ones who can afford to champion the causes of change or, as is most often is the case, defend against them. We're not on the cutting edge here for a reason, and therefore, we don't do that sort of thing here, Mister. You would do well to remember that."

"Really? Since when is trying to get code to put the factual basis on their violation notices, just as one example—I can think of many more—anywhere close to being on the cutting edge of legal practice?"

"Perhaps there's too much of the martyr in you, Cooper. Something of the tragic hero. All that Prometheus sort of thing. That's too bad. While you were in college, did you ever study something of the Classics? Greek drama? Shakespeare? Ever read Hamlet in college?"

"Not that I can recall."

"You didn't major in English, I take it?"

"Poli-sci."

Woo's head tilts up. He grins.

"Ah! Very well then. That explains it, you see. A state school, no doubt. That superficial do-gooder vantage point. Pity. You should have read it. Read it now. Marvelous, all that nonsense 'to thine own self be true'—ha! You know the best part, don't you?"

"To be or not to be?"

Woo scowls.

"Don't be a fool! No!"

Woo waits.

"The best part is that he dies!"

"Who dies?"

"Hamlet, you idiot! All that angst. All that soul-searching, all that torment, and turmoil. All that relentless pot-stirring. For what? For nothing! Nothing, I tell you! That's right, Mister. Think about that. Think about where you're headed."

He leans forward again, tapping a finger on my desk.

"Listen to me, Mr. Cooper. See, all that political correctness you disdain, it serves a good purpose. A very good purpose. It keeps you from doing something stupid, something you might live to regret, or worse. It keeps you from making serious mistakes and doing the stupid things you've been doing."

Woo grimaces.

"But no! Here you are in our very own little world of . . . what did you call it? Oh, yes. I remember now—'make-believe.' There he goes! Our very own Mr. Cooper, right here in our very own little world of make-believe, and off he goes to Washington or so he would imagine, going to fix up our little world. Well, now. Our little world doesn't need to be fixed. You do—and fixed but good—Mr. Cooper! That's the part you so conveniently manage to avoid seeing. Blind zeal does that."

He stands up. Stretches his hands high over his head. Maybe he'll try some yoga next. Nope. He lowers his arms and breathes deeply.

"Well now, Mr. Cooper, tell me, there's so much wrong with our little world of make-believe, so much of it displeases you, why don't you leave us? Pack up and leave. That's right! Go back to the real world. Nothing's stopping you. Is there?"

"Okay, Woo. You want to talk about the real world? How do you think the real world got the way it is? The same way it started here. But here, we can fix. We can do better by everyone. And for all the same reasons you say we can't. Besides, I'm not stupid. I know the shape the economy's in. There's nothing out there. Believe me, I know. I've checked. It's the only part of the paper I read. And you and I both know there's even less out there for men of my age. Age discrimination is illegal everywhere but the legal profession because you and I both know how to get around it."

"Oh, I see. Well now. Lacking some guts, aren't we? Real world a little too tough for you, a little too unfair? Is that it? Seems to me that you are in a bit of a predicament. So heroic yet not quite so heroic enough."

"I don't know what you mean."

"Oh, I think you do, Mister. I think you do. But seeing how you are such a man of detail—and I daresay, *minutiae*—allow me to spell it out for you. We run a tight little ship here, Mister, in our little make-believe world as you so critically notice. And it seems you're stuck on it, and that displeases you. I hope it displeases you all the more when you realize that this predicament of yours is as much of your own doing as it is anyone else's. That's called irony, Mister. It may be lost on you, but it's certainly not lost on me, and I intend to enjoy it fully."

Woo pulls a folded piece of paper from his shirt pocket.

"Now then, I've been mulling it over for some time, what to do with you, given all the trouble you keep causing. Seems here"—he looks at the paper—"Code Enforcement has had their fill of you and your making waves. That doesn't sit well upstairs, Mister, that does not sit well at all. They want someone else. They have been, shall we say, quite vocal about it too."

"I'm not surprised. Keystone Kops couldn't do any worse. Have you bothered to read any of my status emails about the judges' comments on these cases?"

"I have not. There's no need. If you have listened to anything I've said, you'd know that by now. The courts are not our clients."

"Actually, they are. It's in the government code. I can show you if you like."

Woo scowls.

"That won't be necessary. You have the wrong context, as usual. I . . . I misspoke."

"I understand. There's a lot of that going around here too."

"That so? Well now, I sincerely thank you for that insight, Mr. Cooper. I do. I think you have just solved both of my problems. I need to do something with you. You made the office look bad. That's as nearly an unforgiveable sin as there is around here. Admin goes to great lengths to match up the right attorney to the client departments. Now, don't let this go to your head, that's why you were hired. Code was expanding, new leadership was anticipated within Land Use, and Code needed to show some success. You had the right track record. We brought you aboard, and you exceeded their and our expectations. The success of your administrative citation ordinance for Code's use demonstrated as much. Again, do not let that go to your head. But you weren't satisfied to stop there—you kept pushing. Apparently, you failed to take the hints. So you kept pushing, trying to make changes and corrections to things that had succeeded well enough for years."

"Those changes were needed. Read my emails."

"No doubt. Again, you miss the point!"

"Right. Keep the sizzle. Just make damn sure to throw out the steak. Appearance and only appearance matters. God forbid the county actually ever do anything."

"That's exactly right, Mister! Well now, it seems you have been listening! That's very good. I am pleased. There may be some hope for you after all, and once you get this desire for martyrdom out of your system. In fact, I can help you with that. I can help you with that right now, Mister. I have a new assignment for you. But rather than tell you about it, I will let Darryl have the honors. He is your immediate supervisor after all."

"A chain of command thing?"

"Quite right, Mister. I also understand that scuttlebutt has it you and he have quite the rapport."

"Okay."

"Very well. Thank you, Mr. Cooper for allowing me to stop by on such short notice and interrupt you today. Needs of the office, you understand."

He stands, I'm hoping he's about to leave.

"Oh, just one more thing, Mister. It would behoove you to remember that if you truly were so much as a mere pinch—the tiniest pinch off a piece of the lawyer you think you really are—you would not be here. You'd be out there. Your name on the door. Better yet, at the top of a major office building's exterior facade, visible for miles. But it isn't. Never will be. You're just not good enough. Never were, never will be. This is as high as you are ever going to get, Mister. And right here, by your own doing, is where you are going to stay until we are done with you."

Woo is smiling, rubbing his hands together.

"You think you've got it bad, that we've given you a bum deal here? Well, just you wait, Mister. You are at the bottom of the food chain here—a worker bee, a nameless drone—and you're going to like it. You are going to toe the line, and you are going to keep that big mouth of yours shut! From now on, you won't be writing any more memoranda with all your recommendations, corrections, and changes, No more, Mister. Not ever!

"From now on, you are going to bust your ass more than any bosun's ever done on any of my ships back in the day. You are going to take whatever we give you, however jacked up you may think it is, and you are going to handle it in a professional and politically correct manner and without so much as a whimper of a complaint or the slightest wave making. Now hear this, Mister, now hear this! If you don't, I will send you packing out into that big bad real world you can't seem to face on your own. Do you hear me, Mister?"

I glance down at my desk and answer in a low voice, "Loud and clear, sir."

Silence.

I look up. He's frozen in place, staring at me. No, glaring. His face is red. He probably thinks I'm mocking him. I'm not trying to do anything at all.

I close my eyes and lower my head.

Stillness. Silence. I don't mind it at all.

"That's more like it, Mister. It's about time you started showing me more respect. Stay that way. Life will be better for you. Now, I'm very happy we had this little chat. You'll be hearing from Darryl fairly soon, I imagine. Good day."

Woo gets up and leaves.

"Good day."

I don't think he heard me. No matter.

I feel the urge to visit the men's room. I do. I take care of business, wash up, and walk back to my office.

"How ya swinging it, slugger?"

This time, I jump at Darryl's voice.

"Holy crap! What is it with you guys? Are you walking through walls now?"

He's sitting across from my desk.

"All rested? All bright-eyed and bushy-tailed from your revelry in Vegas? All worn out from Woo's ass-chewing? Damn he's a windbag. Normal for a bureaucrat, I suppose."

I shrug. My go-to move.

"Yeah, I suppose."

"Good. I've been talking with him. I suppose he mentioned that."

"I've heard."

"He blames you, you know."

"No, I don't know. Blames me for what?"

"Robby checking out."

"*What*? Oh god."

"You're so easy," Huntington chuckles. "Retirement, bucko. Relax. He ain't dead. Checked himself into a rehab, then something about a twelve-step program in the desert run by Benedictine monks or whatever they are. He's fine."

"Okay."

"You know, Woo's not such a bad guy for a two-bit, piece-a-shit bureaucrat. Although I have to tell you all that navy talk and his mannerisms wear a bit thin. A little dense maybe. Oh, hell. They all are. There's a lot of that going on around here, you may have noticed, but that's another issue. Like I said, we're rethinking your assignment."

He adjusts his necktie. Blood red. Looks like silk.

"Code Enforcement's about to undergo another management overhaul, so it will be a while before they can even think of getting their act together. In any event, none of that concerns you. I suggested moving you over to do hospital collections. Toughen you up for the long haul. Woo and the rest of Admin agree with me. Wholeheartedly."

He smiles.

"Here's the new deal, slugger. You're going to be suing people whose lives are ruined by catastrophic illness and injury for the hospital bills they can't pay. How's that sound?"

"That can't be good."

"No, I didn't think so either. I've been reading up on you, your personnel file. An OR release investigator in Probation. Now there's a bleeding-heart outfit for you. Qualifying arrestees for pretrial detention release from custody. There's some ass-backwards thinking for you. Guess that would be up your alley."

He stares at me.

"Yes, Paul. I'm going to make you a heartless bastard," he grins. "Groom you for bigger and better. Now how's that sound, slugger? Gets me all dewy just thinking about it."

"Sounds like I need a different job."

"Oh? You think?" He crosses his legs. "Well, no shit, Sherlock! You son of a bitch! As I recall, I tried giving you a leg up. I gave you a shot at some real money, something a true litigator would never pass up."

He looks at his watch.

"But you did. Well, now look at you! I understand you now. I was all wrong before. My bad. So be it." He smoothes his necktie. "Go see Melinda. She'll have some files for you."

This is obviously not the hill I want to die on.

"Will do. Any chance of getting some pointers, maybe a seminar or two?"

"No. Forget all that. All you need to know is this. Number one, they owe the money, period. Bottom line? They *owe* the money. It's that simple. You need to understand that."

"They owe the money?"

"They do, indeed. That's your new mantra. Understand your new client department. They're collectors and collectors collect. Period. You want charity, go to church!"

"They owe the money."

He pauses, squints, and says with a sneer, "Indeed, and get that stupid look off your face. The fact that those poor patient debtors can't pay the bill or any of their bills is not our problem. More importantly, for you, it's not your problem. It's their problem, and frankly, I don't care what all their boo-hoo problems are, and neither will you."

He juts out his chin and smoothes his shirt collar.

"It's like this, Paul. If the hospital accounts people want to throw the taxpayers' money away going after insolvent debtors in the hope that they might win a lottery someday and go full-on, whole-hog fangs out after those helpless little bastards, then you're going after them the same way. That's how it works here. Under the powers who be, that's how this county rolls. Geez, what a hot mess. And what do you care? If you intend to succeed here—or anywhere else, for that matter—you won't care. Get my point, Paul? You won't give a damn. You just go through the motions and pass the shit on down the line. You just might make it to retirement. Make sure you understand that."

"Okay."

"The secret is this, Paul—you make it up as you go along. Whatever it takes to prove the debt and the fact that they owe it, that's what you offer as evidence, and you make damn sure it all gets admitted. That's it. That's your whole case in a nutshell. You want pointers? There you go. I gave you pointers." He leans back in the chair. "Litigation 101, slugger. I shouldn't have to tell you any of this."

"Fair enough."

It's never wise to argue with the devil.

"Here's another pointer. Those hospital account people have no concept of the real world. So you're going to educate them. When you do, you're going to bill those assholes for everything. Every call, every question, every email—everything. There's no internal time on this, no covering for them. Ever. You wake up in the middle of the night freaked out over a case, you bill 'em. You fart, you bill 'em. You sneeze, bill 'em. You cough, bill 'em. You catching my drift here, Paul?"

"Bill the asshole bastards."

"That's exactly right. Six-minute increments at $194.00 per hour. If they ask you something and you don't know it—and take the hint, you won't—you tell those bastards, 'That's an excellent question. I will research it, and I promise I will get right back to you.' Then do it, double the time it took you to do it, and bill 'em."

"Bill 'em."

"At $194.00 an hour. Damn right. There are consequences to their asinine arrogance and continuing failure to adequately and fairly negotiate the hospital liens and then demand judgments in full. No provider should get that. Ever. Those bastards need to understand that, and it should cost them big money when they don't."

"Big money. Bill 'em?"

"Damn right." He steeples his fingers at the edge of his chin. "Oh, before I forget. Got some bad news for you."

Like any of this is good news?

Of course, he has bad news, and that isn't news at all. It can always get worse. In my case, it usually does.

He rubs his hands together.

"The situation's changed, Slugger. My work here for the Board is done. Thank God. What a shitfest. Word isn't out yet. Within the next few months, there'll be a new CAO on board, you're truly welcome, and regardless of who it is, they'll no doubt be bringing some of their people over as department heads. That likely includes County Counsel." He smiles like a shark. "Bank on it. There will also be a new Code Chief, and they'll, no doubt, bring over an attorney or two accustomed to doing things the new chief's way, so one of them will be running the nuisance abatement team."

He smiles again.

"Of course, none of that is going to be your problem because starting now, you, my friend, are now the County's one and only collections lawyer. You're starting with unpaid hospital patient accounts. Book up, bucko. In addition to studying, given what I've learned about you, you'll want to stock up on antacids, tranquilizers, and anti-diarrhea meds."

He laughs, apparently finding his remark—if not his awareness of the state of my physical health—rather amusing.

"You're on your own now, slugger." He smooths his collar. "If it's any consolation—and I don't see how it could be coming from that clown—but Woo said to be sure to let you know you're still his guy. Whatever the fuck that means. He expects great things from you. Great things. Right. He's so full of shit. Anyway, point is you'll answer directly to him from now on." He smiles. "You probably figured that one out on your own."

Darryl strokes his chin.

"Guess that means you'll be pounding sand for years to come, like Woo would say. Pity. Not that he's likely to be around any longer than the rest of you. Oh well. Such is life. Such is your life, anyway. And his. And the rest of 'em." He grins. "Speaking of consolation once again—and by the way, don't get all dreamy eyed about it—but you were one of the few people here I found worth saving. So much so, I made special plans for you. But you pissed your chance away, so there's that. Oh! One last thing. I think you've got a couple of trials next week. How's that saying go again? Oh, yeah. What doesn't make you stronger kills you. Something like that. Ha! Good luck, slugger! A thousand deaths await you."

He stands up, smooths his tie this time, and starts whistling a familiar tune.

He stops at the door, points at me, and sings, "And your career might as well be frozen."

He laughs.

"That's a line from your song, isn't it? The one the boys sang at the BBQ?"

I nod.

"Part of the chorus."

"Thought so. Love that line. Funny." He shakes his head. "I love the irony."

He gets up and moves to the door. He stops.

"Do you realize that in the pantheon of lawyers, you're even lower than us bottom feeders working PI? So low, you'll have to spit up just to hit the ground. Do you understand that you do nothing but the crap work, the hospital collections cases? Only newbies and all the never-will-bes on their way out the door do that shit. You realize all that now, right?"

"So you tell me."

"So I've told you." He shakes his head. "I tried to throw you a rope, you know, and you just let it fall."

He just stands there, staring me down.

"So long, slugger."

He walks out.

So long, Darryl, you devil.

Sure enough, I find a foot-high stack of legal-size manila folders on Melinda's desk. A yellow "For Paul" sticky note is stuck on the front of the topmost folder. She's not there. I gather them up and head back to my office.

I go through them. Not a lot of information in any of them. After a while, I figure out there are court notices included. Some give notice of dates set a few months into the future for "orders to show cause re: service" and "orders to show cause re: dismissal" at whatever courtroom the case has been assigned by the court clerk. Others start with dates for trial setting conferences. All the files have a complaint listing various causes of action for what amounts to unpaid county hospital bills. Some of the complaints have admissions forms attached as exhibits.

My stomach is knotting up, and I feel woozy and force myself to concentrate, and finally it dawns on me that a good place to start is calendaring all the court dates and, after that, remembering Darryl's comment about trials and finding out which ones already have trial dates. Now I just need to figure out how to keep my sanity and make it up as I go along.

Chapter 38

Sure enough, there's a trial next week. I delve into the file, and a couple of hours later, I think I have it sorted it out. Or not. There are some documents I need, so I send an email request. I spend the week trying to become a collections lawyer.

My pulse races more every day, and by Friday, I feel another anxiety attack building and it hits me like a tsunami. To think I've been doing so well, and for a second, I think of maybe going out the window. But I'm too light-headed and there's this compulsion to check my email of all things—certainly not my first choice—but it's overwhelming, so I do.

There's one from Jessica Carrigan, my new boss. I delete it unread.

There's one from someone I've never heard of, and it's one of those hospital accounts people. He wants to know why I have his case and if he really needs to appear at trial like he did on the Lewis case and if so, why. Because that's not something he ordinarily has to do, still doesn't understand why he had to do so for the Lewis case, and he wants no part of doing it ever again.

"I don't know yet," I type. "That's an excellent question. Let me look into that. I promise that I will get back to you."

I hit Send. I bill for reviewing and replying to his email. I talk myself into making a note to find the Lewis file and see if it has anything I can use as a roadmap for making it up as I go along. I bill for that too.

Then there's another one, a reply from some other hospital account person replying to my documents request telling me I can't have those documents because that's not how they do things. His email says my request is "unacceptable." That's a new one.

Asshole.

I sit back, close my eyes, and let go in time to enjoy yet another stress-induced light show that I cannot control. And in my surrender, the words just flow:

> And I see the lights that sparkle
> And I see the lights that shine
> And I know that I'd still see them
> Even when
> I'm finally blind
>
> And I hear the voices calling
> Saying I'm to blame
> For the lack of their good fortune
> Their freedom
> And their fame
>
> My my my
> My my my
> Ohh, my
>
> Well I see the light's a flashin'
> From the darkness as it came
> And everything I'm hopin's
> Got me callin' out your name
> And everything I'm dreamin'
> Says I'll never be the same

And I see the lights that sparkle
And I see the lights that shine
And I know that I'd still see them
Even when
I'm finally blind

And I hear the voices calling
Saying I'm to blame
For the lack of their good fortune
Their freedom
And their fame

My my my
My my my
Ohh, my

My my my
My my my
Ohh, my.

And when my retinas finally calm down, I politely reply with a thank-you email, and do as I was told, and bill 'em. I bill 'em jes' like the 'ol boss hawg done said I was to do—$194.00 an hour. Fuckin' A. *Assholes.*

I write down what few words I can remember from I just sang silently to myself in my head. I hope the rest come back. I would really like to get them put to music.

I need some air, so I make a special trip to the courthouse. I wait in line at the attorney window. When it's my turn, I make my request. I'm given a number and told to take a seat. Twenty minutes later, I'm called back to the window. I'm shown the file, make my copy request, and return to my seat. Fifteen minutes later, I have what I need and go back to my office. I bill 'em for all the time I'm gone times two and, for good measure, throw in another half hour for the migraine aura I suffered because of those bastards' incompetence, ignorance, indifference, and insistence on telling me how to practice law.

Fuckin' A. Asshole pricks.

My desk phone rings. A woman's voice starts off real sweet-like, and then before long, the screaming and wailing starts, slapping me hard with her pain. She's grateful the doctors saved her life and all so grateful and how she's making do without her legs—she once had two—and there's nothing I can do or say to explain why the county—and that means me, just me—is suing her for $250,000.00 in unpaid county hospital bills or why her applications for charity care were repeatedly denied.

I have no answer but to go out on a limb and promise to look into it and suggest she reapply. I ask her for her name, and I write it down. I'm so grateful when the sob sister hangs up. So grateful. But it doesn't help me any, and my retinas flame with fierce fireworks. I can barely see; and I shove the phone off my desk, spin in my chair, and grope for the guitar case. I manage to get it open and dump out the guitar with a harsh twang from its strings. I pick it up. It feels familiar, and I can't see for shit, and I don't care. I just strum it up and down, up and down, up and down like a fool on fire.

I close my eyes—there's nothing to see anyway. I just feel the fretboard with my fingers trying to shape chords by feel, knowing I can't do that for shit either, and I don't care. I just let my fingers find their own way and strum. Sometimes it's okay, and mostly it's a crappy sound, and I don't care. But sometimes I get a chord right, and it's music and it's pure. I just need to hear the strings, and I gladly take whatever sounds they care to give me.

I just go on a strummin' and a hummin' to myself, and then words start to flow. So I turn 'em loose and sing and let 'em go.

> You think I must be dreamin'
> As I listen to you screamin'
> How the bills all piled up so high
> And you wanna know the reason
> Because no one's ever told you why.

Well I don't know what to tell you
I don't even know what to say
Seems the County chose to sue you
About some bills you have to pay.

I'm supposed to be a tough old Joe,
I can't be bothered so you know
With all your sobs and cries,
But your babblin' tales of woe
Leave tears a wellin' in my eyes

An' that collections bitch,
So rude and crude
To you
You say,
And how all she really wants
Is someone she can screw
Today.

There's not much I can do
And there ain't much I can say
In case you missed the clue
It's only fair to say
That bitch is out to screw somebody
And it might as well be you.

Well now, that may be-
And I agree
And it does sound so cruel
For her to say--
That you still owe the money
So cough it up, honey
And tell me how much you can pay.

Well I don't know what to tell you
I don't even know what to say
Seems the County chose to sue you
About some bills you have to pay.

I'm supposed to be a tough old Joe,
I can't be bothered, so you know
With all your sobs and cries,
But your babblin' tales of woe
Leave tears a wellin' in my eyes.

They leave tears a wellin' in my eyes.

Look at me—
I'm sobbin'
Sobbin' like a sissy.

"Hey! Der Bingle Boy! Close your damn door, will you, please? Shut up with all your caterwauling! Some of us might be actually be working out here!"

Now that's funny. Like that costume jewelry–janglin' bitch has ever done a full day's work in her whole life. I keep at it until I hear the ol' bat push her chair away from her desk and jump off her jiggly fat ass and huff 'n' puff it on over here and slam my door shut. I laugh. Must mean I've got a helluva good song going. Too bad I can't see clearly enough to write the words down. Oh well. No worries. I'm feeling a little better now.

I keep strumming, and then the chords start flowing. I actually manage to play "Twinkle, Twinkle, Little Star" all the way through and in time, in a slow rhythm. Duh. But it's recognizable as the song. Not exactly a chick-diggin' lick, but it's something. It's real progress. That's the key. This is huge because it has taken me months. I need this milestone.

I'm mindful, and I celebrate this moment that's right here in front of me. Then some other kid's song comes along and then another, and then I'm groovin' around with chords of some major scales. Thank you, God. I keep on jammin' to myself, and no one needs to know I'm feeling groovy. A lot of the pressure is off.

———— ·✦✦✦✦· ————

Come Saturday morning, I'm feeling a whole lot better being gone and away from the Big Suck House, and I breathe freely for a change and I can see just fine. My heart is almost back to normal as I fly down the highway in my soccer-mom sedan.

I just avoid getting rear-ended by some beach-going jackasses in a Beemer as I turn off the highway and under the shade of eucalyptus trees marking the entrance to the bohemian enclave of Calypso Guitars and nirvana.

Norse God's already in rare form. His beard is as packed with sawdust as the expression on his face is packed with his intensity. He's leaning over the counter, staring at a piece of wood.

"Hola, Norse God! I bring gifts and tribute, O intrepid mariner one."

I set down a pink box of two dozen lemon-jelly-filled donuts, his favorite, and an extra-large iced green tea. He's heavy into tea. Beer too, of course. He's a guy. But that comes later in the day. Mornings are all about green tea and donuts. He's young, and he has his health to consider.

He grunts. He blinks. He snaps out of it.

"Oh, hey, man. Thanks."

He runs a hand through his beard, gives it a shake, and sawdust flies everywhere.

"You don't have to keep doing this."

He grins and rips into the box like a Viking scoring fresh plunder.

"I know."

Chapter 39

I know I have to keep doing this because his life is on the edge, like mine. But unlike me, he is okay with that—and for far better, nobler, healthier, and more worthwhile reasons. A little sweetness to take the edge off, even on those good-vibe, creative, inspiring, and productive days is a good thing for those high-energy types who forget to eat; as it is for those of us high-anxiety types who can't eat, albeit for different reasons. I wait for him to take his pick, then I help myself to a donut.

He scarfs down a couple of donuts. He wipes his hands on his apron and picks up the thin board from the counter. He holds it up gingerly by one corner.

"Listen to this," he says, tapping lightly at various spots.

I listen to the faint hum. I can tell the wood is cedar, and from that and the hum, I know this piece will be the top of a guitar, a soundboard.

"We're getting there," he says with his eyes closed. "Getting close now. This is where it gets tricky. I want to shave it down as thin as I can get it without making it brittle or weak. The thicker it is, the stronger it is. The thinner it is, the more it will vibrate and produce its tone. We need both, but there's a trade-off."

He taps it at different places. He explains that's where bracing comes in. He goes off on a tangent about the bracing patterns of his hero guitar makers.

Nirvana.

"The trick is finding that point and going just a hair past it. Then the strength comes from the bracing. The bracing's got to be slender and light and in the right places so we gain the strength without losing the good vibration qualities. Tone is all about getting a good vibration," he grins and carefully puts the board down. "Need to change shavers now."

He scarfs another donut.

"Mmmm. Good cake!"

I spend a glorious day here, mostly watching him and repeating what he does. Later in the afternoon, I even try my hand at bending sides. I break a couple, cringing each time. I suck. I'm stunned that he just laughs it off. He's incredibly patient, which amazes me no end, and he's quite pleased when I get one right. I think even more than I am. That means a lot. Then I feel great. Like anything's possible. Even as I know that can't ever be true.

I treat him and Lani to beer and pizza. I had suggested dinner out, but they nixed that idea. It's beer and pizza and some strumming on a pair of Muses we finished that day. What an incredible high it is to help build a musical instrument, set it up, and then play it.

Lani's got that romantic look in her eye, and I figure that's my cue to hit the road. She gives me a hug, and Norse God says he'll see me next week. I tell him he's got a deal.

In the car and feeling good and brave for a change, I pull out my wallet and find Ria's card. I pull it out and a slip of paper falls in my lap. I call her. My heart's racing as I listen to the ringtone. I don't know why, I'm just calling to ask about some lessons, maybe.

It took a while, but I think I finally got the lesson and Coach thing worked out with Sasquatch at that last appointment. Habits die hard, I guess.

"I'm guessing it wasn't the lessons, so much as the judging, eh?"

"Yep. Nothing was ever good enough. I never knew when I got it right. If I ever did. It was like he was always changing the rules. The few times that I did get it right, unknowingly, I was convinced

I was doing it all wrong and try something else, what I thought he really wanted, and then he'd explode all over me again. Hit me with the ball or the glove. Over and over. One time, he almost used the bat. I bundled up in the dirt and wet my pants. So fuckin' scared."

I tell him I just got hit with another migraine aura. He says he understands and asks me to close my eyes and continue.

"Then the cops showed up. Ugly fuckin' scene, man. Mom screaming at the cops to haul his mean ol' ass away. Them talking to her like it was her fault. I knew they could smell the booze on her. Not on him. Dad hadn't started yet. Pretty sure that saved him. That and maybe I didn't have any bruises to show. Just Mom overreacting to some unorthodox training methods. That's what they said. Anybody could tell he wasn't going to hit the boy. That's what the old fat one kept saying. Wonder who he was protecting."

Sasquatch took a lot of notes. Then he spent some time reading them over and looking out a window. I told him the hitting stopped after that night, all of it. From then on, someone else would give the lessons. He wouldn't be around. He never asked me how I did or how I felt. Except one time—the tap-dancing lessons.

Coach had read somewhere about this all-star second baseman back east who had taken tap-dancing lessons from about the seventh grade on. This all-star bragged about it, saying it was the best training he ever had for balance and timing. He called playing second base "dancing at the hop" because he could anticipate the bad hops the ball would take when smashed right to him or on either side of him. Coach took me to see him play.

"I had had several of those dance lessons by then, and I could see some of the steps in his moves. He was never off balance. He could, quite literally, spin on a dime. And he always—*always*—moved in time with ball. That was the amazing part. No matter where the ball was, where it went, or how hard it was hit or whatever, if it was anywhere close, he was already there, ready, always in the right position to drop or rise in rhythm with the ball. Yep. It really was dancing at the hop. He was so good. So. Damn. Good. Fucking All-Star good. I wasn't."

I shrug.

"Okay, I mean, all in all, it didn't hurt me. I stopped stumbling so much, and I did play better. I got to the point where I could rock upward onto the toes of my shoes like a ballet dancer and hang there like I was floating. It was such a weird sensation too. The closest I've ever come to feeling weightless. Not that I was ever close to being heavy back then. I was really skinny as a kid. But still, I was the only boy in the class. Eventually, all Coach wanted to know was if I felt like a fairy or not."

Overall, it was a good session. Sasquatch said we were done as far as the county was concerned. He gave me the option to continue with him, on my own, or he would be happy to recommend somebody. I told him as long my insurance was good, I'd stick with him. He was fine with that. He said a few more months should get me where I need to be, and then I could follow up with him quarterly and see how I was doing.

I'm disappointed to get Ria's voice mail. Her voice is soothing and joyful, and I'm sad. I mumble like a teenager and totally botch the simple message asking about lessons and describing the DVD I'm working with, but I manage to get my phone number out and ask her to call or to text me when she gets the message.

Yeah. Baby steps.

I put the card back in my wallet and pick up the slip of paper that had fallen out and unfold it. It's a receipt. I stare at it a while. I don't understand why the receipt for Ria's violin is in my wallet. Of course! Danny must have accidentally put it there when he put her card in my wallet.

But why would he do that?

Ouch. No wonder she liked it.

Holy Fuck!

It's a $14,999.00 violin made in Italy. I keep looking at the receipt. Danny signed it. Right, that makes sense. He bought it.

Something doesn't feel right. I take out my credit cards and compare the last four digits shown on the receipt to my cards, and sure enough, there's a match.

What the fuck?

Wait. Deep breath here. This ain't right. How'd the hell this get on my card? I remember he has the same kind of wallet as me. Simple mistake? Breathe. It's a simple mistake. He must have got them mixed up. Huh. Still, it's on my card. Well, okay then. I'll just take care of it Monday at work.

◆ ◆ ◆ ◆ ◆ ◆ ◆

Monday rolls around and I take the receipt to Danny.

"Why is Ria's violin on my card?"

"What are you talking about?"

"My credit card. Ria's $15k violin is on my credit card. I'm asking you why."

"No-ohh! That isn't so, is it?"

"See for yourself."

I give him the receipt.

"Well, that's weird." He has a funny grin. "Your wife seen this?"

"I don't see how. It's not like she's been around much. I didn't even see it until two days ago."

He chuckles to himself and looks up at me.

"Oh. That's . . . good to know." He holds it up. "This is obviously a very simple mistake, Paul. Tell you what, I'll call 'em and get it taken care of. Trust me, Paul. You'll be golden. I promise."

"Okay. I appreciate it. My life is shitty enough now. I sure as hell don't need anything else going wrong."

He holds up a hand even as he's laughing.

"Hey, preachin' to the choir, here, bro. I get it. I'm all over this! Got you covered. Trust me." He's still grinning. "C'mon, it is funny."

"No. Not really. No." I take a moment to breathe. Deep.

"Paul, tell you what. I will fix this right now. Don't move."

"Okay. Fair enough."

"That's right. You breathe easy, bro. I'll take care of this. No hassle."

I nod. "Thanks."

He picks up the phone and dials.

"Hey, yeah, it's me, Danny boy. Hey, listen. Remember Paul? Yeah, the anxious one . . . yeah, that's him"—he covers the phone handset's mouthpiece with his other hand—"how about that, Paul? They remember you!"

He uncovers the mouthpiece.

"No, that's exactly why I called. Paul and I have the same kind of wallet. You're not going to believe this, yeah, I mistakenly used his credit card. Can you believe it? Right. Same credit union. The credit card. Right. I know. I never even looked at it. I bet you didn't either. No, you're right about that. I was most definitely paying more attention to the girl. Wasn't she though? Oh my god, yeah. Total sweetheart. Yeah. Stupid mistake. Shuffled them up big time is right. It is funny. Paul?"

He looks at me from across the desk.

"No, no. He's not taking it so well. He's standing next to my desk as we speak. I think he's about to have a stroke."

He looks at me again.

"Hey, Lago says you need to sit down, everything is going to be okay. What? Hey, right, exactly, I need to fix this right now."

Danny reaches back for his wallet, gives me a funny look, then switches hands on the phone, and goes to the other rear pants pocket. Yep. Sure enough, same kind of wallet. He opens it and pulls out his credit card. Yep. Same credit union.

"Okay, I'm ready, let me know when you're ready."

Danny waits, then slowly reads off his credit card number.

"Yeah, read it back to me. Yeah. That's it. We're good? Excellent. Talk to you soon. You got it. So sorry for the trouble."

Danny exhales and looks up. Big-ass grin on his face.

"We're good?"

"Yep. We're good. Thank you."

"Hey, anything for the Bard! You know, it's kind of funny when you stop and think about it."

Not funny.

The hours tick by, and I don't hear from Ria. I get excited when my office phone rings until I realize she wouldn't be calling that number. The LED says "Reception."

I answer.

"You have a delivery up front."

I hear the click before I can reply. Oh well, what the hell. I go up front, and there's a guy in a sheriff's uniform and he's even way older looking than me. He's wearing brown cowboy boots with pointed toes that don't look right with the uniform. But once again, what the hell do I know?

Maybe he's one of them Berdoo Boys on loan from Barfstow or one of them places. He's all wrinkled and grizzled and ugly. His buzz cut is gray, nearly white in the places that still have hair. His skin looks perpetually sunburned. Nasty-looking old coot. He's got a serious pair of biceps for an old coot, I'll give him that much. There's a glint of gold, and I recognize lieutenant's bars on his collar.

"Cooper?" His voice is raspy, like he gargles gravel with his whiskey.

"Yes, sir."

"Here you, go, son." He grins, walks over, and swats my chest with an envelope. "You are served."

I catch the envelope as it falls.

"Really? Was that necessary?"

"You gonna tell me how to do my job now, are you, lawyer boy?"

I see the name tag.

"Wouldn't do any good, now would it, Hood? Have a safe trip back to the River. Try not to violate anybody's civil rights."

"Ha-ha. You're funny, lawyer boy. God, I love this job. Enjoy your divorce papers, asshole. Hope your ex enemas the livin' shit outta yer pansy pink ass."

Divorce papers?

I take the large envelope back to my desk. Sure enough, divorce papers and a restraining order and what is no doubt a nasty cover letter from some asshole family law attorney. I scan the letter and catch the demand to refund our credit account for the $15k violin.

Breathe!

I do an online search, call, and get Lago on the phone. I tell him plainly about the divorce papers and read aloud the key portion from the nasty cover letter and politely but firmly ask for a prompt credit acknowledgment. He apologizes profusely. He tells me he cancelled my card transaction and that I should call the card company. Shows what I know. My bad for letting Tami handle all the money.

Tami.

I think about calling her. I look at the restraining order.

Hmm. Read the restraining order. I don't remember being served for that hearing. Whatever.

I decide against making the call.

I feel my phone vibrate. Ria's text is short and maybe not so sweet, "Your DVD is fine. Keep working with it. I'm not the right instructor for you. You should know that by now."

Ouch.

I think about calling her too. I decide against it. I think about it, type in, "Thank you." I press Send.

Can't think of any better way to start another week in this hellhole. I grab a file and spread some papers across my desk like I'm working and lean back in my chair. I close my eyes and try to start one of the meditation exercises.

I got nothing.

Danny keeps his word and emails me a copy of the corrected credit purchase and a copy of a polite handwritten note of apology for the error from the Luthiers in Las Vegas. At the end of the note, they even wish me luck.

Gonna need more than luck.

I know what's coming next, and I don't even try to fight it. I lean back and close my eyes again and wait for the fireworks to pass. They don't. They last longer than usual this time.

Well, no shit, worthless. You worthless, worthless . . .

Chapter 40

I chug a handful of extra meds with a half a pitcher of melted chocolate fudge ice cream thinned out to creamy perfection with maple-flavored bourbon. Once I can feel sufficiently, comatosely mellow, I pick up again with the meditation exercises.

I keep up with the meditation exercises twice a day.

I get through the first collections trial, keeping relatively calm. The patient debtor is an elderly man who had made his living as a gardener until an illegal alien, who was driving drunk at the time, nailed him in a crosswalk. He tearfully explains to the court how the hospital saved his life, but he's left without a job and he's facing foreclosure on his home and he has nothing left.

Judge Lakeland discretely dabs at the corner of one eye as she politely rips me for wasting her time suing an elderly man who has no viable assets. Then she rips into me because the purpose of government is to serve its citizens, not tyrannize them by forcing them into bankruptcy and demands to know why the county did not do more to assist him in applying for charity care and lectures me on the inherent unfairness of it all. She apologizes again to the old man and tells him how much she detests these cases because of their inherent unfairness.

That's all well and good, but she's not the least bit interested in my explanation and cuts me off.

With great effort and a slur to his voice and partial paralysis visible on the right side of his face, the old man slowly says he didn't understand the forms or what to do with them. Every time he had called the hospital, he was told they couldn't help him because the accounts were in collections; and every time he called collections, all they did was demand money, ask him if he would like to make a payment, and if he could pay at least fifty dollars a month. He also says they told him that they were collectors and that all they do is collect, that the forms were his problem, and that they don't do application forms. They collect and the only form they use is a voluntary grant of lien on the house—if he owns a house.

He then tells the judge that he told them he had received several foreclosure notices because he was behind on his house payments because he had been recently hospitalized for a stroke.

Judge Lakeland brushes her dark hair behind her ear and adjusts her eyeglasses as the microphone before her picks up the jangling of the silver charms dangling from the shining bracelet on her wrist. Glaring at me, she clears her throat and apologizes to him yet again and explains that she has no choice but to follow the law and to enter judgment, most reluctantly, against him and encourages him to consult with legal aid as soon as possible regarding possible bankruptcy options. She also suggests that he complain to his county supervisor concerning the overzealous conduct of county employees.

She does, however, deny my request on behalf of the county for its attorney's fees finding, first, that it's incredulous that County Counsel charges other county departments "attorney's fees" in the manner of outside counsel when it's just one big county when all's said and done and money never, ever really changes hands. Second, she finds there is no valid contract arising from Mr. Eldridge's signing of the hospital's admission forms. And third, doing so is simply in the interest of justice, as a matter of simple equity between parties.

Sensing that the nuance of billing other departments is how the county in fact allocates a portion of its budget to funding and operating its Office of County Counsel will be utterly lost on

Her Honor, given her umbrage over how two county departments essentially bludgeon the innocent, I decide not to argue the point any further. Maybe this is Woo's idea of flowing with a river's current or some such nonsense.

She also orders me to give Mr. Eldridge the contact information for both the appropriate county supervisor and legal aid before he leaves the courtroom. She clears her throat again and orders me, as an officer of the court, to explain to him what factual information he needs to convey to the legal aid people. She comments once more on how much she detests these cases because "they are so heavy-handed, so one-sided, as to readily appear unfair and unjust," as Her Honor so succinctly said.

She then orders me to prepare the judgment and to submit it no sooner than forty-five days from today. She sets an OSC re: judgment some sixty days out. She says court is adjourned and leaves the bench. I gather up my paperwork and move my chair closer to the old man. I sit down next to him with a pad and a pen and begin to obey the court's orders.

I feel a tap on my shoulder. I turn and the young, bat-faced, mouse-eyed little bean counter, my hospital accounts collection witness, leans down. His loud tie sways close to my face. It's impossible not to see the pattern—US currency.

Now I understand why scissors are not allowed in a courtroom. I take a breath.

"Well?" he demands in a loud, whiny, nasally tone. "How soon do we get our money?"

I blink. It's my turn to clear my throat.

"You know, that's . . . yeah, that's a very good question." I nod as my visual field narrows and my fingertips tingle. There won't be much time before my retinas erupt. "A very good question. Given the court's orders, I will need to look into that and get back to you."

"How long will that take? How much will that cost? I can still record the judgment, though, right?"

"As long as it takes and as much as I bill for it. There's no judgment to record until the judge signs it."

"Then she'll sign it in thirty days."

"No. It will be submitted to the court, at the earliest, in forty-five days. That was the court's order. I don't know when she will actually get it, and when she does, she will sign it when she signs it—if she signs it—and I have no way of knowing when that will be."

"I don't understand. When do we get our money?"

"Again, a very good question. My guess is that you won't get any money. You will, in all likelihood, get a judgment. Judgment is a legal term that for you means nothing but a worthless piece of paper in this instance. Now, if you'll excuse me, I have some court orders to comply with."

"But we won. We get our money in thirty days, right?"

"No, limp dick. You get my bill in thirty days."

I look at the court attendant and shrug. Fortunately, she gets the hint. She gets up from her desk and approaches the beady-eyed grubber.

"Sir, court's adjourned. Your lawyer can stay—in fact, he has to stay—but you need to leave immediately."

"I need to know when we get our money."

"No, sir. What you need is to follow my direction and leave immediately. Your lawyer will advise you at a later time."

"Fine!"

He leaves.

"What a jerk," she says.

"Thank you. I appreciate it."

"Anytime, Mr. Cooper," she smiles.

She walks back to her desk and looks at the clerk.

"Did you see that asshole's necktie?" she asks, her left arm bent at the elbow, her left thumb over shoulder and pointing back toward the door.

"No, why? Was it something gross?"

"Might as well have been. It had little mini dollar bills on it."
She shakes her head.

"Seriously?"

"Yeah. I kid you not."

"That's rather crass. If the judge saw it, I don't think she'd approve."

The attendant looks at me.

"Mr. Cooper, did you know he was coming to court dressed like that?"

I look up from the pad I'm slowly writing on.

"Ma'am, I never know what those idiots are doing."

"I couldn't do your job," says the clerk.

"Most days, I can't even do it, unless heavily medicated."

I take another sheet and carefully note everything I've said to Mr. Eldridge and everything I've written down, figuring I will probably need to do a CYA declaration to the court regarding my compliance with the court's orders on this matter. Not to mention to protect myself from an internal personnel complaint lodged by the collector dudes.

As an afterthought, I decide a copy of what I've written would be in my best interest. I ask for one, explaining why.

"Oh, with pleasure, Mr. Cooper."

The attendant takes it and comes back a few minutes later with two copies and two copies of the court's minute orders for the matter's proceedings. I thank her for both sets.

I finish up with Mr. Eldridge and give him my card. I tell him to give it to the legal aid people. His mind may still be sharp, but his body's wrecked. I decide to call legal aid on my own, as an officer of the court, send them a copy of the minute order, and explain everything directly. I leave the courtroom and sit on a bench in the hall as another light show begins.

✦✦✦

Back at my office, I tap out an email to Woo about how Judge Lakeland detests these hospital collections cases. I attach copies of everything. Another week or so goes by before he replies. I hear the computer go "ding," and I see am email from him and it says he wants to see me.

I also see a fresh batch of emails from Jessica Carrigan.

Oh joy!

Delete. Delete. Delete.

I call Woo. Marcie picks up, annoyed with me as usual. I tell her why I'm calling. She puts me on hold, comes back on a moment later, and then tells to come on up. I do.

Woo's door is open, but I know better and wait in the doorway. He's sitting at his desk, leaning over a tiny vise. He's holding a pair long-nose clamps with the thumb and forefinger of one hand, the arm held up shoulder high and bent sharply at the elbow. With the clamps, he's pulling a line of thread taut from whatever is held by the jaws of the vise. With his other hand, he's holding a small bottle and dripping droplets of what I'm assuming is glue onto whatever is in the vise. Stuff that looks like sewing scraps lie about, littering the desktop, along with little snippets of feather and yarn and something resembling caterpillar fuzz.

I think about knocking, hard and loud. I think better of it, imagining him flinching and squirting glue in my direction if I did. I don't. I quietly pick out a chair and sit down.

He puts the glue bottle down, takes up his tweezers, and picks up a fleck of fuzzy stuff. He wraps it around the glue spot. Then it's another drop of glue, a few bits of this and that, and then a flourish of the hands in a circular motion, tying some sort of knot. He takes a pair of scissors and carefully cuts away the still taut line of thread. He exhales sharply and leans back in his chair.

"Thank you for being so patient, Paul." He takes off his glasses and rubs the bridge of his nose. "I appreciate the courtesy."

"Of course."

"So about Judge Lakeland and her detesting your collection cases." He's still leaning back, his eyes closed.

"Yes."

He waves at me blindly with his glasses.

"First, I do appreciate you keeping me in the loop. Keep doing that."

"Yes, sir."

"However, that said, I'm very concerned to say the least about your recommendation and request for authority to paper a judge under 170.6. Very concerned. First of all, I direct your attention to my prior instructions when we last spoke. Secondly, I'm not sure we really want to set any practice precedents for this sort of thing and start papering judges just because they don't like your cases. That's a tad strong."

"I understand all that well enough, sir."

"Do you? Apart from failing to follow orders."

"Yes, I do. But what about HS 1473 and the *Lara* case, which, as I read it, essentially stands for the proposition that we have a duty to not sue people who are essentially judgment proof?"

He rubs the bridge of his nose again.

"Well, about that, reasonable minds do differ, do they not?"

"Yes, sir, they do. All the time."

"You bet your grandfather's wicker creel they do!" He draws a breath and exhales sharply again. "I mean I would think that you, you of all people, would want to wade into these waters with greater care, so as to——"

"Not make waves?"

"Oh, with even greater care than that! Never underestimate the power and effect of ripples."

"Oh, I don't know. Way I was raised? If it's close, you swing at it. Foul it off if you have to, but don't ever go down on a called strike."

"No. No. Absolutely, no. First of all, I fail to see your analogy. I don't follow it all. Second, we simply cannot have that. We simply cannot. I've never been in a courtroom. However, but even

I know that's simply too aggressive an approach. Third, and most importantly, I think you just have rechannel your efforts and work harder to win over Judge Lakeland. I do. Yes, I really do."

"But what about HS 1473 and *Lara*? I don't think we can just ignore the law."

"Oh, I don't know about that. Has anyone brought it up as a defense?"

"No. Not yet. But they will."

"Fine. Then until someone actually does so, it's not a problem. You—I mean, especially you—do not need to go and make it one."

"But, sir, that's one of the reasons the judges are displeased with these cases. They see them as a waste of their time and a cruel imposition on these people because they're poor to begin with, and whatever they may have had before they were injured or took ill has been lost. The term to remember here is 'judgment proof.'"

"Paul, Paul." Woo shakes his head. "Our job is not to make things right. Haven't you realized that by now? You're not . . . Sir Lancelot or St. George or whomever. No! You're nobody. Nobody. Our job here—and therefore, your job here—is to make damn sure that things flow smoothly for the county departments we serve by advising them as to the law and then letting them do their jobs however they see fit. Right or wrong."

"Even when they're wrong and not following the law?"

"Especially when they're wrong and not following the law! What the hell's the matter with you? Are you not hearing me? All that's on *them*. We don't fall on *their* swords. Not ever! You, my friend, would do very well to remember that! In fact, you may even want to write that down."

"All right."

"You're not writing."

"What?"

"I said, you are not writing." He sits up, hunts around for a pad of sticky notes, picks it up, and tosses it at me.

I watch it sail on by.

"No! Go get that! Write that down. I'm serious. Write it down, Mr. Cooper! Write that down in one quick hurry. That's an order!"

"Yes, sir."

I step out of his office, retrieve the pad, and begin writing.

Woo nods.

"Good. Now, let's start over. I do not wish to be harsh. I do recognize your effort to act in the county's best interest here. I do. Truly. That said, you need to rethink your approach to this matter, Paul. Truly, you do. HS 1473, or whatever it is, is not an issue. Like I said, you're not going to make it one."

My turn to sigh. It's a heavy one.

Woo sits up.

"Finesse, Paul. Finesse." He puts his glasses on. "How many judges are there now in Central Civil?"

"Three."

"That's right, Paul. Three. We most definitely do not want to reduce that number to two or to one because we're papering them. Oh, believe me, I do sympathize with you. But bear in mind, that is the limited, short-term view. Long term? We won't take such chances, I'm afraid. Win the battle and lose the war and all that. Do you see my point?"

"Yes."

"Good! You represent the county when you're in court. You are its face when you're in court. If the judges are displeased with you, they are also displeased with the county. Besides, lots of people have one gripe or another against the county. That's just county life, and you should be well accustomed to it by now."

"No ripples."

Woo nods.

"Absolutely correct." He leans back again. "No ripples. None whatsoever. Still water. Still water runs deep. Remember to mind your manners with the client department. I do hope we're clear on this."

"Crystal."

"Very well. As I say, I was concerned. After all, I am leaving for a month, and I want to come back to find business as usual—what I consider business as usual. I want all our affairs floating smoothly downstream."

"No ripples."

"No ripples. No ripples at all, Mister," he beams. "I'm so pleased you understand. It restores my faith in you. You had me concerned. I'm relieved you came to me for a little chat. I really am. Aren't you?"

"Yes, sir. Of course. Absolutely. A little guidance does go a long way. Thank you."

"Good! See that it does. And, Paul?"

"Yes, sir?"

"Seriously, Paul. No more recommendations. Keep them to yourself until you and I have a chance to chat about them first. Understood?"

"Yes, sir."

"Very well. I'll let this breach slide. You are making strides here, Paul. We all recognize that. Still, we're keeping you on a short leash, nonetheless. The next one, however, will result in discipline."

He nods and returns his attention to the little vise amid the mess of scraps.

I get up to leave.

Now I remember what Coach used to call a guy who lived to fight another day. *Coward.*

I'm beginning to hate myself.

Each day I bury myself more and more in a bottle made of wood and steel strings. I get lost in attempting to master a handful of chords, two strum patterns, and, for now, just one tempo—dead slow. Because, you know, chicks dig licks. There you go.

I'm just outside the door when Woo's phone rings.

"Who?" I hear him ask.

"Cooper!" he yells.

I return to the doorway.

He looks up at me, glaring. He moves the phone handset away from his face and covers the mouthpiece with one of his hands.

"Sit down, Mister! Sit down!"

He focuses his attention on the phone.

"I see. No, no, that's . . . absolutely unacceptable. Of course, no . . . he said . . . what?"

He turns and glares at me again.

"Unbelievable! No. Certainly not. Yes. Yes. Of course. We will proceed in the customary manner . . . through HR, yes. Yes. Yes. Yes. Certainly. Any time. Yes. Thank you."

He hangs up and stares at his phone. Several minutes go by.

"Is there something else?"

He turns. He holds up a hand to motion "stop." He keeps his hand up as he begins to speak.

"Do not say a word. Not a single word. I have just been informed that a certain collector has complained and has filed a personnel complaint to HR against you about your utterly unprofessional, disrespectful treatment at a very recent trial and that you called him a 'limp dick' in open court. You will be notified of further developments in due course. That is all. Please leave immediately."

Fair enough.

Some days, I get stupid email responses from the collections drones. Like another one of those "this is unacceptable" responses to another one of my document copy requests. My stomach churns as I pick up the phone to call the miscreant drone. I make the mistake, yet again, of trying to explain what I need. Apparently, I'm not getting through this time either.

"I'm not a lawyer. I don't pretend to know how anything works in your world. I'm a collector. And collectors collect. You just don't understand. What we need from your office is someone who does what we tell them to do. We really don't need anything else."

"Okay. So enlighten me."

"It's our money. We collect it."

"But they don't have any money. There isn't any money for you to collect. Don't you see the problem there?"

"Again, you're way off target. If you're talking about—for instance, say, the Tina Matthews's file—then she has an asset. She owns a house."

"Okay. Tell me again how that works when the house is in foreclosure by the lender?"

"As the county's collectors, that's not our concern. She is listed on the County Recorder's records as the owner of record for a house. That house is an asset. That's why we always offer our patient account debtors a voluntary grant of lien. That way, they're unencumbered and when the sell the house or refi, we get our money."

"Query. How can it be an asset when she hasn't made a year's plus worth of payments because she was injured in a car wreck, lost her legs in that wreck that wasn't her fault, lost her job because she lost her legs because of the those injuries, and because those injuries have cost her, her job, they now cost her, her home as well. Ergo, she has no money. So why do you insist on suing her?"

"To get our judgment. She has an asset."

"Wait! Do you ever stop to consider or even determine the present status of the asset's value? What if it's, you know 'underwater'?"

"No. We never do that. We just confirm that the patient debtor is an owner of record. Nothing else. Per our admin, that's all we are required to do. As long as she's the owner, we pursue the account until paid in full because we have our judgment. That way, if she ever gets any money in the future—who knows, she could possibly win the lottery someday—we can collect on our judgment. That's why we always get our judgments. That's why we always renew our judgments."

"I see. So what happens when she files bankruptcy? What then?"

"Simple. We close out the file and take the account off our books, same as if paid in full."

"How are you paid in full if you get no money?'

"Simple. We treat a bankruptcy the same as a payment in full. It's off our books. That's all we care about."

"I see. But in that scenario, you don't actually collect any real money. In fact, you don't collect anything. The county gets no money. No money at all. It gets zero. Am I right?"

"Yes and no. We collect a judgment, and if there's money to pay the judgment, then we collect that. Correct."

"Okay, so if I'm understanding you, by your department's method and manner of accounting, a recovery of zero dollars is exactly the same as a recovery of a hundred dollars or a hundred thousand dollars, right?

"If there's a bankruptcy, yes. But only if there's a bankruptcy."

"Whew. That's some system you got there."

You moron!

"It works very well for us, yes."

"So what percentage of these hospital collections cases end up in bankruptcy because you sued people with no money?"

"No. That never happens. We only sue people with assets. So to answer your question, as to how many of those cases end in bankruptcy, I couldn't tell you."

"But it's got to be a rather high number, wouldn't you agree?"

"It's very high, yes."

"But I guess it all works out as long as you look good on paper, is that right?"

"Correct."

"Even though the truth of the matter is the collectors are not actually collecting anything."

"No. We always collect a judgment. We always have our judgment."

"Well, you may think you have a judgment. But in reality, you really don't. I find it as interesting as it is ironic how you people insist on equivocating the term *collect*. 'Having a judgment' and 'collecting on a judgment' are entirely two different things."

"No they're not. Look, I'm just telling you what we do. This is the way we have always done it here. We've never had a problem. And from what I've heard, no one has ever questioned it except you."

"I see."

I fucking hate this job! I can tell I'm going to need more pills, maybe a lobotomy.

I go back to Sasquatch. Apart from the guitar, he says my life is a total train wreck, eh, and refers me to a psychiatrist for real meds.

Well, no shit, Sherlock!

I meet with her, the psychiatrist, a couple of weeks later for about forty minutes. She asks. I answer. No high blood pressure, no liver problems. Social drinker. Antisocial drinker. She prescribes something called a serotonin-norepinephrine reuptake inhibitor.

Whoo-hoo! I'm starting at 30 mg once a day, in the morning, at least one hour before going to work. It's supposed to be effective for the treatment of anxiety and depression. Sounds promising. She also suggests looking at retirement. Sounds depressing.

Unfortunately, retirement is easily a few years away. So for now, it's a Calypso guitar and what I'm calling my "happy, happy pills" because a complete meltdown is not a few years away—it's more like a few hours away.

That, and I treat myself to the very occasional chocolate milkshake with just a wee bit of flavoring—maple-flavored bourbon—for sweetness because life is better with some sweetness. It just is. I want to do it more often, but apparently abusing alcohol and my meds will eat up my liver. Not a good plan.

More trials, more pills, more practice, more nasty letters from Tami's lawyer I don't bother reading, more stupid emails from that Carrigan character which I do enjoy deleting, on and on for months on end and with no end in sight. With only two seasons in southern California, fire season and "getting ready for fire" season, I'm not sure what year it is. But I trust it's that much closer to the end—whatever that turns out to be.

As for calling that collector clown a "limp dick," I manage to get off with a written reprimand for being unprofessional. Apparently, Judge Lakeland took her dim view of the county's collections process and one collector in particular to the presiding judge who then personally cornered the county's CAO for about an hour and regaled him with the facts of litigation life that the county would now face.

I only hope the effects will last. For his part, Woo has his river boatman steering him well clear of the big rocks and the whitewater surging from this incident and appears content to tell me from some objective distance that I need to "face the wind and lean into the current of the river"—whatever that means. He says he's otherwise pleased with my work so far, that Judge Lakeland was sympathetic to my dilemma in handling these cases, that she had very pointed questions concerning both HS 1473 and the *Lara* case, and that, overall, I'm making reasonably good progress in this assignment. Keep at it, he says. He would. The louse. Apparently, performing frustrating exercises in futility in pursuing worthless judgments is absolutely essential to the county's overall litigation strategy.

Who am I to argue? I'm supposed to keep my mouth shut, go along with the program, face the wind, and lean into the current of the river. Whatever that means.

What I need is to find a way to last through the ninth inning and just end this game. In the alternative, I pray for a permanent rain delay.

It's back to Sasquatch, and we talk. We talk quite a bit. Then we talk some more. He reminds me again and again how all these years I've taken all my hard work, all my due diligence, all my conscientious effort and made myself miserable with it because it was in response to what others wanted or demanded from me. He suggests how much better off I'd be if maybe I had simply partied hearty like everybody else, eh. And then I'd have been healthy, wealthy, and maybe even retired and dead by now.

He's got a point, eh.

Who am I to argue? I just nod, not sure whether he's serious or joking or maybe a little of both to get me thinking deeper. He does that, and it drives me nuts. I take it all in and tell him how I been hankerin' for bluegrass and country music since our last visit, and he laughs and says, "Well, hee-haw there, Huckleberry. I'm happy for you, eh."

Then it gets serious again, and he goes over his notes and, with his pen, circles something he's written.

"You touched on something here tonight that I want to get back to. You need to get used to the idea of disappointing the people in your life, eh, or you're never going to break through. The truth is this, Paul, none of them get the privilege of being you."

What privilege?

It takes a while to sink in, and when it does, what he says hits me like a hammer and shatters my denial. There's no choice here. I face up to being fifty knowing that I haven't really lived each one of those fifty years. It hurts to admit that most of my life, I have been a shadow of what I might have been.

It hurts knowing I'm running out of time. My fear that I will wake up one day when I'm sixty-four and know I've never tried doing what I love because I still have no idea what that is because of all the years I've wasted trying so hard to do the things everyone else loves for me hurts me even more.

I catch my breath.

"The truth hurts."

"Yes. It does. It also sets you free. If you choose to accept it and act on it."

"Fair enough."

"Please, Paul, remember that this life that's yours to live, for however long you get to live it, eh, is your show and no one else's, ever. No one else ever gets to be you, so you need to accept that truth and decide once and for all to be true to yourself and no one else."

Okay, that's some heavy stuff. I write it all down so I don't forget, because I always have. And because as much as it shakes me, I know I'll manage to forget it again and lapse back into whatever rut I've cut for myself in the vinyl that has since become the LP of my life.

"Paul, just so we're clear, keep in mind that I'm not talking God here—that's something else entirely, eh. I'm talking flesh and blood, got to put their pants on one leg at a time, unless their flat-backing, ordinary, plain, everyday people like you and me. That's it. All of it, eh. The people you live with, work with, the people you are related to, not related to, 'shoot 'em and they bleed and die' kind of people. Okay? Like none of them matter on this level of self that I'm talking about here, eh."

I take a breath. And another one. Really deep this time.

Chapter 41

"That means you have choices and decisions to make every day, all day long. Is this—whatever this may be—good for me? Am I a better, healthier person if I do this thing? Is this what I want? What am I willing to sacrifice for this? Is that sacrifice fair to me? Is it a fair swap? If I am doing this thing, then who am I really seeking to please? Why? And the last question, because it's the most important one, is doing this thing deep, deep down really what I love to do? If there's so much a single no answer, you must walk away. End of story, eh."

He leans forward and stares straight into my eyes.

"Paul, no one—no one, not me, not Tami, not Coach, not Woo, not your friends, not your enemies, absolutely no one ever—has any say at all as to what is or is not in Paul's best interest. That's your job."

He invites me to write that down too, and I do:

Only Paul decides what is or is not in Paul's best interest

He waits. He looks me in the eye

"You know what a jackass is, eh?"

I resist the urge to roll my fingers into my palms, making fists. Looking down, I mutter, "No. What?"

"A beast for somebody else's burden. Stop being one, eh."

There's a silence, an uncomfortable one for me. I write "Stop being a jackass" on the paper.

"Got it."

I fold it up and put it my wallet.

Then he closes out the session by putting me on an anxiety–depression workbook based on mindfulness.

"Use this. It will help you on many levels, eh, including finding your passion in life, your reason to get up every morning."

As I get up, he throws me for another loop and says I need to start reading Shakespeare.

"Start with *Hamlet*, eh," he tells me.

So it's stop being a jackass, working with the mindfulness workbook, thinking about the Shakespeare thing about some dead guy (why can't it be Hemingway?), more trials, and another couple of visits to the psychiatrist.

She urgently urges me to look at retirement, which I explain will easily take a few more years. She says I may not have a few years, and then she puts me on more pills much more frequently, so I'm up to 60 mg a day now. Oh, joy.

Well then, joy it is, sort of.

After a while, I feel a little calmer. I remember that guy at the guitar store—Kerry, I think it was—who said chicks dig licks. Okay. So who am I to argue? Fair enough. Flow downstream.

So it's more trials, more trips to Sasquatch—whom I've taken to calling my "talking shrink"—more work in the workbook, more trips to my psychiatrist, whom I've taken to calling my "dealer shrink" who prescribes more pills much more frequently. I'm up to 90 mg a day now.

Holy fuckin' yowza, baby!

But it's all good. I'm beginning to understand what *irie* really feels like. No outbursts. No phone bashing. I don't remember the last time I punched a wall. Ain't never been so calm in my whole life.

And more practice. Always more practice. Practice. Practice. And country, folk, and blues. I am a rock, and I be more like a mellow rockin' it irie, mon, which is much to be admired for one so likely off his rocker as me, and I practice mellow. I still can't play for shit, but it bothers me less and less and so that's progress too. I practice because, because . . . chicks dig licks. I vaguely remember somebody telling me that once.

I have the house to myself now. Shelley Lynne says Tami's quit the hospital and is shacked up with Taylor in San Francisco.

Well, shit. Don't that beat all?

I'm amazed at how calm I am just looking out the window. I'm amazed at how blue the sky is. I'm amazed at how much fun it is to watch a woman walk. Hips are amazing, how they move, and everthang like that. You'd really have to be God to invent a woman's hips—and all the rest of her, for that matter.

It'll be so bitchin' learning to play country blues someday. Someday . . . and reggae! Oh my god! Reggae! Who knew, right? And country! Country sounds really good to me now.

I mean real country, the traditional stuff—T-shirts and jeans, beers and babes. Lord have mercy! I want a pickup truck, a red one, with a guitar rack, an ice chest full of beer, and a dog sitting in the front seat. Big-ass, mean-as-fuck German shepherd dog who loves me sitting in the front seat and ridin' shotgun. Mess with me, my truck, or my guitar, and get eaten.

More trials, more stupid shit at work, more time with the workbook, and back to Sasquatch.

"You're fifty-one now, eh. The wounds will heal with acceptance," he says. "It's okay to allow yourself that acceptance—acceptance that no one was ever going to please the Coach. Not even you, eh. Acceptance that you didn't fail him. Not once. Not ever. He failed you. Acceptance that as a child you were not able to know or process any of this information. As an adult, sure."

He pauses and gives me the once-over.

"Coach wanted restored to himself what he deeply believed was his—something that he believed had been taken from him. The problem was, he had no say in that. Unfortunately, it's a risk all athletes on the verge of a professional career must face. I see it all the time in my practice," he says.

"Paul, it doesn't matter what Coach thought. It's called life. In my work, we say, 'shit happens,' eh. He suffered for it. You did too. That's not your fault. That's all on him. He probably couldn't help himself. Even if he wanted to. I'm sure he would have wanted to, if he knew. If he understood. He didn't know how. Nobody in his life did. No way they could know. That's why all those beers, all those horrible years. He was trying to kill the pain. Just like you trying to please everybody and their dog, eh," he says.

"That's the takeaway here. Which brings us back to acceptance, acceptance that none of it was ever your fault. None of it can ever be your fault," he says. "Acceptance, Paul. Let the Coach go. Let the Coach do Coach. Even in death. As for you, Paul? Go do you, eh. Go do you for a change. It's never too late for that. That's your job now. Go do you. That's what you'll be on the hook for from now on. Believe me. It's enough."

My hands do their own version of the kneejerk, scrambling through all my pockets for a pen. I always feel naked without a pen.

So how come I never have one when I need one?

Sasquatch hands me a cheap pen, then a small pad of sticky notes. Then he hands me a whole box of the cheap pens.

"You might want to hang onto these, eh."

I nod.

Good thinking.

I start scribbling. I scribble faster before the memory of what he just said falls out of my ear for good.

Shit!

It's gone.

"Why does this keep happening?

"Resistance from prior programming is powerful stuff, eh."

"You heard me?"

"You're the one talking, eh."

"But I was just thinking to myself."

"Out loud."

"Oh, yeah. I do a lot of that. Too much. Way too much." I put the pen down. Heavy sigh. "I got nothing."

Sasquatch hands me a small stack of printed index cards. They're all laminated. Each one's got text, some of which is even highlighted. Everything he just said is on these cards.

Oh, this guy's good! He gets me!

"Okay. This works."

Sasquatch nods. "I made more if you lose any of them. They're ten bucks apiece. Consider it an incentive to hang onto this first set."

"Yeah. That works too."

"I hope so. For your sake, eh."

"Yeah. I hope so too."

"Good. Start there, Paul. You've got a lot of work to do to record a newer version of that soundtrack of your life as you call it. If it were a vinyl LP, then I don't see how there could be any vinyl left, eh. Fifty-one-plus years of cutting the same groove. Time you finally cut a new master, eh?"

"Fair enough."

Still more trials. Still more—much more—stupid shit at work. Naturally, that means more time with the workbook, systematically repeating new neurolinguistic programming affirmations, working on releasing and letting go of all the old tapes from Coach—fifty-plus years' worth—and then back to Sasquatch, wondering if I'm ever going to break clean.

I tell him I want to live. I ask for ice time. He enthusiastically agrees, so we go for ice time. I want to try skating with a stick. He's game.

I get the notion of using the stick for balance. He tells me I'm not there yet, but do I listen?

Hell no.

I find out using a hockey stick for balance is really tricky. That and tap-dancing, what little I remember of it, doesn't work all that well on skates. Your torso goes one way; your legs go their own separate ways. It's like trying to skate on three legs when the universe knows you only have two and it really doesn't work. I have seventeen stitches on the back of my head to prove it.

I should have seen it coming when my helmet flew off after one fall and Sasquatch told me to put it back on. And did I listen?

Hell no.

I also know now that my blood is the most beautiful shade of red that I have ever seen, and it looks so really good on pure white hockey rink ice. So beautifully graphic. Like abstract art.

I know, right? I get it.

It also feels so warm and soothing sliding down the side of my face. This is like, you know, so totally amazing to me; so naturally, I tell Sasquatch all this while he squeezes my head with his bare hands the whole time to slow the bleeding while we're waiting for the ambulance. I think he's swearing loud and fast. Not sure. Sounds like swearing, eh. Sounds Canadian—really pissed Canadian. And he's mumbling something about how can anyone so thickheaded bleed so damn much.

That's funny!

When he gives me to the paramedics, he wastes no time getting my dealer shrink on the line. They talk. Something about holding me steady at 90 mg. I was so looking forward to going to 120 mg with the happy, happy pills. That is so not happening now. Well, shit. Okay. Fair enough.

But I just want to be so mellow.

I have alarms set on my phone now to remind me to robot up, go to work, go to court, and do all that step-in-time, "march to some other drummer" crap and try the cases with what little information I'm allowed to try them with and see how far I can get with that.

And it's all good, like a continuing science experiment in self-destruction where you get zapped (high voltage is good voltage, the higher the better) and you get back up, shake it off, get ready to do it all over again, and ask yourself, "Okay and let's see what happens when I stick *this* into Mr. Light Socket's little mouth."

Ryan checks on me now and then. He's like the best mother ever. He won't cop to it, of course; but secretly, I think he's gay. He's a really great dude.

I don't see anybody else.

Not even at the office. Pretty much everybody avoids me like a leper. Even got a new office. I'm just four doors done the hall away from Woo. Sweet. Ignorant bastards downstairs all think I'm in line for a promotion.

Fuck them.

Woo hounds me like, you know, a hound. He keeps reminding me that sob sister's jury trial is coming up. I keep telling him I'm on it.

I keep wondering if Chrome Dome will consider this a real case.

Sob sister's real name is Melanee Amber Hathaway. She's a thirty-one-year-old professional dancer—as in a bona fide freelancer—who had last worked for a ballet company based in San Francisco.

She changed freeway lanes to avoid being rear-ended by a speeding car only to get nailed by the car that the speeder was racing against, spun like a dreidel, and sent careening down an embankment into a bridge abutment. Traumatic amputations, one leg above the knee, the other below the knee. One haul-ass, tree-level, Vietnam-style helicopter flight among urban treetops from the freeway all the way to county hospital.

Three and a half weeks in the hospital, seven or eight surgeries, yada yada yada, and the brain-dead bean counters at county are suing her for about a quarter of a million dollars, all told, for her unpaid hospital bills. Correction. The bean counters are making *me* sue her for about a quarter of a million dollars, all told, for her unpaid hospital bills. Naturally, neither racer is insured nor do either of them have any real assets. No lie. Go ahead. Tell me life isn't cruel and doesn't suck.

I'll wait.

Understandably, Ms. Hathaway is an exemplary and extremely sympathetic witness at trial. She sits in silence in her wheelchair, zoned out, unable to see past the space where the rest of her legs used to be. So naturally, it gets worse. Despite my legitimate objections, argumentative, assumes facts not in evidence, lack of foundation, what have you—her shrewd lawyer gets a county collections witness (guess who?) to admit the county is suing her solely on the speculation that she may win the lottery someday. The county's collections folk are rather fond of that idea, apparently. It's a complete clusterfuck circus of a trial.

Any redirect with this particular witness would be utterly useless. Finally, defense counsel rests. There's a brief recess. I get glares of hatred from some of the jurors as they file back in and take their seats. I smile, nod, and let the light show takeover.

I choose to keep my closing short, almost perfunctory. I pop some more meds for good measure and spill water down my chin.

I smile politely at the jury.

"Ladies and gentlemen, the calculus here is quite simple."

I pause. I pause, first, for effect. Second, because it's hard to stand up with abdominal cramping. Juror 12 has her eyes closed. Her chin dangles just above the vee of her collar bones.

"Four years ago," I begin, "this—all this absolutely horrible, tragic stuff—happened to Ms. Hathaway. I can't undo that. None of us can. We all want to, though, don't we? Of course, we do. We all do. Human nature. None more than Ms. Hathaway, certainly. Ms. Hathaway had been working before the accident as a freelance ballet dancer in the Bay Area up north. Most regrettably, she did not have health insurance. The county cannot fix that. None of us can. Now it is too late. The county can't change it or undo it. It is what it is. We have to be honest here."

Juror 7 is leaning over and writing on the steno pad balanced across her knees and making noises of disgust. She doesn't bother looking up. She pushes her shoulder-length, brown hair behind her left ear.

"I get it. I do. I can see that some of you refuse to listen to me, even now, despite the oath you have all taken. I can understand that. We are all human. As such, we all have our limits of what we can bear. Please hear me out, please, to be fair, just hear me out."

Chapter 42

I take a deep breath. This will be the hard part.

"In all that time, what has Ms. Hathaway done about it? Sadly, she did nothing. Nothing. Did she or anyone, for that matter, ever apply for any kind of aid? Medi-Cal, Medicaid, charity care, anything? No. No one ever did."

I pause.

"Did the county provide a reference sheet to her with that information? Yes, it did. Several times."

I pause again.

"Did the hospital provide her care as it was required to do by law? Yes it did. Of course it did. Were the charges reasonable? Yes, they were."

I pause again and move.

"Now for the hard part. Does she owe the money? Yes. Yes, she does. Does she have to pay it? The law says she does. The jury instructions will spell all that out. As horrible as it may sound, she willingly signed the admissions form acknowledging her financial responsibility. That's it. That's all of it."

I take a deep breath. Time to finish up.

"That's the hard part that I know you don't want to hear. But hear it, you must. You are the jury. You have to listen to it. Because it's the truth. You have to listen to it because you are the jury here.

There it is. The absolute truth. It really is that simple. It's what all of this comes down to."

I touch the counsel table to steady myself.

"No matter what else you might think today, no matter what all of us may want for her, nothing else is relevant today. Today. Now. This is purely an action on a debt. Nothing else. Ms. Hathaway owes the money. Period."

Another breath.

"Whether she can pay it or not is not at issue here. Not today. I'm asking you, in fairness, to follow the law and find in the county's favor and then give the county the judgment it's entitled to, and we can all go home. That's all. Thank you."

Hathaway's ever-snazzy lawyer—that self-appointed, self-serving, sawed-off captain of justice—leaps to his feet before Chrome Dome can tell him that it's his turn.

"We can all go home? Go home? Are you kidding me? Unbelievable! Look at her, ladies and gentlemen!"

He tugs at the shiny gold cuff link at his left wrist.

"Look at her! Unbelievable, isn't it, that we're even here? Huh?"

He points at me.

"Did you hear this guy? Did you listen to him? That, ladies and gentlemen, is your government talking! Can you believe it? Have you ever heard such blatant, insufferable arrogance? That, ladies and gentlemen, is your meager tax dollars at work! Every penny of it wasted. And yet they still want more. Unbelievable. Unforgiveable!"

He parades before the jury box.

"Unbelievable! Unforgivable! Enough of this ridiculous charade! Enough of this insulting, despicable behavior! That such nonsense ever be tolerated in a court of law is utterly beyond me. Someone"— he looks first my way, then at Chrome Dome—"owes you an apology for wasting your time. Someone"—he looks my way again—"owes my client a great deal, a very great deal, in damages on her cross-complaint. You must, you absolutely must, compensate my client for all she has suffered because of this stupidity, this charade."

"Objection."

"Sustained. Mr. Eckstein, we have discussed this. We have a bifurcation on this matter. Good lord, man! Stay within the proper scope of argument!"

Ignoring Chrome Dome, Eckstein maintains his momentum.

"Forget the debt the county claims that she owes," he says, waving both of his arms over his head. "Forget it! The county is not entitled to one thin dime, not even one red cent—not now, not ever, not for what they've put my client through!"

"Objection."

"Overruled. That's about as far as you get to go, Mr. Eckstein."

"Don't give them anything." He backs up, as he's pointing at his client, until he's beside her. "And why not? You know exactly why not! Every one of you good and decent people knows why not. Because of the county's stupidest stunt of all, ladies and gentlemen"—he puts one hand gently on his client's shoulder and points at the gallery—"there, right there, stand up, Mr. Bucksworth. Yeah, you! Stand up!"

Bucksworth stands. He starts to speak, but Eckstein screams at him.

"Stop! Stop! Stop right there! You have already testified in this trial, Mr. Bucksworth! Not another word from your foul mouth!"

"Your Honor."

"Overruled. Good lord, tread lightly, Mr. Eckstein."

Eckstein's at the rail, still ignoring Chrome Dome.

"Look at him, ladies and gentlemen! Yes, that man, standing up right there! That one with that smug look! The chubby, grubby one! He'd make Scrooge a saint! Wouldn't he?"

Some juror laughs.

"Yes, that clown! That collector clown! That automaton, that two-bit bureaucrat, had the utter audacity to admit in front of you good, fair, and decent people—admit to you under oath that the only reason the county has for proceeding with this ridiculous action is that someday, someday, some 'only God knows when' day, my client might, might, *might* win the lottery!"

He struts, hands on hips, chest out, to face the jury.

"Let that sink in for a moment, please. I beg you."

Now it's his turn to pause for effect.

"Now I ask you. Could the county's minions say anything more insipid, more stupid, more sinister, more cruel, more asinine, more offensive, or more inhumane?"

Another pause for effect.

"No! I don't think so!"

He turns from the jury, walks back toward me, and leans over my side of the counsel table and stares at me. He rambles on about my expert, and I get up and go to sit in his chair.

"Hold it! Mr. Eckstein, step away from the counsel table. That's an order! Mr. Cooper, you may return to your seat."

We each comply with the judge's direction.

Eckstein goes back to the front of the jury box and starts in again on the lottery angle. This goes on a while. I hope he keeps at it till the jury finally sees through his well-rehearsed charade, gets worn out—the effect wears off—and they no longer care.

He continues whining about the circus, the sideshow, deftly ignoring the part about how he's orchestrated the whole sideshow the whole time. Shrewd. I think he's done this before. Eventually, he stops and thanks the jury profusely. Finally, I can savor a brief silence.

"Any rebuttal, Mr. Cooper?"

"Yes, please. If I may."

"Proceed."

"Damn the torpedoes," as somebody once said. I rush to the gig bag behind the bailiff's desk. He's leaned back in his chair, snoring. I grab the bag and rush back to my place at counsel table.

"Ladies and gentlemen, Mr. Eckstein has adamantly insisted the county has done nothing but put on a charade, a circus of sorts. In fact, yes, *circus*—I think that's the word he's been tossing around the past week throughout his dog-wagging diatribe of a tale. But here's the truth. The simple and honest truth. There's been no circus other than that of his own making. He gave you the gong show, not the county. In fact, Mr. Eckstein wouldn't know a circus if he rode in here on an elephant and got off it over there somewhere and then bent over just so we can see the elephant pickin' peanuts off his ass."

"Objection!"

"Sustained! Good lord, Cooper! Decorum!"

"Okay, fine. To illustrate my point, I'll give you one. I'll give you a circus!"

I open the gig back and take out the mini dreadnought. Instinctively, I raise it toward my nose for a deep whiff. *Mmm.* A real mahogany top, probably sapele sides and back, mahogany neck. A sweet little acoustic. I sit on the edge of the counsel table and start strumming the chords, mostly minor sevenths and a few cowboy chords. Hell, nobody here's likely gonna know.

The rhythm's slow but good. The practice is paying off. I'm feelin' irie! This case is in the toilet, so what the hell? I might as well go for the straight flush. I get an idea and strum with it.

I have no idea what tune I'm strumming, if any. I start singing a parody, making up the lyrics as I go, based on the facts of this case, singing to the tune of the song in my head, ignoring whatever tune it is that I am actually strumming:

> I am a lawyer for the county
> And I'm suing Ms. Hathaway for all she owes
> Hoping I'll hit yet another motherlode!
>
> I hear she's been callin' me a liar,
> An Eckstein here, just screams and whines
> But I'm still the county lawyer and I'm workin' overtime!
>
> I know y'all want your spring vacations, but y'all just
> missed your planes
> An' if you go, ol' Chrome Dome here will just haul yo
> asses back again!

And I need you more than want you.
And I want you, this one time
So this county lawyer can be chillin'
If your verdict's in on time!

A quick turnaround and once more with feeling:

And I need you more than want you.
And I want you, this one time
So this county lawyer can be chillin'
On the taxpayers' silver dimes!

I strum a few chords more and end with a C major.

"There. Eckstein wanted a circus? Fair enough. What I just did right there, that's a circus. That's what a circus looks like. That's what a circus sounds like. You finally got the circus Mr. Eckstein has promised you throughout this entire trial. But as we all know, if—if we are completely honest here—the whole circus thing is a lie. All of Mr. Eckstein's grandstanding shenanigans are a lie. A big butt-ugly lie."

I approach the jury box.

"The ugly truth that we all must face, the truly butt-ugly circus elephant in the room, is that neither the county nor I have done anything wrong here. We followed the law. Now, I respectfully ask you to do the same. That's it. Just follow the law. Thank you."

All in all, I'm pleased with how I played. It wasn't great, sure. Hell, it wasn't even proficient by any real standard. But by beginning student standards, it was passable. Okay, maybe it wasn't. It was the only thing that's gone right in this trial and I sit down.

Eventually, the deputy retrieves his guitar and puts it back into his gig bag and takes it back to his desk, giving me the stink eye all the while. I smile back at the smug, fat, lazy bastard. He's probably a workers' comp case transfer from the river.

Chrome Dome comes out of the ozone and goes through all the formalities, the jury instructions, verdict forms—all of it.

I'm thinking of chord changes.

Eckstein and I rise as the jury goes out, escorted to their jury room next to chambers for deliberations. I sit down. He wheels Ms. Hathaway around so the jury can see her a wee bit longer.

Good for him.

They're only out forty minutes, and Eckstein and I rise as they get escorted back in at ten to five. I sit down again.

Defense verdict. Elation. Tears. Chrome Dome thanks them for their service. They're discharged and excused. Jurors hug Ms. Hathaway. She's oblivious.

My esteemed and evil colleague vigorously shakes my hand.

"Gutsiest closing I've seen in a long time, counsel. I don't think anyone could have done any better trying to turn my charade argument around. It was never going to work, as you well know, but hey, kudos to you, pal. You gave it one helluva shot. I'll give you points for that."

"Thank you."

Juror 4 walks past and says I need more lessons. I thank her instead of asking her what kind.

Chrome Dome stares at me from the bench. He stands, breaks into a grin, shakes his head, announces that trial on the cross-complaint begins tomorrow at 10:00 a.m., and walks off.

I pack up and go back to the office.

Woo has already heard about my closing argument. Apparently, it's the talk of the office, and he's none too happy about it. Decorum, no doubt. He's waiting for me at the elevator. He's livid.

"Are you nuts? Have you lost what little mind you have? What the hell were you thinking?"

How 'bout you just shut the hell up and gargle my balls.

I keep walking. He follows me. Now he's the one yelling, drawing a crowd as we pass the long, gray line of surplus metal file cabinets.

"That is not how we at County Counsel conduct our trials before the superior court of this county!"

"Yeah? How the fuck would you even know? You said it yourself. You've never been in a courtroom."

His ballooning face reddens.

"I am severely disappointed in you, Paul! Severely disappointed! I-I'm appalled!" He catches his breath. "I will take this to HR, Mister. There will be discipline. By god, there will be discipline! You've gone too far, Mister! Mark my words on this, Mister! You've gone too far this time! There will be discipline!"

I drop my catalog case and walk right up to him and get in his face. He stumbles back. I keep going.

"Good. I hope so. Put me on admin leave, again. Effective immediately. While you're at it, dole some of that shit out for yourself. You've never even tried a case, not once in your whole worthless, fly-fishing life. You puffed-up little poser. That's right—poser. Putting people like you in charge of people like me is a crime. Put that in your fuckin' email to HR."

Chapter 43

Woo is crimson.

He can barely stutter, "I shall, Mister!"

"Oh, wait! There's more!" I say. My turn for a deeper breath. "What an incestuous, cloistered little bunch you all are! You bring in the subspecialists like me that you need to get the real work done—all because none of you can do it yourselves. You make us deal with the fallout that in the end is nothing more than the fruits of your own deliberate, incompetent indifference."

I take a breath.

"You sit on your asses all day with your séance sessions divining how the board is likely to feel on this, that, and the other thing. Pick up the fuckin' phone once in a while and just ask the bastards!"

Yeah, I'm on a roll.

"You gleefully turn a blind eye to the ignorance and utter ineptitude of everybody else in the county and then smugly sit back and insulate yourselves from any real consequences. And then, as if that's not enough, once we catch on to your little secret, you punish us for zealously doing what you brought us here to do in the first place!"

A quick breath.

"You're right about one thing, Woo. You are never going to allow any of us to accomplish real change because it would upset too many of the many apple carts that all of you keep your hands in! Any advancement in this office is kept to the carefully chosen few, those just lucky enough to be in the right place at the right time and get admitted to your private little club! And what's the membership fee?"

"Hold on there, Mister!"

"You hold on! You all can talk a good game while making damn sure you never step onto the field. You people sure are content to ride other counties' coattails. Otherwise, it's just so much window-dressing smoke and mirrors, ain't it, sailor? Well, fuck it, thanks for the rides to all the battles I've won for you. Think I'll get off your little boat now. I'm fed up! Time for you to go row it yourself a while."

"Get out! Get out!"

"Pipe down, sailor. You don't have to tell me twice. I'm outta here."

He leaves in a huff, as they say, and I saunter on into my office.

Shelley Lynne's in my chair. Way. Too. Cool! I can't help but smile. It's a nice change.

"Hey, there, kiddo. Wazzup?"

"Papa!" She gets up and hugs me. "Papa? That's a lot of commotion. I heard you yelling. Is everything okay?"

"No. Yeah. Ah fuck, I don't know anymore. It's all good. Everything is just . . . peachy. Peaches and cream, kiddo. It's all good."

"Are you sure?"

"Scout's honor."

"Okay," she smiles and holds up what looks like concert tickets. "Let's roll."

I drop the work crap onto the floor, get my keys and personal stuff, and we jet.

In the parking lot, she says we're going to a Duggie Meadows concert. Fine with me. We waste no time leaving.

I didn't know there was going to be a concert anywhere near here. Turns out it's not here and nowhere anywhere near here, but we go anyway. Truckin' on down the road, she asks if I had already taken time off from work.

"Yeah. In a manner of speaking, sure. Anyway, that's their problem."

Aw hell, pretty sure I'm probably already on another round of admin leave. I don't need to let Shelley Lynne know about all that. Let Woo and the wee little wankers stick somebody else with the trial on the cross-complaint for a change. Not my fault these sheep have no grasp of the hypomanic edge. Whatever. No matter. I know I'm hosed.

On the way, I call Norse God for his blessing, and he says, "Hell yeah, but be back next week," because he needs the help. I promise I'll be there. It's not often that I'm ever needed.

Except for Norse God and Shelley Lynne, I don't remember ever being needed in my whole life.

I don't remember getting to the Red Canyon Amphitheatre either. I think there might have been a plane ride—not sure—but hot damn, she got us here and here we are—wherever the hell *here* is— and we're where the concert venue is on a giant-ass bluff overlooking this awesome river that's way the hell down yonder over there. I let Shelley Lynne handle everything. Even my meds. I sometimes lose count. Never did like math. Everything is totally mellow now, thanks to my meds and Shelley Lynne. She's like the totally best daughter ever.

Duggie is freakishly shorter than I thought he'd be but so awesome at the meet and greet. We even share a few laughs. Imagine that—me and the Calypso crooner getting on like old buds. Nice! He's like the best bud ever. I tell him about Norse God and Calypso Guitars. He says he'll check him out and then signs my book. He's a totally rad dude. We're chatting on, and I begin to understand why so many people want to be around him, why they can't get enough of him. Then his jaw drops as he looks past me.

Chapter 44

"Tami? Tami Parker?" Duggie calls out. "Is that you?"

He looks at me.

"Gimme a second, mate. Yuh life gonna be irie from now on," he says, giving me a hug.

He blows by me like a zephyr. I don't even mind. I'd have been grateful if he had just given me a wave.

I turn, and there's my Tami—Tami Marie Cooper, née Parker, and she's like totally hot as hell in a pair of ass-squeezin' cut-off Daisy Dukes shorts and a pink blouse (naturally), tied in front (holy shit, look at them taters!), just below her blue-ribbon rack. Oh. That baldo jackass is with her.

Well shit. Isn't that just awesome?

"Holy shit, gyal! Don't you ever age?" Duggie asks, doing a little monkey hop thing on one leg. "Wah gwaan wid yuh todeh? Damn you look fine, gyal!"

He catches a glimpse of the stiff standing next to her.

"Who's your beau?"

He does a take.

"No way! No friggin' way, mon! Who dah duppy?"

He smacks the stiff playfully on the shoulder. Then he rubs the shaved head.

"Yow, bredda! Mickey? Little Mickey Lynne Lawrence? Oh, mon, is it really you? Tell me duh truut."

Taylor's still a statue, an indignant one.

"Kindly unhand me! My name is L. Michael Taylor. I'm an associate justice for the United States Court of Appeals for the Ninth Circuit."

Of course he is. He would be. Pompous baldo bastard. Too fuckin' inflated to know that nobody within a hundred miles of here gives a fuck.

Duggie leans away. His eyes are open big and wide. One eyebrow is jacked way up.

"Dat so? Okay, duppy mon."

"No, really, Duggie. It's him. I thought it be good therapy for him to see you," Tami says. "Go easy, he doesn't remember much."

Duggie steps back, squints with concern.

"Dat so? Oh, mi hav fi big up Mickey duh Michael mon now. Irie, Irie! It's good to see you again. You're most welcome here. Even if mi bredda duppy mon nuh remember me."

Tami laughs.

"You never change. All these years and you're still talking all that crazy, stupid Caribbean shit," she laughs again.

"Dat beso." He looks around. "Hey!"

Immediately some staffer in dreads runs over.

"Yo, Duggie, whatcha need man?"

"These are my guests, Tami and—"

"Michael," Tami says, hugging the baldo bastard.

"Get 'em set up for duh bashment, Jamrock style, full access VIP badges, everting."

"I'm on it." He snaps their photos with his phone and disappears.

"Mother? How do you know Duggie Meadows?"

Duggie turns to Shelley Lynne.

"Who are you?"

"Duggie, this is my daughter, Shelley Lynne Parker—well, it's Cooper now."

"Who be Cooper?"

"I be Cooper, mate," I say with a wave and a nod, strumming a G chord on a fun little guitar I picked up from the chair I decided to lounge in as I no longer have the strength to stand.

Shit, I can barely breathe.

"He's my real dad," adds Shelley Lynne, pointing at me.

"Shelley Lynne, it's time you met your real father, Michael."

Duggie does another take.

"Ooh, mon! I didn't see that one coming."

"I'm sorry to spring this on you all at once, Duggie. I didn't know my daughter and ex-husband would be here."

"Mom, he's not your ex-husband yet, and Baldo here isn't my father!" Shelley Lynne takes off.

That's my girl.

Tami hugs Taylor tighter.

"She doesn't mean it, honey. She's a teenager."

I struggle to get up with the guitar. I sort of stumble, walk by Duggie.

"Gimme a second, mate."

"Duggie, I'm so sorry," says Tami.

I follow Shelley Lynne, but she's moving too fast. I have no idea what the rush is. I wander around a bit, and I see her by the corner of the stage. The crew is doing various soundchecks and some of the audience is trickling in. I walk over, lean down, and gently kiss her on the forehead.

I look out at a sea of people—okay it's a small sea, but they're here and many are cheering. My guts are churning. My left leg's doin' the sewing machine shake.

Why not? I got no particular place to go. I meander further out onto the stage and plop my bony butt onto the stool and start strumming. Pretty soon, I hear the strumming go out to the crowd, and then I hear myself coming through the speaker in front of me. Somebody brings over a microphone stand and adjusts it so that the microphone is at my lips but not interfering with my playing.

What the hell. Why not? Chicks dig licks. There must be some out there, right?

I get a familiar groove going—a simple one, so slow and oh so simple mon, G and C and D, with a little D7 thrown in for seasoning—and I go for it. This one's for me. Me and Shelley Lynne and my Duggie dude.

> Duggie, Duggie, you're the star
> I like to listen to in the bar
>
> Up above the stage you fly
> Down below we're gettin' high
>
> Duggie, Duggie, you're the star
> I like to listen to in the bar.

The crowd likes it. Especially the "gettin' high" part. Duh. Hey, whatever works and gets your audience feelin' the groove and gettin' irie is what you do.

It's what you do, mon.

So I do it again. And again. It's easy fun, a fun, easy groove; and everyone is getting into it and singing along.

> Mellow mellow mon, you're the king
> Keep us dancing,' make us sing
>
> You're hangin' ten on waves so high
> As babes in their woodies go cruisin' by
>
> Duggie, Duggie, you're the king
> Keep us dancing,' make us sing.

"Thank you! Good night!"

That last one cracks up the crowd. It ain't nowhere near dark yet, and the concert doesn't start for another couple of hours. Oh well, what the hell. It's all good. I think about trying a sea chanty or two or something about Moby Dick, the duppy mon. Maybe not. No worries. I'm effin' stoked big time.

Hey, I played a real song to a real audience, eh. Okay. It was a quick song, and it wasn't my audience. But still, they're here, and maybe they liked it or maybe they're just glad all over 'cause, you know, it's all over. I can't tell. No matter. No worries, mon.

The air just feels electric even as I get off the stool and one of Duggie's fans is cheering somewhere. That's nice. It takes me a second to realize it's Shelley Lynne. I feel charged with lightning. I'm short of breath and realize I am sweating. I feel like I can fly, and for an instant, I feel like I'm going to just float off like I'm on a hot air balloon like maybe I'm dreaming. Dreaming like I be the dreamin', geezer, guitarded, irie mon, irie. It's only been a few minutes, but it feels like hours have passed.

"Papa!" She waves the backstage pass hanging from a lanyard around her neck that some staffer has given her. "I've got one for you, too!"

"Hey, Princess! Okay!" The air still feels electric, and I'm in the clouds again. "That was amazing. I mean, it's nothing to anybody else, but I did it! I had fun!"

"You did great, Papa."

She looks sad.

"Papa," she says, "Mother wants to talk to you."

"Really? How extraordinarily odd."

I look around, and sure enough, thar she be and not more than maybe twenty feet away; and she's still draggin' that dead white whale, and she's smiling, and I must be dreaming, and I mosey on over on new sea legs. She's still smiling even as she shakes her head and her ponytail swirls around her neck.

"You ever let go of that thing?"

"Huh?" I realize I'm still carrying the guitar. "Oh, yeah. No. Not ever. Why?"

"Whatever. I see you managed to put on a little show of your own. Pretty gutsy of you," she laughs.

"Yeah?"

"Yeah. For a guy with no talent, yeah, I'd say so. For a sound check, maybe it's not so bad after all. Not so good either, to be honest. Whatever. I don't care. It'll do," she laughs.

"Thanks!"

I reach out to hug her and move in to kiss her, and I feel her finger against my lips, and I feel my heart skip a few beats. There's something in my throat, and it's difficult to speak.

"No," she says.

"Yes." That's all I can manage to say.

"No! I'm sorry, Paul."

I force the words. "But you said it'll do."

She gently pushes me away.

"Paul," she says, smiling, looking radiant. "There's somebody I really want you to meet."

"Really? There's no point. I met him when you introduced him to Duggie. Obviously, the three of you are all connected somehow. Okay, I guess this can't get any more weird than it already is. Fuck it. I'll bite. Fess up. How?"

Tami smiles and gets all gushy.

"In high school. We met in San Diego. My parents had an apartment there they never used, so I'd sneak off on weekends with Mickey. We met Duggie at some concerts. He needed a place to stay, so I gave him a key."

"So then you all go back a ways."

"Yes, Duggie and me, we go way back with Mickey—well, Michael, now. His family—"

"Changed his name, put him in an institution. Something about electric shock treatments. Yeah, I know. I remember bits of his yawn talk at the bar dinner. Guess this means you're really serious about the whole judge thing."

Chapter 45

"Oh, Paul. You're such a card. It's so much more than that."

She reaches into the bag slung over her shoulder. She takes out an envelope from a book, opens the envelope, and removes a small photograph and hands it to me.

"Here. A picture's worth a thousand words. This one explains everything."

I stare at the image.

"How old were you?" I ask without looking up.

I can't look at anything but this snapshot of her and some skinny boy with long, curly, blond hair, even longer and prettier than hers.

Shit!

He even looks like a girl. They're both smiling, and her chin rests on his shoulders and she has her arms wrapped around his bony chest. She's sitting on a picnic table, and he's in front of her and his hands are in front of his waist and wrapped around the neck of an electric guitar, a black-and-white electric guitar, holding it just below the headstock.

"Seventeen."

In my peripheral vision, I notice the man at her side. Only now can I look up. Her smile is the same as in the snapshot. I realize in all the years we've been married, she's never smiled at me like this.

"You're even prettier now."

She blushes.

"That's so lovely of you to say, Paul."

My eyes well up.

"I mean it. Every word."

"I know."

Her eyes are welling up too. Seeing that makes me hurt even more and gives me hope that I fear will fade. She puts her arm around the great white duppy mon whale, and he responds in kind, and all my hopes start to fade.

I look at Taylor and then at the picture.

"This is you?"

"Yes."

"Seriously?"

I can't punch this SOB cuz he's sure to have bodyguards very nearby, bein' a federal justice and all. But that doesn't mean I can't have a little fun with him.

"Yes."

He doesn't attempt to hide his annoyance.

I shrug.

"You had a lot more hair back then."

"Oh, you think?"

"And from the looks of it, a rather fine electric guitar, apparently."

"That's what they tell me."

He's easing back on the annoyance.

"I see." I glance at him and look at the photo again. "My guess is, your electric guitar has aged a lot better than you."

That brings a snooty look to his face. Got the annoyance meter pegged!

"Paul!"

I look at Tami.

"So tell me, is he's where Shelley Lynne gets her musical talent?"

The annoyance meter isn't helping. I feel weak.

"Yes. I'm sorry, Paul."

I nod.

"Well, thanks for saying so. I get it now. All these years"—I have to stop and breathe—"you've been waiting for the chance to love him."

And not me.

"Yes! Yes! I knew you'd understand."

I give her back the photo.

"Well, shit." I feel like such a chump. "All these years, did you ever really love me?"

"Of course I did. But it was, so . . . you know . . . different. I tried to make that clear. Shelley Lynne needed a father. I was getting desperate. And you and I, we dated a few times, and I could tell . . . that I could make it work. You adored me, and she adored you. You were so good to her. You still are. Anyway, I do, you know, love you for that. But it's different for us. It's so different. Even more so now. You. You're different to me."

I believe the term is jackass. *Whatever.*

"Why? It doesn't have to be." I make a futile, last-ditch effort.

"Paul, c'mon. Please, don't do this. It's different. It just is." She moves away. "I'm sorry. I have to go."

They move.

"Why are you here?"

"When I heard you and Shelley Lynne were going to be here, well, you know."

"What do you mean you heard we'd be here? How did you hear we'd be here?"

"I got a call from somebody at your office named Danny, I think. Yeah, Danny, that was it."

"Oh? Danny! Yeah. Guess he would be the one to call you. Oh, he's just full of surprises, that Danny."

"Anyway, as I was saying, I thought it would be a good chance to introduce the two of you and, you know, for the three of us—Duggie, Mickey, and me—to catch up on old times."

"Oh, right. Good therapy and all that." I feel like I've hit by yet another runaway train. "So what about Shelley Lynne? Does she know?"

Tami stops and turns toward me.

"She knows."

"It's okay, Papa. I'm right here."

She's putting a pink envelope into her back pocket and walking toward me.

Her voice is soft and gentle, and I feel her arm slide along my back, and I hold my daughter as she holds me.

"We need to go," says Tami, and she leaves with Taylor.

They blend into the backstage crowd, round a corner together, and disappear.

"You played really well, Papa. I'm so proud of you."

I feel the squeeze of her arms and her head against my chest.

"You're on your way now, Papa."

"Maybe," I hear myself say. "One more thing to try."

I almost tell her but catch myself and stop before I do.

"You were about to say something stupid, weren't you, Papa?"

"Oh, I hope not."

"But I know you. You're such a dreamer, Papa. You never give up. I love that about you, you know." She hugs me tighter. "She's going to break your heart again, Papa. She's good at it."

"I'm hoping not. I'm hoping she'll see *me* this time."

"I know. Hey, it's not like the divorce papers means she's serious, right?" She eases upon her grip. "You don't have to do this, you know, whatever it is you're thinking of doing."

"Actually, kiddo, I kinda do."

"Why? For her?"

"More for me."

"Oh my god! Men! Okay, Papa, but don't make me regret telling you this. They're going to the Rainbow Barn. It's a coffee house about an hour from here, and there's an open mike night tonight.

She wanted me to go with them. Part of her therapy trip to get her Mickey back. I told her I'm not leaving you."

I lean down and kiss the top of her head.

"That's so sweet of you, Princess."

"You wrote something for her, didn't you?"

"Yep."

"I knew it. It's not gonna work, Papa."

"I know."

"But you're gonna try anyway, aren't you?"

"I am."

"Papa, please! You really don't have to do this! She's just gonna knock your dick in the dirt like always." She hugs me tighter still. "Do you need me to go with you?"

"No, Princess. I'm good. Besides, you deserve so much to be here now and to enjoy this concert."

"I love you, Papa. Please text me when it's over. I'll be here."

She lets go and hands me a business card.

"This is where they'll be. Directions are on the back. Text me if you get lost. Text me when you get there. Text me if you wise up and change your mind."

"I will, Princess. I promise."

"Wait, better yet, she said something about a shuttle. Yes, there's a shuttle for Duggie's crew into town. Your pass is all you need. Here. It'll get you into the coffee house too."

"Thank you, Princess." I hug her tight.

I take the shuttle into town. It's a scenic ride. For the first time in a long while, I feel free. I take out my phone and stare at it a while.

Yeah. It's time.

Chapter 46

I compose an email to all of Admin. I make sure it's all prim and proper like with just enough gonzo for flavoring. I add a separate line text and add CalBar to the recipient list. Deep breath. Send it. Slide, hop, strum, let 'er ring!

I'm done.

Sure enough, the shuttle stops in front of the Rainbow Barn, which is not a barn at all but a butt-ugly, rundown diner. I'm not sure what to do when I walk in. But somebody spies the concert all-access pass hanging from my neck and the guitar case at my feet with the guitar I borrowed from Duggie, and the next thing I know, I'm in line to go on stage. And then it's my turn for reals.

I see and grab a stool and bring it on stage with me because I'm still having trouble playing standing up and need to see more of the fretboard, and that just can't happen standing up. Naturally, I manage to drop it. Then hit it with the headstock of my guitar as I bend over to pick it up.

Smooth move there, you totally klutz-butted dipshit.

Naturally, people laugh.

"Okay. So I wrote this one for my wife, who is also here," I say onstage, drawing more laughter, though I'm not trying to.

I take another breath—a deep one.

"Only, she's with some other guy. A duppy mon."

That gets a round of laughs from several men in the audience.

"So I'm gonna try and win her back."

Crickets on that one.

Huh.

Someone in the back cheers. Another breath, and I start strumming.

Someone from somewhere else in the back yells out, "Give it up, hoser!"

Then I see her. In the front row.

Shit.

I'm fumbling. I'm all fumbles. She's changed clothes. A black pullover sweater with a V-neck and those uber-tight fashionably blue designer jeans that look spray-painted on. Italian leather boots with spiked heels.

I mumble something about the key of A, a good guitar key, and keep going. I hear Ria's voice and remember soft hands and guiding fingers. I start strumming an A. This song starts with an A for two bars, letting 'er ring; then a slide and a hop to make the switch to the D, strum it for two bars, letting 'er ring; then I repeat that sequence for four alternating lines to match the lyrics. I'll keep that sequence for the chorus that starts this song, and for the two verses that follow, until I hit the minor chord verse or bridge in the middle. I find the rhythm and go with it.

It feels irie, mon.

I close my eyes for a moment and sing the chorus silently in my head, remembering my voice will rise at the end of the second and fourth lines. Same with the first two verses.

Eyes still closed, I relax and pretend I'm just that nice clean-cut kid I always wanted to be, hanging out in the malt shop and singing to his girl, way back in the day.

> Tami, oh, Tami- whoo!
> You're my star so bright
> Let me keep on loving you
> Each and every night.

So what if I'm guitarded
That's no reason to be alone
You know I'm open-hearted
Let me climb up to your throne.

And let me be free
And love me as I am
I'm hoping then you will see
I still can be your man.

Tami, oh, Tami- whoo!
You're my star so bright
Let me keep on loving you
Each and every night.

I keep strumming.

"If anybody out there's got a good harmonica solo, now's the time."

I throw this out there cuz this is the instrumental or lead guitar part that transitions to the moodier, sadder bridge and I can't do it, cuz I don't know what is. I also can't play harmonica yet.

Anyway, my comment gets a pretty good chuckle from the otherwise subdued crowd. That'll do. Of course, Tami would laugh the loudest.

Damn.

She's joined the hecklers, now?

Focus!

Now comes the minor chord bridge. From the A major chord shape, I move my fretting fingers left, one string each, relative to the plan view of a chord chart, give this new chord—I don't know what it's called, maybe B-sus something or C/B, I don't know. I just know it's a bit deeper cnd darker than an A, and I give it a couple of down-up-down strums and switch to E minor, which is good and melancholy, and strum that chord for two bars, keeping the same rhythm.

Then I switch to A minor for two bars, which is good and melancholy too, but with a different sound and shade of sadness, and I'm still well within the key of G major—the "love and blessings" key—so even with a melancholy bridge, I can't go wrong. I repeat that sequence to accompany this bridge with these next four lyric lines:

> Once we made a bargain
> To get us through some years
> An' all it's ever brought us
> Was measured by our fears.

I try to keep my voice even to maybe slightly lower on the second and fourth lines, in contrast to the upbeat chorus and verses. I strum another bar each of E minor and A minor without singing, thinking harmonica and fiddle would be good about now, getting the song out of sad and back to happy, and immediately get back to the A and D sequence, picking up the tempo as I do, which makes this part of the song feel like a reward. Which is I want.

> So let me stay free
> Just love me as I am
> Then I'm sure you'll see
> I still can be your man.

Okay. Last chance. I'll show them all a hoser. Here goes, and so once more with feeling and a faster, stronger strum. Just the chorus now.

> Tami, oh, Tami- whoo!
> You're my star so bright
> Let me keep on loving you
> Each and every night.

People are likin' the "whoo!" part.
Well, they should. The bastards.

Tami, oh, Tami- whoo!
You're my star so bright
Let me keep on loving you
Each and every night.

Each and every night,
Each and every night,
Whoo!

Each and every night!

I drag out the words a little on the last line, stretching the word *night* as I sing it, raising the pitch of my voice as I do, as best I can. I let my voice fade out; strum one last down-up-down hard, with all my pent-up feelings; and stop.

Chapter 47

And then it's over.

I let the last chord ring a while. It's a clean one too, and I enjoy the sound. This guitar has good sustain. I feel good. I feel irie. I let the sound fade and then mute my strings and look up. I know I probably still sucked overall, but even so, I don't think I sucked that bad. Could have been a lot worse. I've sure played a lot worse. I've had lots of people tell me so.

I can't hear Baldo's snort. Don't need to. I can see the gesture plain enough even in this dim haze and despite the glare of the makeshift lights for this little stage. I see Tami give him the look, the one she usually gives me; and in the same instant, I'm both jealous and glad.

I can faintly hear her telling him, "Don't be an ass, Mickey."

Yeah! You go, girl!

Her voice gets softer.

"You used to be like that, only you played a lot better, for sure. Do you remember? That's why I brought you here tonight. We used to sneak out to places like this, remember?" She looks at him. "No. Of course you don't. You can't. It will be okay."

She hugs him.

"We'd listen to each set, then we'd hang out in the parking lot, and you'd mimic them with your guitar, matching every riff, every solo, every tune, chord for chord, lick for lick. So beautiful. So incredible. And you always said it was because of me. You were the best ever. And you always will be. You'll see. You'll get it back. I'll make sure of that, I totally promise."

All she gets from him is a blank stare of what I'm assuming must be self-righteous boredom. Getting to play god in a courtroom guarantees it. It gets even worse the higher up you go.

She takes his arm and snuggles closer. Their bodies merge in the darkness, oblivious to all the pairs of hidden eyes gazing upon them.

"It's okay, Michael. I'm here for you now."

The whole room has fallen silent but for her sweet and gentle voice.

"It'll be better soon," she says. "I promise. I'm still your muse, Mickey. You'll see."

She gets up—damn, she's so tall—and then she leans down and kisses his cue-ball head.

"It will be just like before. You'll see."

Well, shit. Isn't this just awesome.

She makes her way around the table and walks toward the stage and to me.

"Damn it, Paul."

She reaches for my face, and I freeze, not sure what's coming. But I feel her warm palm caress my cheek.

She sighs.

"I do, you know, love you."

She sighs again and shakes her head.

"And I need you . . . to love me."

Yes!

"I need you to love me so much . . . that you'll let me go."

Wait. What? What the hell'd you just say?

"If I go with you, part of me will always stay empty. I've been empty long enough, Paul. I'm not doing empty anymore. I just . . . can't. I need Mickey"—she shakes her head—"Michael. And yes, he really needs me now. You can see that, can't you? Please. Don't make me choose, Paul. Don't. I'm begging you. Love me enough to let me go. Will you do that? Can you do that? For me?"

Tami's eyes are so blue, so inviting—not at all icy like they've always been before. Like I always remember them. I do love her. I love her so much, and I want her to be happy, and I want to be happy, and I want her to be happy with me, and I don't want to be reminded how much that hurts because I want her to be happy more. I'm tired of hurting, and I'm tired of waiting, and I'm tired of chasing all the damn carrots in my life when all I ever get is the stick.

God, how I hate carrots.

I don't want to, but I can't help it. I glance at that glistening cue ball head of his and force myself to look away and close my eyes, and some part of me wants nothing more right now than to bust him deep into a corner pocket somewhere. But I feel Tami's warmth on my face instead, and I melt into her presence.

I feel her breath, her calm, and even her joy.

She's happy with him.

I get it. Whole fuckin' universe gets it. Sure, chicks dig licks, but only champions get the trophies. And no matter what happens, once a champion, always a champion. Coach was right. And I'm no champion. Not today. Not tomorrow. And probably not the next day and maybe not ever and certainly not ever soon enough to ever make any fuckin' difference.

I feel trapped.

I'm about to choke on the words I can't hold back, so I let go of them and that choking feeling goes with them, and I hear myself say them because I read somewhere that love means never being selfish, which means letting go.

"Goodbye," I tell her.

And like that, snap your fingers, the words are gone.

I can't believe I just said what I said. Inside, part of me is already up and screaming.

What the hell'd you do that for?

You moron!

You can't let a babe like that just walk! You'll never get another one and you know it!

Get her back! Right now! Do it!

These words—my silent, raging words—hit me like bullets, and I feel myself stagger as if I had begun to bleed out.

She hugs me, squeezing me, almost squealing with joy. Only, it's just not my joy.

My arms move instinctively around her to the small of her back, and I hear her whisper, "Thank you. You're a saint. I will always love you for this moment, Paul. Always."

These words, her words—so fresh, so real, so sincere—just wash over me like a cold wave on a sun-hot rock; and all I can feel is the shock.

She pulls away.

"Thank you, Paul, for trying so hard for so long, to be a good friend, and . . . more. You were a good husband, and I tried to love you as one. Believe me, Paul. I did try, in my own way," she sighs. "I never promised I'd ever really fall in love with you. I admit that I did leave that door open."

Her voice trails off.

"And I'm so, so sorry that I ever did that. That was so unfair. I never meant to do that."

She shrugs.

"What can I say? My daughter needed a daddy, and she fell for you. You were—no, you *are* the perfect daddy for her, Paul. Even so, I never stopped telling you not to get your hopes up. I'm so sorry I couldn't. I can't love you any more than I did."

Waves of words—I hear them, feel them pounding me, pounding me, pounding me, and then receding. I don't bother to look. I turn away in silence because I have no words for this moment, and I'm not at all into sainthood. Sainthood sucks. Saints suffer. Then they die.

And nobody gives a fuck.

I feel no pain. I am numb like rock.

I can hear the steady click of the heels of her all-too-fashionable designer boots, good rhythm, and I try hard not to imagine those silky long legs so shapely in designer denim, so toned, so tanned, and once wrapped in white terry cloth just for me.

It feels like a movie from too long ago, and I focus on holding up my guitar as I sort of stumble to my knees and feel around for the case with my free hand. I can hear mingled voices from the audience and clinking glasses and the usual sounds of this place coming back to life.

I stop for a moment after the snapping sound from opening the last latch on the case, and I listen. I don't hear her boots. I wait another moment anyway and choose to not turn around and look. I put the guitar away instead. My knees are stiff, and I'm awkward, struggling to getting up, like an old man. But I manage and shuffle off the tiny stage. I dare look. Somebody has moved the stool.

Yep. She's gone.

All gonna be a matter of time now.

There's a curtain I don't remember seeing and behind it, a chair. So I go there. It's as good a place as any. It's not like I'm here with anyone.

She's gone.

I sit down and cradle the guitar case upright between my legs and lean my head against the neck of the case. I feel dizzy and weightless and hang on to the guitar case as if it's all that keeps me from floating aimlessly away, and I feel like another me altogether is dying off in the distance. All I hear in my head is silence. It is a relief.

"Now's probably not a good time, but I wanted to say hello before I go. Hope you don't mind."

I open my eyes and look up at Ria.

Her smile fades.

"Yeah. Not a good time. I'm so sorry."

Not a good time, but I am still numb and there's been more than enough pain to go around.

"Thanks." I look around. "What are you doing here?"

She smiles.

"Connie met some kid, and they dragged me out here to join up for a Duggie Meadows concert. He's okay and all, I like a little more folk and country, but I sure as hell don't care for the crowds. I'm not a kid anymore. I want comfort. That's why I'm hanging out here, killing time. And then you show up." She shakes her head. "Damn if that don't beat all."

"Small world."

"Ain't it, though?" She moves closer. "Quite a show. For a minute, I thought you won her back. I swear—all that sincerity, all that vulnerability. I think you might have won over every woman in the house," she says, looking at the crowd.

She looks down.

"I'm sorry it didn't happen for you. I mean that. Anyway, you have a wonderful sense of humor, and I see your playing's improved some. You need to know that, and you need believe it."

She brushes her hair back.

"That's what I came up here to tell you."

She stands close, facing me, looking down, her hands coupled loosely below her belt.

"That and there's more feeling to it now, the way you play. It's more natural like it ought to be. And I had no idea you had such a fun way with words."

"They're just words, Ria. They're not enough."

"Could have fooled me."

"That's not what I meant."

"Then what did you mean?"

"I mean, I meant what I said—yeah, of course I did. I meant every word. It just wasn't enough. But it's just, I'm just not that good at saying it is what I mean."

I leave out the part about champions.

"Don't sell yourself short like that."

I don't have a comeback, and I really don't care. But I want to be nice. I remember it's important to be nice. I nod.

"Thank you. I appreciate it."

"You're welcome, Paul," she smiles.

The stage boss is moving around, helping another player settle in. I don't look at her, although she has a nice guitar with a sunburst finish on the soundboard. I get the hint and get up to make room. The space here is a bit too cozy. I move around the curtain, and there's some applause and that feels weird. So I nod and keep going. There's a spot at the end of the counter near the entrance, so I aim for it, trying not to bump people with my guitar case as I float toward the open spot at the counter. Ria's following me. I save her a seat.

"Hey, I was thinking of getting something. You want something?" I ask.

"Sure." She sits.

"Sweet. What do you want?"

"Whatever you're having is fine."

"Yeah? Okay." I wave, and the guy comes over.

He's got a towel on his shoulder, and he's grinning and shaking his head.

"You got balls, man. I just got to tell you that. Whatever you want, man, it's on the house. What can I get ya?"

I have to think about it.

"Okay. I'm not a coffee guy, so you got anything like hot apple cider and maybe some maple bourbon to go with it, anything like that?"

That raises a few eyebrows. He looks around.

"Yeah, I can probably come up with something, no problem. Give me a couple of minutes. I'll fix you up."

"Sweet. Make it two, please."

Then I remember my meds.

Shit!

"Something wrong?" he asks.

Chapter 48

"No. I'm fine."

It's just one drink, for God's sake, for a little sweetness. I think my liver can handle that.

"You said two, right?" He grins, noticing Ria move in closer. "She with you?"

"Yes."

"Geezus! All right, big guy. You're on." He glances at Ria. "Two somethings with cider and maple-flavored bourbon. Sure thing."

I nod.

The new player is strumming. Sounds like an A, maybe an A. I don't know. Now she's doing some fingerpicking. It sounds carefree and gentle, maybe a little bit like bluegrass, and her voice is high and happy. But I listen to the voice of her guitar's tone woods, the spruce and the rosewood. Pretty sure it's rosewood.

I look at Ria and smile.

"I like that."

"Me too."

"You ever do that—I don't mean that song necessarily—but you know, play onstage in a place like this?"

"Sometimes. Not so much now."

"What's it like?"

Ria's eyebrows shift. She has a curious look on her face.

"You were just up there. What was that like?"

I shrug.

"Fuck. I don't know. Like death. Maybe. Can't feel anything. Can't be the same. That was all about Tami. I don't remember anything else."

I feel awkward—stupid, even. Thank God the ciders are here. I take a sip, it's too hot, and I spill some and put the cup down and spill some more.

Whoopsy.

Ria moves her mug closer to her.

"You okay?" she asks.

I nod and grab a napkin.

"Well, maybe you should try it again and find out."

"You mean now?"

"I don't know. Maybe. If you feel up to it."

Chapter 49

I look at the stage. I turn to her.

"Nah. I don't think so."

"Okay. Some other time then. You know, to find out what it's like, for its own sake or for the music or whatever."

"Yeah, maybe I can do that. Seems a little scary, though, thinking about it."

"It's like that sometimes."

"What do you do? I mean, if it's ever like that for you."

"I don't think about it. I just let myself get lost in the moment of the song, listen to sounds of the chords and feel the song, and then let go and be free."

I wonder what that would be like.

"Yeah. I think I'd love some of that."

I think about it.

"Definitely want some of that," I mumble, and now I'm overthinking it as usual.

I try to remember what it was like doing that sound check on Duggie's stage playing for the early diehards charging in to pick their spots up close. I'm still numb, and I've got nothing. It wasn't more than an hour and a half ago, two at the most, and I'm struggling to remember it. But it's like it never happened.

I look past all the silhouetted heads in front of me to the woman playing the sunburst guitar.

I turn to Ria and ask her, "Think it's wrong for me to want this?"

She glances away for a second before looking at me.

"Probably not a good idea to give up the day job just yet."

"Ohh! We're way too late for that now, lil' darlin'."

Ria's eyebrows arch, and those luscious mahogany brown eyes get big.

"Oh!"

"But not for this. I'm not that stupid. I went for something else. Why?"

"Oh, well, in that case," she hesitates. "Look, your song was so good because it was sincere and real, and for a moment, I felt like you were singing to me. Every woman in here thought you were singing just to them too, I'm sure. But obviously, you weren't, and the truth is—you can't sing."

She purses her lips. She squints a bit and holds me with a steady gaze like she's given me bad news I can't bear and waiting to see what I do with it.

"Yeah, I know. My wife—okay, my immediate ex-wife-to-be?— she always said as much. That's not the part I care about, and as far as that goes, I know I'm not good enough. I'm pretty sure all the lessons in the world won't change that."

I catch myself.

"Wait. I didn't mean that. No offense."

She smiles.

"None taken."

"I meant, you know, I'll never be good enough, and I'm okay with that."

"Hey. You don't know that, world-conquering rock star. Okay, that's one thing. Making a living playing professionally, sure, that's another thing. Being good enough to play what you like whenever you want to? For yourself? That's altogether different. That's something that matters, and that's always in reach. Yes, you can have that much, Paul. You're almost there now."

She wraps her hands around her mug and blows softly across the top.

"That's the part I hope you care about. And for that, you are good enough. You proved it tonight. You just need to keep at it. Stick with it. Get good at the songs you know, and then learn some more. And yes, lessons can be a part of that. And you don't have to make a job out of it either. Please don't make another job out of it. Just chill out and use some common sense."

"Yeah, I want the good enough part. I want to feel alive—as alive as the stuff I hope to learn to play. And maybe something like what you said about being free."

Our eyes meet again.

"Think it's wrong for someone like me to want something like that?"

"No," she says, smiling, patting my hand. "I can see some promise here."

"Yeah. Me too." I look at her hand, resting on mine.

The warmth of her hand feels good.

"Anyway, I like thinking so . . ."

I feel woozy, and I breathe one deep breath and let it go, just as another one of my light shows hits my brain.

"Sweetheart, are you okay?"

I see the crescent of brilliant white flashes cascading across my darkened eyelids. I feel her hand on my arm.

"Yeah. I'll be fine."

"Are you sure?"

I nod.

"Okay."

She gets up and moves around behind me, wrapping her arms around me, resting her head against mine.

I feel her warm cheek against mine.

"You're a good man with a good heart, Paul Cooper." She gives me a squeeze and a soft kiss on my cheek. "It's not easy for me to say this. I really am sorry it didn't work out for you the way you wanted."

"Thank you. It's good to know." I catch my breath. "Ria?"
"Yeah?"
"About those lessons."
My voice leaves me.

Chapter 50

"We can work something out."

"Fair enough."

Accustomed to the light show and Ria's wraparound grip, my thoughts drift like clouds moving across a window, among macaws and margaritas, to jamming with Shelley Lynne, to silk robes with red dragons, then to the chill and thrill and spill of bloody good ice time, back to jamming with Shelley Lynne, and then hanging out in Ryan's barn, being the Bard and writing stuff down.

My thoughts drift on to spruce and ebony and cedar and walnut of making Calypso Spirit and Muse guitars with Norse God and a hope of someday introducing him to the Luthiers at Las Vegas, of my dream of making a pilgrimage to Nazareth, and past the pure joy of strumming a clean chord.

I hope for happiness and the grace to let go.

I hope to never go on television ever again.

I wonder what it'll be like when the numbness wears off, when there are no more light shows flashing in my head, when the magic moment comes back. If it ever comes back.

I wonder what it might be like to finally let go and fully commit to doing whatever brings me the most joy and makes my life meaningful for a change, once and for all.

I feel Ria let go and move back to her seat. I finish my drink and wonder what it might be like when my chord changes are easier, faster, more fluid, and full of feeling.

"Here. You can have the rest of mine." Ria leans in and kisses me on the other cheek. "You earned it, you sweet little pup."

She smiles and pushes one of her arms into the sleeve of her leather jacket. She pulls the jacket up over her shoulder.

I help her with the other sleeve. It's a tight fit and looks good on her. The brown leather goes well with her dark orange top and the dark cinnamon tint of her hair. She reaches back and flips her shoulder-length hair over the collar.

"Call me someday when you're ready for a lesson," she says.

"I will."

She smiles, and I study her as she turns, her butt making a cute little swish, and she leaves.

I turn around and finish her drink and then watch the next couple of performers. After that, I figure it's time to move on. I make my way to catch the last shuttle and climb aboard.

I feel my phone buzz. I want to ignore it, but I know I won't. I can't. I check it. It's nothing. But when in Rome . . . I start what becomes a rambling text to Norse God, think better of it, and then delete it altogether.

I pull up my favorite picture of Tami, thinking maybe it's time to delete it. My head explodes with loud voices telling me not to. Can't really blame them. She's just so icy hot.

What the hell.

I'll keep it. No matter what, I'll always have that night at the Mission Inn. That and the sound in my head of the crashing crescendo of the G/Fadd9 chord or whatever chord it was that heralded a triumphant night after a long hard day, both for me and for what became a celebrated pop song of the '60s. I will always cherish it with a smile and a damn good reason to remember it. Always.

I text Shelley Lynne the news that I do not doubt she expected all along. The news everybody's expected all along. The news that I've been denying all along.

I'm a stubborn ass . . .

I stare out the window and begin to lose myself in the hum of the motor of the rumbling shuttle and the nearly golden shine from the streetlamps and the bright neon lights of the bars and nightlife spots, each glistening off the glowing, wet pavement below as we pass by them on the long ride back to the concert venue.

I think of Robby.

Jesus. Of all the people to think of, why him? Why now?

He's out there, somewhere, drying out with the Benedictine monks; and the thought hits like a gut punch, and I'm reminded to get right with God again and clean out my gutter mouth once and for all.

I close my eyes again and make another effort at letting go.

After a while, I start feelin' irie again.

And this time, I'm content to float along the boozy backwaters of my own mind for a change and imagine what it will be like making my own cookies from now on, not feeling like I'm somebody's unfinished figure drawing or something always under construction by others, just writing my own songs and stuff and building guitars because I effin' feel like it—how my life is really gonna be irie from now on—and strumming the simple and peppy cowboy chords of a goofy little song about life at the beach and a coconut burrito with ham and pineapple.

I imagine what it might be like to finally be at peace, to be strumming the chords of that goofy little burrito song I love to some irie gyal who's looking mighty fine. And who knows? Maybe she's some bouncy brown-eyed honey of a woman in a yellow sundress who's dancing in her cowgirl boots and stops now and then to bow her fiddle, a woman who's never been afraid to tutu, who still yearns, at times, for sweetness—a trophy of a woman I'm guessing might know a thing or two about champions and sweethearts and such.

Epilogue

Sidney Woo continues to rake in the deferred comp and monitor the county's legal business while stoically sucking up to the new County Counsel in her transition to her new position.

Marcie hasn't changed much either.

Kerry is the manager at the new Strummin' City store in Riverside, California. The San Gorgonio store was closed as a result of corporate downsizing.

The frazzled woman, whose real name is Aubrie Baudin, is frazzled no more. She's enjoying a better life. With the help of anonymous donors, she owns and operates a small French-Canadian bakery and cafe in Oak Glen, California. She and her son, "Shithead Jr."—which, it turns out, he never was—and whose real name is Henri Baudin, live together in a modest two-bedroom apartment on the second floor of the café building.

Henri is homeschooled at The Barn (i.e., Ryan's house) with other gifted children from the vicinity. He is a voracious learner of all things guitar and has developed a strong taste for the "gypsy jazz" style of guitar popularized in Paris in the '20s. He can also seriously shred heavy metal. Who knew? Thanks to music, he excels in and loves math. He often plays in his mother's café on weekends. He shares his tips with her fifty-fifty. It was his idea.

Darrell Huntington has resumed being the most preeminent trial lawyer in the nation, pursuing seriously "real money."

Judge Corley "Oh Good Lord" O'Halloran has found his niche hearing a criminal calendar of long cause matters involving only *pro-per* defendants. He thoroughly enjoys regaling this captive audience with tedious war stories of his past trials, his history of almost always prevailing on appeals—*by God*—and his consummate knowledge of civil and criminal law and procedure, all without interruption.

Millicent Camille O'Halloran and Barbara Ann Parker are both back in rehab in a residential long-term care detox facility in Palm Springs, California. They play cards together in the same bridge and gossip club. Neither one of them can stand each other.

Hamilton Langhorne Parker IV, long retired from active practice, is enjoying the fruits of having wisely invested most of his exorbitant attorney's fee awards won at past trials. He continues to spoil his only grandchild Shelley Lynne with exorbitant gifts. He entertains himself with frequent flights to Las Vegas, Nevada, for some high-stakes poker games at various casinos on the Strip.

Paul's former secretary from hell still remains on paid administrative leave, pending yet another appeal to the county's civil service folks for her termination for using her county-assigned office computer to conduct her personal online business selling cosmetics and costume jewelry.

Myrtle Edith Potts is the new deputy county counsel for Code Enforcement. She's thoroughly appalled about it all.

Jessica Elizabeth "Betsy" Carrigan was promoted to Chief Deputy County Counsel shortly after her election to the city council for the City of San Gorgonio. She is on her third nanny and is already pregnant with her second set of twins. She predominantly telecommutes and chairs a variety of committees within the office, including the Diversity Committee and the Holiday Committee.

She is also very active in numerous state bar events, her tier-one law school's alumni association, and regularly publishes a blog and newsletter about women's rights for millennial moms in the professional workplace. She is also pursuing legal specialization in women's rights and elections law.

Jenny Ellen Curtis is on television every afternoon at four. *Duh.* Check local listings.

Sheriff's Lieutenant Rawlings Rodney Hood retired from the county. He lives alone in a mobile home park backed up to the Colorado River on the Arizona side. He works part-time for his drinkin' buddy, Billy "Kid" Cavanaugh, managing Billy's Bluffin' Billy Bluster's Brewhouse Marina & Bar.

Hood will be sitting in a lawn chair on the sand next to the marina's dock with an ice chest of cold beers on each side and a sawed-off .30-30 Winchester lever-action rifle (commonly known to gunners as a "mare's leg") holstered to his right leg in the manner of his favorite TV show from the 1950s.

Lt. Col. Timothy Cleveland Seville, USAF (call sign "Hawg Boss"), has returned home to Whiteman AFB, Missouri, to begin his service separation duties for retirement. An excellent pilot with an exemplary combat service record, he served several combat tours flying out of Kandahar, Afghanistan, as a squadron commander for the 303rd Expeditionary Fighter Squadron, flying the Republic A-10C Thunderbolt II "Warthog" (a.k.a., the "Hawg") close air support fighter/bomber in support of US ground forces fighting in Afghanistan. A-10 pilots are commonly identified as "hawg drivers."

Colonel Seville hasn't touched a guitar since graduating high school in Las Vegas, Nevada, and entering the United States Air Force Academy at Colorado Springs, Colorado, for his "Doolie Summer" immediately thereafter.

After the divorce and a black-tie wedding among elite San Francisco society, Tami Astrid Marie Cooper, née Parker, gleefully wed Lynne Michael Taylor, her duppy mon, the great bald whale.

They are honeymooning harmoniously on a luxury catamaran, complete with crew and two divers, cruising among the Hawaiian Islands for the next several weeks.

Shelley Lynne Cooper has graduated from UCD and is part of Duggie's tour management team. For the summer months, Duggie Meadows, born Douglas Ethan Hale McHenry Meadows, is on tour throughout the Caribbean. Shelley Lynne will be traveling with the tour and working in the logistics support group. Her summer promises to be ridiculous and utterly epic.

Next fall, Shelley Lynne begins a course of study in music composition for guitar at Duggie's alma mater. Tuition and all expenses have been prepaid, courtesy of the Duggie Meadows Organization.

Maria Templeton is a popular music teacher at a private girl's school in Brentwood, California. She is a popular singer-songwriter with a growing fanbase among the area night clubs in West Hollywood and around Los Angeles, California.

Together as Danny & Friends, AJ, Danny, Paul, Robby, and Ryan recorded one eponymous album of songs built from Paul's lyrics and poems. AJ produced the album, which was recorded at Ryan's barn.

They maintain personal ownership, individually and collectively, of the publishing rights to the album's twelve songs through their own publishing company, created prior to their television appearance on *The Jenny Curtis Show*, thereby receiving all royalties earned. The album is garnering a respectable amount of both critical and financial success. However, there is no plan for any promotional tour for the album.

Retired and living in his converted barn, snuggled deep in a wooded canyon, Ryan Seamus O'Byrne is delighted to be leading a surging renaissance among the burgeoning bohemian community of visual and performing artists, sculptors, writers, musicians, playwrights, yoginis, herbalists, and the proliferation of other various artisans, as well as the ubiquitous and sustainable organic growers of truly excellent herb, in the heart of Apple Country in Oak Glen, California. The expansive barn and related structures support a charter school for the performing arts and a playhouse, in addition to his soon-to-be state-of-the-art recording studio.

Daniel Aaron "Danny" Schaefer has left the county and joined a private Century City, California, boutique law firm, specializing in transactional, intellectual property law as a full equity partner. Danny represents performing artists, primarily singers and musicians. He lives on a lovely sailboat in a private slip in Marina del Rey, California.

Retired from his accounting practice, Aaron Joseph "AJ" Goldman still makes his weekly visits to his parents' gravesites in Culver City, California. He owns and operates a recording studio in West Hollywood, California. It's highly regarded within the music recording industry as the mecca for LA-area jazz musicians for whom he often fills in as a percussionist and drummer during their recording sessions.

Retired from his government law practice, Robert Earl "Robby" Sherwood has been clean and sober for 153 days at last count. He is a recent convert to Buddhism, and he is training to become a Buddhist monk. He lives in a monastery in Tibet.

Robby's personal and legal affairs are handled by Danny's firm. Robby's 1950s-era classic single-cutaway electric guitar is stored securely in a vault in Danny's law office.

Karl and Lago, the Luthiers at Las Vegas (their full names have been withheld by request) remain thoroughly successful in all aspects of their business.

Through Paul's efforts, they have since met and taken quite a liking to the energetic young luthier, Eric March Gregersen, and they have eagerly taken him under their professional wings.

Eric's wife Leilani "Lani" Gregersen, née Tonono, a.k.a., Hula Babe, keeps a close eye on her beloved luthier hubby and particularly the Calypso books when she's not throwing pots, surfing, or enjoying Las Vegas whenever Eric is being tutored by Karl and Lago in all things guitar making.

After an early retirement from the county, changing his state bar status to inactive and going slightly bohemian himself, Paul Edward Cooper has begun taking shop courses in basic woodworking at Laguna Canyon Community College.

He hangs his hammock at Calypso Guitars in Laguna Beach, California, where he serves as the volunteer, night watchman, and as a day apprentice to Eric.

Paul spends most of his time at the Calypso shop. He frequently strums an acoustic guitar that he helped Eric build. It's a Spirit model but with a longer scale length and without any cutaway. The bridge, fingerboard, and headstock cover plate of the guitar are all ebony. The neck is Honduran mahogany. There is no pickguard. Paul paid Eric's standard retail price for the build, plus the additional costs for the ebony and mahogany tone woods.

Paul pens his poetry and potential song lyrics in his ever-present spiral-bound notebook. He occasionally gets guitar lessons from Ria, and he also attends some of her shows. He has also written several sets of lyrics, inspired by thinking about Ria and their common interests, as potential material for future songs.

Paul is feelin' irie.